AMONG THE HIDDEN

MW01074744

Also by Margaret Peterson Haddix

The Missing series
Found
Sent

The Shadow Children series
Among the Hidden
Among the Impostors
Among the Betrayed
Among the Barons
Among the Brave
Among the Enemy
Among the Free

The Girl with 500 Middle Names
Because of Anya
Say What?
Dexter the Tough
Running Out of Time
The House on the Gulf
Double Identity
Don't You Dare Read This, Mrs. Dunphrey
Leaving Fishers
Just Ella
Turnabout
Takeoffs and Landings
Escape from Memory
Uprising
Palace of Mirrors

Among the Hidden

MARGARET PETERSON HADDIX

SIMON & SCHUSTER BOOKS FOR YOUNG READERS
NEW YORK   LONDON   TORONTO   SYDNEY

For John and Janet

If you purchased this book without a cover, you should be aware that this book is stolen property. It was reported as "unsold and destroyed" to the publisher, and neither the author nor the publisher has received any payment for this "stripped book."

SIMON & SCHUSTER BOOKS FOR YOUNG READERS
An imprint of Simon & Schuster Children's Publishing Division
1230 Avenue of the Americas, New York, New York 10020
This book is a work of fiction. Any references to historical events, real people, or real locales are used fictitiously. Other names, characters, places, and incidents are products of the author's imagination, and any resemblance to actual events or locales or persons, living or dead, is entirely coincidental.
Text copyright © 1998 by Margaret Peterson Haddix
Illustration copyright © 1998 by Cliff Nielsen
All rights reserved, including the right of reproduction
in whole or in part in any form.
SIMON & SCHUSTER BOOKS FOR YOUNG READERS
is a trademark of Simon & Schuster, Inc.
For information about special discounts for bulk purchases, please contact
Simon & Schuster Special Sales at 1-866-506-1949
or business@simonandschuster.com.
The Simon & Schuster Speakers Bureau can bring authors to your live event.
For more information or to book an event, contact the Simon & Schuster Speakers Bureau
at 1-866-248-3049 or visit our website at www.simonspeakers.com.
Also available in a hardcover edition.
Book design by Heather Wood
The text for this book is set in Elysium.
Manufactured in the United States of America
1009 OFF
First paperback edition March 2000
50 49
The Library of Congress has cataloged the hardcover edition as follows:
Haddix, Margaret Peterson.
Among the hidden / Margaret Peterson Haddix
p.   cm.
Summary: In a future where the Population Police enforce the law limiting a family to only two children, Luke has lived all his twelve years in isolation and fear on his family's farm, until another "third" convinces him that the government is wrong.
ISBN 978-0-689-81700-7 (hc)
[I. Science Fiction.] I. Title.   PZ7.H1164Am   1998
[Fic] dc21   97-33052
ISBN 978-0-689-82475-3 (pbk)
ISBN 978-0-689-84807-0 (eBook)

CHAPTER ONE

He saw the first tree shudder and fall, far off in the distance. Then he heard his mother call out the kitchen window: "Luke! Inside. Now."

He had never disobeyed the order to hide. Even as a toddler, barely able to walk in the backyard's tall grass, he had somehow understood the fear in his mother's voice. But on this day, the day they began taking the woods away, he hesitated. He took one extra breath of the fresh air, scented with clover and honeysuckle and—coming from far away—pine smoke. He laid his hoe down gently, and savored one last moment of feeling warm soil beneath his bare feet. He reminded himself, "I will never be allowed outside again. Maybe never again as long as I live."

He turned and walked into the house, as silently as a shadow.

"Why?" he asked at the supper table that night. It wasn't a common question in the Garner house. There were plenty of "how's"—*How much rain'd the backfield get? How's the planting going?* Even "what's"—*What'd Matthew do with the five-sixteenth wrench? What's Dad going to do about that busted tire?* But "why" wasn't considered much worth asking. Luke asked again. "Why'd you have to sell the woods?"

Luke's dad harrumphed, and paused in the midst of shoveling forkfuls of boiled potatoes into his mouth.

"Told you before. We didn't have a choice. Government wanted it. You can't tell the Government no."

Mother came over and gave Luke's shoulder a reassuring squeeze before turning back to the stove. They had defied the Government once, with Luke. That had taken all the defiance they had in them. Maybe more.

"We wouldn't have sold the woods if we hadn't had to," she said, ladling out thick tomatoey soup. "The Government didn't ask *us* if we wanted houses there."

She pursed her lips as she slid the bowls of soup onto the table.

"But the Government's not going to live in the houses," Luke protested. At twelve, he knew better, but sometimes still pictured the Government as a very big, mean, fat person, two or three times as tall as an ordinary man, who went around yelling at people, "Not allowed!" and "Stop that!" It was because of the way his parents and older brothers talked: "Government won't let us plant corn there again." "Government's keeping the prices down." "Government's not going to like this crop."

"Probably some of the people who live in those houses

will be Government workers," Mother said. "It'll all be city people."

If he'd been allowed, Luke would have gone over to the kitchen window and peered out at the woods, trying for the umpteenth time to picture rows and rows of houses where the firs and maples and oaks now stood. Or had stood—Luke knew from a sneaked peek right before supper that half the trees were now toppled. Some already lay on the ground. Some hung at weird angles from their former lofty positions in the sky. Their absence made everything look different, like a fresh haircut exposing a band of untanned skin on a forehead. Even from deep inside the kitchen, Luke could tell the trees were missing because everything was brighter, more open. Scarier.

"And then, when those people move in, I have to stay away from the windows?" Luke asked, though he knew the answer.

The question made Dad explode. He slammed his hand down on the table.

"Then? You gotta stay away *now*! Everybody and his brother's going to be tramping around back there, to see what's going on. They see you—" He waved his fork violently. Luke wasn't sure what the gesture meant, but he knew it wasn't good.

No one had ever told him exactly what would happen if anyone saw him. Death? Death was what happened to the runt pigs who got stepped on by their stronger brothers and sisters. Death was a fly that stopped buzzing when the swatter hit it. He had a hard time thinking about himself in connection with the smashed fly or the dead pig, gone stiff in the sun. It made his stomach feel funny even trying.

"I don't think it's fair we've got to do Luke's chores now," Luke's other brother, Mark, grumbled. "Can't he go outside some? Maybe at night?"

Luke waited hopefully for the answer. But Dad just said, "No," without looking up.

"It's not fair," Mark said again. Mark was the second son—the lucky second, Luke thought when he was feeling sorry for himself. Mark was two years older than Luke and barely a year younger than Matthew, the oldest. Matthew and Mark were easily recognizable as brothers, with their dark hair and chiseled faces. Luke was fairer, smaller-boned, softer-looking. He often wondered if he'd ever look tougher, like them. Somehow he didn't think so.

"Luke don't do nothing nohow," Matthew jeered. "We won't miss his work at all."

"It's not my fault!" Luke protested. "I'd help more if—"

Mother laid her hands on his shoulders again. "Hush, all of you," she said. "Luke will do what he can. He always has."

The sound of tires on their gravel driveway came through the open window.

"Now, who—" Dad started. Luke knew the rest of the sentence. Who could that be? Why were they bothering him now, his first chance all day to sit down? It was a question Luke always heard the end of from the other side of a door. Today, skittish because of the woods coming down, he scrambled up faster than usual, dashing for the door to the back stairs. He knew without watching that Mother would take his plate from the table and hide it in a cupboard, would slide his chair back into the corner so it looked like an unneeded spare. In three seconds she would hide all evidence that Luke existed, just in time to step to the door and offer a weary smile to the fertilizer salesman or the Government inspector or whomever else had come to interrupt their supper.

CHAPTER TWO

T here was a law against Luke.

Not him personally—everyone like him, kids who were born after their parents had already had two babies.

Actually, Luke didn't know if there was anyone else like him. He wasn't supposed to exist. Maybe he was the only one. They did things to women after they had their second baby, so they wouldn't have any more. And if there was a mistake, and a woman got pregnant anyway, she was supposed to get rid of it.

That was how Mother had explained it, years ago, the first and only time Luke had asked why he had to hide.

He had been six years old.

Before that, he had thought only very little kids had to stay out of sight. He had thought, as soon as he was as old as Matthew and Mark, he would get to go around like they did, riding to the backfield and even into town with Dad, hanging their heads and arms out the pickup window. He had thought, as soon as he got as old as Matthew and Mark, he could play in the front yard and kick the ball out into the road if he wanted. He had thought, as soon as he got as old as Matthew and Mark, he could go to school. They complained about it, whining, "Jeez, we gotta do homework!" and, "Who cares about spelling?" But they also talked about games at recess, and friends who shared candy at lunchtime or loaned them pocketknives to carve with.

Somehow, Luke never got as old as Matthew and Mark.

The day of his sixth birthday, Mother baked a cake, a special one with raspberry jam dripping down the sides. At supper that night she put six candles on the top and placed it in front of Luke and said, "Make a wish."

Staring into the ring of candles—proud that the number of his years finally made a ring, all around the cake—Luke suddenly remembered another cake, another ring of six candles. Mark's. He remembered Mark's sixth birthday. He remembered it because, even with the cake in front of him, Mark had been whining, "But I wanna have a party. Robert Joe had a party on his birthday. He got to have three friends over." Mother had said, "*Ssh*," and looked from Mark to Luke, saying something with her eyes that Luke didn't understand.

Startled by the memory, Luke let out his breath. Two of his candles flickered, and one went out. Matthew and Mark laughed.

"You ain't getting that wish," Mark said. "Baby. Can't even blow out candles."

Luke wanted to cry. He'd forgotten even to make a wish, and if he hadn't been surprised he would have been able to blow out all six candles. He knew he could have. And then he would have gotten—oh, he didn't know. A chance to ride to town in the pickup truck. A chance to play in the front yard. A chance to go to school. Instead, all he had was a strange memory that couldn't be right. Surely Luke was thinking about Mark's seventh birthday, or maybe his eighth. Mark couldn't have known Robert Joe when he was six, because he would have been hiding then, like Luke.

Luke thought about it for three days. He trailed along behind his mother as she hung wash out on the line, made strawberry preserves, scrubbed the bathroom floor. Several times he started to ask, "How old do I have to be before people can see me?" But something stopped him every time.

Finally, on the fourth day, after Dad, Matthew, and Mark scraped back their chairs from the breakfast table and headed out to the barn, Luke crouched by the kitchen's side window—one he wasn't supposed to look out because people driving by might catch a glimpse of his face. He tilted his head to the side and raised up just enough that his left eye was above the level of the windowsill. He watched Matthew and Mark running in the sunlight, the tops of their hog boots thumping against their knees. They were in full sight of the whole world, it seemed, and they didn't care. They were racing to the front door of the barn, not the side one off the backyard that Luke always had to use because it was hidden from the road.

Luke turned around and slid to the floor, out of sight.

"Matthew and Mark never had to hide, did they?" he asked.

Mother was scrubbing the remains of scrambled eggs out of the skillet. She turned her head and looked at him carefully.

"No," she said.

"Then why do I?"

She dried her hands and left the sink, something Luke had almost never seen her do if there were still dirty dishes left to be washed. She crouched beside him and smoothed his hair back from his forehead.

"Oh, Lukie, do you really need to know? Isn't it enough to know—things are just different for you?"

He thought about that. Mother was always saying he was the only one who would ever sit on her lap and cuddle. She still read bedtime stories to him, and he knew Matthew and Mark thought that was sissified. Was that what she meant? But he was just younger. He'd grow up. Wouldn't he be like them then?

With unusual stubbornness, Luke insisted, "I want to know why I'm different. I want to know why I have to hide."

So Mother told him.

Later, he wished he'd asked more questions. But at the time it was all he could do to listen to what she told him. He felt like he was drowning in the flow of her words.

"It just happened," she said. "You just happened. And we wanted you. I wouldn't even let your dad talk about... getting rid of you."

Luke pictured himself as a baby, left in a cardboard box

by the side of a road somewhere, the way Dad said people used to do with kittens, back when people were allowed to have pets. But maybe that wasn't what Mother meant.

"The Population Law hadn't been around long, then, and I had always wanted lots of kids. Before, I mean. Getting pregnant with you was like—a miracle. I thought the Government would get over their foolishness, maybe even by the time you were born, and then I'd have a new baby to show everyone."

"But you didn't," Luke managed to say. "You hid me."

His voice sounded strangely hoarse, like it belonged to someone else.

Mother nodded. "Once I started showing, I didn't go anywhere. That wasn't hard to do—where do I go, anyway? I didn't let Matthew and Mark leave the farm, for fear they'd say something. I didn't even say anything about you in letters to my mother and sister. I wasn't really scared then. It was just superstition. I didn't want to brag. I thought I'd go to the hospital to give birth. I wasn't going to keep you secret forever. But then…"

"Then what?" Luke asked.

Mother wouldn't look at him.

"Then they started running all that on TV about the Population Police, how the Population Police had ways of finding out everything, how they'd do anything to enforce the law."

Luke glanced toward the hulking television in the living room. He wasn't allowed to watch it. Was that why?

"And your dad started hearing rumors in town, about other babies..."

Luke shivered. Mother was looking far off into the distance, to where the rows of new corn plants met the horizon.

"I always wanted a John, too," she said. " 'Matthew, Mark, Luke, and John, bless the bed that I lie on.' But then I thank the Lord that I have you, at least. And it's worked out, the hiding, hasn't it?"

The smile she offered him was wobbly. He felt he had to help her.

"Yes," he said.

And somehow, after that, he didn't mind hiding so much anymore. Who wanted to meet strangers, anyway? Who wanted to go to school, where—if Matthew and Mark were to be believed—the teachers yelled, and the other boys would double-cross you if you didn't watch out? He was special. He was secret. He belonged at home— home, where his mother always let him have the first piece of apple pie because he was there and the other boys were away. Home, where he could cradle the new baby pigs in the barn, climb the trees at the edge of the woods, throw snowballs at the posts of the clothesline. Home, where the backyard always beckoned, always safe and protected by the house and the barn and the woods.

Until they took the woods away.

CHAPTER *THREE*

Luke lay on his stomach on the floor and idly ran the toy train back and forth on the track. The train had belonged to Dad when he was a little boy, and his own father before him. Luke could remember a time when his greatest longing had been for Mark to outgrow the train so Luke could have it all to himself. But it wasn't what he wanted to play with today. There was a beautiful day unfolding outside, with fleecy clouds in a blue, blue sky, and a mild breeze rustling the grass in the backyard. He hadn't left the house in a week now, and he could almost hear the outdoors calling to him. But now he wasn't even allowed in the same room as an uncovered window.

"Are you *trying* to be discovered?" Dad had bellowed at Luke just that morning, when he'd held the shade a few inches back from the kitchen window and peeked out longingly.

Luke jumped. He'd been so busy thinking about running barefoot through the grass that he'd half-forgotten there was anyone or anything behind him, in the house.

"No one's out there," he said, glancing again to be sure.

He'd been trying not to look beyond the ragged edge of the backyard to the bulldozed mess of branches, trunks, leaves, and mud that had once been his beloved woods.

"Yeah?" Dad said. "Did it ever occur to you that if there is, they might see you before you see them?"

He grabbed Luke by the arm and jerked him back a good three feet. Freed from Luke's grasp, the bottom of the shade banged against the windowsill.

"You can't look out at all," Dad said. "I mean it. From now on, just stay away from the windows. And don't go into a room unless we've got the shades or curtains pulled."

"But then I can't see anything," Luke protested.

"Better that than to get turned in," Dad said.

Dad sounded like he might feel sorry for Luke, but that only made things worse. Luke turned around and left, scared he might cry in front of Dad.

Now he gave the toy train a shove, and it careened off the track. It landed upside down, wheels spinning.

"Who cares?" Luke muttered.

There was a harsh knock on his door.

"Population Police! Open up!"

Luke didn't move.

"That's not funny, Mark!" he shouted.

Mark opened the door and bounded up the stairs that led to Luke's room proper. Luke's room was also the attic, a fact he had never minded. Mother long ago had shoved all the trunks and boxes as far as they could go under the eaves, leaving prime space for Luke's brass bed and circular rag rug and books and toys. Luke had even heard Matthew and Mark grumble about Luke having the biggest room. But they had windows.

"Scared you this time, didn't I?" Mark asked.

"No," Luke said. Nothing would force him to admit that his heart had jumped. Mark had been playing the "Population Police" joke for years, always out of their parents' earshot. Usually Luke just ignored Mark, but now, with Dad acting so skittish…What would Luke have done if it really had been the Population Police? What would they do to him?

"Matt and me, we've never told anyone about you," Mark said, suddenly serious, which was strange for him. "And you know Mother and Dad don't say anything. You're good at hiding. So you're safe, you know?"

"I know," Luke muttered.

Mark kicked the toy train Luke had crashed. "Still playing with baby toys?" he asked, as if to make up for slipping and being nice.

Luke shrugged. Normally, he wouldn't have wanted Mark to know he played with the train anymore. But today everything else was so bad that that didn't matter.

"Did you come up here just to bug me?" Luke asked.

Mark put on an offended look.

"Thought you might want to play checkers," he said.

Luke squinted.

"Mother told you to, right?" he asked.

"No."

"You're lying," Luke said, not caring how nasty he sounded.

"Well, if you're going to be that way—"

"Just leave me alone, okay?"

"Okay, okay." Mark backed down the stairs. "Jeez!"

Alone again, Luke felt a little sorry he'd been so mean. Maybe Mark had told the truth. Luke should apologize. But he didn't really feel like it.

Luke got up and started pacing his room. The squeak of the third board in from the stairs annoyed him. He hated having to duck under the rafters on the far side of his bed. Even his favorite model cars, lined up on the shelves in the corner, bothered him today. Why should he have model cars? He'd never even sat in a real one. He never would. He'd never get to do anything or go anywhere. He might as well just rot up here in the attic. He'd thought about that before, on the rare occasions when Mother, Dad, Matthew, and Mark all went somewhere and left him behind—what if something happened to them and they never came back? Would someone find him years from now, abandoned and dead? He'd read a story in one of the old books in the attic about a bunch of kids finding a deserted pirate ship, and then a skeleton in one of the rooms. He'd be like that skeleton. And now that he wasn't allowed in rooms with uncovered windows, he'd be a skeleton in the dark.

Luke looked up automatically, as if to remind himself that nothing lit the rafters but the single bulb over his head. Except—there was light at either end of the ceiling, leaking in under the peak of the roof.

Luke stood up and went to investigate. Of course. He should have remembered. There were vents at each end of the roof. Dad grumbled occasionally about heating the attic for Luke—"It's just like throwing money out those vents"—but Mother always fixed him with one of her stares, and nothing changed.

Now Luke climbed on top of one of the largest trunks and looked down through the vent. He could see out! He could see a strip of the road and the cornfield beyond, its leaves waving in the breeze. The vent slanted down and limited his view, but at least he was sure nobody would ever be able to see him.

For a moment, Luke was excited, but that quickly faded. He didn't want to spend the rest of his life watching the corn grow. Without much hope, he stepped down from the trunk and went to the other end of the attic, the portion that faced the backyard. He had to slide boxes around and drag an old step stool from the opposite end of the attic, but finally his eyes were level with the back vent.

The view was not of the backyard—it was too close—but of the former woods. He'd never realized it before, but the land there sloped away from his family's house, so he had a clear view of acres and acres that once had been covered with trees. The land was abuzz with activity now. Huge yellow bulldozers shoved brush back from a rough road that had been traced out with gravel. Other vehicles

MARGARET PETERSON HADDIX

Luke couldn't identify were digging holes for huge concrete pipes. Luke watched in fascination. He knew tractors
and combines, of course, and had seen his dad's bush hog
and manure spreader and gravity wagons up close, in the
barn. But these machines were different, designed for different jobs. And they were all operated by different people.

Once, when Luke was younger, a tramp had walked up
to the house and Luke had only had time to hide under the
sink in the mudroom before the man was in the house,
begging for food. The door of the cabinet was cracked, so
Luke had been able to peek out and see the man's patched
trousers and holey shoes. He'd heard his whiny voice: "I
ain't got no job, and I ain't et in three days.... No, no, I
can't do no farmwork for my food. What do you think I
am? I'm sick. I'm starving...."

Other than that tramp and pictures in books, Luke had
never seen another human being besides his parents and
Matthew and Mark. He'd never dreamed there was such
variety.

Many of the people running the bulldozers and shovel
contraptions were stripped of their shirts, while others
standing nearby even wore ties and coats. Some were fat
and some were thin; some were browned by the sun and
some were paler than Luke himself, who would never be
tan again. They were all moving—shifting gears and lowering pipe, waving others into position or, at the very
least, talking at full speed. All that activity made Luke
dizzy. The pictures in books always showed people still.

Overwhelmed, Luke closed his eyes, then opened them again for fear of missing something.

"Luke?"

Reluctantly, Luke slid down from his step stool perch and scrambled over to recline innocently on his bed.

"Come in," he called to his mother.

She climbed the stairs heavily.

"You okay?"

Luke dangled his feet over the side of the bed.

"Sure. I'm fine."

Mother sat on the bed beside him and patted his leg.

"It's—" she swallowed hard. "It's not easy, the life you've got to live. I know you'd like to look outside. You'd like to go outside—"

"That's okay, Mother," Luke said. He could have told her then about the vents—he didn't see how anyone could object to him looking out there—but something stopped him. What if they took that away from him, too? What if Mother told Dad, and Dad said, "No, no, that's too much of a risk. I forbid it"? Luke wouldn't be able to stand it. He kept silent.

Mother ruffled his hair.

"You're a trooper," she said. "I knew you'd hold up all right."

Luke leaned against his mother's arm, and she moved her arm around his shoulders and hugged him tight to her side. He felt a little guilty for keeping a secret, but mostly reassured—loved and reassured.

Then, more to herself than to him, Mother added, "And things could be worse."

Somehow, that wasn't comforting. Luke didn't know why, but he had a feeling what she really meant was that things were going to get worse. He snuggled tighter against Mother, hoping he was wrong.

CHAPTER FOUR

L uke found out what Mother meant a few days later
when he came down for breakfast. As usual, he opened
the door from the back stairs to the kitchen only a crack.
He could remember barely a handful of times in his entire
life when someone had dropped by before breakfast, and
each time Mother had managed to send Matthew or Mark
up to warn Luke to stay out of sight. But he always
checked. Today he could see Dad and Matthew and Mark at
the table, and knew from the sound of frying bacon that
Mother must be at the stove.

"Are the shades closed?" he called softly.

Mother opened the door to the stairs. Luke started to
step into the kitchen, but she put out her arm to keep him
back. She handed him a plate full of scrambled eggs and
bacon.

"Luke, honey? Can you eat sitting on the bottom step
there?"

"What?" Luke asked.

Mother looked beseechingly over her shoulder.

"Dad thinks—I mean, it's not safe anymore to have you

in the kitchen. You can still eat with us, and talk to us and all, but you'll be...over here."

She waved her hand toward the stairs behind Luke.

"But with the shades pulled—" Luke started.

"One of those workers asked me yesterday, 'Hey, farmer, you got air-conditioning in that house of yours?'" Dad said from the table. He didn't turn around. He didn't seem to want to look at Luke. "We keep the shades pulled, hot day like today, people get suspicious. This way is safer. I'm sorry."

And then Dad did turn around and glance at Luke, once. Luke tried to keep from looking upset.

"So what'd you tell him?" Matthew asked, as if the worker's question was only a matter of curiosity.

"Told him of course we don't have air-conditioning. Farming don't make nobody a millionaire."

Dad took a long sip of coffee.

"Okay, Luke?" Mother asked.

"Yes," he mumbled. He took the plate of eggs and bacon, but it didn't look good to him now. He knew every bite he ate would stick in his throat. He sat down on the step, out of sight of both kitchen windows.

"We'll leave the door open," Mother said. She hovered over him, as if unwilling to return to the stove. "This isn't too much different, is it?"

"Mother—" Dad said warningly.

Through the open windows, Luke could hear the rumble of several trucks and cars. The workers had arrived for the day. He knew from watching through the vent the past few days that the caravan of vehicles came up the road like a parade. The cars would peel off to the side and unload the nicer dressed men. The more rugged vehicles pulled on in to the muddiest sections, and the people inside would scatter to the bulldozers and backhoes that had been left outside overnight. But the vehicles barely had time to get cold, because the workers were there now from sunup to sundown. Someone was in a hurry for them to finish.

"Luke—I'm sorry," Mother said, and scurried back to the stove. She loaded a plate for herself, then sat down at the table, beside Luke's usual spot. His chair wasn't even in the kitchen anymore.

For a while, Luke watched Dad, Mother, Matthew, and Mark eating in silence, a complete family of four. Once, he cleared his throat, ready to protest again. *You can't do this— it's not fair—* Then he choked back the words, unspoken. They were only trying to protect him. What could he do?

Resolutely, Luke stuck his fork in the pile of scrambled eggs on his plate and took a bite. He ate the whole plateful of food without tasting any of it.

CHAPTER *FIVE*

L uke ate every meal after that on the bottom step. It became a habit, but a hated one. He had never noticed before, but Mother often spoke too softly to be heard from any distance, and Matthew and Mark always made their nasty comments under their breath. So they would start laughing, often at Luke's expense, and he couldn't defend himself because he didn't know what they had said. He couldn't even hear Mother saying, "Now, be nice, boys." After a week or two, a lot of the time, he didn't even try to listen to the rest of the family's conversation.

But even he was curious the hot July day when the letter arrived about the pigs.

Matthew brought the mail in that day from the mailbox at the crossroads a mile away. (Luke had never seen them, of course, but Matthew and Mark had told him there were three mailboxes there, one for each of the families that lived on their road.) Usually the Garners' mail was just bills or thin envelopes carrying curt orders from the Government about how much corn to plant, which fertilizer to use, and where to take their crop when it was harvested. A letter from a relative was a cause to celebrate, and Mother always dropped whatever she was doing and sat down to open it with trembling hands, calling out at intervals, "Oh, Aunt Effie's in the hospital again...." or, "Tsk, Lisabeth's going to marry that fellow after all...." Luke almost felt he knew his relatives, though they lived hundreds of miles away. And, of course, they didn't even know he existed. The letters Mother wrote back, painstakingly, late at night, when she'd saved up enough money for a stamp, contained plenty of news of Matthew and Mark, but never once had mentioned Luke's name.

This letter was as thick as some from Luke's grandmother, but it bore an official seal, and the return address was an embossed DEPARTMENT OF HUMAN HABITATION, ENVIRONMENTAL STANDARDS DIVISION. Matthew held the letter at arm's length, the way Luke had seen him hold dead baby pigs when they had to be carried out of the barn.

Dad looked worried the minute he saw the letter in Matthew's hand. Matthew put the letter down beside Dad's silverware. Dad sighed.

"Can't be anything but bad news," Dad said. "No use ruining a good meal. It can wait."

He went back to eating chicken and dumplings. Only after his last belch did he turn the envelope over and run a dirt-rimmed fingernail under the flap. He unfolded the letter.

" 'It has come to our attention…,' " he read aloud. "Well, so far I understand it." Then he read silently for a while, calling out at intervals, "Mother, what's 'offal'?" and, "Where's that dictionary? Matthew, look up 'reciprocity.' " Finally, he threw down the whole thick packet and proclaimed, "They're going to make us get rid of our hogs."

"What?" Matthew asked. More serious than Mark, he had talked for as long as anyone could remember about, "When I get my own farm, it's going to be all hogs. I'll make the Government let me do that, somehow…." Now he looked over Dad's shoulder. "You mean they're just going to make us sell a lot at one time, right? But we can build the herd back up—"

"Nope," Dad said. "Those people in them fancy new houses won't be able to stand pig smell. So we can't raise hogs no more." He threw the letter out into the center of the table for all to see. "What'd they expect, building next to a farm?"

From his seat on the stairs, Luke had to hold himself back from going to fish the edge of the letter out of the chicken gravy and looking at it himself.

"They can't do that, can they?" he asked.

Nobody answered. Nobody needed to. Luke felt like a fool for asking as soon as the words were out of his mouth. For once, he was glad of his hiding place.

Mother twisted a dishrag in her hand.

"Those hogs are our bread and butter," she said. "With

grain prices the way they are…what are we going to live on?"

Dad just looked at her. After a moment, so did Matthew and Mark. Luke didn't know why.

CHAPTER SIX

he tax bill arrived two weeks later, the day that Dad, Matthew, and Mark loaded the hogs onto the livestock trailer and took them all away. Most were going to the slaughterhouse. The ones too young and too small to bring a decent price were going to an auction for feeder pigs. Luke watched through the vent at the front of the house as Dad drove by in the battered pickup with each load. Matthew and Mark sat in the back of the pickup, making sure the trailer stayed hitched right. Even three stories up, Luke could see Matthew's hangdog expression.

Then when the three of them came into the house for dinner, after washing the last of the hog smell off their hands in the mudroom, Dad handed Mother the tax bill without comment. She put down the wooden spoon she'd been using to stir the stew and unfolded the letter. Then she dropped it.

"Why, that's—" she seemed to be doing the math in her head as she bent to retrieve it. "That's three times what it usually is. There must be a mistake."

Dad shook his head grimly. "No mistake. I talked to Williker at the auction."

The Willikers were their nearest neighbors, with a house three miles down the road. Luke always pictured them with monster scales and fierce claws because of the number of times he'd been cautioned, "You don't want the Willikers to see you."

Dad went on. "Williker says they raised everyone's taxes because of them fancy houses. Makes our land worth more."

"Isn't that good?" Luke asked eagerly. It was strange— he should hate the new houses for replacing his woods and forcing him to stay indoors. But he'd half-fallen in love with them, having watched every foundation poured, every wooden skeleton of walls and roofs raised to the sky. They were his main entertainment, aside from talking to Mother when she came upstairs for what she called "my Luke breaks." Sometimes she pretended his room needed cleaning as badly as the bread needed baking or the garden needed weeding. Sometimes she just sat and talked.

Dad was shaking his head in disgust over Luke's question.

"No. It's only good if we're selling. And we ain't. All it means for us is that the Government thinks they can get more money out of us."

Matthew was slumped in his chair at the table. "How are we going to pay?" he asked. "That's more than we got for all the hogs, and that was supposed to carry us through for a long time—"

Dad didn't answer. Even Mark, who normally had a smart-alecky comeback for everything, was stupefied.

Mother had turned back to her stew.

"I got my work permit today," she said softly. "The factory's hiring. If I get on there, I can maybe get an advance on my paycheck."

Luke's jaw dropped.

"You can't go to work," he said. "Who will—" He wanted to say, *Who will stay with me? Who will I talk to all day when everyone else is outside?* But that seemed too selfish. Luke looked around. No one else looked surprised by Mother's news. He shut his mouth.

CHAPTER SEVEN

y mid-September, Luke's days had fallen into a familiar pattern. He got up at dawn just for the chance to sit on the stairs and watch the rest of his family eat breakfast. They all rushed now. Mother had to be at the factory by seven. Dad was trying to get all the machinery in working order before harvest. And Matthew and Mark were back in school. Only Luke had time to linger over his undercooked bacon and dry toast. He didn't bother asking for butter because that meant someone would have to stand up and bring it over to him, all the while pretending for the sake of the open window that they'd just forgotten something upstairs.

As soon as the rest of his family had stomped out the door, Luke went back to his room and watched out the vents—first out the front, to see Matthew and Mark climb onto the school bus, then out the back, where the new houses were practically finished. They were mansions, as large as the Garners' house and barn put together. They gleamed in the morning sunlight as though their walls were studded with precious jewels. For all Luke knew, maybe they were.

Hordes of workmen still arrived every morning, but almost all of them worked indoors now. They headed into the houses first thing, carrying rolls of carpet, stacks of drywall, cans of paint. Luke couldn't see much of them after that. He spent more time now watching a new kind of traffic: expensive-looking cars driving slowly down the newly paved streets. Sometimes they pulled into a drive-way and went into one of the houses, usually trailing a woman who appeared to be talking nonstop. It had taken Luke a while to figure it out—he certainly hadn't dared ask anyone else in his family—but he thought maybe the people were thinking about buying the houses. Once he realized that, he studied each potential neighbor carefully. He'd overheard Mother and Dad marveling that the people moving into the new houses were not just going to be city people, but Barons. Barons were unbelievably rich, Luke knew. They had things ordinary people hadn't had in years. Luke wasn't sure how the Barons had gotten rich, when everybody else was poor. But Dad never said the word "Baron" without a curse word or two in front of it.

The people streaming through the houses did look different from anyone in Luke's family. They were mostly thin, beautiful women in formfitting dresses, and heavyset men in what Luke's dad and brothers called sissy clothes—shiny shoes and clean, dressy pants and jackets. Luke always felt a little embarrassed for them, showing up like that. Or maybe he was embarrassed for his family, that they never looked like any of the Barons. Luke preferred it when the adults had children with them and he could concentrate on them. The smallest ones were always as dressed up as their parents, with hair bows and suspenders and other geegaws Luke knew his parents would never buy. The older kids usually seemed to be wearing whatever they'd grabbed first out of their closet that morning.

Though he knew no one would dare show up with three kids, he always counted: "One, two..." "One..." "One, two..."

What if a family with just one kid moved in behind them, and he sneaked into their house and pretended to be their second child? He could go to school, go to town, act like Matthew and Mark....

What a joke—Luke living with Barons. More likely he'd be shot for trespassing. Or turned in.

When he began thinking things like that, he always jumped down from his perch by the vent and grabbed a book from one of the dusty stacks by the eaves. Mother had taught him to read and do math, as much as she knew herself. "At least we have a few books for you...," she often mumbled sadly when she left in the morning. He'd read all their books dozens of times, even the ones with titles like *Diseases of the Porcine Species* and *Common Grasses of Our Countryside*. His favorites were the handful of adventure books, the ones that let him pretend he was a knight fighting a dragon to rescue a kidnapped princess, or an explorer sailing on the high seas, holding tight to a mast while a hurricane raged about him.

He liked to forget he was Luke Garner, third child hidden in the attic.

Sometime around noon he'd hear the door from the mudroom to the kitchen swing open and he'd go down and eat at the same time as his dad. Without Mother there were no homemade pies now, no mashed potatoes, no roasts that sent good smells throughout the house. Dad always made four sandwiches, checked to make sure no one could see him, then handed two of them to Luke in the stairwell.

Dad never talked—he'd explained that he didn't want anyone overhearing him, and wondering. But he did turn the radio on for the noon farm report, and there was usually a song or two after that before Dad silenced the radio and went outside to work again.

When Dad left, Luke went back to his room to read or watch the houses again.

At six-thirty Mother came home, and she always stopped in and said hi to Luke before rushing out to do a whole day's work in the few hours before bedtime. Usually Matthew or Mark came up to visit him, too, but they could never stay long, either. They had to help Dad before supper, then do homework afterwards. And they always had been nicest to Luke outdoors. Before the woods came down, the three of them often had played kickball or football or spud in the backyard, after school and chores. Matthew and Mark always fought about who got to have Luke on his team, because, even if Luke wasn't very good, two boys together could always beat the third.

Now they played halfhearted games of cards or checkers with Luke, but Luke could tell they'd rather be outside.

So would he.

He tried not to think about it.

The best part of the day came at the end, when Mother tucked him in. She'd be relaxed then. She'd stay for an hour sometimes, asking him what he'd read that day, or telling him stories about the factory.

Then one night, when she was telling how her plastic glove had gotten stuck in a chicken she'd de-gutted that day, Mother suddenly stopped in the middle of a sentence.

"Mother?" Luke said.

She answered with a snore. She'd fallen asleep sitting up.

Luke studied her face, seeing lines of fatigue that hadn't been there before, noticing that the hair around her face now held as much gray as brown.

"Mother?" he said again, gently shaking her arm.

She jerked. "—but I cleaned that chicken al— oh. Sorry, Luke. You need tucking in, don't you?"

She fluffed his pillow, smoothed his sheet.

Luke sat up. "That's okay, Mother. I'm getting too old for this any"—he swallowed a lump in his throat— "anyway. I bet you weren't still tucking Matthew or Mark in when they were twelve."

"No," she said quietly.

"Then I don't need it, either."

"Okay," she said.

She kissed his forehead, anyhow, then turned out the light. Luke turned his face to the wall until she left.

CHAPTER *EIGHT*

One cool, rainy morning a few weeks later, Luke's family left in such a rush, they barely had time to say good-bye. They dashed out the door after breakfast, Matthew and Mark complaining about their packed lunches, Dad calling back, "I'm going to that auction up at Chytlesville. Won't be home until supper." Mother hurried back and handed Luke a bag of cracklings and three pears and some biscuits from the night before. She muttered, "So you won't get hungry," and gave him a quick kiss on the head. Then she was gone, too.

Luke peeked around the stairway door, surveying the chaos of dirty pans and crumb-covered plates left in the kitchen. He knew not to look out as far as the window, but he did, anyway. His heart gave a strange jump when he saw the window was covered. Someone must have pulled the shade the night before, to try to keep the kitchen warm, and then forgotten to raise it in the morning. Luke dared to lean out a little further—yes, the shade was down on the other window, too. For the first time in almost six months, he could step out into the kitchen and not worry about being seen. He could run, skip, jump—dance, even—on the vast linoleum without fear. He could clean up the kitchen and surprise Mother. He could do anything.

He put his right foot out, tentatively, not quite daring to put his full weight on it. The floor squeaked. He froze. Nothing happened, but he retreated, anyway. He went back up the stairs, crawled along the second-floor hallway to avoid the windows, then climbed the stairs to the attic. He was so disgusted with himself, he could taste it.

I am a coward. I am a chicken. I deserve to be locked away in the attic forever, ran through his head. *No, no*, he countered himself, *I'm cautious. I'm making a plan.*

He climbed up onto the stool on top of a trunk that served as his perch for watching out the back vents. The neighborhood behind his house was fully occupied now. He knew all the families and had come up with names for most of them. The Big Car Family had four expensive cars sitting in their driveway. The Gold Family all had hair the color of sunshine. The Birdbrain Family had set a row of thirty birdhouses along their backyard fence, even though Luke could have told them it was pointless to do that until spring. The house he could see best, right behind the Garners' backyard, was occupied by the Sports Family. Two teenaged boys lived there, and their deck overflowed with soccer balls, baseball bats, tennis rackets, basketballs, hockey sticks, and apparatus from games Luke could only guess at.

Today, he wasn't interested in games. He was interested in seeing the families leave.

He had noticed before that all of the houses were empty by nine in the morning, with kids off to school and grown-ups off to work. Three or four of the women didn't seem to have jobs, but they left, too, returning late in the afternoon with shopping bags. Today, he just had to make sure no one was staying home sick.

The Gold Family left first, two blond heads in one car, two blond heads in another. The Sports Family was next, the boys carrying football pads and helmets, their mother teetering on high heels. Then there was a flurry of cars streaming from every driveway onto the still-sparkling new streets. Luke counted each person, keeping track so carefully that he made scratches on the wall, and counted the scratches twice again at the end. Yes—twenty-eight people gone. He was safe.

Luke scrambled down from his chair, his head spinning with plans. First, he'd clean up the kitchen; then he'd start some bread for supper. He'd never made bread before, but he'd watched Mother a million times. Then maybe he could pull the shades in the rest of the house and clean it thoroughly. He couldn't vacuum—that'd be too loud—but he could dust and scrub and polish. Mother would be so pleased. Then, in the afternoon, before Matthew or Mark or the kids in the neighborhood got back, he could put something on for supper. Maybe potato soup. Why, he could do this every day. He'd never considered housework or cooking particularly thrilling before—Matthew and Mark always scoffed at it as women's work—but it was better than nothing. And maybe, just maybe, if this worked, he could convince Dad to let him sneak out to the barn and help there, too.

Luke was so excited, he stepped into the kitchen without a second thought this time. Who cared if the floor creaked? No one was there to hear it. He gathered up dishes from the table and piled them into the sink, scrubbing everything with extraordinary zeal. He measured out flour and lard and milk and yeast and was putting it all in a bowl when it occurred to him it might be okay to turn on the radio, very softly. Nobody'd hear. And if they did, they'd just figure the family had forgotten to turn it off, just as they'd forgotten to raise the shades.

The bread was in the oven and Luke was picking up lint by hand from the living room rug when he heard tires on the gravel driveway. It was two o'clock in the afternoon, too early for the school bus or Mother or Dad. Luke sprinted for the stairs, hoping whoever it was would just go away.

No luck. He heard the side door creaking open, then Dad exclaiming, "What the—"

He was back early. That shouldn't matter. But hiding on the staircase, Luke suddenly felt like the radio was as loud as an entire orchestra, like the smell of baking bread could fill three counties.

"Luke!" Dad yelled.

Luke heard his father's hand on the doorknob. He opened the door.

"I was just trying to help," Luke blubbered. "I was safe. You left the shades down, so I thought it was okay, and I made sure everyone was gone from the neighborhood, and—"

Dad glared. "You can't be sure," he snapped. "People like that—they get deliveries all the time, they get sick and come home from work, they have maids come during the day—"

Luke could have protested, no, the maids never come before the kids get home from school. But he didn't want to give himself away any more than he already had.

"The shades were down," he said. "I didn't turn on a single light. Even if there were a thousand people back there, nobody would know I was here! Please—I've just got to do something. Look, I made bread, and cleaned up, and—"

"What if a Government inspector or someone had stopped by here?"

"I would have hidden. Like always."

Dad was shaking his head. "And leave them smelling bread baking in an empty house? You don't seem to understand," he said. "You can't take any chances. You can't. Because—"

At that precise moment, the buzzer on the oven went off, sounding as loud as a siren. Dad gave Luke a dirty look and stalked over to the oven. He pulled out the two bread pans and tossed them on the stove top. He flipped off the radio.

"I don't want you in the kitchen again," he said. "You stay hidden. That's an order."

He went out the door without looking back.

Luke fled up the stairs. He wanted to stomp, angrily, but he couldn't. No noise allowed. In his room, he hesitated, too upset to read, too restless to do anything else. He kept hearing *You stay hidden. That's an order,* echoing in his ears. But he'd been hidden. He'd been careful. To prove his point—to himself, at least—he climbed back up on his perch by the back vents and looked out on the quiet neighborhood.

All the driveways were empty. Nothing moved, not even the flag on the Gold Family's flagpole or the spokes on the Birdbrain Family's fake windmill. And then, out of the corner of his eye, Luke caught a glimpse of something behind one window of the Sports Family's house.

A face. A child's face. In a house where two boys already lived.

CHAPTER *NINE*

Luke was so surprised, he lost his balance and almost fell backwards off the trunk. By the time he recovered and righted himself, the face was gone. Had he imagined it? Was it just one of the Sports Family brothers home early from school? Kids got sick, like Dad said, or they decided to play hooky. Luke tried to remember every detail of the face he'd seen, or thought he'd seen. It had been younger than either of the Sports Family brothers'. Softer. Hadn't it?

Maybe it was a thief. Or a maid, come early.

No. It had been a child. A—

He didn't even let himself think what another child in that house would be.

He stared for hours at the Sports Family's house, but no face reappeared. Nothing happened until six, when the two Sports Family boys drove in in their jeep, unloaded their football gear, and carried it into the house. They didn't run out screaming about being robbed.

And he'd seen no thief leave. He'd seen no maid leave.

At six-thirty, Luke reluctantly climbed down from his

perch when he heard his mother's knock on the door. He sat down on his bed and muttered a distracted, "Come in."

She rushed to hug him.

"Luke—I'm sorry. I know you were just trying to help. And everything is amazingly clean. I'd love it if you could do this every day. But your father thinks—I mean, you can't—"

Luke was so busy thinking about the face in the window that at first he couldn't figure out what she was talking about. Oh. The bread. The housecleaning. The radio.

"That's okay," Luke mumbled.

But it wasn't, and it never would be. His anger came back. Why did his parents have to be so careful? Why didn't they just lock him in one of the trunks in the attic and be done with it?

"Can't you talk to him?" Luke asked. "Can't you convince him—"

Mother pushed Luke's hair back from his face. "I'll try," she said. "But you know he's just trying to protect you. We can't take any chances."

Even if the face in the window of the Sports Family house was another third child, so what? Luke and the other kid could live right next door all their lives and never meet. Luke might never see the other kid again. And he'd certainly never see Luke.

Luke lowered his head.

"What am I supposed to do?" he asked. "There's nothing

for me to do. Am I supposed to just sit in this room the rest of my life?"

Mother was stroking his hair now. It made him feel itchy and irritable.

"Oh, Lukie," she said. "You can do so much. Read and play and sleep whenever you want.... Believe me, I'd like to live a day of your life right about now."

"No you wouldn't," Luke muttered, but he said it so softly, he was sure Mother couldn't hear. He knew she wouldn't understand.

If there was a third child in the Sports Family, would he understand? Did he feel the way Luke did?

CHAPTER *TEN*

When Luke went down to supper, he saw that Mother had set his two loaves of bread out on the china plate she used for holidays and special occasions. She was showing off the bread the way she used to tape up the crooked drawings Matthew and Mark brought home from school when they were little. But something had gone wrong—maybe Luke hadn't used enough yeast, or he'd kneaded the dough too much or too little—and the loaves had turned out flat. They looked lopsided and pathetic in the center of the table.

Luke wished Mother had just thrown them away.

"It's cold out now. Nobody'd notice if you pulled the shades. Why can't I sit at the table with all of you?" he asked when he reached the bottom of the stairs.

"Oh, Luke—" Mother started.

"Someone might see your shadow through the shade," Dad said.

"They wouldn't know it was mine," Luke said.

"But there'd be five. Someone might get suspicious," Mother said patiently. "Luke, we're just trying to protect you. How about a big slice of your bread? There's cold beef and canned beans, too."

Resignedly, Luke sat down on the stairs.

Matthew asked about the auction Dad had gone to.

"I drove all that way for nothing," Dad said disgustedly. "I waited four hours for the tractors to come up, and then I couldn't even afford the first bid."

"At least you got home in time to fix that back fence before dark," Mother said, cutting the bread.

And yell at me, Luke thought bitterly. What was wrong with him? Nothing had changed. Except he'd maybe seen a face that maybe belonged to someone like him—

Matthew and Mark suddenly noticed the bread Mother was doling out.

"What's wrong with that?" Mark asked.

"I'm sure it will taste fine," Mother said. "It's Luke's first try."

Luke muttered, "And my last," too softly for anyone to hear. There were advantages to sitting on the other side of the room from everyone else.

"Luke made bread?" Mark said incredulously. "Yuck."

"Yeah. And I put special poison in one of the loaves, that only affects fourteen-year-olds," Luke said. He pantomimed death, clutching his hands around his own neck, letting his tongue hang out of his mouth, and lolling his head to the side. "If you're nice to me, I'll tell you which loaf is safe."

That shut Mark up but earned Luke a frown from

Mother. Luke felt strange about the joke, anyway. Of course he'd never poison anyone, but—if something happened to Matthew or Mark, would Luke have to hide anymore? Would he become the public second son, free to go to town and to school and everywhere else that Matthew and Mark went? Could his parents find some way to explain a "new" child already twelve years old?

It wasn't something Luke could ask. He felt guilty just thinking about it.

Mark was making a big ceremony out of bringing the bread to his mouth.

"I'm not scared of you," he taunted, and took a big bite. He swallowed with great difficulty and pretended to gag. "Water, water—quick!" He gulped down half his glass and glared at Luke. "Tastes like poison, all right."

Luke bit into his bread. It was dry and crumbly and tasteless, not like Mother's at all. And everybody knew it. Even Dad and Mother had pained expressions on their faces as they chewed. Dad finally pushed his slice away.

"That's okay, Luke," he said. "I'm not sure I'd want any son of mine getting too good at baking, anyhow. That's what a man gets married for."

Matthew and Mark guffawed.

"Getting married soon, Luke?" Mark teased.

"Sure," Luke said, struggling to sound as devil-may-care as Mark. "But don't think I'd invite *you* to the wedding."

He felt a cold, hard lump in his stomach that wasn't the

bread. Of course he'd never get married. Or do anything. He'd never leave the house.

Mark switched to teasing Matthew, who evidently did have a girlfriend. Luke watched the rest of his family laughing.

"May I be excused?" Luke asked.

Everyone turned to him in surprise. Usually he was the last one to make that request. Mother often begged Matthew and Mark, "Can't you wait, and talk to Luke a little bit longer?"

"Done already?" Mother asked.

"I'm not very hungry," Luke said.

Mother gave him a worried look but nodded, anyway.

Luke went to his room and climbed onto the stool by the back vents. In the dark, it was easier than ever to see into the houses of the new neighborhood. Their windows were lit up against the night. Some families were eating, like his. He could see one set of four people around a dining room table, and one set of three. Some families had their curtains or shades drawn, but sometimes the material was thin and he could still see shadows of the people inside.

Only the Sports Family had all their windows totally blocked, covered by heavy blinds.

CHAPTER *ELEVEN*

L uke watched the Sports Family house constantly after that. Before, he had just looked out the back vents in the early morning and late afternoon, when he knew people were about. But he'd seen the face at two o'clock. Maybe the other kid knew the rhythms of the neighborhood, too, and let his guard down only during times he considered safe.

For three long days, Luke saw nothing.

Then on the fourth day, he was rewarded: One panel of one of the blinds on an upstairs window flipped quickly up and down at eleven o'clock.

The seventh day the blinds in a downstairs window were left up in the morning. Luke saw a light go on and off at 9:07, two full hours after the last of the Sports Family had left. A half hour later, the Sports Family mother drove in in her red car and stomped into the house. Two minutes later, the blind in the downstairs window went down. The mother left immediately.

The thirteenth day was unseasonably warm, and Luke sweated in his attic. Some of the Sports Family's windows were left open, though still covered by the blinds. The wind blew the blinds back a couple times. Luke saw lights on in some of the rooms some of the time, in other rooms as the day wore on. Once he even thought he saw a glow of a TV screen.

He had no doubts anymore. Someone was hiding in the Sports Family house.

The question was, what could he do about it?

MARGARET PETERSON HADDIX

CHAPTER *TWELVE*

Harvest came. Matthew and Mark stayed out of school to help Dad bring the crops in, the three of them working some days from dawn until midnight. Mother's factory got busier, too, and she began working two or three hours of overtime every day. She brought up a store of food to Luke's room so he wouldn't get hungry while they were all away.

"There!" she said cheerfully, lining up boxes of crackers and bags of fruit. "This way, you won't even miss us."

Her eyes begged him not to complain.

"Uh-huh," he said, trying to sound game. "I'll be fine."

He watched the Sports Family house only sporadically now. What other proof did he need? What good did it do him to know about the other third child? What did he expect—that the other kid would run out in his backyard and yell, "Hey, Luke, come out and play!"?

He munched his solitary apples. He ate his crackers alone.

And in spite of himself, a crazy idea grew in his mind, sprouting new details daily.

What if he sneaked into the Sports Family house and met the other third child?

He could do it. It was possible. Theoretically.

He spent entire days plotting his route. He'd be hidden by bushes and the barn through much of his yard. It was only about six feet from there to the nearest tree in the Sports Family's backyard. He could crawl on his stomach. Then he'd be hidden by the fence the Sports Family shared with the Birdbrain Family—all those birdhouses might actually help. After that, it was only three steps to the Sports Family house. They had a sliding-glass door at the back, and on warm days they'd been leaving it open, with just a screen. He could go in there.

Would he dare?

Of course he wouldn't, but still, still—

The first time he looked out the vents and saw maple leaves shot through with shades of red and yellow, he panicked. He needed those leaves to hide him on his way to the Sports Family house. If he waited too long, the leaves would be gone.

He began waking up every morning in a cold sweat, thinking, *Maybe today. Do I dare?*

Just thinking about it made his stomach feel funny.

It rained three days in a row in early October, and he was almost relieved because that meant he couldn't go on those days, didn't even have to think about going. He couldn't risk leaving footprints in the mud. And Dad and Matthew and Mark were in the way, hanging around the house and the barn, grumbling because they couldn't get into the fields.

Finally the rain stopped and the fields dried up and Dad and Matthew and Mark went back to their combine and tractors, acres away from the house.

The backyard and the Sports Family's backyard were dry, too.

And it was warm again. The Sports Family left their sliding-glass door open.

The rain hadn't knocked all the leaves off the backyard trees, but the next rain probably would.

On the third morning after the rain, Luke's stomach churned as he sat on his perch watching the neighborhood empty out. He knew without question that today was the day he'd have to go, if he ever intended to. He couldn't wait until spring. He wouldn't be able to stand it.

He watched twenty-eight people leave in eight cars and one school bus. Hands trembling, he made scratches on the wall again and recounted, once, twice, three times. Twenty-eight. Yes. Twenty-eight. Yes. Twenty-eight. The magic number.

He could hear the blood pounding in his ears. He moved in a daze. Off his perch. Down the stairs. Into the kitchen. And then—out the back door.

CHAPTER *THIRTEEN*

H e had forgotten what fresh air felt like, filling his nostrils and lungs. It felt good. With his back pressed against the house, he stood still for a moment, just breathing. All the months he'd spent inside suddenly seemed like a dream. He'd been like some confused animal hibernating during nice weather. The last real thing that had happened to him was being called inside when the woods were coming down. Real life was outdoors.

But so was danger. And the longer he stayed out, the greater the danger.

He forced himself down into a crouch and half-crawled, half-ran alongside the house and the hedges and the barn. At the back edge of the barn he hesitated, staring into the seemingly endless gulf between the barn and the trees at the boundary between his backyard and the Sports Family's.

Everybody's gone, he told himself. *There's not a soul around to see you.*

Still, he waited, staring at the blades of grass just beyond his feet. He'd been taught all his life to fear open spaces like the one in front of him. It faced dozens of windows. He'd never stepped foot in any place that public, even if it was deserted.

Still hidden by the barn, he made himself inch his foot forward. Then he drew it back.

He turned around and looked at his family's house, so safe and secure. His sanctuary. He heard his mother's voice in his head: *Luke! Inside. Now.* It seemed so real, he remembered something he'd read in one of the old books in the attic about telepathy—supposedly if people really loved you, they could call out to you from miles away if you were in danger.

He should go back. He'd be safe there.

He took a deep breath, looking forward toward the Sports Family's house, then back again toward his own. He thought about returning home—trudging up the worn stairs, going back to his familiar room and the walls he stared at every day. Suddenly he hated his house. It wasn't a sanctuary. It was a prison.

Before he had time to think again, he pushed himself off into a sprint, recklessly streaking across the grass. He didn't even stop to hide at any trees. He ran right to the Sports Family's door and tugged at the screen.

It was locked.

CHAPTER *FOURTEEN*

I n all his plottings, Luke had never thought of the screen door being locked. Though he knew his own parents locked up at night—when they didn't forget—the doors at his house had always been open for him. And he'd never been near anyone else's door.

"Idiot," he muttered to himself.

He tugged harder on the door, but he couldn't concentrate enough to make his hands work together. Each second that passed made the hair on the back of his neck stand up more. He'd never been so exposed in his entire life.

Hurry, hurry, hurry. Get out of sight....

The door didn't budge. He'd have to turn around. Now.

That was what his brain said. What his hand did was plunge through the screen. He pulled the wire away from the frame and reached through. The screen scraped the back of his hand and his arm, but he didn't stop. He fiddled with the lock inside until he heard it click.

He silently slid the screen door back and stepped past the hanging blinds into the Sports Family's house.

Even with the blinds blocking every window, the room he entered was airy and bright. From the freshly painted walls to the sparkling glass tables to the polished wood floor, everything looked new. Luke stared. Almost all the furniture in his own house had been around as long as he could remember, and whatever patterns and designs it originally carried had long ago been worn away. At his house, even the once-orangish couch and the once-greenish chairs were now all a matching sort of brownish gray. This room was different. It reminded him of a word he'd never heard, only read: "pristine." Nobody had ever stepped on these white rugs with manure-covered boots. Nobody had ever sat on those pale blue couches with corn-dust-covered jeans.

Luke might have stood by the door forever, in awe, but someone coughed in another room. Then he heard a strange *be-be-be-beep*. He tiptoed forward. Better to discover than to be discovered.

He went down a long hallway. The beeps had turned into a drawn-out "buzzzzz," coming from a room at the end.

Holding his breath, Luke stopped outside the door to that room and gathered the nerve to peek in. His heart pounded. There was still time to escape unseen, to go back to his house and attic and normal, safe life. But he'd always wonder—

Luke leaned forward slowly, moving a fraction of an inch at a time, until he could just barely see around the door.

Inside the room was a chair and a desk and a big apparatus that Luke vaguely recognized as a computer. And at the computer, typing away furiously, sat a girl.

Luke blinked, thrown off. Somehow he'd never thought about the Sports Family's third child being a girl. She was mostly facing away from Luke, and she wore jeans and a gray sweatshirt not much different from what the Sports Family brothers always wore. Her dark hair was almost as short as Luke's. But there was something about the curve of her cheek, the tilt of her head, the way her sweatshirt clung or didn't cling to her body—all of that made Luke certain she wasn't like him.

He blushed. Then he gulped.

The girl turned her head.

"I—" Luke croaked.

Before he had a chance to think of another word, the girl was across the room and had knocked him down. Then she pinned him to the floor, his arms twisted behind his back, his face buried in the carpet. Luke struggled to turn his head to breathe.

"So," the girl hissed in his ear. "You think you can sneak up on a poor, innocent, unsuspecting girl, who's home all alone? Guess nobody told you about our alarm system. A call went out to our security guards the minute you stepped on our property. They'll be here any second."

Luke panicked. So this was how he'd die. He had to explain. He had to escape.

"No," he said. "They can't come. I—"

58   MARGARET PETERSON HADDIX

"Oh, yeah?" the girl said. "Who are you to stop them?"

Luke raised his head as much as he could. He said the first words that came into his mind.

"Population Police."

The girl let go.

CHAPTER *FIFTEEN*

Luke sat up, checking his arms to make sure she hadn't broken anything.

"You're lying," the girl said.

But she made no effort to tackle him again. She crouched, looking puzzled for a few moments. Then she grinned.

"I got it! You're another one. Great code word. I'll have to think about using that for the rally."

Now it was Luke's turn to squint in confusion.

The girl giggled.

"I mean, you're another shadow child. Right?"

"Shadow—?" Luke wondered why his brain seemed to be slowing down. Was it just because she seemed several miles ahead of him?

"That's not the term you use?" she asked. "I thought 'shadow child' was universal. But, you know, an illegal, someone whose parents broke Population Law 3903. A third."

"I—" Luke couldn't bring himself to confess. He'd broken so many taboos today, leaving the house, standing in the open yard, talking to a stranger. Why did one more violation matter?

"You can say it," the girl coaxed. " 'I'm a third child.' Why should there be anything wrong with that?"

Luke was spared having to answer her, because she suddenly sprang to her feet, exclaiming, "Oh, no! The alarm!"

She raced down the hall and around the corner. Luke followed to find her jerking open a closet door, then punching buttons on a panel of colored lights.

"Too late. Drat!"

She ran to a phone, Luke following breathlessly. She dialed. Luke watched in amazement. He'd never talked on a phone. His parents had told him the Government could trace calls, could tell if a voice on a phone was from a person who was allowed to exist or not.

"Dad—" She made a face. "I know, I know. Call the security company and get them to cancel the alarm, okay?" Pause. "And might I remind you that the penalty for harboring a shadow child is five million dollars or execution, depending on the mood of the judge?"

She rolled her eyes at Luke while she listened to what seemed to be a long answer.

"Oh, you know. These things happen." Another pause. "Yeah, yeah. Love you, too. Thanks, Dad."

She hung up. Luke wondered if he should run back to his house immediately, before the Population Police really did show up.

"They can find you now," Luke said. "Just from the phone—"

The girl laughed.

"They *say*. But everybody knows the Government's not that competent."

Luke started inching toward the back door, just in case.

"But there really was an alarm?" he asked. "And you have security guards?"

"Sure. Doesn't everyone?" the girl took another look at Luke. "Oh. Maybe not."

She winced apologetically as soon as she'd said that. Luke decided to ignore the insult.

"Do the security guards know you're here?" he asked.

"Of course not," the girl said. "If they came, I'd have to hide. Personally, I think my family just has the alarm system to make sure I stay in the house. They don't know I can disable it. But"—she gave him an evil grin—"I set it off sometimes just for fun."

"That's fun?" Luke asked. He'd thought another third child would understand him, be just like him. This girl sure wasn't. "Aren't you scared the guards might find you?"

"Not really." The girl shrugged. "And see, doing it on purpose every now and then helped us today—my dad didn't really even ask why the system needed to be stopped. He just thought it was me making trouble again."

In a twisted way, she kind of made sense. But trying to figure everything out made Luke's head hurt. He glanced toward the door. If he could just get safely home, he'd never complain about being bored again. Here, he felt as baffled as Alice in Wonderland from one of the old books in the attic. Or—he remembered something he'd read in a nature book—maybe he was like the prey of a snake that hypnotized its victims before it ate them. He didn't think the girl would hurt him, but she might keep him confused and fascinated until the Population Police or the security guards or someone else arrived.

The girl saw where he was looking.

"Am I scaring you?" she asked. "Shadow kids can be so jumpy. You're safe, you know. How about if we start over? Would you care for a seat, uh—what's your name, any-way?"

Luke told her.

"Nice to meet you," the girl said, shaking his hand in a way that made him feel like she was kind of making fun of him. Then she led him to sit down on a couch in the room he'd first entered. She perched beside him. "I'm Jen. Really, it's Jennifer Rose Talbot. But do I look like a Jennifer?"

She shook her head and spread out her arms as if Luke should understand something from her rumpled sweat-shirt and messy hair.

Luke frowned.

"I don't know," he said. "I don't know any Jennifers. Just Matthew and Mark and Mother and Dad." He knew his parents' real names were Edna and Harlan, but he won-dered if he shouldn't keep that secret. Just in case. Probably he shouldn't have even mentioned Matthew and

Mark, but he was surprised into it, thinking suddenly about how there was a world full of people outside his house, with a world full of different names he'd never heard of.

"Hmm," the girl said. "Then I have to explain—a Jennifer's supposed to be, like, really girly and prissy. So the joke's on Mom. She wanted some frilly little girl she could put in lacy dresses and sit in the corner. Like a doll." She paused. "Are Matthew and Mark your older brothers?"

Luke nodded.

"So you've never met anyone outside your immediate family?"

Luke shook his head no. Jen looked so amazed, he felt he had to defend himself.

"And you have?" he asked, with almost the same taunting voice he sometimes used with Mark.

"Well, yeah," she said.

"But you're a third child, too," Luke protested. "A shadow child. Right?"

He suddenly felt like it might be easy to cry, if he let himself. All his life, he'd been told he couldn't do everything Matthew and Mark did because he was the third child. But if Jen could go about freely, it didn't make sense. Had his parents lied?

"Don't you have to hide?" he asked.

"Sure," Jen said. "Mostly. But my parents are very good at bribery. And so am I." She grinned wickedly. Then she squinted at Luke. "How *did* you know I was a third child? How did you know I was here?"

Luke told her. Somehow it seemed important to start with the woods coming down, so it turned into a very long story. Jen interrupted frequently with questions and comments—"So you've never been away from your house except to go to your backyard or barn?"; "You've stayed inside for six months?"; and "Gosh, you must really hate these houses, huh?" And then, when he got to the part about seeing her face in the window, she bit her lip.

"My dad would kill me if he knew I'd done that. But the mirrors were messed up, and Carlos bet me I didn't even know what the weather was outside, and—"

"Huh?" Luke said. "Mirrors? Carlos?"

Jen waved away his questions.

"Luke Garner," she announced solemnly, "you have come to the right place. Forget that hiding-like-a-mole stuff. I'm your ticket out."

CHAPTER SIXTEEN

"Want any more potatoes, Luke?" Mother offered that night at supper. "Luke?" Her voice got more insistent. "LUKE?"

Luke jerked his attention back to his family. Mother was holding the bowl of mashed potatoes out to him.

"Er—no," Luke said. "No thanks. I've still got some."

"More for me!" Mark crowed.

Luke tuned them out again. He'd barely eaten his first serving of potatoes, he'd been so busy thinking about his secret visit to the Sports Family house. He couldn't believe he'd dared to go. Just the thought of his run through their yard made his heart beat fast, remembering fear and pride. He'd really done it.

And then meeting Jen was—amazing. There was no other word for it. He was so overwhelmed with wonder at everything he'd seen at her house, everything she'd told him, that he started to say, "Did you know that Jen—"

At the last minute, he clamped his teeth shut, holding the words in. He thought he'd burst. He could feel his face flush red with the effort of keeping still. He bent his head low over his plate so nobody would see. How could he ever manage to keep Jen secret? But he had to, because if he told, they'd forbid him to go back.

And he had to go back.

"We'll set up a signal," Jen had said. "Something I can see—"

"But you don't have vents to look out like I do," Luke protested. "You can't look out the windows."

"Oh, when the mirrors work, it's not a problem. Look." She took him over to a window near the sliding-glass door and showed him a mirror that reflected a wide view of the Talbots' backyard and the landscape beyond. It showed just the corner of the Garners' barn, but when Jen turned it a bit, the entire Garner house came into view. Luke wondered if his parents could set up the same kind of system. Then he looked at the mirror again and decided it might be expensive. And, anyway, how would he explain where he'd gotten the idea?

"So, let's see," Jen said. "A signal. I've got it—how about if I look out every morning at nine, and if you can come over, you shine a flashlight at me. I'll shine one back if everything's safe."

"We don't have any flashlights," Luke said. "Not that work, I mean."

Jen frowned.

"Why not?"

"We haven't had any batteries in, I don't know, four or five years," Luke explained. In fact, he felt proud even to remember what a flashlight was.

"Okay, okay," Jen said. "No flashlight, no computer—"

"Oh, we have a computer," Luke said. "My parents do. And I think it still works. But it's in Dad's office in the front of the house, and I'm not allowed in there. And, anyhow, I'd never be allowed to touch the computer." He remembered once when he was very young, maybe three or four, and he'd followed Mother into Dad's office while she was cleaning. The rows of letters on the computer keyboard had looked like a toy to him, and he'd reached one finger up and tapped the space bar, over and over again. Mother had turned around and freaked out.

"They can find you now!" she'd screamed. "If they were watching—"

And for weeks after that, she'd hidden him even more carefully than ever, locking him in his room when she had to go outside.

Jen rolled her eyes.

"Don't tell me your family believes that Government propaganda stuff," she said. "They've spent so much money trying to convince people they can monitor all the TVs and computers, you know they couldn't have afforded to actually do it. I've been using our computer since I was three—and watching TV, too—and they've never caught me. How about a candle?"

"What?" It took Luke a minute to realize she was talking about the signal again. "The candles—they're all in the kitchen, and I'm not allowed—"

Jen mimicked the words as he said them: "—to go in there."

"They've got you on an awfully short leash, don't they?" she asked.

"No. I mean, yes. But they're just trying to protect me—"

Jen shook her head. "Yeah, I've heard that one. Ever hear of disobeying?"

"I—" Luke started defensively. "I'm here, aren't I?"

Jen laughed. "Got me. But, listen, if you can't do candles or a flashlight, how about just turning on a light that I can see?"

Luke was quicker this time figuring out that she was still talking about the signal.

"The one by the back door," Luke said. "You can't miss it."

He wasn't allowed to turn that on, either, but he didn't dare say "not allowed" again.

Now Luke toyed with his mashed potatoes. His entire conversation with Jen had been like that—she mocked, he defended, but she always got her way.

Of course—he defended her to himself—she knew and had seen so much more than him. After he'd finished his story on the couch, she'd told him hers.

"First," she'd said defiantly, "my parents had me on purpose. Thirteen years ago. Mom already had Bull and Brawn from her first marriage—"

"Your brothers?" Luke asked.

"Yeah. Buellton and Brownley, really, but what kind of names are those for knuckleheads like them? Mom was going through some snobbish upper-class phase with husband number one."

"She's had more than one husband?" Luke asked. He didn't know that was possible.

"Sure," Jen said. "Dad—who's really my stepdad—is number three."

Luke found that so confusing, he just kept his mouth shut.

"Anyhow," Jen said. "Mom was dying to have a little girl, so when she and husband number two got together, she went and paid some doctor lots of money so she could get pregnant."

"What if you'd been a boy?" Luke asked.

"Oh, they got in on the beginning of the gender selection experiments." Luke must have given Jen a particularly blank look, because she explained it. "That means they made sure I was a girl. Doctors can do that, you know, but the Government outlawed the procedure because they were afraid it'd throw the population even more out of whack. I'm sure my parents paid a lot for it. Were your mom and dad trying for a girl?"

Luke thought about it. He remembered Mother saying she'd wanted four boys, but would she have wanted a girl even more? Someone like Mother? He couldn't really picture a girl in his house.

"They weren't trying for anything," he said. "I was a surprise. Luck."

Jen nodded. "I didn't think they paid for you," she said. Then she put her hand over her mouth. "That sounded really terrible, didn't it? I didn't mean anything by it. It's just—you're the first person I've met who wasn't a Baron."

"How do you know I'm not?" Luke asked stiffly.

"Well—" Jen waved her hand in a way that made Luke even more aware of the contrast between his ragged flannel shirt and patched jeans, and Jen's perfect house. "Look, don't be mad. It doesn't matter. Or maybe it does, but I think it's cool that you're not a Baron. You can help me even more."

"Help?" Luke asked.

"With the rally," Jen said. She bit her lip. "Should I— there's no way you could be an infiltrator, is there? Can I trust you?"

"Of course you can," Luke said. He felt insulted again.

Jen leaned her head back and stared at the ceiling, as if an answer were written there. Then she looked back at Luke.

"I'm sorry. I'm botching this. I'm not used to really talking, just on the Net. Look, I trust you, but I'm not the only one involved. So let's wait, okay?"

"Okay," Luke said. But he couldn't help sounding injured.

Jen leaned over and gave his shoulders a quick shake.

"Oh, don't say it like that. Say, 'Okay, Jen, I respect your judgment.' Or, 'Okay, Jen, whatever you think is best.'" She giggled. "That's what Dad tells me I should say when I disagree with him. Can you believe it? Lawyers!"

Luke was glad the subject had changed. "Your dad's a lawyer?" he asked.

Jen rolled her eyes. "Yeah, all Mom's husbands have been. Strange taste, huh? Number one was an environmental lawyer, of all things; number two was corporate—that's how they had enough money to get me. And number three, Dad, is with the Government. High up, I might add."

"But—if you're an illegal—" Luke hadn't thought he could get any more confused.

Jen laughed.

"Haven't you learned? Government leaders are the worst ones for breaking laws. How do you think we got this house? How do you think I got Internet access? How do you think we live?"

"I don't know," Luke said, fully honest. "I don't think I know much of anything."

Jen patted his head, as if he were a little kid or a dog.

"That's okay," she said. "You'll learn."

It wasn't long after that that Luke said he had to leave, because he was afraid Dad or Matthew or Mark might come in for lunch a little early. He dreaded the trip back. Jen walked him to the door, chattering the whole way.

"I'll fix the screen and deal with the security system, so

no one will ever know you were here," she said. "And—oh, no!"

Luke followed her gaze. She was staring at three pinpoints of blood on the carpet.

"I'm sorry," Luke said. "That must be from when I scraped my hand. I'll clean it up. There's still time—"

Secretly, he was glad of the delay.

"No, no," Jen said impatiently. "I don't care about the carpet. It's just that Mom and Dad will know, and when they see I don't have any cuts—"

And then, before Luke even knew what she was doing, she thrust her hand toward the torn part of the screen. The jagged edge didn't cut immediately, so she held the screen with her right hand and raked it across her left. When Jen pulled her hand back, Luke saw a gash even deeper than his. Jen squeezed out a few drops of blood and let them fall to the carpet.

"There," she said.

Stunned, Luke backed out the door.

"Come back soon, farmer boy," Jen said.

Luke turned and ran, blindly, not even slowing down to creep alongside the barn. He went straight to the back door of his house, yanked it open, and let it bang shut behind him.

Now, sitting at supper, he felt his heart pounding again as he thought of how dangerous that had been. Why hadn't he looked first? Why hadn't he crawled? He poked his fork into his potatoes, now gone cold and congealed. He watched Mother gathering up dirty dishes while Dad, Matthew, and Mark leaned back in their chairs, talking of grain yields. Jen had scared him—that was why. Seeing her cut her hand had terrified him. How could she do something like that for him, when they'd just met?

CHAPTER *SEVENTEEN*

Luke spent practically every second of the next three days either reliving his secret visit to Jen or planning another one. The first day, a Government inspector came out to examine the Garners' crop, so Luke stayed in his room the entire day. The second day it rained, and Dad spent the morning doing book work in the house. The third day, Dad was back in the fields, but when Luke crept over to the back door promptly at 9 A.M. and daringly flipped the light switch, he got no answering flash from Jen's house. Maybe the clocks in her house were slow. He left the light on for fifteen whole minutes, terrified the whole time that someone besides Jen might see it. Finally, heartsick, he switched it off and climbed with shaky legs back to his room.

What if something had happened to Jen? What if she were sick—dying, even—alone in her house? What if she'd been caught or turned in? Just from the little time Luke had spent with her, he could tell: She took a lot of risks.

It never had occurred to him that knowing another

person would give him someone else to worry about.

He steadied himself by leaning against the wall at the top of the stairs and reminded himself of less frightening possibilities: Maybe one of her parents was just out running errands, not working, so they were going to be home soon. Maybe...he tried to think of another safe reason Jen hadn't signaled for him to come. But he had so much trouble picturing her ordinary life that his imagination failed him.

He found out the next day, when he risked a dash to Jen's house as soon as Jen answered his signal.

"Where were you?" he asked instantly.

"When? Yesterday?" She yawned, sliding the door shut behind him. "Did you try to come over? I'm sorry. Mom had a free day and made me go shopping."

Luke gaped at her. "Shopping? You went out?"

Jen nodded nonchalantly.

"But I didn't see you leave—" Luke protested.

Jen looked at him as if she seriously wondered if he had a brain. "Of course not. I was hiding. The backseat of our car is hollowed out—Dad had it custom-built."

"You went out—" Luke repeated in awe.

"Well, it's not like I saw anything until we got to the mall. Two hours of riding in the dark is not my idea of fun. I hate it."

"But at the mall—you got out? You didn't have to hide?"

Jen laughed at his amazement.

"Mom got me a forged shopping pass a long time ago.

Supposedly, I'm her niece. It's good enough to convince store clerks, but if the Population Police ever found me in a roadside stop, I'd be dead. There you have it, my mother's priorities. Shopping is more important than my life."

Luke shook his head and sat down on the couch because his knees were feeling a little shaky.

"I didn't know," he said. "I didn't know thirds could do that."

What if Mother and Dad got him a forged pass? For a minute he could almost picture it—they could hide him under burlap bags in the pickup truck bed until they got into town.

Everybody in town knew Mother and Dad. Everybody knew Mother and Dad had only two sons. Matthew and Mark.

"You went to the city," he said.

"Well, yeah," Jen said. "You don't see any malls around here, do you?"

"What was it like?" Luke almost whispered.

"Boring," Jen said. "Really, really boring. Mom wanted to buy me a dress—who knows why—so we went to one store after another, and I had to try on all these dresses that scratched and pricked and poked me. And then she made me get a bunch of bras—oh, sorry," she said when Luke blushed a deep red. "I guess you don't talk much about bras at your house."

"Matthew and Mark do, sometimes, when they're being...dirty," Luke said.

"Well, bras aren't *dirty*," Jen said. "They're just torture devices invented by men or mothers or something."

"Oh," Luke said, looking down.

"But, anyway," Jen said, with a bounce that propelled her off the couch. "I checked you out on the computer and you're all right, you don't exist. Not officially, anyway. So you're safe. And—"

Hearing Jen say that so flippantly—*you don't exist*—made Luke feel funny.

"How do you know I'm safe?" he interrupted.

"Fingerprints," Jen said. When Luke gave her a blank look, she explained. "My brother Brawn went through this phase where he wanted to be a detective—not that he ever would have been smart enough for it—and I remembered he still has a fingerprinting kit. So I dusted for your fingerprints on things you touched, just like on TV. I got a really good print off the wall. Then I scanned that into the computer, linked into the national file of fingerprints and, *voilà*, I discovered your fingerprints don't exist, so neither do you. Officially."

She made a mocking face for emphasis. Luke wanted to ask, *The Population Police can't find me because of what you did, can they?* But he understood so little of what she'd explained that he didn't think it would help to ask anything. And Jen was already onto the next thought.

"And, anyhow, you seem trustworthy. So-oo, now that I know you're safe, I can tell you about the rally and show you our secret chat rooms and everything—"

Jen was already leaving the room, so he had to follow just to hear the rest of her sentence.

"Want something to eat or drink?" she asked, hesitating at the doorway to the grand kitchen. "I was so surprised, I forgot to be a good hostess the last time. What'll it be? Soda? Potato chips?"

"But those are illegal," Luke protested. He remembered reading something about junk food in one of the books in the attic and asking his mother about it. She'd explained that it was something people used to eat all the time, until the Government shut down the factories that made it. She wouldn't tell him why. But, as a special treat, she'd brought out a bag of potato chips she'd been saving for years and shared them, just with him. They were salty, but hard to chew. Luke had pretended to like them only because Mother seemed to want him to.

"Yeah, well, we're illegal, too, so why shouldn't we enjoy ourselves?" Jen asked, thrusting a bowl of chips at him. To be polite, Luke took one chip. And then another. And another. These potato chips were so good, he had to hold himself back from grabbing them by the handful. Jen stared at him.

"Do you go hungry sometimes?" she asked in a low voice.

"No," Luke said in surprise.

"Some shadow children do because they don't have food ration cards, and the rest of their family doesn't share," she said, opening a refrigerator that was bigger than every appliance in the Garners' kitchen put together. "My family can get all the food we want, of course, but"—she looked at him in a way that once again made him conscious of his ragged clothes—"How does your family get food for you?"

The question puzzled Luke.

"The same way they get it for themselves," he said. "We grow it. We have a garden—I used to work in it a lot, before, you know. And then, we have the hogs, or used to, and I guess sometimes we'd trade a butchered hog for someone else's butchered steer, so we'd have beef—"

Those were all shadowy transactions in Luke's mind. He had to strain his brain to remember overhearing Dad or Matthew reporting to Mother, "Ready to cook some steak? Johnston up near Libertyville wants some ham..."

Jen dropped a plastic bottle full of brown liquid. "You eat *meat*?" she exclaimed.

"Sure. Don't you?" Luke asked.

"When Dad can get it," Jen said, bending to pick up the bottle. She poured a glassful for Luke and one for herself. Both drinks fizzed and bubbled. "Even his clout isn't *that* great. The Government's been trying to force everyone, even the Barons, to become vegetarians."

"Why?" Luke asked.

Jen handed him his glass.

"Something about vegetables being more efficient," she said. "Farmers have to use a lot more land to produce one pound of meat than to produce a pound of—what's it called?—soybeans."

Luke wrinkled his nose at the thought of eating soybeans.

"I don't know," he said slowly. "We always fed our hogs the grain we couldn't sell because it didn't meet Government standards. But since the Government made us get rid of our hogs, Dad just lets that grain rot in the field."

"Really?" Jen grinned as if he'd just announced the overthrow of the Government. She thumped him on the back just as he took his first sip of soda. Between the bubbly drink and her enthusiastic pounding, Luke started coughing. Jen didn't seem to notice. "See, I told you you'd be a big help. I'm going to go post that on a bulletin board right now!"

"Wait—" Luke sputtered between coughs. He didn't know what she was talking about. But he couldn't let her get his family in trouble. He chased her down the hall, catching up just as she was sliding into the chair in front of the computer. She switched it on, and it made the *be-be-be-be-beeep* sounds Luke had heard the last time. Luke stood to the side, carefully out of sight of the screen.

"It's not going to bite you," Jen said. "Grab a chair. Sit down."

Luke inched back.

"But the Government—" he said.

"The Government's incompetent and stupid," Jen said. "Get it? Believe me, if they were watching through my computer screen, I'd know by now."

Meekly, Luke pulled over a padded chair and sat down.

He watched as Jen typed in, "If the Government let farmers feed their animals the grain they can't sell, there'd be more meat."

Luke was relieved that she hadn't mentioned his family. But, unless the Government was spying on them, he couldn't understand what difference it made for her to write that.

"Where'd that go?" he asked as the words disappeared. "Who's going to see it?"

"I put it on a Department of Agriculture bulletin board. Anyone with a computer can find it now. Maybe a Government worker with half a brain will see it and actually think for the first time this decade."

"But—" Luke squinted in confusion. "Why does it matter?"

Jen fixed her gaze on Luke.

"You don't even know, do you?" she asked. "You don't know why they passed the Population Law."

"N-no," Luke admitted.

"It's all about food," Jen said. "The Government was scared we'd all run out of food if the population kept growing. That's why they made you and me illegal, to keep people from starving."

Luke suddenly felt doubly guilty for the potato chips he was still cramming into his mouth. He swallowed hard and lowered his hands to his lap, instead of back into the chip bowl.

"So if I didn't eat, my food would go to someone who

was legal," Luke said. But in his family, that would just be Matthew or Mark, and they were hardly starving. Matthew was even starting to sport the same roll of fat around his waist that Dad had. Then Luke remembered the tramp from long ago, saying, "I ain't et in three days...." Was that Luke's fault?

Jen laughed.

"Stop looking so worried," she said. "That *is* what the Government thinks, but they're wrong. My dad says there's plenty of food, it's just not distributed right. That's why they've got to stop the Population Law. That's why they've got to recognize you and me and all the other shadow kids. That's why we're going to have the rally."

As ignorant as he was, Luke could tell from the way she said it that the rally was important.

"Can you tell me about the rally now?" he asked humbly.

"Yes," Jen said. She pushed away from the computer and twirled on her chair. "Hundreds of us—all the shadow children I could track down—are going to march on the Government in protest. We'll go right to the president's house. We won't leave them alone until they give us the same rights everybody else has."

Just my luck, Luke thought. I finally meet another third child, and she's absolutely crazy.

"And"—Jen said, as bubbly as the shaken soda—"You can come, too. Won't it be great?"

CHAPTER *EIGHTEEN*

—" Luke said. He couldn't look at Jen's triumphant grin. "I don't think I—"

He thought about how terrifying it was just running back and forth between his house and Jen's. Even this morning, on his third run through their yards, his heart had pounded so hard, he'd wondered if it could burst from fear. And in the yard at least, he was sure—or as sure as he could be—that no one was watching. How could Jen think he would dare go out in public, where he knew people could see him—people in Government, no less—and say, "I am a third child! I want to be treated like everyone else!"

"Scared?" Jen said softly.

Luke could only nod.

Jen turned back to the computer.

"Well, I am, too," she said matter-of-factly. She typed something, then looked back at Luke. "Some. But don't you think it'll be a relief? No more hiding, no more pretending, just—being free!"

Luke wondered if he'd always misunderstood the meaning of the word "relief." Jen's rally sounded like his worst nightmare.

"You can think about it," she said. "You don't have to decide anything today. Now, ready to chat?"

Luke looked back at the computer screen, where rows of words were unfurling:

Carlos: It's 105 here, and my parents think it's a waste to run the a.c. during the day. Can you say heartless?

Sean: Why don't you just crank it up, then turn it off again right before they get home? That's what Pat and I do. They'll never know.

Carlos: Yeah, but my parents probably read their electric bill.

Yolanda: So what are they going to do? Ground you?

Carlos: Good point. I'm searching for the temp control right now.

Yolanda: Where's Jen?

Sean: You know she never gets up this early.

Carlos: Curses—my parents have the temp control locked somehow. Told you they were evil. Where is Jen? I can't wait for her sarcarstic comment.

Luke read the words Jen was typing: "I'm right here, and, Sean, I do so get up early. I just don't always choose to see *you* first thing. And Carlos—what's wrong? Is there sweat in your eyes? There's only one 'r' in 'sarcastic.'"

She hit another key, and the words appeared right up

with everyone else's. They were followed quickly by another line:

Sean: Good morning to you, too, Jen. Glad to see you're still among the living.

Jen typed quickly: "No, just among the hidden. Not the same thing at all!!!!" Then she sent it, too.

"What is this?" Luke asked. "Some sort of game?"

He remembered Jen mentioning a Carlos before, and never explaining who he was. Were these some sort of computerized imaginary friends?

"Carlos, Sean, Yolanda—they're all other third children. Sean's even got a brother, Pat, who's a fourth child. This is how I talk to them."

Luke watched the next line of type appear: "Carlos: Thanks for the sympathy, Jen."

"But how—?" Luke asked, still doubtful.

"Oh, you know. It's the Net," Jen said. "If you've got a spare hour or two sometime, I'll give you the technical gobbledygook to explain it. All I care about is that it works. I'd die without someone to talk to."

She was typing even as she talked. Luke craned his head to see what she wrote: "Guess what? The kid I told you about, Luke, is here with me."

Quickly, three "Hi, Luke"s appeared on the screen.

Luke fought down panic.

"But the Government—" he said. "They'll find me—"

Jen playfully slugged his arm. "Chill, okay? Nobody from the Government can get in this chat room. We all use a password. Just third children know it. And, anyhow, even if someone else read this, what would they know? Just that somewhere in the world, there's a kid named Luke. Big deal."

"But they can trace you through the computer, and then they'd find me, too." Luke's heart was still pounding.

"Look, if they could trace people through the computer, or through this chat room, wouldn't they have found me a long time ago?" Jen asked.

Luke tried to think clearly. "Your parents," he said. "You said they bribe people. So you're safe. But mine—"

Jen was shaking her head.

"No, I'm not safe," she said grimly. "Even my parents couldn't bribe the Population Police if they found me. Maybe to keep them from looking—but maybe not even that. The Population Police get some ridiculously big reward for every illegal they find. Why do you think I hide at all? Why do you think we have to have the rally? *Everybody* ought to be safe. And nobody should have to use bribes just to walk down the street or go to a mall or take a ride in a car...."

Luke glanced back at the computer screen, where the conversation continued.

"How did all those people find out the password?" he asked. "How did you?"

"Well, I created the chat room, so I made it up," Jen said.

"And I knew a couple other shadow kids, and I got my parents and their parents to get the password to them. And then some of those kids spread the password to other kids they knew. Last time I counted, I had contact with eight hundred kids."

Luke shook his head. He didn't think even his parents knew that many people.

"So what is the password?" he asked.

" 'Free,' " Jen said. "It's 'free.' "

CHAPTER *NINETEEN*

Luke left Jen's that day with a pile of books and computer printouts clutched to his chest.

"Some reading material for you," she'd said. "So you'll understand."

Back in his own room, Luke sat down on his bed and opened the first book. It was thick and carried its title in ominous black letters: THE POPULATION DISASTER. The type inside was small and closely spaced. Luke read a sentence at random: "While debate continues over the carrying capacity of the earth—" He skipped ahead. "If the Total Fertility Rate in industrialized countries had remained at or below 2.1—" Luke saw that reading this book would be like puzzling out the letters Dad got from the Government. He glanced at the other two books: *The Famine Years Revisited* and *The Population Reversal*. They looked no easier. The computer printouts were at least brief, but both "The Problem of the Shadows" and "The Population Law: Our Country's Biggest Mistake," were full of big words.

Luke sighed. He was tempted to put the books aside and just ask Jen to explain them to him. And he might have, except for what she'd said as she'd begun handing them to him. "Oh, my gosh! I didn't think—you can read, can't you?"

"Of course," Luke had answered stiffly. "I was reading in the chat room, wasn't I?"

"Yes, but you could have been—oh, never mind. I've offended you again, haven't I? Me and my big mouth. It wouldn't have been anything to be ashamed of, even if you couldn't. Oh, I'm making things worse. I'll shut up. Here."

And it had seemed to Luke that she'd pulled even bigger books off the bookshelves after that.

Now he resolutely turned to the beginning of *The Population Disaster* and began reading: "Since some elements of the overpopulation crisis were foreseen in the 1800s, an uninformed observer could only wonder why humankind came so near to total annihilation. But—"

Luke reached for the dictionary and settled in for the long haul.

It rained for the next several days, so Luke read constantly, not even tempted to race over to Jen's instead. He could hear Dad banging around downstairs, stomping in and out from the barn or the machine shed. Now that the harvest was in, Luke thought Dad might be bored without the pigs to take care of. So Luke read cautiously, always ready to shove his population book under his pillow and replace it with one of his adventure books. The preparation paid off on the fourth day, when he heard Dad's footsteps on the stairs.

"Hey, Luke, what're you up to?"

"Nothing," Luke said, turning *Treasure Island* right side up at the very last moment. Dad didn't notice.

"Want to play cards?"

They played rummy on Luke's bed. Luke could feel the corner of *The Population Disaster* poking his back throughout the entire game. And he kept wanting to ask Dad about what he was learning. He spent most of the first game biting his tongue. Dad won.

"Again?" Dad asked, shuffling the cards.

"If you don't have any work you've got to do."

"In November? With no livestock? Only work I've got now is figuring out how we're going to pay our bills once the hog money runs out."

"Isn't there some way to grow stuff inside during the winter? Like down in the basement, with special lights, lots of water and extra minerals. And then you could sell it?" Luke asked without thinking. He'd just finished reading a chapter in the population book about hydroponics.

Dad squinted.

"Seems I did hear tell of that once."

Luke won the next hand. Dad didn't seem to be concentrating. At the end, Dad said, "Mind if we quit now?"

Luke was terrified Dad would ask where he'd heard of hydroponics. So he just said, "No problem."

Dad left muttering, "Growing food inside...hmmm..."

Luke wished he'd had the nerve to ask about the Population Law, or the famines, or even some family history.

Once he got past the dense language, the books Jen had loaned him were full of revelations. As best he could understand it, the world had simply gotten too full of people about twenty years earlier. Poor countries had it particularly bad, and people there often starved or were malnourished. But then something worse happened: Terrible droughts struck the parts of the world that always grew the most food. For three years, they grew almost nothing. People everywhere starved. In Luke's country, the Government began rationing food, only allowing people to have 1,500 calories a day. And, to make sure there was food, they seized control of all food production. They forced factories that had made junk food to crank out healthy food instead. They forced farmers to move to land that would be more likely to produce. *(Is that why we don't live near our grandparents?* Luke wanted to ask his parents.) But the Government didn't think that was enough. They wanted to make sure there would never again be more people than the farmers could feed. So they passed the Population Law, too.

In the evenings, spooning in his stew or cutting up his meat, Luke felt pangs of guilt now. Perhaps someone was starving someplace because of him. But the food wasn't *there*—wherever the starving people were—it was *here*, on his plate. He ate it all.

"Luke, you're so quiet lately. Is everything all right?" Mother asked one night when he waved away second helpings of cabbage.

"I'm fine," he said, and went back to eating silently.

But he was worrying. Worrying that maybe the Government was right and that he shouldn't exist.

Only when he got to the two computer printouts did he begin to feel better. One of the articles began, "The Population Law is evil." The other said, "Hundreds of children are hidden, mistreated, starved, neglected, abused—even murdered—for no reason. Forcing children into the shadows can be counted as genocide."

"How can this be?" he asked Jen a week later when he finally got a chance to go back to her house. "How can the books and the articles be so different?"

She handed him a glass of soda.

"What do you mean?" she asked.

Luke pointed to *The Population Disaster.* "This book says the human race would have gone extinct if we hadn't had the Population Law. And this"—he held up and shook "The Problem of the Shadows" article—"this says the Population Law was totally unnecessary and cruel. It says there was plenty of food, even during the famines, except that the Barons were hoarding it." Belatedly, he remembered that Jen was a Baron. "Sorry."

Jen shrugged, not the least bit offended.

"So what's the truth?" Luke asked.

Jen shook potato chips into a bowl.

"Well, think about it. The Government allowed those books to be published—they probably even paid for them. So of course they're going to say what the Government wants people to believe. They're just propaganda. Lies. But the articles, the authors of those probably put themselves at risk getting the information out. So they're right."

Luke pondered that. "Then why'd you make me read the books?" he asked.

"So you'd understand how stupid the Government is," Jen said. "So you'd understand why we have to make them see the truth."

Luke looked at the stack of thick books on the Talbots' kitchen counter. They looked so official, so important—who was he to say they weren't true?

CHAPTER *TWENTY*

Luke feared he'd have to wait months between visits to Jen once the snow started. But the weather proved kind that winter—most days were dry and clear. He didn't have leafy trees to hide behind, but he began to feel safe, anyway, crawling through his and Jen's backyards. By mid-January he could make the entire journey without his heart beating abnormally at all. The odds against someone watching from one of the other Baron houses seemed too astronomical to worry about. His only concern was Dad.

Dad usually hung around the house a lot during the winter. Without the hogs to tend to, he could easily have been there even more than usual, preventing Luke from ever sneaking out. But suddenly Dad had taken to heading to town many mornings, yelling up to Luke, "I'm going to the library. You've got something up there to eat for lunch, don't you?" or, "There's some plastic tubing over to Slyton I want to check out. Tell the boys when they get in from school, you hear?"

"It's that hydroponics notion," Luke bragged to Jen one day in late January while they were sitting at the computer together. "I got Dad all excited about it, and now he's too busy with that to notice what I do."

"What's hydroponics?" Jen asked.

"It was in one of your books—you know, growing plants indoors, without soil, just using water and special minerals."

"Oh," Jen said. "Does he think the Government would actually let him do that?"

"I guess so," Luke said. "Why wouldn't they?"

Jen shrugged. "Why does the Government do anything?"

Luke didn't have an answer to that. Jen turned back to the computer chat room, where everyone was debating fake I.D.'s.

Carlos: Mom says they won't buy me one until I'm 18, because she thinks the Gov. wouldn't challenge an adult's as much. And maybe they'll be cheaper then.

Pat: Maybe Sean and I will get ours by the time we're ninety. Dad and Mom have been saving for them as long as we can remember.

Yolanda: My dad sez he's waiting to find one that's fool-proof. He sez there are too many bad ones out there.

Jen began typing furiously. "Who needs a fake I.D.? Carlos, they'd probably get one for you that says 'John Smith,' and you'd have to spend the rest of your life trying to pass for an Anglo. My parents have been begging me to get a fake I.D. for years, but I won't until I can have one that says 'Jen Talbot' and is really *mine*.

"Have you all forgotten the rally? We're all gonna get real I.D.'s that say who we really are!!!! WE AREN'T FAKES! WE SHOULDN'T HAVE TO HIDE!"

She jabbed the Enter button so hard, the computer shook.

"But, Jen," Luke said timidly, "I thought you used a fake I.D. to go shopping with your mom. It said you were her niece."

Jen turned her fierce gaze to Luke.

"No, that was just a shopping pass," she said. "I don't like using that, either, but I figured I can't fight my parents about everything. What they're talking about"—she pointed at the computer screen—"is taking on a fake identity permanently. Most shadow kids do that eventually—they go live with another family and pretend to be someone they aren't for the rest of their lives."

"So you'd rather hide?" Luke asked. He thought about using a different name, living in a different family, being a different person. He couldn't imagine it.

"No, of course I wouldn't rather hide," Jen said irritably. "But getting one of those I.D.'s—that's just a different way of hiding. I want to be me and go about like anybody else. There's no compromise. Which is why I've got to convince these idiots that the rally's their only chance."

There was a shocked blankness on the computer screen after Jen's entry. Then Carlos ventured, "Um, Jen, got any of your parents' blood pressure medicine handy? Sounds like you need it."

Jen stabbed the power button on the computer. The screen instantly went dark. She spun around in her chair and clenched her fists.

"Argh!" she screamed, with a grimace of frustration.

"Jen?" Luke asked. He leaned away from her in case she decided to use those clenched fists.

Jen turned to Luke in surprise, as though she'd forgotten he was there.

"Don't you ever feel like saying, 'I can't take this anymore'?" she asked. She leaped up and began pacing the floor. "Don't you ever want to just walk out into the sunshine and say, 'Forget hiding! I don't care!'? Am I the only one who feels this way?"

"No," Luke whispered.

She whirled around and pointed at the computer.

"Then what's wrong with them? Why don't they understand? Why aren't they taking this seriously?"

Luke bit his lip.

"I think," he said, "people just have different ways of expressing what they feel. Those kids make jokes and complain. You run around screaming your head off and tackling people."

He was proud of himself for figuring that out, considering he really only knew five people in the whole world. But for the first time, he wondered how the rest of his family would cope if any of them had to hide. Dad would get grumpy. Mother would try to make the best of it, but you'd be able to tell that she was really unhappy. Matthew would be quiet, but would look sad all the time, the way he looked every time anyone mentioned the pigs they couldn't keep anymore. Mark would gripe so much that he'd make everyone miserable. For the first time, Luke felt a glimmer of pride, that he dealt with hiding better than anyone else in his family would. He thought.

Jen snorted at his explanation. "Whatever," she said. She slid back into her chair by the computer. "But the rally's in April. I've got three months to make sure everyone's ready."

She switched on the computer and began typing furiously again.

Luke slipped away a few hours later. He wasn't sure Jen noticed him leaving.

CHAPTER *TWENTY-ONE*

I n February, Dad got the letter from the Government forbidding him from trying to grow anything indoors.

"It has come to our attention that you have been purchasing excess amounts of plastic pipe, such as is used in the germination, cultivation, and development of vegetative matter in an interior structure," the letter began. "Due to the preponderance of such agricultural methods in the cultivation of illegal substances, we order you to cease and desist immediately...."

Luke read the letter at supper, after everyone else in the family had had a stab at trying to figure out what it meant. Somehow, after reading all the big books that Jen had loaned him, he didn't find the fancy words so daunting.

"They want you to stop," Luke said. "They're scared you're going to grow something illegal. And this part"— he pointed at the letter, although everyone else was at the table, several feet away, and he was in his usual spot on the stairs—"this part, where they say, 'render all such materials for our adjudication,' that means you have to turn over all the stuff you bought and they'll decide if they're going to fine you or not."

The rest of the family looked at Luke in amazement. Then Mark started giggling.

"Drugs," he said. "They think you're going to grow drugs."

Dad flashed him a look of pure disgust.

"Think it's funny? We'll see what you think next year when your feet grow and we don't have money for new shoes."

Mark stopped laughing.

"We'll get by," Luke's mother said quietly. "We always have."

Dad shoved back from the table.

"Why didn't I get a permit?" he asked no one in particular. "Maybe if I just get a permit—"

By then, Luke had read the rest of the letter.

"They don't give out permits for hydroponics," he said. "This says it's always illegal."

This time he only got a glare from Dad.

Luke felt his father's disappointment, and seeing his parents so worried about money made a small voice whisper in the back of his head, *Maybe if they didn't have you, they could afford everything they want.* But he didn't eat that much, and all of his clothes were hand-me-downs from Matthew and Mark. And how much could it cost to heat his attic room? Sometimes he found ice crystals on the chair he sat in to watch the neighborhood. He tried to ignore the voice.

What bothered him more was that, without the hydro-ponics idea to keep him busy, Dad barely left the farm for the rest of the winter. Luke made it over to Jen's only once in all of February, and twice in March, when Dad began driving around looking for the best seed corn prices.

But each time, Jen greeted him with big hugs and acted genuinely thrilled to see him. Her tantrum in January seemed forgotten. One day, the two of them made a huge mess of the Talbots' kitchen baking cookies.

"Won't your parents mind?" Luke asked when Jen scolded him for attempting to clean the flour handprints off the cabinets and refrigerator and stove.

"Are you kidding? I want this preserved. They'll be thrilled to see any sign of domesticity on my part," Jen said.

Another time, they played board games all morning, sprawled out on the floor of the Talbots' family room.

The third day, they just spent the whole time talking. Jen kept Luke enthralled with stories of places she'd been, people she'd met, things she'd seen.

"When I was little, Mom used to take me to a play group that was all third children," Jen said. She giggled. "The thing was, it was all Government officials' kids. I think some of the parents didn't even like kids—they just thought it was a status symbol to break the Population Law and get away with it."

"What'd you do at the play group?" Luke asked.

"Played, of course. Everybody had a lot of toys. And one

of the kids had a dog he brought with him sometimes, and we all took turns feeding it dog biscuits."

"These people had pets, too?" Luke asked incredulously.

"Well, you know, they were Barons," Jen said.

Luke frowned. He slid down in the soft couch, so different from anything in his own house.

"My dad says that when he was little, just about everyone he knew had pets. He had a dog named Bootsy and a cat named Stripe. He talks about them all the time. Why'd the Government make pets illegal?"

"Oh, you know, the food thing," Jen said. She took a chocolate chip cookie from a pack they were sharing and waved it for emphasis. "Without dogs and cats, there's more food for humans. My dad says if it weren't for the Barons breaking the law, lots of species would have gone extinct."

Luke looked at the cookie in his own hand. So now was he supposed to feel guilty about eating food that should have gone to animals, as well as to other people?

Jen saw his expression. "Hey, don't go dopey on me," she said. "It's all a scam, remember? There's more than enough food in the world, especially now that there aren't enough babies being born."

"What?" Luke asked.

"Well, besides passing the Population Law, the Government went on this big campaign to make women think it was something evil to get pregnant and have kids. They put posters up in all the cities, with things like, 'Who's the worst criminal?' under a picture of a pregnant lady and, I don't know, some tough-looking crooks. And then if you read the whole sign it'd tell you the woman was the worst of all. Another one"—Jen giggled—"it had a picture of a huge pregnant belly, with the label, 'Ladies, do you want to look like this?' And women aren't allowed to go anywhere once they get pregnant. So now, my dad told me, there are so few babies being born that the population's going to be cut in half."

Luke shook his head, confused as usual. "So why doesn't the Government take down the signs and let people have as many babies as they want?"

Jen rolled her eyes. "Luke, you've got to quit thinking this makes any sense," Jen said. "It's the Government, remember? That's why we've got to have the rally—"

Luke changed the subject as quickly as he could. "What do women do if they can't go anywhere the whole time they're pregnant? I don't know about humans, but pigs take almost four months to have a baby. Do the women stay home all that time?"

"Hiding like us, you mean?" Jen asked. But she took the distraction. "Lots of them pretend they're just getting fat. My mom said she went shopping the day before I was born, and nobody noticed. But that's my mom and shopping."

And then she was off on a tale about her mother taking Jen shopping in a city ten hours away, just because she'd heard a store sold good purses there.

"That's probably the only reason my brothers don't turn me in," Jen said. "If she didn't have me, my mother would drag them around shopping. Can you see those two gorillas with shopping bags?"

Jen did an impression, walking around with her arms dragging from imaginary loaded-down bags. Even though Luke had only seen her brothers from a distance, he caught the resemblance and laughed.

"Your brothers would never turn you in," he protested. "Would they?"

"Of course not," Jen agreed. "They lo-ove me." She hugged herself mockingly and flopped back onto the couch beside Luke. "Anyhow, they wouldn't be smart enough to figure out how to turn me in without getting the rest of the family in trouble. What about your brothers?"

"They're not stupid," Luke said defensively. "Or—do you mean—"

"Would they ever betray you?" Jen narrowed her eyes, truly curious. "Not now, necessarily, but, say, years from now, if your parents were dead and it wouldn't hurt anybody but you, and they'd get lots of money for it—"

It was a question Luke had never considered. But he knew the answer.

"Never," he said, his voice cracking with earnestness. "I can trust them. I mean, we grew up together."

It was strange how he could be so sure, because they barely took time even to tease him anymore. Matthew was getting very serious with his girlfriend, and spent every spare moment at her house. Mark had suddenly gone basketball-crazy, and talked Dad into nailing an old tire rim to the front of the barn for a hoop. Luke could hear him outside, throwing balls late into the night. No matter how certain he was of their loyalty, Luke sometimes felt like his brothers had outgrown him. He missed them.

But it didn't matter. He had Jen now.

Luke kept Jen from talking about the rally the rest of that day, and they didn't even go near the computer. They just had fun. He crawled back to his house a few hours later, thinking that he didn't mind at all anymore, having to hide. He could go on this way forever, as long as he got to visit Jen. The leaves would come back to the trees soon, and he'd feel even safer on his trips to her house. And when planting season started, Dad would be out in the fields all day, and Luke could see Jen all the time.

But April came before planting season.

CHAPTER *TWENTY-TWO*

I t rained the first two weeks of April, and Luke was in a tizzy wondering when he would ever get to see Jen again. Finally the ground dried out, and Dad headed out to the fields to plow. Luke raced to Jen's house.

"Oh, good!" she greeted him. "You can get the advance battle plans. I was afraid we were just going to have to pick you up Thursday night and fill you in then."

Luke carefully slid the door shut behind him and straightened the blinds so he and Jen would be totally hidden. Then he turned to face her.

"What are you talking about?" he asked. But he knew. His heart began to thump harder than it had in his rush through the backyards.

"The rally, of course," Jen said impatiently. "Everything's set. I'm taking one of my parents' cars, and I'm picking up three other kids on my way. But I made sure there'd be room for you. You should feel lucky—lots of kids are just going to walk. We're all meeting at the president's house at 6 A.M."

Luke clutched the cord to the blinds.

"Do you know how to drive?" he asked.

"Well enough." She flashed him a wicked grin. "My brothers told me how. Come on."

She waved him over to the couch. He sank into it while Jen perched on the edge.

"What if the Population Police stop you before you get to the capital?" he asked.

"Us, you mean. We. You're going, too, remember? Don't worry—nobody'll stop us." She giggled. "I checked the national employee staffing schedules through the computer. Let's just say several of the Population Police got some unexpected days off."

"You mean you changed their schedules? You can do that?"

Jen nodded, a wicked gleam in her eye.

"It took me a whole month to figure out how, but you are now looking at an accomplished hacker."

Dimly, Luke realized why Jen had seemed so relaxed and happy on his last several visits. They'd been vacations for her, breaks from intense work on plans for the rally. He looked closer and saw the fatigue in her eyes. She looked like a younger version of Mom after a twelve-hour shift in the chicken factory, or Dad after a long day of baling hay. But there was something more in her expression—his parents had never looked so feverishly giddy.

"What if someone finds out what you did? And changes it back?"

Jen shook her head. "They won't. I was very selective—

I coordinated everyone's travel plans and only eliminated the police who had to be eliminated. Aren't you excited? We're going to be free after all these years." She leaned down and pulled a sheaf of papers out from under the couch. "Best hiding place in the world. The maid's too lazy to clean under there. Now, let's see, I'll pick you up at 10 P.M., and—"

Luke was glad she was looking at the papers instead of him. He wouldn't have been able to meet her eyes.

"Okay, okay, so nobody's going to be caught on the way to the capital. But once you're there, at the president's house, someone will call the Population Police, and then—" Luke felt panicky just thinking about it.

Jen wasn't fazed. "So what?" she asked. "I don't care who gets called once we're there. Heck, I may call the Population Police myself. They're not going to do anything to a crowd of a thousand, especially not when lots of us are related to Government officials. We'll make them listen to us. We're a revolution!"

Luke looked away. "But your friends—you were mad at them because they weren't into it—what if they don't show up?"

"What do you mean?" Jen's voice was fierce.

Luke could barely speak for the panic welling inside him. "In the chat room, they were making jokes. Carlos and Sean and the others. You said they weren't taking it seriously."

"Oh, *that*. That was—a long time ago. They're all on

board. They're psyched. Why, Carlos is my lieutenant in all of this. You wouldn't believe how much he's helped. So, okay, ten o'clock, and then it's eight hours to the capital, and—" she consulted her papers again. "What kind of sign do you want to carry? 'I deserve a life' or 'End the Population Law now!' or—this is one I found in an old book—'Give me liberty or give me death'?"

Luke tried to imagine what Jen seemed to be taking for granted. He could get in a car. He'd sat in the pickup in the barn—a car wasn't much different. And for eight hours, that would be all he had to do—sit. Not that difficult. Except that panic would be coursing through him for the entire eight hours because of where the car was going. And then to get out, in public, at the president's house? And carry a sign? His imagination failed. He broke out in a cold sweat.

"Jen, I—" he started.

"Yes?"

Jen waited. The silence between them seemed to be growing, like a balloon. Luke struggled to speak.

"I can't go."

Jen gaped at him.

"I can't," he said again, weakly.

Jen shook her head briskly. "Yes, you can," she said. "I know you're scared—who isn't? But this is important. Do you want to hide all your life, or do you want to change history?"

Luke made a stab at humor.

"Isn't there another choice?"

Jen didn't laugh. She sprang from the couch.

"Another choice. Another choice." She paced, then jerked back to face Luke. "Sure. You can be a coward and hope someone else changes the world for you. You can hide up in that attic of yours until someone knocks at your door and says, 'Oh, yeah, they freed the hidden. Want to come out?' Is that what you want?"

Luke didn't answer.

"You've got to come, Luke, or you'll hate yourself the rest of your life. When you don't have to hide anymore, even years from now, there'll always be some small part of you whispering, 'I don't deserve this. I didn't fight for it. I'm not worth it.' And you are, Luke, you are. You're smart and funny and nice, and you should be living life, instead of being buried alive in that old house of yours—"

"Maybe I just don't mind hiding as much as you do," Luke whispered.

Jen faced him squarely, her gaze unwavering.

"Yes, you do. You hate walls as much as I do. Maybe more. Have you ever listened to yourself? Every time you talk about how you used to go outdoors and work in the garden or something, you glow. You're alive. Even if you don't want anything else, don't you want to get the outdoors back?"

What Luke wanted was to get away from Jen. Because she was right. Everything she said was right. But that couldn't mean he had to go. He huddled deeper in the couch.

"I'm not brave like you," he said.

Jen grabbed his shoulders and peered into his eyes.

"Oh, yeah?" she said. "You dared to come over here, didn't you? And here's something—why are you always the one who makes the trip? Ever think of that? If I'm so much braver, how come I'm not risking my life to see you?"

There were a thousand answers to that. *Because I found you first. Because your house is safer than mine. Because I need you more than you need me. You've got your computer and all your chat room friends. And you go places.* Luke squirmed away.

"My dad hangs around my house too much," he said. "It's safer this way. I'm—I'm just protecting you."

Jen backed up. "Thanks for the chivalry," she said bitterly. "I've got enough people protecting me. If you care so much, why don't you help me get free? You say you won't come to the rally for yourself—so do it for me. That's all I'll ever ask of you."

Luke winced. When she put things that way, how could he not go? Except—he couldn't.

"You're crazy," he said. "I can't go, and neither should you. It's too dangerous."

Jen flashed him a look of pure disgust.

"You can leave now," she said coldly. "I don't have time for you."

Luke could feel the ice in her words. He stood up.

"But—"

"Go," Jen said.

Luke stumbled toward the door. He stopped by the blinds and turned around.

"Jen, can't you understand? I do want it to work. I hope—"

"Hope doesn't mean anything," Jen snapped. "Action's the only thing that counts."

Luke backed out the door. He stood on the Talbots' patio, blinking in the sunlight, breathing in the smell of fresh air and danger. Then he turned and ran home.

CHAPTER *TWENTY-THREE*

Luke let the kitchen door slam behind him and didn't care. He was so mad, his eyes blurred. The nerve of her, saying *I don't have time for you.* Who did she think she was? He tramped up the stairs. She'd always thought she was better than him, just because she was a Baron, showing off with her soda and her potato chips and her fancy computer. So what? It didn't mean she was special, just because her parents had lots of money. It wasn't like she'd earned it or anything. Who was she, anyway? Just some dumb old girl. He wished he'd never gone over there. All she did was brag, brag, brag and show off. That's all the rally was, anyhow, showing off: *Hey, look, I'm a third child and I can go to the president's house and nobody will hurt me.* He hoped someone shot her. That would show her.

Luke stopped in the middle of pulling the attic door shut behind him. No, no, he took it back. He didn't want anyone to shoot her. His knees went weak, and he had to sit down on the stairs, all his anger suddenly turned to fear. What if someone did shoot her? He remembered the sign she'd asked if he wanted to carry: "Give me liberty or give me death." Was she serious? Did she expect to—? He stopped himself from thinking the rest. What if she never came back? He should go, if only to protect Jen. But he couldn't—

Luke buried his face in his hands, trying to hide from his own thoughts.

Mother found him there, hours later, still crouched on the stairs.

"Luke! Were you getting impatient waiting for me to get home? Did you have a nice day?"

Luke stared at her as though she were a vision from another life.

"I—" he started, ready to spill everything. He couldn't hold it all in.

Mother felt his forehead.

"Are you sick? You're so pale—I worry about you, Luke, all day long. But then I remind myself, you're safe here at home, out of harm's way." She gave him a weary smile and ruffled his hair.

Luke swallowed hard and recovered himself. What was he thinking? He couldn't tell anyone about Jen. He couldn't betray her.

"I'm fine," he lied. "I just haven't been out in the sun for a while, remember. Not that I'm complaining, of course," he added hastily.

Hiding again.

CHAPTER *TWENTY-FOUR*

For three days, Luke agonized. Sometimes he decided he had to stop Jen, to persuade her not to go. Sometimes he decided he ought to go with her. Sometimes he was mad again, and thought he should just stalk over there and demand an apology.

But anything he might do required seeing Jen, and that wasn't possible. It poured every day, the rain coming down in long, dreary sheets that made Luke feel worse as he watched from the attic vents. Downstairs he could hear Dad stomping around, muttering every now and then about the time and topsoil being lost with every raindrop. Luke felt like a prisoner.

Thursday night he went to bed convinced he'd never be able to sleep for imagining Jen and the others in her car, getting farther and farther from him and closer and closer to danger. But he must have dozed off, because he woke to total darkness. His heart pounded. He was sweaty. Had he dreamed something? Had he heard something? A floor-board creaked. His ears roared as he tried to listen. Was that someone else's breath or just his own, loud and scared? A beam of light swept across his face.

"Luke?" A whisper.

Luke bolted up in bed.

"Jen? Is that you?"

She switched off her flashlight.

"Yes. I thought I'd kill myself coming up your stairs. Why didn't you tell me they were so narrow?" She sounded like the same old Jen, not mad. Not crazy.

"I didn't know you'd ever be climbing them," Luke said.

It was insane to be talking about stairs now, in the middle of the night, in his room. Every word either of them spoke was dangerous. Mother was a light sleeper. But Luke was delighted not to be moving on, not to be talking about what Jen had really come to talk about.

"Your parents didn't lock your doors," Jen said. She seemed to be stalling, too. "Guess I'm lucky the Government outlawed pets. Didn't farmers always used to keep big guard dogs that would chomp people's heads off in one bite?"

Luke shrugged, then remembered Jen couldn't see him in the dark. "Jen, I—" He wasn't sure what he was going to say until he said it. "I still can't go. I'm sorry. It's something about having parents who are farmers, not lawyers. And not being a Baron. It's people like you who change history. People like me—we just let things happen to us."

"No. You're wrong. You can make things happen—"

Luke sensed, rather than saw, Jen shaking her head. Even in the dark, he could visualize each precisely cut strand of hair bouncing and falling back into place.

"I'm sorry," she continued. "I didn't come here to harp at you. This is dangerous, and no one should go unwillingly. I was too hard on you the other day. I just wanted to say—you've been a good friend. I'll miss you."

"But you'll be back," Luke said. "Tomorrow—or the next day—after the rally. I'll be over to visit. If your rally works, I'll be walking in the front door."

"We can hope," Jen said softly. Her voice faded away. "Good-bye, Luke."

CHAPTER *TWENTY-FIVE*

Luke lay awake the rest of the night. At first light, he got up and quietly scrubbed away the mud Jen had tracked in and up the stairs. Trust her not to think about mud. He fervently hoped she'd thought of all the details about the rally.

Luke was just finishing the last of the kitchen floor when he heard the toilet flushing upstairs. He hid the muddy rags in the trash and scrambled back to his place on the stairs just in time to meet Mother coming down.

"'Morning, early bird." She yawned. "Were you up during the night? I thought I heard something."

"I had trouble sleeping," Luke said truthfully.

Mother yawned again.

"And you're up early...feeling okay?"

"Just hungry," Luke said.

But he picked at his food. Everything he ate stuck in his throat.

After the rest of his family left, he risked sneaking over and turning the radio on low. There were weather reports and commercials for soybean seed and lots of music.

"Come on, come on," he muttered, keeping one eye on the side window, watching for Dad.

Finally the radio voice announced the news. Someone's cattle had gotten out and caused a minor car wreck. Nobody hurt. A Government spokesman predicted a poor planting season because of all the rain.

Nothing about the rally.

Dad came back toward the house. Luke snapped off the radio and bolted for the stairs.

At lunch, Dad forgot to turn the radio on, and Luke had to remind him. The announcer promised a big story after the commercials. His sandwich gone, Dad reached over to turn the radio off.

"No, no—wait!" Luke said. "This might be interesting—"

Dad harrumphed, but waited.

The announcer came back. He cleared his throat and declared that new Government statistics proved last year's alfalfa harvest had set a record for the decade.

It was like that for days. Luke kept waiting, desperate to hear anything. But the few times he could get to the radio, it said nothing.

Every time Dad left the house for any length of time, Luke switched on the light by the back door, his old signal to Jen. He stared so hard, willing her answering light to go on, that he thought he would go blind. But there was nothing.

He took to watching her house as obsessively as he had when he had first discovered her existence. There was no sign of her. The rest of her family came and went as usual. Did they look sadder? Happy? Worried? At peace? From a distance, he couldn't tell.

He got so desperate, he asked Mother if she'd thought about going over to visit the new neighbors, to welcome them to the area. She looked at him as if he were deranged.

"They've been there for months. They're hardly new anymore. And they're *Barons*," she said. She laughed in a way that didn't hide her bitterness. "Believe me, they don't want us visiting."

And what was she supposed to do, say, "Nice to meet you. Now, tell me everything about the child you never talk about"?

After a week, Luke did feel deranged. Every time anyone spoke to him, he jumped. Mother asked him, "Are you all right?" so many times, he took to avoiding her. But he couldn't just sit in the attic, waiting. He paced. He fidgeted. He chewed his fingernails.

He came up with a plan.

CHAPTER TWENTY-SIX

Finally, finally, a week and a half after the rally, a day dawned that was so clear and dry, Luke knew Dad would be in the fields all day. Without hope, Luke turned on the light by the back door. After five minutes without a response, he turned it off and quietly slipped out the door.

The cool air was a jolt, and for the briefest time, he paused. This was more dangerous than ever.

"But I have to *know*," he muttered fiercely, and crept alongside the barn before making his dash for Jen's house.

He had to rip the screen and break the pane of one of the Talbot's windows, which he felt bad about. But it didn't matter. If Jen was there, she could think of an excuse. And if she wasn't...if she wasn't, he'd never be back at the Talbots' again.

Once inside, he knew he had to do something about the alarm quickly. Jen had explained it to him once, told him the exact sequence of buttons to hit to disable it. He ran to the hall closet, yanked open the door, and punched buttons quickly, afraid he'd forget the sequence if he hesitated even a second. Green-blue-yellow-green-blue-orange-red.

The lights blinked out before he hit the last button, and that spooked him. Was that how it worked before?

"Hurry, hurry," he urged himself. The words kept replaying in his brain.

"Jen?" he called. "Jen?"

He went up and down stairs, looking in every room.

"Jen? You don't have to hide. It's me. Luke."

The house was enormous, three floors and a basement. He couldn't search everywhere, but if Jen was there, why would she hide? Against reason, he kept hoping she was.

"Jen? Come on. This isn't funny."

He found the bedrooms—huge, elegant rooms with beautifully carved beds and long, mirrored closets. He couldn't even tell which one was Jen's.

Finally, he admitted defeat and rushed down to the computer room.

He hurried over to the keyboard and typed in the same sequence of letters he'd watched Jen type so many times. His fingers were clumsy, and he kept messing up. Finally, he got to the chat room password. F-E-R-E. No. Erase. F-E-E-R. No. At last he got it. F-R-E-E.

The screen went blank, with none of the friendly banter that had magically appeared every time he'd watched Jen. Had he done something wrong? Frantically, he exited and entered the chat room again, his hands shaking. Still nothing. Timidly, using only his right index finger, he typed, "Where's Jen?" He had to hold one hand with the other to steady his finger enough to hit the Enter button.

Almost instantaneously, his words vanished and reappeared at the top of the screen. He waited. Nothing. The
screen stayed blank below his question.

Because nothing was worse than doing nothing, he
typed again, "Hello? Is anybody there?"

Still nothing. He slammed his fist down on the computer desk so hard, it hurt.

"I have to know!" he shouted. "Tell me! I can't go home
until I know!"

He heard the door too late to react. And suddenly a
voice boomed behind him: "Turn around slowly. I have a
gun. Who are you and why are you here?"

CHAPTER *TWENTY-SEVEN*

Luke stifled his instinct to run. He turned around as slowly as he could. Guns had been outlawed for everyone but Government officials long before he was born. But he recognized the object pointed at him from books and Dad's descriptions. Dad had always talked about hunting rifles and shotguns, big guns to bring down deer or wolves. This gun was smaller. Meant to kill humans.

All that flashed through Luke's mind before he looked beyond the gun, to the man holding it. He was tall and fleshy, his expensive clothes only partially hiding his bulk. Luke had seen him only from a distance before.

"You're Jen's dad," he said.

"I didn't ask who I was," the man snapped. "Who are you?"

Luke exhaled slowly.

"A friend of Jen's," he said cautiously.

Only because he was watching very, very closely did he see the man lower the gun by a fraction of an inch.

"Please," Luke said. "I just want to know where she is."

This time the man clearly relaxed his gun hand. He circled around behind Luke and snapped off the computer.

"Jen says you have to park the hard drive before you do that," Luke said.

"How do you know about Jen?" the man asked. He narrowed his eyes.

Luke blinked. The man was bargaining, he realized, offering to negotiate. He wanted something from Luke before he would tell Luke anything about Jen. But what?

"I'm a third child, too," Luke said finally. The man's expression didn't change, but Luke thought he saw a flicker of interest in his eyes. "I'm a neighbor. I found out about her, and I started coming over, when I could."

"How did you know she was here?" the man said.

"I saw—" Luke didn't want to get her in trouble. "I saw lights when I knew everyone was gone. I guessed. I—I really wanted there to be another third child for me to meet."

"So Jen was careless," the man said, with an edge to his voice that Luke didn't understand.

"No," Luke said uncertainly. "I was observant."

The man nodded, only to accept Luke's answer. Then he sat down in the chair by the computer desk, and rested the gun on his leg. Luke took that as a sign that the conversation might last long enough for him to find out something.

"Did Jen teach you how to disable our alarm system?" the man asked.

Luke saw no point in lying. "Yes. But I must have screwed up, since you came—"

"No," the man said. "If you'd screwed up, the security

guards would have come. But I have it set so I'm automatically notified if the system's shut down while I'm away.... Given the circumstances, I decided to investigate myself."

Luke longed to ask what "circumstances" he meant, but the man was already asking another question. "So what else did you and Jen do together?" the man said. Luke couldn't understand why he sounded so accusatory.

"Nothing," Luke said. "I mean, we talked a lot. She showed me the computer. She—she wanted me to go to the rally, but I was too scared."

Too late, Luke thought to wonder if the man knew about the rally. Was Luke betraying Jen's confidence? But the man didn't seem surprised. He was studying Luke as intently as Luke had been studying him.

"Why didn't you stop her?" the man asked.

"Stop Jen? That's like trying to stop the sun," Luke said.

The man gave Luke the faintest of smiles, one that contained no happiness. "Just remember that," he said.

"So where is she?" Luke asked.

The man looked away.

"Jen's—" His voice broke. "Jen is no longer with us."

"She—?"

"She's dead," the man said harshly.

Somehow Luke had known without wanting to know. He still stumbled backwards, in shock. He bumped into the couch and sagged into it.

"No," he said. "Not Jen. No. You're lying."

His ears roared. He thought crazy things. *This is a dream.*

A nightmare. I will make myself wake up. He remembered Jen talking a mile a minute, gesturing wildly. How could she be dead? He tried to picture her lying still, not moving. Dead. It was impossible.

The man was shaking his head helplessly.

"I'd give anything to have her back," he whispered. "But it's true. I saw. They gave us...they gave us the body. Special privilege for a Government official." His voice was so bitter, Luke could barely listen. "And we couldn't even bury her in the family plot. Couldn't take a bereavement day off work. Couldn't tell anyone why we're going around with red eyes and aching hearts. No—we just had to pretend to be the same old family of four we'd always been."

"How?" Luke asked. "How did she...die?"

He was thinking, if the car had wrecked, it wouldn't be so bad. Or maybe it had nothing to do with the rally. Maybe she just got really sick.

"They shot her," Jen's father said. "They shot all of them. All forty kids at the rally, gunned down right in front of the president's house. The blood flowed into his rose-bushes. But they had the sidewalks scrubbed before the tourists came, so nobody would know."

Luke started shaking his head no, and couldn't stop.

"But Jen said there'd be too many people to shoot. She said there'd be a thousand," Luke protested, as if Jen's words could change what he was hearing.

"Our Jen had too much faith in the bravery of her fellow hidden," Jen's father said.

Luke flinched. "I told her I couldn't go," he said. "I told her! It's not my fault!"

"No," Jen's dad said quietly. "And you couldn't have stopped her. It's not your fault. There are plenty of other people who deserve the blame. They probably would have shot a thousand. Or fifteen thousand. They don't care."

His face twisted. Luke thought he had never seen such pain, not even the time Matthew dropped a sledgehammer on his foot. Tears began to spill down Jen's father's face.

"What I don't understand is—why did she do this, this Children's Crusade? She wasn't stupid. We'd been warning her about the Population Police all her life. Did she really think the rally would work?" he said.

"Yes," Luke assured him. Then, unbidden, the last words she'd spoken to him came back to him: *We can hope*—after she'd told him hope was worthless. Maybe she knew the rally would fail. Maybe she even knew she would probably die. He remembered the first day he'd met her, when she'd cut her hand to cover the drops of his blood on the carpet. There was something strange in Jen he couldn't quite understand, that made her willing to sacrifice herself to help others. Or to try to.

"I think at first she thought the rally would work," Luke told Jen's dad. "And then, even when she wasn't sure…she still had to go. She wouldn't call it off."

"Why?" Jen's dad asked. He was sobbing. "Did she want to die?"

"No," Luke said. "She wanted to live. Not die. Not hide. Live."

The words played over and over again in his brain: "Not hide. Live. Not hide. Live." As long as he held on to them, he felt like Jen was there. She'd just left the room for a minute, to get more potato chips, maybe, and soon she'd be back to lecture him again about how they both deserved a better life than hiding. He could believe it was her voice echoing in his ears.

But if he let go, let the words stop for a minute, he was lost. He felt like the whole world was spinning away from him, and he was all alone. He wanted to cry out, "Jen! Come back!"—as if she could hear him, and stop the spinning, and come to him.

As if from a great distance, Luke heard Jen's father heave a sigh and blow his nose in a businesslike way.

"You may not be ready to hear this," he said. "But—"

Dizzily, Luke raised his head and listened halfheartedly.

"When you logged into that chat room," Jen's father said, "a buzzer went off in a room in Population Police headquarters. They're monitoring the chat room very closely—they found it after the rally. I've managed to…uh, cover up things about Jen, but they'll trace your message back to our computer. The Population Police are backlogged right now, following leads from the rally, so I should have a day or two to come up with a plausible-sounding explanation. But if they investigate too carefully, you may be in danger."

"More than usual?" Luke said sarcastically.

Jen's dad took the question seriously.

"Yes. They will begin actively looking for you. They'll search every house around this one. It wouldn't take them long to find you."

A chill ran down Luke's spine. So he would die, just like Jen. Or not like her—she had gone bravely. He would be caught like a mouse in its hole.

"But if you'll let me," Jen's dad continued, "I can get you a fake I.D. You can be miles away before they come looking."

"You would do that for me?" Luke asked. "Why?"

"Because of Jen."

"But—how?"

"I have connections. You see"—Jen's dad hesitated—"I work for the Population Police."

CHAPTER *TWENTY-EIGHT*

Luke began screaming and couldn't stop. Suddenly his brain didn't seem to have any control whatsoever over what his body did. He felt his legs spring up and propel him toward Jen's dad. He saw his own hand grab for the gun and wrestle it away. He heard a voice he barely recognized as his own scream, again and again, "No! No! No!"

"Stop!" Jen's dad yelled. "Stop, you little fool, before you get us both killed—"

Somehow, the gun was in Luke's hand. Jen's dad lunged at him, and Luke could picture Jen's dad tackling him, just as Jen had tackled him all those months ago. But this time Luke stepped to the side at the last moment, and Jen's dad crashed uselessly into the far wall. Luke pointed the gun at him and struggled to hold it steady.

Jen's dad turned around slowly.

"You can shoot me," he said, holding his hands helplessly up in the air. "I might even welcome the chance to stop missing Jen. But it would be a mistake. I swear to you, in the name of everything that's sacred—in Jen's name— I'm on your side."

Jen's dad stared into Luke's eyes, waiting. Luke felt a surge of pride that he'd gotten the upper hand, that he had earned the right to decide what happened next. But how could he know what was right? Surely Jen's own father wouldn't lie in her name. Would he?

Luke squeezed his eyes shut. Then he lowered the gun to his side.

"Good," Jen's dad said, audibly releasing his breath.

Luke let Jen's dad walk toward him, gently take the gun, and lay it on the desk.

"I was going to explain," Jen's dad said, panting a little. He sat down. "I only work at Population Police headquarters. I don't agree with what they do. I try to sabotage them as much as I can. Jen never understood, either— sometimes you have to work from inside enemy lines."

Jen's dad talked and talked and talked. Luke thought he was repeating everything he said two or three times, but that was okay, because Luke's brain was functioning so slowly, he needed the extra help.

"Do you know much history?" Jen's dad asked.

Luke tried to remember if there were any history books among his family's collection in the attic. Did adventure stories of long ago count?

"Just—" He cleared his throat. "Just from the books Jen loaned me."

"Which ones?"

Luke pointed to the ones on the shelves above the computer.

"And she gave me some articles, printouts from the computer."

Jen's dad nodded. "So you got the propaganda from both sides," he said. "No truth."

"What do you mean?" Luke asked.

"The Government publications are trying to convince people of one thing, so they stretch the facts. And the underground is just as extreme in its own way, making statistics match their cause. So you know nothing."

"Jen said the stuff from the computer was true," Luke said defensively. Just saying her name made him wince. And now she was dead. How could she be dead?

Jen's dad waved that away impatiently.

"She believed what she wanted to. But I'm afraid—" He stopped, and Luke was afraid Jen's dad might start crying again. Then he swallowed hard and went on. "I'm afraid I encouraged her. I passed along some slanted information. I wanted to give her hope that someday the Population Law would be repealed. I didn't know she'd...she'd..."

Luke knew he wouldn't be able to bear seeing Jen's dad break down again.

"So what should I know?" Luke asked. "What is the truth?"

"The truth," Jen's dad muttered, catching onto those two words as though Luke had thrown him a lifeline. He recovered himself quickly. "Nobody really knows. There have been too many lies for too long. Our Government is totalitarian, and totalitarian governments never like truth."

That made no sense to Luke, but he let Jen's dad go on talking.

"You know about the famines?"

Luke nodded.

"Before that, our country believed in freedom and democracy and equality for all. Then the famines came, and the government was overthrown. There were riots in every city, over food, and many, many people were killed. When General Sherwood came to power, he promised law and order and food for all. By then, that was all the people wanted. And all they got."

Luke squinted, trying to understand. This was grown-up talk, pure and simple. No, it was worse than the grown-up talk he was used to, because all his parents ever talked about was the corn harvest and bills and the likelihood of frost at the end of May. Those Luke understood. Governments being overthrown, cities rioting—they were beyond his comprehension.

"Barons got more," he blurted, then blushed because it sounded so rude.

Jen's dad laughed. "True. You noticed. I know it's not fair, and I'm not proud of it, but…Government officials made a conscious decision to allow one class of people to have special privileges—Jen probably introduced you to junk food, didn't she?"

Luke nodded.

"That's a good example. Officially, it's illegal, but no one ever got arrested for supplying Barons with junk food. Which is mighty convenient, considering that all the powerful Government officials are Barons." The cynicism in his voice sounded so much like Jen that Luke almost gave in to grief again. But he forced himself to focus on what Jen's dad was saying.

"The Government justifies keeping everyone else in poverty because people seem to work the hardest when they're right on the edge of survival," he continued. "The Government does try to make sure that most people—the ones who cooperate—do survive. If you've heard your parents talking about other farmers, you'll know that nobody loses their farms anymore. But, also, nobody ever makes enough to live comfortably."

Luke thought about his parents' constant worries about money. Was it all unnecessary? Were they just being manipulated? He felt a spark of anger, but buried that, too, because he had other questions.

"But even Barons have to follow the Population Law," he said. "Is that because"—he gulped—"because it's necessary? Were there too many people? Are there?"

"Probably not," Jen's dad said. "If food had been distributed fairly...if people hadn't panicked...if we'd had good leaders being honest about the need for everyone's cooperation...we could have survived the crisis without curtailing anyone's rights. And now—it shouldn't be a problem if some people choose to have three or four kids, as long as some other people choose to have none. But the Population Law became General Sherwood's proudest accomplishment. That's why even Barons aren't exempt. He points to that and says, 'See how much control I have over my people's lives.'"

"So it is wrong," Luke said, trying to grasp the point.

"I believe so. Yes," Jen's dad said.

Luke felt a strange sense of relief, that it wasn't truly wrong for him to exist, just illegal. For the first time since he'd read the Government books, he could see the two things being separate. Maybe that was why he'd been too scared to go to the rally. If he'd truly believed, the way Jen had, then he might have gone.

And would he have been killed, as she was?

It was all too confusing and scary to think about.

Jen's father looked at his watch.

"I need to get back to work. I can only hide so much. If you want it, I can have the fake I.D. for you by tomorrow night. In the meantime, I'd advise you to—"

He broke off. Luke knew why: a sound from his worst nightmares—pounding on the door, and then the command, "Open up! Population Police!"

CHAPTER *TWENTY-NINE*

Before Luke had a chance to move, Jen's dad had picked him up and thrust him into the closet.

"There's a secret door at the back," he hissed. "Use it."

Luke groped blindly, fighting through what felt like piles of hair. Behind him, he could hear Jen's dad yelling, "I'm coming! I'm coming! That's a twelve-thousand-dollar door. If you break it down, you're going to pay!" Then Luke heard the computer making its *be-be-be-beeep!* and Jen's dad muttering, "Fine time for them to discover efficiency. Come on, come on, connect—"

The pounding at the door grew louder, and a gruff voice yelled out, "You have three seconds, George!"

Luke dug deeper into the closet. He couldn't even find the back wall, let alone any secret door. And then he heard a splintering sound from the front of the house. Seconds later, there were stomping footsteps in the computer room.

"What is the meaning of this?"

It was Jen's dad's voice coming from the hall, full of outrage. If he hadn't witnessed it himself, Luke never would have guessed that Jen's dad had been crying only moments before. He sounded too forceful, too assured, too confident that he was right and anyone who opposed him was wrong. The stomping stopped. From deep inside the closet, Luke heard someone snicker.

"Caught you with your pants down, eh, George?"

"Yes, yes, very funny," Jen's father replied, not sounding the least bit amused. There was a sound that could have been a zipper being zipped. "Has it come to this? A man can't even go to the bathroom without his door being broken down by a bunch of morons with power complexes? And you will pay for that door, I assure you."

If Luke had been one of the Population Police, Jen's dad would have scared him to pieces. Luke would have backed out, muttering, "I'm sorry. I'm sorry." He never would have believed that Jen's dad was hiding a third child. Hopefully, Luke paused in his burrowing into the Talbots' closet.

But the voice that answered Jen's father carried only the slightest edge of doubt.

"Come off it, George. You know we're entitled to search and seizure. We have reports of that computer being used for illegal purposes. Just a half an hour ago."

"You're even bigger fools than I thought," Jen's dad answered. "Don't any of you read your memos? I reported to Central Command this morning that I was going to continue my sting operation in the illegal chat rooms. See, I wrote, 'Where's Jen?' and, 'Hello? Is anybody there?', which is what some lost, confused, third child who missed the rally might write. Are you so low-ranking that you don't know I was pretending to be the guerrilla leader Jen all along? Did you miss the commendation ceremony where I was rewarded for the disposal of forty illegals?"

Luke wondered that Jen's dad could say her name without his voice giving him away. If Luke didn't know Jen—hadn't known her, he corrected himself with a wince—and if he didn't know how much she'd trusted her father, he would have been certain that Jen's father had double-crossed her. As it was, his head swam with the fear that Jen's father still might betray him. How could he trust anyone who spoke so coldly of the "disposal" of third children? Luke struggled on through the closet, reaching a stack of blankets at the back. Finally he touched the wall, but everything he felt was smooth. Jen's father said there was a door. There had to be a door.

The voices from outside the closet were muffled now.

"—see the memo—"

"I'm sure it's on your desk back at the office, with all the paperwork you never read." Jen's dad raised his voice, so Luke could hear him clearly. "Or can you even read?"

The Population Police officer ignored the insult.

"Show us on the computer."

"Very well."

Luke prayed that Jen's dad had something to show them. He could not find the door, though he ran his fingers along the wall, again and again. His heart was beating so loudly, he was sure the Population Police could hear him.

All he could hear of the Population Police and Jen's father were mutterings. Then the one officer's voice rang out, "You're lying, George. We're going to search."

"Just because of a computer malfunction? Fine. It's not my problem." Luke was stunned by the indifference in Jen's father's voice. "But when you don't find anything— and you won't—you know that I'm entitled to the Illegal Search and Seizure Benefits granted to Barons, and I will press charges. Should I use the extra money on caviar or champagne?"

"Aw, George, you wouldn't really sue."

"You don't think so? Then go ahead. Start here."

Suddenly the closet was flooded with light. Luke stifled a gasp. How could Jen's father have flung open the door of the very place Luke was hiding? Desperately, Luke yanked a blanket over his head.

None of the Population Police answered Jen's father, but the pattern of shadows that fell on Luke's blanket made him think the Population Police were standing right in the doorway of the closet. He heard hangers scraping against a metal bar. And then the Population Police walked away.

Confused and terrified, Luke remained huddled under the blanket. He could hear muffled footfalls elsewhere in the house, and was certain they'd be returning to the com- puter room any minute. Before they killed him, he hoped they let him go back to his parents and tell them how much he loved them. He could apologize to Matthew and Mark, too, for not appreciating the checkers and card games they played with him when he knew they'd rather be outside. And probably he should apologize to his parents for disobeying, and coming to Jen's house in the first place. Except, even scared to death of being found, he couldn't scrape up full regret for that.

Anyhow, it wasn't likely that they'd let him see his parents before they killed him. He'd have to protect his parents, and refuse to even reveal who they were....

Luke's mind was still racing with frantic plans when he heard someone coming back to the computer room. There was only one set of footsteps, so he dared to hope—

"You could have swept up the glass on your way out!"

It was Jen's dad. Luke strained to hear an answer, but none came. Were the Population Police gone?

Luke kept his head down. He heard Jen's dad wading into the closet. Then he pulled the blanket off Luke and clamped his hand over Luke's mouth. Luke started to struggle until he read the words on the paper Jen's dad held in front of his face:

They're gone.

You're safe,

but

DON'T TALK!!!

Luke relaxed and nodded to show he would obey. Jen's dad released him, flipped the paper over, and began writing furiously.

House bugged now.

Luke gave Jen's dad a puzzled look.

"B—" he started to say, then remembered and stopped. He took the pen from Jen's dad and wrote, *Bugged? Ants? Roaches?*

Jen's dad shook his head frantically. *Bugs = little listening devices—Population Police hear everything. That's why can't talk. They do that when a bust's unsuccessful. Even left one bug on me.*

Jen's dad turned around and pointed, and Luke saw a small disc sticking to the back of his collar.

Luke frowned and wrote on the paper, *Why not take off?*

Jen's dad shook his head. *Safer this way. Long as they think they hear everything, they won't come back.*

Jen's dad pointed to the hairy lumps on the hangers behind him.

Bribed them with fur coats. Very rare, very valuable.

Luke looked at the coats. There did seem to be a lot fewer of them now. Were they animal skins? Why would anyone want such a thing? He couldn't ask, though, because Jen's dad was already scribbling more.

Just bought time. My goose probably cooked now—I didn't file that memo. They'll find out.

Luke reached for the pen. *What will they do to you?*

Jen's dad shook his head. *Don't know,* he wrote. *I've survived this kind of thing before. But everything's chancy now. The fact they got here so fast = they have it in for me.*

Weakly, Luke leaned his head back against the closet wall. That reminded him of his frantic search along its surface. He reached for the paper and wrote, *Where's the door?*

Jen's dad pulled out a new sheet of paper. Shaking his head, he wrote, *Isn't one. Just wanted to get you to back of closet.*

Luke buried his face in his hands. Jen's dad was a good liar, there was no doubt about that. How could Luke trust him? Luke raised his head and watched as Jen's dad scribbled something else on the paper. His expression was full of concern, and Luke knew, somehow, that he was trustworthy. He easily could have turned Luke in, and gotten praise and another commendation ceremony. But how confusing, to never know when someone was lying.

Jen's dad turned the paper to face Luke. It said, *So. Want fake I.D. or not?*

Luke gulped. After a minute, he wrote back, *Am I safe if I don't?*

Jen's dad seemed to be weighing the question. He narrowed his eyes and wrote, *Probably. They're after me now, not you. If they really thought there was an illegal here, they wouldn't take bribe. Or would take it and you, too. But I'd advise—get I.D.*

Luke wrote back, *Can't I wait? Think about it for a while?*

That was what Luke wanted. Or not even to think, but to hide from thinking for a while. He wanted to remember Jen, and grieve for her by himself. He didn't want to have to think about what parts of the Population Law were good, and what parts were bad, or why his family didn't have more money. He didn't want to have to figure out Jen's dad, and other people like him, who could pretend to be so many different things. He didn't want to have to decide something now that could change the rest of his life.

But Jen's dad had written back, *Don't know. May be case of 'now or never.'*

Luke scrawled, *Why?*

Jen's dad wrote for a long time. Then he turned the paper to Luke. It said: *I have power now. Tomorrow, probably. Next week????? Next year????? Can't tell with our Gov't. Favored lackey one day,* persona non grata *the next. Never know. No guarantees.*

Luke stared at the paper until the words blurred together. He had to decide. Now.

He thought about reading and daydreaming in the attic the rest of his life. His parents were kind to him, even if they weren't around much. And as much as Matthew and Mark had always teased him, he was pretty sure they would take care of him if his parents couldn't someday. His life was very limited—he understood that now more than ever. But he was used to it. It was safe. He could make himself be happy.

Except...

Luke remembered how bored he'd felt before meeting Jen, how desperate he'd been to do something—anything!—besides read and daydream. He'd been so desperate that he'd risked his life for the chance of meeting another third child. Did he want to spend the rest of his life feeling that desperate? Did he want to just...waste it?

But even if he got a fake I.D., what would he do?

The answer was there instantly, as if he'd known it all

along and his brain was just waiting for him to come looking.

He could do something to help other third children come out of hiding. Not with another big dramatic rally, like Jen had tried, or by finding fake I.D.'s the way Jen's dad did. Maybe there was something smaller and slower he could do. Studying ways to grow more food, so no one would go hungry, no matter how many kids people had. Or changing the Government so that farmers were allowed to raise pigs or use hydroponics, and ordinary people, not just Barons, could have better lives. Or figuring out ways for people to live in outer space, so they wouldn't be too crowded on Earth and chop down beautiful woods just for houses. He didn't know exactly how he could do those things, or even what the right thing to do was. But he wanted to do something.

He remembered what he'd told Jen, the last time he'd seen her: *It's people like you who change history. People like me— we just let things happen to us.* And he'd believed it. That was how his family had always lived. But maybe that was wrong. Maybe he could succeed where Jen had failed precisely because he wasn't a Baron—because he didn't have her sense that the world owed him everything. He could be more patient, more cautious, more practical.

But he'd never be able to do anything staying in hiding.

He bit his lip. His hand shook as he wrote his answer.

I want a fake I.D. Please.

CHAPTER *THIRTY*

ee Grant settled into the car that would take him away from the farm where he'd found refuge, after running away from home. He'd gotten lost—he'd certainly never intended to end up *here*. He surveyed the dusty barnyard in front of him, the ugly ruts of dried mud where tractors and trucks had left their tracks. He stared at the ramshackle barn and the peeling paint on the weathered house, sights that should have been entirely foreign to him, but weren't. He—

Luke gulped, unable to keep thinking in his new identity quite yet. It was too soon, too hard, when his shoulders still felt the warmth of Mother's last hug. He looked down at his hands, clenched together in his lap, and they already seemed like someone else's against the background of his crisp new trousers. No more ragged blue jeans and hand-me-down flannel shirts for him—he had a whole suitcase in the trunk full of the same kind of fancy Baron clothes he'd laughed at all those months ago. He didn't care about the clothes, but he wished they'd let him keep his name, at least. Yet Jen's father had been proud that he'd gotten to keep the same initials.

"A rush job like this, it's a wonder you're not stuck with Alphonse Xerxes," he'd bragged in the letter he'd dropped off the night before, pretending he was just coming to ask Luke's parents to cut back the willow tree that draped over onto the Talbots' land.

The real Lee Grant was a Baron. He had died in a skiing accident just the night before. His parents wanted nothing to do with Luke—"too painful," Jen's father had explained—but they had agreed to donate their son's name and identity card the way people had once donated hearts and kidneys. Some secret group that helped third children had arranged it. The group also had agreed to pay for Luke to go to a private school as a boarder, year-round. Supposedly he was transferring in during the middle of a term as punishment for running away. He'd read about such places in the old books in the attic. It seemed a strange way to live, without family, but he was just as glad not to have to pretend to love another set of parents.

Now Luke looked back at his family's porch, where Mother and Dad and Matthew and Mark were standing and already waving. Dad and Matthew looked gruff, and Mark merely looked serious—strange enough for him—but tears were streaming down Mother's face.

She'd cried, too, the night Luke had told his parents everything.

He'd started with his first visit to Jen's house, and Mother had immediately scolded, "Oh, Luke, how could you? The danger...I know you're lonely, but honey, promise us, never again..."

"That's not all," Luke said.

He told the rest of the story without looking at her, until he reached the end and his decision to get a fake I.D. Then the sound of her sobbing made it impossible to avoid looking. She was red-eyed, devastated.

"Luke, no. You can't," she'd gasped. "Don't you know how we'd miss you?"

"But, Mother, I don't want to go," Luke said. "It's just that...I have to. I can't spend the rest of my life hiding in the attic. What will happen when you and Dad can't take care of me anymore?"

"Matthew or Mark will," she replied.

"But I don't want to be a burden on them. I want to do something with my life. Figure out ways to help other third kids. Make—" All the things he'd thought of sounded too childish to explain, in the face of Mother's sobbing. So he finished weakly, "Make a difference in the world."

"I'm not saying you can never do that," she answered. "But that's years away. We'll figure out some way to get a fake I.D. for you when you're grown up. Somehow." She turned to Luke's father. "Tell him, Harlan."

Dad sighed heavily.

"The boy's right. He needs to go now, if he can."

Luke could tell his father's words came out painfully, but they still stabbed at him. Maybe part of him had been secretly hoping his parents would forbid him to go, would lock him in the attic and keep him as their little boy forever.

"I've checked around some, quietlike, to see if anyone's heard of a third child getting to live a normal life. Around here, they can't," Dad said. "Far as I can tell, he's not going to get another chance."

Luke turned back to his mother, because it was too hard to look at Dad while he was saying that. But the pain twisting Mother's face was worse.

"Then I guess we don't have a choice," she'd murmured.

That had been two days ago, and ever since then she'd called in sick to work and stayed home, spending every second with Luke. They'd played board games and cards, but she'd interrupted every move with, "Do you remember..." or, "I remember..."

The coos he'd made as a baby. His first steps. His delight in discovering dirt the spring he was two. The first time he'd hoed a straight row. The zucchini he'd grown as long as his arm. The bedtime stories and tucking-ins.

She was filling him up with memories, he knew, for the times when he'd have no one to talk to about his childhood. But it was hard to listen to. He wished they could just move their Monopoly pieces and pretend the time wasn't ticking away.

But all too soon this morning had come. Jen's dad had pulled up in his fancy car, and sprang out to shake hands with Luke's parents.

"Mr. Garner, Mrs. Garner, thank you very much for reporting this boy's arrival immediately. From what I hear, the Grants were worried sick." He turned to Luke. "Young man, what you did was irresponsible and reckless. The only smart thing you did was remember to take your I.D. card. I guess you must have heard that the Population Police shoot first and ask questions later."

He clapped Luke on the back and slid his hand down to slip something into Luke's pocket. Luke reached down to touch the stiff edge of an I.D. card. His I.D. card.

"Do we have to start pretending already?" Luke's mother whispered, the tears beginning in her eyes.

Jen's dad was shaking his head sternly and patting his chest, as if looking for something in a hidden pocket.

"Bugged," he mouthed.

When Luke's parents nodded to show they understood, he stopped patting and pulled out an official-looking paper.

"Ah, here they are. Your travel papers. Your parents are sending you to Hendricks School for Boys. And if you don't shape up—" Jen's dad gave him a stern look that somehow also conveyed his sympathy.

"Would"—Mother cleared her throat—"Would it be all right if we gave him a good-bye hug? We've gotten kind of fond of him in...in the time he's been here."

Jen's father nodded, and then both Luke's parents held him tight and released him.

"Be a good boy, now, you hear?" Mother said. Luke could tell she was trying to make it jokey, the way she might talk to some other mother's runaway son. But for the life of him, he couldn't come back with a joking response. He only nodded, blinking hard.

And then he stumbled to the car and tried to be Lee.

Jen's dad circled the car and slid in on the driver's side. He started the car and pulled out.

"You're just lucky you're getting such a highly paid chauffeur," he said. "If I weren't a personal friend of your father's cousin—"

Luke wasn't sure if there was a hidden message in the words, or if Jen's dad was just talking for the sake of the bug. He decided he couldn't analyze it yet. He peered back at his frantically waving family until they were out of sight. Soon the car was passing the other side of the barn and the field beyond, views Luke had never seen, though he'd lived his entire life within a hundred yards of them. In spite of the fear gnawing in his stomach and the anguish of missing his family—already—he felt a thrill of excitement. There was so much to see. He'd have to tell Jen—

Jen. The grief he'd been avoiding for days welled over him again. But, "I'm doing this for you, too, Jen," he whispered, too softly for Jen's dad or the bug to hear over the car's hum. "Someday when we're all free, all the third children, I'll tell everyone about you. They'll erect statues to you, and name holidays after you...." It wasn't much, but it made him feel better. A little.

Luke stared back at his family's farm as long as he could. He could see just the roof of Jen's house beyond the sparse line of trees. And then, in no time at all, it seemed, everything familiar disappeared over the horizon.

Lee Grant turned around to see what lay ahead.

— THE MISSING —

"Fans of Haddix's Shadow Children books will want to jump on this time travel adventure. . . . An exciting trip through history." —*Kirkus Reviews*

MARGARET PETERSON
HADDIX

AVAILABLE NOW FROM
SIMON & SCHUSTER BOOKS FOR YOUNG READERS

ENTER THE WORLD OF

EREC REX

Books 1 and 2 in stores now

THE DRAGON'S EYE

THE MONSTERS
OF OTHERNESS

And Book 3 coming in June 2009

THE SEARCH FOR TRUTH

Travel into magical new worlds with

The Chronicles of the Imaginarium Geographica!

HERE, THERE BE DRAGONS

THE SEARCH FOR THE RED DRAGON

THE INDIGO KING

THE SHADOW DRAGONS

Among
the Impostors

MARGARET PETERSON HADDIX

SIMON & SCHUSTER BOOKS FOR
YOUNG READERS

NEW YORK LONDON TORONTO SYDNEY SINGAPORE

For John and Janet

If you purchased this book without a cover, you should be aware
that this book is stolen property. It was reported as "unsold and destroyed"
to the publisher, and neither the author nor the publisher has received
any payment for this "stripped book."

This book is a work of fiction. Any references to historical events, real people,
or real locales are used fictitiously. Other names, characters, places,
and incidents are the product of the author's imagination, and any resemblance
to actual events or locales or persons, living or dead, is entirely coincidental.

First Aladdin Paperbacks edition October 2002

Text copyright © 2001 by Margaret Peterson Haddix

Simon & Schuster Books for Young Readers
An imprint of Simon & Schuster
Children's Publishing Division
1230 Avenue of the Americas
New York, NY 10020

All rights reserved, including the right of
reproduction in whole or in part in any form.

Also available in a Simon & Schuster Books for Young Readers hardcover edition.
Designed by Heather Wood
The text of this book was set in Elysium.
Printed in the United States of America
30 29

The Library of Congress has cataloged the hardcover edition as follows:
Among the impostors / Margaret Peterson Haddix.
p. cm.
Sequel to: Among the hidden
Summary: In a future where the law limits a family to only two children,
third-born Luke has been hiding for the entire twelve years of his life,
until he enters boarding school under an assumed name and
is forced to face his fears.
ISBN 0-689-83904-9 (hc.)
[1. Fear-Fiction. 2. Interpersonal relations-Fiction. 3. Science fiction.] I. Title.
PX7.H1164 Ap 2001   [Fic]-dc21   00-058325
ISBN-13: 978-0-689-83908-5 (ISBN-10: 0-689-83908-1)

0310 OFF

For Connor

CHAPTER ONE

Sometimes he whispered his real name in the dark, in the middle of the night.

"Luke. My name is Luke."

He was sure no one could hear. His roommates were all asleep, and even if they weren't, there was no way the sound of his name could travel even the short distance to the bed above or beside him. He was fairly certain there were no bugs on him or in his room. He'd looked. But even if he'd missed seeing a microphone hidden in a mattress button or carved into the headboard, how could a microphone pick up a whisper he could barely hear himself?

He was safe now. Lying in bed, wide awake while everyone else slept, he reassured himself of that fact constantly. But his heart pounded and his face went clammy with fear every time he rounded his lips for that "u" sound—instead of the fake smile of the double "e" in Lee, the name he had to force himself to answer to now.

It was better to forget, to never speak his real name again.

But he'd lost everything else. Even just mouthing his

name was a comfort. It seemed like his only link now to his past, to his parents, his brothers.

To Jen.

By day, he kept his mouth shut.

He couldn't help it.

That first day, walking up the stairs of the Hendricks School for Boys with Jen's father, Luke had felt his jaw clench tighter and tighter the closer he got to the front door.

"Oh, don't look like that," Mr. Talbot had said, pretending to be jolly. "It's not reform school or anything."

The word stuck in Luke's brain. Reform. Re-form. Yes, they were going to re-form him. They were going to take a Luke and make him a Lee.

It was safe to be Lee. It wasn't safe to be Luke.

Jen's father stood with his hand on the ornate door-knob, waiting for a reply. But Luke couldn't have said a word if his life depended on it.

Jen's father hesitated, then pulled on the heavy door. They walked down a long hallway. The ceiling was so far away, Luke thought he could have stood his entire family on his shoulders—one on top of the other, Dad and Mother and Matthew and Mark—and the highest one still would barely touch. The walls were lined, floor to ceiling, with old paintings of people in costumes Luke had never seen outside of books.

Of course, there was very little he'd ever seen outside of books.

He tried not to stare, because if he really were Lee, surely everything would look familiar and ordinary. But that was hard to remember. They passed a classroom where dozens of boys sat in orderly rows, everyone facing away from the door. Luke gawked for so long that he practically began walking backwards. He'd known there were a lot of people in the world, but he'd never been able to imagine so many all in one place at the same time. Were any of them shadow children with fake identities, like Luke?

Jen's father clapped a hand on his shoulder, turning him around.

"Ah, here's the headmaster's office," Mr. Talbot said heartily. "Just what we were looking for."

Luke nodded, still mute, and followed him through a tall doorway.

A woman sitting behind a mammoth wood desk turned their way. She took one look at Luke and asked, "New boy?"

"Lee Grant," Jen's father said. "I spoke with the master about him last night."

"It's the middle of the semester, you know," she said warningly. "Unless he's very well prepared, he shan't catch up, and might have to repeat—"

"That won't be a problem," Mr. Talbot assured her. Luke was glad he didn't have to speak for himself. He knew he wasn't well prepared. He wasn't prepared for anything.

The woman was already reaching for files and papers.

"His parents faxed in his medical information and his

insurance standing and his academic records last night," she said. "But someone needs to sign these—"

Jen's father took the stack of papers as if he autographed other people's documents all the time.

Probably he did.

Luke watched Mr. Talbot flip through the papers, scrawling his name here, crossing out a word or a phrase or a whole paragraph there. Luke was sure Jen's father was going too fast to actually read any of it.

And that was when the homesickness hit Luke for the first time. He could just picture his own father peering cautiously at important papers, reading them over and over before he even picked up a pen. Luke could see his father's rheumy eyes squinted in concentration, his brow furrowed with anxiety.

He was always so afraid of being tricked.

Maybe Jen's father didn't care.

Luke had to swallow hard then. He made a gulping noise, and the woman looked at him. Luke couldn't read her expression. Curiosity? Contempt? Indifference?

He didn't think it was sympathy.

Jen's father finished then, handing the papers back to the woman with a flourish.

"I'll call a boy to show you your room," the woman said to Luke.

Luke nodded. The woman leaned over a box on her desk and said, "Mr. Dirk, could you send Rolly Sturgeon to the office?"

Luke heard a roar along with the man's reply, "Yes, Ms. Hawkins," as if all the boys in the school were laughing and cheering and hissing at once. Luke felt his legs go weak with fear. When this Rolly Sturgeon showed up, Luke wasn't sure he'd be able to walk.

"Well, I'll be off," Jen's father said. "Duty calls."

He stuck out his hand and after a moment Luke realized he was supposed to shake it. But he'd never shaken hands with anyone before, so he put out the wrong hand first. Jen's father frowned, moving his head violently side to side, and glaring pointedly at the woman behind the desk. Fortunately, she wasn't watching. Luke recovered. He clumsily touched his hand to Jen's father's.

"Good luck," Jen's father said, bringing his other hand up to Luke's, too.

Only when Mr. Talbot had pulled both hands away did Luke realize he'd placed a tiny scrap of paper between Luke's fingers. Luke held it there until the woman turned her back. Then he slid it into his pocket.

Jen's father smiled.

"Keep those grades up," he said. "And no running away this time, you hear?"

Luke gulped again, and nodded. And then Jen's father left without a backward glance.

CHAPTER *TWO*

L uke wanted to read the note from Mr. Talbot right away. He was sure it would tell him everything—everything he needed to know to survive Hendricks School for Boys. No—to survive anything that might come his way in this new life, outside hiding.

It was just one thin scrap of paper. Now that it was in his pocket, Luke couldn't even feel it there. But he had faith. Jen's father had hidden Luke from the Population Police, double-crossing his own employer. He'd gotten Luke his fake I.D., so he could move about as freely as anyone else, anyone who wasn't an illegal third child. Jen's father had risked his career helping Luke. No, it was more than that—he'd risked his life. Surely Mr. Talbot would have written something incredibly wise.

Luke slid his hand into his pocket, his fingertips touching the top of the note. Ms. Hawkins was looking away. Maybe—

The door opened behind Luke. Luke jerked his hand out of his pocket.

"Scared you, didn't I?" a boy jeered. "Made you jump."

Luke was used to being teased. He had older brothers,

after all. But Matthew and Mark's teasing never sounded quite so mean. Still, Luke knew he had to answer.

"Sure. I'm jumpy like a cat," Luke started to say. It was an expression of his mother's. Being cat-jumpy was good. Like being quick on his feet.

Just in time, Luke remembered he couldn't mention cats. Cats were illegal, too, outlawed because they might take food that was supposed to go to starving humans. Back home, Luke had seen wild cats a few times, stalking the countryside. Dad had liked having them around because they ate rats and mice that might eat his grain. But if Luke were really Lee Grant, filthy-rich city boy, he wouldn't know a thing about cats, jumpy or otherwise.

He clamped his mouth shut, closing off his "Sure—" in a wimpy hiss. He kept his head down, too scared to look the other boy right in the eye.

The boy laughed, cruelly. He looked past Luke, to Ms. Hawkins.

"What's wrong with him?" the boy asked, as if Luke weren't even there. "Can't talk or something?"

Luke wanted Ms. Hawkins to stick up for him, to say, "He's just new. Don't you remember what that's like?" But she wasn't even paying attention. She frowned at the boy.

"Rolly, take him to room one fifty-six. There's an empty bed in there. Just put his suitcase down. Don't waste time unpacking. Then take him back to Mr. Dirk's history class with you. He's already behind. Lord knows what his parents were thinking."

Rolly shrugged and turned around.

"I did not dismiss you!" Ms. Hawkins shrieked.

"May I be dismissed?" Rolly asked mockingly.

"That's better," Ms. Hawkins said. "Now, get. Go on with you."

Luke picked up his suitcase and followed, hoping Rolly's request for dismissal would work for both of them. Either it did, or Ms. Hawkins didn't care.

In the hallway, Rolly took big steps. He was a good head taller than Luke, and had longer legs. It was all Luke could do to keep up, what with the suitcase banging against his ankles.

Rolly looked back over his shoulder, and started walking faster. He raced up a long stairway. By the time Luke reached the top, Rolly was nowhere in sight.

"Boo!"

Rolly leaped out from behind the newel post. Luke jumped so high, he lost his balance and teetered on the edge of the stairs. Rolly reached out, and Luke thought, *See, he's not so bad. He's going to catch me.* But Rolly pushed instead. Luke fell backwards. He might have tumbled down all the stairs, except that Rolly's push was crooked, and Luke landed on the railing. Pain shot through his back.

Rolly laughed.

"Got you good, didn't I?" he said.

Then, strangely, he grabbed Luke's bag and took off down the hall.

Luke was afraid he was stealing it. He galloped after Rolly.

Rolly screamed with laughter, maniacally.

This was not what Luke had expected.

Rolly dodged around a corner and Luke followed him. Rolly discovered a secret about Luke's bag that Luke had missed—it was on wheels. So Rolly could run at full-speed with the bag rolling behind him. He careened this way and that, the bag zigzagging from side to side. Luke got close enough to tackle it if he wanted, but he hesitated. If the bag had been full of his own clothes, all the hand-me-down jeans and flannel shirts he'd gotten after Matthew and Mark outgrew them, he would have leaped. But the bag held Baron clothes, stiff shirts and shiny pants that were supposed to make him look like Lee Grant, instead of Luke Garner. He couldn't risk ruining them. He focused on Rolly instead. Instinctively, Luke dove over the bag to catch Rolly's legs. It was like playing football. Rolly fell to the ground with a crash.

"Just what is the meaning of this?" a man's voice boomed above them.

Rolly was instantly on his feet.

"He attacked me, sir," Rolly said. "I was showing the new boy his room and he attacked me."

Luke opened his mouth to protest, but nothing came out. He'd learned that from Matthew and Mark: Don't tattle.

The man looked dismissively from Rolly to Luke.

"What is your name, young man?"

Luke froze. He had to stop himself from saying his real name automatically. Then he had a split second of fearing he wouldn't be able to remember the name he was supposed to use. Was he taking too long? The man's glare intensified.

"L-L-Lee. Lee Grant," Luke finally stammered.

"Well, Mr. Grant," the man snapped. "This is a fine way to begin your academic career at Hendricks. You and Mr. Sturgeon each have two demerits for this disgraceful display. You may report to my room after the final bell to do your time."

"But, sir, I told you," Rolly protested. "He attacked me."

"Very well, Mr. Sturgeon. Make that three demerits for each of you."

"But—" Rolly was undeterred.

"Four."

Rolly was going to complain again. Luke could tell by the way he was standing. But the man turned away and began walking down the hall, as if Rolly and Luke were both too unimportant to bother with, and he'd wasted enough time already.

Luke's head swam with questions. What were demerits? When was final bell? Where was this man's room? Who was he, anyway? Luke tried to muster up the nerve to call after the man—or to ask Rolly, which seemed even more dangerous. But then he was blindsided with a shove that sent him crashing into the wall.

"Fonrol!" Rolly exploded.

Luke slumped against the wall. His shoulder throbbed. Why did Rolly seem to hate him so much?

"Well, come on, you little exnay," Rolly taunted. "Want to get demerits from Mr. Dirk, too?"

He stepped backwards, tugging on Luke's suitcase. Then he shoved it through a nearby doorway. Luke looked up and saw 156 etched on a copper plaque on the door. Relief overwhelmed him. Finally something made sense. This was his room. The rest of the day would be horrible—he'd already resigned himself to that. But eventually it would be night, and he'd be sent to bed, and he could come to this room and shut the door. And then he could read the note from Jen's dad, if he didn't get a chance to read it before bedtime. Come nightfall, he'd know everything and be safe, alone in his own room.

Imagining the haven that awaited him in only a matter of hours, he got brave enough to peek around the corner.

The room held eight beds.

Seven of them were made up, with rich blue spreads stretched tautly from top to bottom. Only one, a lower bunk, was covered just by sheets.

Luke felt as desolate as that bed looked. He knew it was his. And he knew he wouldn't get to be alone in this room.

He probably wouldn't be safe, either, not if any of his seven roommates were anything like Rolly.

He edged his hand into his pocket, his fingers brushing the note from Jen's dad. What if he just pulled it out and read it now, right in front of Rolly?

He didn't dare. The way the last ten minutes had gone, Rolly would probably rip the note to shreds before Luke even had it completely out of his pocket.

And Jen's dad had acted like it was secret. If Ms. Hawkins wasn't supposed to see it, there was no way Rolly could be trusted.

Rolly hit Luke on the shoulder.

"Tag! You're it!" he hollered, and took off running. Panicked, Luke chased after him.

CHAPTER *THREE*

L uke managed to keep up with Rolly only because Rolly slowed to a dignified walk when he began passing classrooms instead of sleeping quarters. But it was a fast dignified walk, and Luke was terrified that Rolly might dart around a corner unexpectedly and disappear. Then Luke would be totally lost. So Luke dared to jog a little, hoping to keep pace.

A tall, thin man with a skimpy mustache came out of one of the rooms as Luke passed by.

"Two demerits, young man," he said to Luke. "No running allowed. You know the rules."

Luke didn't, and didn't have the nerve to say so.

Rolly smirked.

The thin man went back into his classroom. Luke knew he'd have to risk asking Rolly a question.

"Wha—" he began. But just then Rolly opened a tall, wooden door to one side of the hall and slipped through. Luke's reflexes weren't fast enough. The door shut behind Rolly and then Luke had to fumble with the knob. It was ornate and gold, and had to be turned further to the right than all the doorknobs at home.

Home . . .

For the second time in less than an hour, Luke was overcome with an almost unbearable wave of home-sickness.

Stupid, Luke chided himself. *How can you be homesick for doorknobs?*

Blinking quickly, he shoved on the door and it gave way. Blindly, he stepped in.

He was at the back of a huge classroom. Boys sat in row upon row upon row, dozens of them, it seemed to Luke, all the way to the front of the room. There, the tall, thin man who'd just given Luke demerits was writing on the wall.

Or was it the same man? Luke squinted, confused. Oh. There was a door at the front of the room, too. That was the door the man had used. But had Luke and Rolly really walked so far between the doors? Suddenly, Luke wasn't sure of anything.

Luke scanned the row of boys in front of him, looking for Rolly. He was supposed to stay close to Rolly, so that's what he'd do. But now he couldn't even remember if Rolly had brown hair or black, short or long, curly or straight. He'd really never looked that closely at Rolly, just followed him and gotten beat up by him. Any of the heads in front of him might belong to Rolly.

The man at the front of the class turned around.

"And the Greeks were—sit down—" he interrupted himself impatiently.

He was looking at Luke.

"M-Me?" Luke squeaked. "W-Where should I sit?"

His voice wasn't much more than a whisper. There was no way the man could have heard him, all the way at the front of the room. Probably the boy sitting a foot away hadn't even heard him. But suddenly every boy in the room turned around and stared at Luke.

It was awful. All those eyes, all looking at him. It was straight out of Luke's worst nightmares. Panic rooted him to the spot, but every muscle in his body was screaming for him to run, to hide anywhere he could. For twelve years—his entire life—he'd had to hide. To be seen was death. "Don't!" he wanted to scream. "Don't look at me! Don't report me! Please!"

But the muscles that controlled his mouth were as frozen as the rest of him. The tiny part of his mind that wasn't flooded with panic knew that that was good—now that he had a fake I.D., the last thing he should do was act like a boy who's had to hide. But to act normal, he needed to move, to obey the man at the front and sit down. And he couldn't make his body do that, either.

Then someone kicked him.

"Ow!" Luke crumbled.

Rough hands jerked him backwards. Miraculously, he landed on the corner of a chair, barely regained his balance, and managed not to fall completely. He slid to his right and was solidly in the seat.

"*Thank* you," the man at the front said with exaggerated,

mocking gratitude. "See me after class. As I was saying before I was so rudely interrupted, the Greeks were quite technologically advanced for their time. . . ."

Then Luke could no longer hear the man's words over the buzzing in his ears. His heart kept thumping hard, as if it, at least, still thought Luke would be wise to run. But Luke resolutely gripped the edge of the chair. He was acting normal now. Wasn't he? The boys who had been staring at him slowly began turning back to face the teacher again. Luke wiped sweat from his forehead and looked around for whoever had kicked and pulled and shoved him. Had they been trying to help him? Luke desperately wanted to believe that. But all the boys near him were looking at the teacher, nonchalantly, as though Luke weren't even there. And if they'd been trying to help, wouldn't they be trying to catch Luke's eye, to get him to say thanks?

Luke really didn't know. He knew how his family would act—Mother and Dad, Matthew and Mark. Mother and Dad would never kick him, and his older brothers would be poking him now, taunting him, "Want us to kick you again?"

The only other people Luke had ever met before today were Jen's dad—who was practically as big a mystery as the boys sitting beside him now—and Jen. And Jen would . . .

Luke couldn't bear to think about Jen.

A bell rang suddenly, and it was such an alarming sound that Luke's heart set to pounding again.

"Remember! Chapter twelve!" the teacher called as all the boys scrambled up.

Luke meant to go see the teacher, as he'd been instructed. This had to be the end of the class. But the tide of boys swept him out the back door of the classroom before he quite knew what was happening. By the time he got his feet firmly on the ground, and felt like he might be able to break away, he was around a corner and down another hall. He fought his way back to what he thought was the original hallway. But then he couldn't figure out which way to turn. He looked all around, frantically searching for either the teacher or Rolly—as nasty as he'd been, Rolly was at least sort of familiar. But all the faces that flowed past him were strangers'.

Of course, the way Luke's mind was working, both Rolly and the teacher could have paraded past Luke five times and he might not have even recognized them.

The crowd in the hall was thinning out. Luke began to panic again.

"Get to class," an older boy standing nearby ordered him.

"Where?" Luke said. "Where's my class?"

The boy didn't hear him. Luke thought about asking again, louder, but the boy seemed to be some sort of guard, someone in charge, like a policeman.

Like the Population Police.

Luke put his hand over his mouth and veered away, down another hall. Another bell rang and boys started running, desperate to get into their classrooms. Hopelessly, Luke followed a group of three or four through a doorway, into another classroom. At least, he thought it was another classroom. For all he knew, he might have circled around and gone into the same one all over again. Maybe that was good. Maybe after class this time, he could make it up to talk to the teacher—

It was a short, fat man who stood up to talk this time. As confused and panicky as Luke felt, even he could tell it wasn't the same teacher.

Luke hastily sat down, terrified of drawing attention to himself again. He resolved to listen carefully this time, to pay attention and learn. He owed it to everyone—to Mother and Dad, to Jen's father, even to Jen herself.

It was ten minutes before he realized that the man at the front was speaking some other language, one Luke had never heard before and didn't have a prayer of understanding.

CHAPTER *FOUR*

When the bell rang after this class, Luke didn't even try to go against the crowd. This time the flow of traffic carried him to a huge room with tables instead of desks, and bookshelves instead of portraits on the wall. All the other boys sat down and pulled out books and paper and pens or pencils.

Homework. They were doing homework.

Luke felt brilliant for figuring that out. How many times had he watched his older brothers groan over math problems, stumble over reading assignments, scratch out answers in history workbooks? Matthew and Mark did not like school. Once, years ago, Luke had been peering over Mark's shoulder at his homework, and noticed an easy mistake.

"Isn't eight times four thirty-two?" he'd innocently asked. "You wrote down thirty-four."

Mark stuck out his tongue and pushed so hard on his pencil that the lead broke.

"See what you made me do?" he complained. "If you're so smart, why don't you go to school for me?"

Mother was hovering over them.

"Hush," she said to Mark, and that had been the end of it.

Luke's family didn't dwell on what they all knew: Because Luke was the third born, he was illegal, violating the Population Law with every breath he took and every bite of food he ate. Of course he couldn't go to school, or anywhere else.

But here he was, now, at school. And it wasn't Matthew and Mark's little country school, but a grand, fancy place that only the richest people, Barons, could afford. Rich people like the real Lee Grant, who had died in a skiing accident. His family had concealed his death and secretly given his identity card to help a shadow child come out of hiding.

Couldn't everyone tell that Luke was an impostor?

Luke wished the real Lee Grant were still alive. He wished that he, himself, were still at home, hiding.

"Young man," someone said in a warning voice.

Luke glanced around. He was the only one still standing. Quickly he slipped into the nearest vacant chair. He didn't have any books to study or work to do. Maybe this was the time to read the note from Jen's dad.

But as he reached into his pocket he knew it wasn't safe. The boy across the table from him kept looking up, the boy two chairs down kept whispering and pointing. Though Luke kept his head down, he could feel eyes all around him. Even if no one was looking directly at him, Luke felt itchy and anxious just being in the same room with so many other people. He couldn't read the note. He could barely keep himself from bolting out of his chair, running out the door, finding some closet or small space to hide in.

And then everybody would know that he wasn't really Lee Grant. Everybody would know that all he knew was how to hide.

Luke forced himself to sit still for two hours.

When a bell went off again, everyone trouped down a hall to a huge dining area.

Luke hadn't eaten since breakfast at home—his mother's lightest biscuits and, as a miraculous farewell treat, fresh eggs. Luke could remember the pride shining in her eyes as she had slid the plate in front of him.

"From the factory?" he had asked. Eggs usually were not available for ordinary people, but his mother worked at a chicken factory, and if her supervisors were in a good mood, sometimes she got extra food.

Mother had nodded. "I promised them forty hours of overtime in exchange. Unpaid."

Luke had gulped.

"Just for two eggs for me?"

Mother had looked at him.

"It was a good trade," she'd said.

Remembering breakfast gave him a lump in his throat as big as an egg. He wasn't hungry.

But he sat down, because all the other boys were sitting. Instantly another boy turned on him and glared.

"Seniors only," he said.

"Huh?" Luke asked.

"Only seniors are allowed at this table," the boy said, in the same kind of mocking voice that Mark always used with Luke when Luke had said something dumb.

"Oh," Luke said.

"What are you, some kind of a lecker?" another boy asked.

Luke didn't know how to answer that. He was so eager to get up, he tripped and crashed into the next table.

"Juniors only," a boy said there.

Luke tried to swallow the lump in his throat, but it had grown even bigger.

He went from table to table, not even bothering to try to sit down. At each table, someone said in a bored voice, "Sophomores only," or "Freshmen only," or "Eights only" . . . Luke didn't know what he was, so he kept moving.

Finally he reached an empty table and sat down.

A bowl of leaves and what looked like germinating soybeans sat in front of him. Was this supposed to be food? The other boys were eating it, so he did, too. The leaves were clammy and bitter and stuck in his throat.

Luke let himself think about potato chips. Nobody was supposed to have junk food, because of the food shortages that led to the Population Law. But Jen had given him potato chips when he'd gone over to her house, secretly, at great risk. He could still taste the salt, could still feel the crisp chips against the roof of his mouth, could still hear

Jen saying, when he protested that potato chips were illegal, "Yeah, well, we're illegal, too, so why don't we enjoy ourselves?"

Jen. If Jen were here now, she wouldn't put up with bitter leaves and tasteless bean sprouts for supper. She'd be standing up, demanding decent food. She'd go to any table she wanted. She'd march up to the person in charge—the headmaster?—and say, "Why won't anyone tell me what classes to go to? What are demerits? What are the rules, anyway? You're not running this school very well!" She'd punch Rolly right in the eye.

But Jen wasn't there. Jen was dead.

Luke bent his head low over his food. He stopped even pretending to chew and swallow.

After supper everyone was herded into another vast room. A man stood at the front talking about how glorious the Government was, about how their leaders' wisdom had kept them all from starving.

Lies, Luke thought, and marveled that he had the will even to think that.

Finally another bell rang and the other boys scattered. Luke walked uncertainly up and down strange halls.

"To your room," a man warned him. "Lights out in ten minutes."

Luke was so eager to get to his room, he actually found his voice.

"I-I'm new. I don't know where my room is."

"Well, then, find out."

"How?" Luke asked.

The man sighed, and rolled his eyes.

"What's your name?" he asked, slowly, as though Luke might be too stupid to understand the question.

"L—" Somehow Luke couldn't bring himself to claim his fake identity. "I know my room number. One fifty-six. I just don't remember where it is."

"Why didn't you say so?" the man growled. "Up those stairs and around the corner."

Even with the man's directions, Luke got turned around and had to search and search. By the time he finally saw the engraved 156, his legs were trembling with exhaustion and his feet were blistered from walking in the stiff, unfamiliar shoes. Luke was used to going barefoot. He was used to sitting in the house all day, not walking up and down stairs and through labyrinth-like halls.

He stepped through the doorway and headed straight for his bed. It had a spread on it and looked like all the others now. All Luke wanted to do was fall into it and go to sleep and forget everything that had happened that day.

"Did you ask permission?" someone barked at him.

Luke looked around. He was so tired, he hadn't even noticed that seven boys were sitting on the floor in a circle, playing some sort of card game.

"Per-Permission?" he asked.

One of the boys—probably the one who'd spoken—threw back his head and laughed. He was tall and thin, and older than Luke. Maybe even as old as Luke's brother

Matthew, who was fifteen. But Matthew was familiar, known. Luke couldn't read this boy's expression. He had a strange cast to his dark eyes, and his face was oddly shaped. Something about him reminded Luke of the pictures he'd seen in books of jackals.

"Hey!" the boy said. "They sent us a voice replicator. Amazingly human-like form. Voice is a little off, though. Let's try another one. Repeat after me: 'I am an exnay. I am a fonrol. I am a lecker. I don't deserve to live.'"

Most of the other boys were laughing now, too, but quietly, as if they didn't want to miss Luke's answer.

Luke hesitated. He'd heard those words before: Rolly had called him an exnay and a fonrol, and someone had called him a lecker at dinner. Maybe they were from that foreign language the short, fat teacher had been speaking. Luke had no idea what the words meant, but he could tell that they were probably bad things. Thanks to Matthew and Mark, he could spot a setup.

Luke shook his head.

The jackal boy sighed in exaggerated disappointment.

"Broken already," he said. He stood up and knocked his fist against Luke's side the way Luke had seen his father tap on the engine of broken tractors or trucks. "You just can't get good junk nowadays."

Luke pulled away. He stepped toward his bed.

Jackal boy laughed again.

"Oh, no, not so fast. Permission, remember? Say, 'I am your servant, O mighty master. I shall do your bidding forever. I will not eat or sleep or breathe unless you say it is to be so.'"

The boy moved between Luke and his bed. The others leaned forward, menacingly. *Like a pack of jackals*, Luke thought.

Jackals were nasty, vicious animals. Luke had read a book about them. They tore their prey limb from limb sometimes.

These were really boys, not jackals, Luke reminded himself. But he was too tired to fight.

"I am your servant," he mumbled. "I—I don't remember the rest."

"Why do they always send us the stupid ones?" the jackal boy asked. He looked down at Luke. "Bet you don't even know your own name."

"L-Lee," Luke whispered, looking down at his shoes.

"Lee, repeat after me. 'I—'"

"I—"

"'Am—'"

"Am—"

The jackal boy fed him each word and Luke, hating himself, repeated it. Then the boy made him touch his elbow to his nose. Cross his eyes. Stand on one foot while reciting, "I am the lowest of the low. Everyone should spit on me," five times. The lights flickered and went out in the middle of this ordeal, and still the jackal boy continued. Finally he yawned. Luke could hear his jaw crack in the dark.

"New boy, you bore me," he said. "Remove yourself from my presence."

"Huh?" Luke said.

"Go to bed!"

Meekly, Luke slipped beneath his covers. He was still wearing his clothes—even his shoes—but he didn't dare get back up to take them off. The unfamiliar pants bunched up around his waist, and he silently smoothed them out. Touching his pocket reminded him: He still hadn't read the note from Jen's dad.

Tomorrow, Luke thought. He felt a little bit of hope return. Tomorrow he would read the note, and then he would know how to find out what classes to go to, how to deal with boys like Rolly and his roommates, how to get by. No—not just to get by. Luke remembered what he'd hoped for, leaving home—was it only that morning? It seemed so long ago. He'd been thinking about making a difference in the world, finding some way to help other third children who had to hide. Luke didn't expect the note from Jen's dad to tell him how to do that, but it would give him a start. It would make that possible.

All he had to do was go to sleep and then it would be tomorrow and he could read the note.

But Luke couldn't sleep. The room was filled with unfamiliar sounds: first the other boys whispering, then breathing deeply, in sleep. The beds creaking when someone turned over. Some vent somewhere blowing air on them all.

Luke ached, missing his room at home, his family, Jen.

And his own name. He felt his lips draw together.

"Luke," he whispered soundlessly, in the dark. "My name is Luke."

He waited silently, his heart pounding, but nothing happened. No alarm bells went off, no Population Police swooped in to carry him away. His feeling of hope surged, even more than the fear. His name was Luke. He was nobody's servant. He was not the lowest of the low. He was Dad and Mother's son. He was Matthew and Mark's brother. He was Jen's friend.

Or—he had been.

CHAPTER *FIVE*

uke didn't get a chance to read the note from Jen's dad the next day. Or the next. Or the next.

In fact, an entire week went by with him resolving every night in bed, "Tomorrow. Surely I'll find a way to read the note tomorrow." But the next nightfall found him still stymied.

At first, he thought there was an easy solution. The bathroom, for example. He could go in, shut the door, read the note.

But none of the bathrooms at Hendricks were like the bathroom at home, closed-in and private. The Hendricks bathrooms were rows of urinals and commodes, right out in front of everyone. Even the shower was communal, just an open, tiled room with dozens of spigots sprouting from each wall.

Luke could barely bring himself to lower his pants with everyone watching, let alone read the note. He always lingered until most of the other boys were gone, but he never found a bathroom that fully emptied out. Finally, after three days had passed and he was getting desperate, he resolved to wait in the bathroom for as long as it took, regardless of bells or classes. The bell rang for breakfast and still he remained, pretending to be very concerned with scrubbing his face.

Finally it was just Luke and another boy, standing by the door.

"Out," the boy said.

The boy was mean-faced and muscular. Luke's legs trembled, but he didn't shut off the water.

"I'm not done," Luke mumbled, trying to sound nonchalant, unconcerned. He failed miserably.

The boy grabbed Luke's arm.

"Didn't you hear me? I said OUT!" The boy jerked so hard on Luke's arm that Luke felt pain shoot through his whole body. Then the boy shoved Luke out the door. Luke landed in a heap on the hallway floor. A hall monitor looked down at him in disgust.

"You're late for breakfast," he said. "Two demerits."

Luke feebly looked from the hall monitor to the other boy, who was now standing menacingly in the bathroom doorway. Then he understood: They were alike. There were guards in all the bathrooms, as well as in all the halls. He couldn't read the note in either place.

He wondered about trying to read the note in his room. He would get there first at bedtime, he decided. The first several days this was impossible because, no matter how hard he tried, he couldn't ever remember which way to go. Left at the top of the stairs, then right, then right, then left? Or was it right, then left, then left, then right? Most nights, it was a miracle if he found the room at all before lights out. Though that was just as well, because it reduced the amount of time that jackal boy could spend tormenting him.

Finally, in the middle of Luke's second week at Hendricks, he sat at the back of the hall during the evening lecture, so he was the first one up the stairs. Holding his breath, he counted off the turns. Right—yes. Right—yes. Left. And there—yes! Room 156.

Luke rushed in past the hall monitor. He slipped behind the door, out of sight, and jammed his hand in his pocket. And heard, "So my servant's reporting for duty early tonight, eh?"

It was jackal boy, lounging on his bed.

Luke had to bite his lip to keep from screaming.

That night jackal boy was crueler than ever.

Luke had to repeat, "I am a fonrol," fifty times. He had to hop up and down on one foot for five minutes. He had to do one hundred push-ups. (He'd never seen anyone do a push-up before. All the other boys howled with laughter when he stammeringly confessed, "I—I don't know how.") He had to push a marble across the floor with his nose.

Lying in bed that night, Luke despaired. His shoulders ached from the push-ups; his side was still bruised from being thrown out of the bathroom.

I'll never get to read the note, he thought. *I'll never be alone.*

It wasn't just that he wanted to read the note. It was maddening to always be around other people, to know that his every action might be observed, to never have a second of privacy.

How could he long to be alone, and feel so lonely, all at once?

CHAPTER SIX

Luke got by.

It wasn't really that hard, as long as he didn't let himself want anything.

As long as he didn't linger in the bathroom or halls, as long as he sat down promptly when he entered a classroom, as long as he didn't try to eat at the wrong table, nobody bothered him except jackal boy. And jackal boy's torture was bearable, even at its worst.

The problem was, Luke couldn't always stop himself from wanting more.

He wanted home and he wanted his family and he wanted Jen alive again. And he wanted all the third children to be free, so he didn't have to go around pretending to be someone else anymore.

Those were impossible dreams, little fantasies that he played with in his mind in the middle of the night when he couldn't sleep.

The glow of those fantasies always made reality seem even bleaker the next morning.

But everything else he wanted seemed impossible, too.

He wanted to be able to climb into bed each night without even looking at jackal boy—without saying, "I am the dumbest lecker alive," a hundred times, without doing a single push-up, pull-up, sit-up, or toe-touch. Once during a nightly session, he dared to mumble, "Leave me alone," to jackal boy. But when Luke looked up, jackal boy was laughing hysterically.

"Did you—did you say what I thought—you said?" he sputtered between laughs. "'Leave me alone.' Oh, that's a good one, you stupid fonrol. You going to make me? Go ahead. Make me."

Jackal boy had his fists up, a taunting grin smeared across his face. Behind him, their other roommates gathered, eager for a fight. Eager, it seemed, to help jackal boy pound every shred of courage out of Luke.

Luke sized up the height and weight difference just between him and jackal boy. Never mind the rest of the boys. Nobody had to swing a single punch. Luke's courage was already gone.

At least jackal boy tortured Luke only once a day.

Three times a day, in the cavernous dining hall, Luke longed for food that tasted good. Mouthing bitter greens and mealy bread, he dreamed of Mother's stews, her biscuits, her apple pies. He could remember the exact sound of her voice asking him, "Want to lick the bowl?" whenever she made a cake. And then the taste of sweet batter.

He could remember every detail of the one time that he and Jen had made cookies together. They'd used special chips made of chocolate, and when the cookies were done and hot from the oven, the chips were melted and sweet on his tongue. He and Jen sat in the kitchen laughing and talking and eating cookie after cookie after cookie.

That was one of the best visits he'd ever had with Jen.

It was also one of the last.

He tried to forget that, but he couldn't. He knew that if he sat down in the Hendricks dining hall and someone put a whole plateful of the Jen cookies in front of him, they'd taste every bit as bitter as the greens. He wouldn't be able to eat a bite.

And Mother's biscuits, flown in fresh—if that were possible—would crumble in his mouth just like the mealy bread. Nothing could taste good when you ate alone in the midst of hundreds of boys who didn't even know your name. Who didn't care.

For Luke wanted a friend at Hendricks, too. Sometimes he forced himself to stop daydreaming and start paying attention to the other boys. He wasn't brave enough to speak to any of them, but he thought if he listened, then someday . . .

He couldn't tell the boys apart.

Maybe it had something to do with being in hiding all those years. He wasn't blind—he could tell that some of them had different-colored hair, even slightly different-colored skin. Some were taller, some were shorter; some were fatter, some were thinner. Some of them were older even than Luke's brothers; others were a few years younger than Luke himself. But Luke could never fix any of them in his mind. Even jackal boy was unrecognizable outside of their room. Once he came up to Luke and said, "Ah, my servant! Just when I need a pen. Give me yours, kid." And Luke stared, openmouthed, for so long that jackal boy just eased the pen out of Luke's hand and headed off, muttering, "Fine time to turn statue on me."

Another time, during breakfast, he overheard boys joking at a nearby table.

"Oh, come on, Spence," one boy said to another.

Luke stared. *Spence,* he repeated to himself, memorizing the boy's features. *That boy's name is Spence. Now I know who he is.* It gave him a warm glow all morning, to think that he'd be able to recognize somebody now.

At lunch he watched Spence slip into his seat. Luke practically smiled. Then Spence knocked over his water glass, dousing the boy beside him.

"Ted, you lecker!" the other boy exclaimed.

Ted? But—

At dinner, the boy Luke would have sworn was Spence looked up when someone called out, "Hey! E. J.!"

"Not now," Spence/Ted/E. J. said irritably. Or was he simply E. J., and Spence and Ted were totally different boys?

Luke gave up trying to keep track of anybody's names. He thought he noticed other boys responding to multiple names, too, but he could never be sure.

Why was he so easily confused?

It was like the halls of the school, which always seemed to double back on themselves. From one day to the next, Luke could rarely find his way to the same classroom twice. So it didn't matter that he was never sure which class he was supposed to be sitting in—he'd never be able to get to the right place, anyhow. The teachers didn't seem to notice Luke, or anyone else. They'd occasionally point at a boy and declare, "Two demerits," but they almost never called anyone by name.

Luke wondered about sneaking up to his room during classtime, and reading the note from Jen's dad, since nobody cared where he was, anyway. But the hall monitors guarded the stairs, too. They guarded everything.

So, Luke reflected gloomily, the note that could save him was doomed to turn to lint in his pocket. And Luke was doomed to endlessly wander the halls of Hendricks, unnoticed, unknowing, unknown.

In bed at night, Luke took to having imaginary conversations with his family, Jen, Jen's dad. His part was all apologies.

I'm sorry, Mr. Talbot. You risked your life to get me a fake I.D., and I wasn't worth it. . . .

I'm sorry, Jen, I'm not doing anything for the cause. . . .

I'm sorry, Mother. This was the hardest one of all. *You wanted me to stay but I said I had to go. I said I was going to make a difference in the world. But I can't. I wanted to make sure there was enough food for everyone in the world, so third children could be legal again. But I can't even understand a word my teachers say. Even the ones who are speaking my language. I'll never learn anything. I'll never be able to help anyone.*

I'm sorry, Mother. I should have never left you. I wish—

But Luke wished for so much, he couldn't go on.

He was so busy longing for big, impossible changes, he never gave a thought to wanting anything smaller or more practical. Like an open door.

But that was what he got.

CHAPTER SEVEN

L uke saw the door one morning on the way to class. He'd barely slept the night before, so he was groggy and stupid. He was shuffling along looking for a familiar classroom to duck into before the hall monitor yelled at him. Between classrooms, he stared down at his feet, too miserable to lift his head. But just as he turned a corner, someone bumped into him. Luke looked up in time to see the other boy barrel past without an apology. Then, as Luke turned his head forward again, he saw it.

The door was on the outside wall. Luke couldn't have said if he'd passed it a hundred times before, or never. It was solid wood with a brass knob, just like dozens of other doors in the school. It was barely even ajar.

But beyond it, Luke could see grass and trees and sky. Outdoors.

He didn't think. He didn't even pause to make sure a hall monitor wasn't watching him. In a flash, Luke was out the door.

Outside, Luke stood still, his back to the wall of the school. He was breathing hard. *Read the note and get back inside!* some tiny, rational part of his brain urged him. *Before someone sees you!*

But he couldn't move. It was May. The lawn ahead of him was a rich green carpet. Redbuds were blooming, and lilacs. He thought he even smelled honeysuckle. His mind played a trick on him, and suddenly he was almost a whole year back in time, standing outside for what he had thought might be the last time in his entire life. The Government workers were just starting to cut down the woods behind his family's house, and his mother was fearfully ordering him, "Luke! Inside. Now."

And when the woods were gone, Jen's house replaced it.

His mind skipped ahead, and he remembered his first trip to Jen's house. He'd stepped outside and felt paralyzed, just like now. And he'd marveled at the feel of fresh air on his face, just like now.

And he'd been in danger.

Just like now.

Luke looked back at the school, hopelessly. Anyone could easily look out a window and see him, and report him. Maybe they'd just give him more of those meaningless demerits. Or maybe this would make them realize that he really wasn't Lee Grant, that his papers were forged, that by the laws of the land, he deserved to die.

Strangely, Luke could see no windows. But the door was opening.

Luke took off running. He raced as blindly as he had that first day, trying to keep up with Rolly Sturgeon. Luke was crashing through the undergrowth of a small woods before his mind fully registered that there was a woods. Brambles tore at his arms and legs and chest, and he kept running. He whipped willow branches out of his way. He was so frenzied, he felt like he could run forever.

Then he tripped over a log and fell.

Silence. Only now that he'd stopped did Luke realize how much noise he'd been making. So stupid. Luke lay facedown in ferns and moss, and waited for someone to grab him and yell and punish him.

Nothing happened. Over the pounding of his pulse, Luke could hear nothing but birdsong. After what seemed like a very long time, he cautiously raised his head.

Trees formed a canopy over his head. A flash of movement caught Luke's eye, but it was only a squirrel jumping from branch to branch. Branches swayed, but only because of the wind.

Slowly, Luke inched back the way he had come. Finally he crouched, hidden by the underbrush, and spied on the school.

Nobody was in sight.

Luke peered at the door. It moved out again, and he stiffened, terrified. But then it moved in.

In, out, in, out—so slow—it was like the school was breathing through the door. Suddenly Luke understood.

Nobody had pushed the door open. It was the wind, or maybe the change in air pressure as the boys walked past.

Luke stuck his head out a little further. He could see one whole side of the school building this way. And he realized for the first time: There were no windows in any part of the wall. It was solid brick, up and down.

How could that be?

Luke thought about all of the rooms he'd been in, since coming to Hendricks, and it was true—he couldn't remember a single window in any of them. Even the room he shared with jackal boy and his minions was windowless. Why hadn't he ever noticed before?

And why would someone build so many windowless rooms?

Suddenly Luke didn't care. There were no windows, nobody was coming out of the door—he was safe.

"I can read the note now!" he said aloud, and chuckled. It was strangely thrilling to hear his own voice—not timid, not stammering—Luke's voice, not the pretend-Lee's.

"I'm going to read it right over there!" he said, speaking just for the pleasure of it. "Finally!"

He strolled deeper into the woods, and sat down on the very log he'd tripped over before. Slowly, ceremoniously, he slipped the note from Jen's dad out of his pocket. Now he would know everything he needed to do.

He unfolded the note, which had grown worn from all the times he'd palmed it, secretly transferring it from the pocket of one pair of pants to another. Then he stared, trying to make sense of Mr. Talbot's scrawl.

The note only held two words:

Blend in

CHAPTER *EIGHT*

"**N**o!" Luke screamed.

That was it? "Blend in"? What kind of advice was that? Luke needed help. He'd been waiting weeks.

"I was counting on you!" Luke screamed again, past caring who might hear.

The "B" on "Blend" blurred before his eyes. Desperately, he turned the note over, hoping there was more on the other side. The real message, maybe. But the other side was blank. What he held was just a small, ragged scrap of paper, not much more than lint. Even Mother—who saved everything, who reused envelopes—even she wouldn't think twice about tossing this useless shred in the trash.

And this tiny piece of nothing was what Luke had pinned all his hopes on.

Too furious to see straight, Luke ripped the note in half. In fourths. In eighths. He kept ripping until the pieces of paper were all but dust. Practically microscopic. Then he threw them as far away as he could.

"I hate you, Mr. Talbot!" Luke yelled.

The words echoed in the trees. Even the woods seemed

to be making fun of him. That was probably all Mr. Talbot had meant to do, too, when he'd handed Luke the note that first day. Luke could just imagine Mr. Talbot chuckling as he drove away from Hendricks after leaving Luke. He probably thought it was funny to drop off a dumb farm boy at a snobby Baron school and tell him, "Blend in." He probably laughed about it all the time. If Jen were still alive, she probably would have laughed at Luke, too.

No. Not Jen . . .

Luke buried his face in his hands and slipped down to the ground, sprawled beside the log. Without the note to count on, he didn't even have enough backbone of his own to sit.

CHAPTER NINE

Luke wouldn't have thought he could have fallen asleep there in the woods, in danger, boiling mad. But somehow he found himself waking up some time later, stiff and sore and confused. The birds were still singing, a mild breeze ruffled his hair—before he remembered everything, Luke actually smiled. What a pleasant dream. But why did he feel so unhappy?

Then he sat up and opened his eyes and everything came back to him. The note he'd believed in so fervently was worthless dust now—no matter how hard he peered off into the underbrush, he couldn't see a single sign of it. He was out in the woods, violating who knew how many rules of the Hendricks School for Boys. And he had no idea how long he'd been gone—squinting at the sun, Luke guessed that it was at least mid-afternoon. They must have noticed him missing by now. He should be thinking up his excuse now. He should sneak back so at least they wouldn't find him out here. It wouldn't look so bad. Maybe he could convince them that he'd started to run away—the real Lee Grant had done that, supposedly—then repented and turned around. But that story depended on him going back *now*.

Luke didn't move.

He didn't want to go back to school. Not now, not ever. There wasn't anything there for him. He knew that now. No friends, no helpful teachers, no good choices. He was just like some windup toy there, marching mindlessly from class to class, meal to meal, trying not to be watched.

Just the thought of school made his stomach churn.

"You can't make me go back," Luke muttered, though he wasn't sure who he thought he was defying.

That was settled. So where else could he go?

Home . . .

Luke was overcome with a stronger longing than he'd ever felt before. To see Mother again, to see Dad . . . This was how miserable Luke felt: He even missed his brothers. He watched a chipmunk race across the ground. The chipmunk's feet barely seemed to touch. It could be just that easy for Luke, going home. All he had to do was start walking.

But.

He didn't know how to get there. Even if he had a map, he wouldn't be able to find his parents' farm on it.

He didn't have his fake I.D. card with him. He didn't carry it at school. He could picture it clearly, tucked in the pocket at the back of his suitcase. He couldn't go back for it. And getting caught without an I.D. card was as good as admitting, "I'm a third child. Kill me."

Luke tried to pretend those weren't obstacles. He still couldn't picture a perfect homecoming.

Even if he managed to find his family's farm without running into the Population Police first, he'd just be bringing danger with him. The penalties for harboring an illegal child were almost as harsh as the penalty for *being* an illegal child. Every second he'd lived with his parents, he'd put their lives in jeopardy. And now there was a record of his existence. If he disappeared now, someone would have to look for him. And when they found him, cowering in his family's attic, they'd be sure to find out the truth as well.

Luke picked up a pebble and threw it far into the woods. It wasn't fair. His only choices were to be miserable at school or a virtual murderer at home. He threw another pebble, and another. Not fair, not fair, not fair. He ran out of pebbles and switched to bark chips, peeled off the log beside him. Some of the pebbles and bark chips hit tree trunks with a satisfying thud. Luke began aiming.

"Take that!" he yelled, forgetting himself.

Then, terrified, he clapped his hand over his mouth. How could he be so stupid?

He froze, listening so hard, his ears began to buzz. But there was no sound of anyone tramping through the woods looking for him. There was no sound from the school at all. Peering around at the ferns and the trees and the sunlight filtering through the branches, Luke could practically convince himself the school didn't exist at all.

It was a shame he couldn't just stay here.

Luke had a moment of hope—he could live on nuts and berries. He could hide in the trees whenever they came looking for him.

But that was a childish plan. He dismissed it immediately. If he stayed in the woods, he'd be caught or starve.

He glanced around again, this time regretfully. The trees looked friendlier than any of the boys or teachers at schools. He was a farm boy who'd spent most of his life outdoors, until the woods were cut down behind his house. Just being outside was a joy. And no matter how much he'd risked, running out here, it was wonderful to be alone, not packed in and watched at every turn.

Luke dug the toe of his fancy Baron shoe into the dirt and stood up. He'd come to a decision without realizing it. He had to go back to school. He owed it to his family, and Jen's dad, and maybe even Jen herself.

But nothing could stop him from visiting the woods again.

CHAPTER *TEN*

L uke put off returning to school as long as possible. His stomach growled and he ignored it. The angle of the sun's rays grew sharper and sharper, but he consoled himself, "It's still daylight. It just starts looking like twilight sooner, when you're deep in the woods."

Finally he could ignore the truth no longer. It was getting dark. And even if nobody had noticed his absence so far, he'd be missed at bedtime. Jackal boy was sure to complain if Luke wasn't there for him to pick on.

Strangely, that thought almost made him feel good.

Luke didn't stop to figure that one out. He strode to the edge of the woods, looked around carefully, then took off running across the lawn.

Halfway to the school, he was struck by a horrible thought: What if the door was locked?

A few steps later, he was close enough to tell: The door wasn't open anymore. It wasn't even ajar.

Luke dashed even faster across the lawn, as if he could outrun his panic. His heart pounded, and it wasn't just from running. He'd been so stupid, going out the door in the first place. Or, if he'd had to step outside, why hadn't he gone back right away? Why had he risked everything for a day in the woods?

He knew why.

Luke was finally close enough to touch the doorknob. He reached out with a trembling hand, prepared for the worst.

Stay calm, stay calm, he told himself. *If it's locked, maybe you can find another door that works. Maybe you can still slip back in undetected. Maybe . . .* Luke didn't have much faith in "maybes."

Hopelessly, he twisted the knob.

The knob turned easily.

Barely daring to believe his luck, Luke pulled the door open a crack. He couldn't see anyone, so he slid in and let the door close behind him. It was dark at this end of the hall. He appreciated the shadows.

Luke was tiptoeing past vacant classrooms when he heard the shout.

"Hey! What are you doing down here?"

It was one of the hall monitors.

"I—I got lost," Luke said, not stammering any more than he would have under normal circumstances. And the excuse was entirely plausible—hadn't he been lost a million times so far at school? But he didn't know what he was missing. Supper? The evening lecture? Lights out?

The hall monitor peered at him suspiciously.

"Nobody's supposed to be in this wing of the building

right now," he said. "Why did you leave the dining hall?"

Luke got a sudden inspiration.

"I got sick," he said. "I ran out to go to the bathroom. Then I got lost when I was going back."

The hall monitor looked skeptical.

"The bathroom's right across from the dining hall," he said.

"I—I wasn't paying attention. I'm new. I was sick." Luke tried to look dumb enough—and queasy enough—to have made such a stupid mistake.

The hall monitor took a step back, like he didn't want to catch anything.

"Okay," he relented. "Go back immediately."

Relieved, Luke turned to go. Then he stopped. Only the day before, he would have obeyed unthinkingly. But now he had a secret to protect. Now he had to be crafty. He turned back to the monitor.

"I don't know how to get there. Remember?"

"Oh, for crying out loud. Why do I have to baby-sit all the leckers?" He took Luke's arm and jerked him to the right. "Go that way. Turn left at the first hallway, then left and right again. Just get out of here!"

The hall monitor sounded a little panicked himself. The day before, Luke wouldn't have noticed, but now he had to pay attention. *Something about that door,* Luke thought. *Why is the hall monitor so desperate to get me away from it?*

Luke was still pondering that question when he reached the doors to the dining hall. They burst open, and boys streamed out. Luke's timing was perfect: He'd gotten there just as everyone was heading toward the evening lecture. He blended in. *See, Mr. Talbot?* he thought bitterly. *I am following the only bit of advice you saw fit to give me. Aren't you proud? Mighty generous of you, I'm sure.*

But some of Luke's bitterness had eased. The note had been worthless, but he had the woods to think about now. And if the note had led him to the woods—well, he did have reason to be grateful to Jen's dad, didn't he?

Nobody challenged Luke as he walked into the lecture room and sat down. Nobody asked, "Where have you been all day?" Nobody ordered him, "Never leave this building again!"

He'd gotten away with it. He could get away with it again.

CHAPTER *ELEVEN*

uke longed to race straight to the woods as soon as he woke up the next morning. It was torture to stand patiently beside all the other boys, splashing water on his face. It was torture to sit still and slowly spoon in the lumpy oatmeal, when he longed to gulp it down and get out of there. (Though, since he'd missed two meals the day before, it was amazing how delicious the oatmeal seemed for once.) It was torture waiting for the cafeteria doors to open and release everyone else to classes, and Luke to the woods.

As soon as breakfast was over, he took off, all but running. Surprisingly, given how confused he usually got in the Hendricks halls, he managed to make a beeline straight for the door, without once making a wrong turn and having to retrace his steps. Approaching the door, he slowed down, waiting for the crowd to clear in the hall. Finally, there was only Luke and a hall monitor, several yards away. The door wasn't open today, but Luke was confident that it wasn't locked. He was confident that he could slip out quickly enough. He glanced back. The monitor was looking the other way. Now! Luke reached for the doorknob—

—and then drew back.

At the last minute, it was like someone or something screamed, *"No!"* in his mind. Mother had talked about God sometimes—maybe that's who it was. Or maybe it was Jen's spirit, come to help Luke when her father's note hadn't. Maybe it was just Luke's own common sense. Luke didn't know what he thought about God or ghosts or even his own intelligence, but he knew: He couldn't risk going to the woods today.

Luke walked on, pretending to be casually dawdling.

"Get to class," the monitor growled.

Luke nodded, and stepped into the next classroom he passed. He felt as disappointed as if he'd discovered bars on the door. What was he—a coward?

Luke remembered all the mind games he'd played with himself trying to get up the nerve to go to Jen's house that first time. He'd waited weeks, always telling himself he was just waiting for the right moment. He had been a coward then.

But he wasn't being a coward now. Sinking into a seat, as anonymous as every other boy in the room, he actually felt brave, clever, crafty.

Probably he'd just gotten lucky the day before. If he wanted to be able to go the woods again and again and again, without getting caught, he'd have to be smart about it. He'd have to pay attention to everything. Maybe he'd even have to figure out why the hall monitor the night before had been so panicky. Before he went back again, he'd have to know it was safe.

Luke looked around the room. Up front, the teacher was drawing complicated-looking mathematical formulas on the chalkboard. Luke couldn't have solved any of them if his life depended on it. But for once, instead of sinking into despair and staring down at the desk in front of him, Luke got the nerve to peer around at the other boys. A few were watching the teacher. A few were taking notes—er, no, they were drawing pictures of naked girls. Some were blatantly sleeping, their mouths slack-jawed. And some were sitting off to the side, their arms clutched around their legs, rocking.

Luke stared. He didn't have much to go on, since he'd only known six people before in his entire life, but that rocking certainly didn't seem like normal behavior.

Eventually the bell rang, and he stumbled into another class. It was the same there: some boys acting normal, some boys rocking endlessly.

Why hadn't he noticed anything like that before?

He knew why. Every other time he'd looked directly at any of the other boys, he'd glanced quickly, then looked away, for fear that they might actually look back.

You could miss a lot, doing that.

Walking through the hall to his next class, Luke tried an experiment: He stared directly into the eyes of every single boy who went past him.

It was terrifying—even worse than running blindly

across a lawn. Luke's stomach seized up, and he thought he might actually throw up his breakfast oatmeal. He thought his legs might crumple under him, in fear.

But it was also interesting.

Most of the other boys he passed looked away as soon as Luke made eye contact. Some of them seemed to have a sort of sixth sense that warned them off from letting Luke look at them in the first place. Only two or three stared boldly back, their eyes locked on Luke's just as Luke's were locked on theirs.

Remember them, Luke ordered himself. But it took all his willpower just to keep himself from looking away.

When he finally arrived in a classroom doorway, Luke was shaking all over.

I gave something away, just then, he thought. *Now they'll know.*

But he didn't know who "they" were.

CHAPTER *TWELVE*

Luke made himself wait an entire week before he went back to the woods. But in that time, no matter how closely he paid attention to everything, the mysteries only seemed to multiply.

For example, by the end of the week, Luke was even more baffled by the lack of windows than ever before. Because he'd discovered: There wasn't a single window in the entire place.

To learn that, Luke had to make himself figure out the floor plan of the entire school. He had to be sure that he peeked into every classroom, every sleeping room, every office. One morning at breakfast, he even pretended to get turned around and plowed straight into the kitchen. Two cooks screamed, and Luke was given a stern lecture and a record ten demerits, but he found out what he wanted to know: Even the kitchen lacked windows.

Why? Why would anyone build a windowless school?

Luke wondered if there'd been something unusual about his family's house, that it had had windows, and he'd just accepted it as the norm. But, no—all the houses and schools and other buildings Luke had seen in books had had windows. And when the Government built Jen's neighborhood, all the houses there had windows. And Jen's family and their neighbors were Barons—if Baron houses had windows, why didn't Baron schools?

Luke couldn't figure out the other boys, either. There were rocking boys in most of his classes, he realized now. Several times, Luke practically hypnotized himself staring at them. But they seemed harmless enough.

The boys who worried Luke were the ones he called "the starers"—the ones who looked back when he looked at them.

All the hall monitors were starers.

So was jackal boy.

Luke tried to tell himself that the starers bothered him only because he'd spent so much time in hiding. Of course he didn't like being stared at. They were probably just acting normal, and he was in danger of giving away his real identity by getting disturbed by it.

Somehow he couldn't believe that.

At night when jackal boy tormented him, Luke kept his eyes trained carefully on the ground. But he could feel jackal boy's gaze on the side of his face as definitely as he would feel a slap or a punch.

"Say, 'I am an exnay of the worst order,'" jackal boy ordered him as usual one evening.

Luke mumbled the words. He wondered what would happen if he looked up and unleashed his questions on jackal boy: Why do you stare? Why aren't there any windows? Why do we never go outside? Why was the door open that one day? And finally: Are there any other shadow children here?

But of course he couldn't ask jackal boy. Jackal boy thought it was funny to make Luke wave his arms for five minutes straight. Jackal boy was only interested in humiliating Luke. He'd probably think it was amusing to tell the Population Police, "I know where you can find a third child. How big's my reward?"

So Luke bit his tongue and gritted his teeth and touched his finger to his nose fifty times, as ordered. He jogged in place until his legs ached. He reached for his toes again and again, until jackal boy said in a bored voice, "Get out of my sight."

Luke crawled into bed unsure whether to be relieved that he hadn't blown his cover, or disappointed that he hadn't found the answers to his questions.

That night in bed, he was too busy puzzling over all his mysteries to even think about whispering his own name. When he had his pretend conversations, he asked advice, instead of offering apologies.

What do you think, Jen? What's wrong with this place? Is there something wrong? You went out into the world on fake passes all the time. Do people everywhere act like the boys at Hendricks?

And, *Mother, Dad, what's your opinion? Is it okay if I go out into the woods again?*

But it was ridiculous to feel like he had to get permission from parents he'd never see again. Or to ask advice from a friend who was dead. It was just too bad that that was all he had.

Luke swallowed a lump in his throat. He couldn't solve the school's mysteries. But he was going back to the woods no matter what.

CHAPTER *THIRTEEN*

uke worked out a plan for leaving the school every day after lunch, and coming back right before dinner. It was sort of a compromise—he thought he ought to go to some classes, no matter how little sense they made to him. And this way he wouldn't miss any meals. He was already hungry all the time. He already had trouble keeping his fancy Baron pants hitched up on his scrawny frame.

The first day he left, he slipped out while the hall monitor was looking the other way. He knew now that none of the other boys would even notice.

So easy, Luke thought to himself as he jogged across the lawn to the woods. *Why don't all the boys escape out here?*

He decided it wasn't worth troubling himself with unanswerable questions.

The sun was shining, and he could tell that even the leaves that had been curled up and tiny a week earlier were full grown and spread out now. High overhead, the arc of tree limbs in some parts of the woods blocked out the sky completely. *It's like a cave,* Luke thought. But that reminded him of hiding and cowering indoors. He moved out into a clearing, where grass struggled to grow through last fall's dead leaves. It looked like there were raspberry plants, too, mostly buried in tangled brush.

"Raspberries," Luke whispered, his mouth watering. Mother grew raspberries, back home, and every June she kept the whole family stuffed with raspberry pies and cakes and breads. She made raspberry jam, too, and spread it on their toast and spooned it into their cornmeal mush all year long.

Luke eagerly searched the branches in front of him—tasting a raspberry would be like visiting home, just for a minute. But there weren't any berries yet, only an occasional bud. And it was likely the weeds would choke out those buds before they matured.

Unless Luke cleared the brush around them.

It only took Luke ten or fifteen minutes to pull the weeds and give the raspberry plants room, but by the time he was done, he had a full-blown idea in his head.

He could grow a whole garden out here. Surely no one would mind, or even find out. In his imagination he saw neat rows of sweet corn, tomato plants, and peas. He could put strawberries and blueberries over at the side of the clearing, where they'd get some shade. He'd want beans, too. Squash wasn't practical, because it wasn't much good raw. But there was always cucumber and zucchini, cantaloupe and watermelon . . . Luke's stomach growled.

Then he remembered seeds. He didn't have any.

Luke's dream instantly withered. How stupid was he that he thought he could grow a garden without seeds? Luke could imagine how Matthew and Mark would make fun of him if they knew. Even Dad and Mother would have a hard time not laughing. Just a month away from home and he'd already forgotten what you needed for a garden.

Luke stared at the measly raspberry plants in disappointment. Then he could almost hear Mother's voice in his ears: *Make the best of what you've got.* How many times had he heard her say that?

Even one raspberry would be delicious.

And maybe he could find blueberry or strawberry plants somewhere in the woods, and transplant them.

And maybe he could get seeds from some of the food at school. The bean sprouts they were always feeding him, for example—could he plant those? He didn't know what kind of beans they would grow into, but even if they were soybeans, Jen had told him once that the Government thought those were edible. Roasted, maybe. He could build a fire.

And maybe later in the summer, they would serve tomatoes or cantaloupe or watermelon, and he could smuggle the seeds to his room somehow. It would be too late for planting by then, but he could save the seeds for next year. . . .

It made Luke's throat ache to think of staying at Hendricks School a whole year. A whole year without his family, a whole year of grieving for Jen, a whole year of not speaking to anyone but jackal boy. A whole year of having nothing but a fake name and clothes that didn't fit.

Luke stood up and planted his feet firmly on the ground.

"I have the woods," he said aloud. "I'll have the garden. This is mine."

CHAPTER *FOURTEEN*

B y the end of the week, Luke had a nice plot of land cleared. The raspberry plants were at the center, and he had straight lines of bean sprouts planted on either side. It was Dad he pretended to appeal to most now.

"What do these look like to you, Dad?" he'd say aloud, as though Dad were really there to answer. "Am I just wasting my time? Or will I have a good crop come fall?"

Luke truly wasn't sure. But he felt so proud, looking at the neat little garden. He kept meaning to explore more of the woods, but he was always too busy digging and weeding, tending his plot. Anxiously he shooed away squirrels and chipmunks, and wished that he could stay out and guard his garden all the time.

But each afternoon he kept a close eye on the Baron watch he now wore on his wrist, so he could run back to the school promptly at six o'clock. He'd found the watch in his suitcase, and faced quite a chore figuring out how to read it. Those lines and "V's" and "X's" on it were numbers, he knew, but different from what he was used to. Why did Barons always have to make everything so fancy and complicated? Back home Mother and Dad had just a single dig-ital clock, in the kitchen. It blinked off the minutes as clear as could be. This watch was like a foreign language to Luke. But he stared at the angle of the rays of sun, he studied the digital clocks at school and compared them with the watch on his wrist—eventually he understood the Baron watch as well as any other.

That made him feel proud, too.

So did his next accomplishment.

One day at lunch they served baked potatoes in the school dining hall. They were so undercooked, they practi-cally crunched. Luke bit into a raw end that hadn't even had its eye removed. Spitting it out, he complained to himself, *I'd rather plant this than eat it.*

Plant this. Of course. How many springs had Luke spent cutting up potatoes for planting? He and Mother, perched over a three-gallon bucket, knives flashing. When he was little, he'd always tried to rest his feet on the top of the bucket, the same way Mother did, but he was never tall enough. Even when he was tall enough, he never balanced things right. He'd tip the whole bucket over. Mother would look at him sternly and sigh, "Pick it up." But then she'd smile, like she wasn't really mad. She'd talk to him the whole time they worked: "Careful with the knife—don't cut toward your hand. You're making sure there's an eye in every potato, aren't you? Nothing will grow without an eye."

But potatoes would grow without a seed. He just needed a raw potato.

Covertly, Luke used his fork to separate the cooked and raw part of his potato. The raw part he dropped into his hand, and slipped into his pocket. Probably nobody had ever used Baron pants for transporting potato parts before, but Luke didn't care.

As soon as the bell rang for the end of lunch, Luke moved quickly among the tables, grabbing the left-behind potato pieces wherever he could. His pockets were stuffed in a matter of minutes.

He walked stiffly down the hall and out his door, trying not to smash the potatoes.

Nobody noticed.

Out in the woods, Luke dumped out his pockets and examined his treasure. He had eight potato pieces that looked like good candidates for planting. He wished he'd thought to smuggle a knife out of the dining hall, too, but that couldn't be helped. He halved as many of the potatoes as he could using his fingernails and brute force. Then he planted them in a row beside the beans.

When he was done, Luke sat back against a tree trunk and surveyed his work. It looked good. In a few days he'd know if anything was going to grow. He thought the bean sprouts looked bigger. At least they weren't withering yet.

After a few minutes of rest, Luke walked down to a creek that ran through the woods and cupped his hands in it, making trip after trip to bring back water for his garden. If only he had one of those three-gallon buckets now! Even a cup would help. Maybe he could bring one from the dining room.

In the meantime, he really didn't mind using his hands. Walking back and forth between the creek and his garden, Luke felt a strange surge of emotion, one he hadn't felt in so long that he'd practically forgotten what it was.

Happy, he thought in amazement. *I'm happy.*

CHAPTER FIFTEEN

The very next day Luke raced out to his garden even more eagerly than ever. It was too soon to tell anything about the potatoes, but if the beans still looked good, he could probably be sure that they would live and grow and produce. And would the raspberries have any more buds today?

Luke reached his clearing and stopped short.

His garden was destroyed.

The raspberry branches were broken off at odd angles; the bean plants were trampled, smashed flat in the mud. There hadn't been any potato shoots to be ruined, of course, but the garden was so messed up, Luke couldn't even tell where he'd planted them.

"No," Luke wailed. "It can't be."

He wanted to believe that he'd accidentally walked into the wrong clearing. But that was crazy. There was the maple tree with the jagged cut in its trunk on one side of the clearing, the oak with the sagging limb on the other side, the rotting trunk in the middle—this *was* his garden. Or—it had been.

Who wrecked it?

His first thought was animals. Back home, back when his family still raised hogs, there had been a couple of times when the hogs had escaped and found their way to the garden. They'd rooted around like crazy, and Mother had been furious over the damage.

But there weren't any hogs in the woods. Luke hadn't seen anything bigger than a squirrel. And for all his shooings and worrying, he knew squirrels couldn't have done this kind of damage.

And squirrels didn't wear shoes.

Luke winced. He'd been too distraught to notice before: Instead of animal tracks, the garden was covered with imprints of the same kind of shoes Luke was wearing. Smooth-soled Baron shoes had stomped on his raspberries, trampled his beans, kicked at his potato hills. They had walked all over his garden.

For a crazy instant, Luke wondered if he himself was to blame. Had he been careless leaving the garden yesterday? Could he have stepped on his own plants by mistake? That was ridiculous. He'd never do such a thing.

What if he'd sleepwalked, and come out here in the night without even knowing it?

That was even more preposterous. He would have been caught.

And he didn't wear shoes to bed.

Anyhow, he could tell by stepping next to the other footprints: Some of the imprints were made by shoes that were bigger than Luke's. Some of the imprints were made by shoes that were smaller.

Lots of people had been in Luke's garden. Lots of people had been there destroying it.

Luke sank to the ground by the tree trunk. He buried his face in his hands.

"This was all I had," he moaned. Once again he was pretending to talk to someone who wasn't there. But it wasn't Mother or Dad, Jen or Mr. Talbot he appealed to now. It was Matthew and Mark, his older brothers. He had to apologize to them. He had to explain why he, Luke Garner, a twelve-year-old boy, was crying.

CHAPTER SIXTEEN

L uke went back to school early that afternoon. What good would it do to stay in the garden? He'd only make himself more miserable. It wasn't worth trying to clean up, to replant. Whoever did this would only come back and destroy his garden again.

Washing his face in the creek before leaving, Luke tortured himself with questions. Who had done this? Who were the—vandals? The criminals? Luke couldn't even come up with a harsh enough word to describe them. Then he thought of the insults that had been hurled at him for the past month. Yes. The guilty ones were fonrols. Exnays. Leckers.

Luke wiped his face off on his sleeve, and it left a streak of mud. Who cared?

He circled wide leaving the creek so he didn't have to see his poor butchered garden again.

He didn't even bother running across the wide expanse of lawn back to the school. He trudged.

At the door, his brain woke again. He couldn't go back in now, in the middle of classes. He'd be noticed wandering the halls alone. How many people had yelled at him and

Rolly that first day? Luke looked at his watch and puzzled out the time. It was only one-thirty. It probably would be another half an hour before classes let out, and Luke could slip into the stream of other boys walking between rooms.

Luke leaned hopelessly against the rough brick wall beside the doorway. He almost welcomed the pain it brought, scraping his arm, pressing into his forehead. Maybe he should run back to the woods, where he could hide better, be safer. But he didn't care. He'd given up his name, his family—everything—for safety. Right now it didn't look like such a great deal.

Anyway, the woods didn't seem the least bit inviting anymore. They weren't his. They never had been.

Standing stoically before a closed door, Luke suddenly understood the clues he'd been too dense or blind—or hopeful—to notice before. Of course some of the other boys visited the woods. That's why the hall monitor had been so panicked that first night, when he saw Luke near the door. The monitor wasn't guarding the hall. He was guarding the door. Some boys had been planning to sneak out, that night, and the monitor was making sure it was safe. Probably they sneaked out to the woods all the time.

Luke could imagine how they'd acted, discovering the garden.

"Hey, look!" he could hear one boy calling to another. "Let's rip this up!"

And then they did—a horde of boys stomping the potatoes and yanking up the raspberries and hurling uprooted bean plants across the garden. Luke's garden.

"I'm going to find you," he whispered. "I'm going to get you."

CHAPTER *SEVENTEEN*

Promptly at two o'clock, Luke eased the door open a crack and peeked in. His timing was good—boys were walking to and from classes, their heads bowed, their eyes trained on the ground. But a hall monitor stood directly across from the door. Luke ducked back.

Look away, look away, Luke mentally commanded the monitor. Luke waited. Then, just when he moved over, ready to peek again, he saw the door slide shut.

Oh, no. Luke tried to figure out what had happened. Had the monitor seen the door open, thought that one of his marauding gang had forgotten to close it, and merely shut it to save his own skin?

Or did he know Luke was out there?

Stay calm, Luke commanded himself, uselessly. His panic boiled over. And his anger. He hated that monitor. He was probably one of the boys who'd trampled Luke's garden.

Luke could have looked for another door. He could have waited another hour, in hopes that a different hall monitor would be manning this spot, and not paying as much attention. He could have even gone back to the woods and waited until his usual time to come back.

But he didn't. He grabbed the doorknob and yanked.

As the door swung open, Luke saw that the hall monitor wasn't looking directly at the door just then. If Luke was sneaky enough, he could slip in without drawing attention to himself. But Luke let the door slam behind him. A cluster of boys with their eyes trained on the ground were jolted by the noise and even looked up briefly. Some of them started running, as panicked as if someone had fired a gun. Other boys didn't even glance Luke's way.

The hall monitor jerked his head around immediately. Luke quickly joined the slow-moving group of boys with their heads down. But just before he lowered his own head, Luke caught the hall monitor's stare. Their eyes locked for just an instant. Luke waited for the monitor to grab him by the collar, to yell, to haul him off to the head-master's office. Luke could feel his shoulder hunching into a cower.

Nothing happened.

Luke shuffled forward with the other boys, and dared to look up again. The hall monitor was carefully looking past Luke.

He knows I was outside, Luke thought. *And he knows I know he knows. Why isn't he doing anything?*

It was like a chess game, Luke realized. He remembered one winter when Matthew and Mark had brought home a chess set from school. They'd had a blizzard after that, and they'd been snowed in for a long time, so Matthew and Mark spent hours playing chess. Luke had been a lot younger then, maybe only five or six. The game that fascinated his brothers only puzzled him.

"Why don't all the pieces move the same way?" he had asked, picking up the horse-shaped piece. "Why can't this one go in a straight line like the castle?"

"Because it can't," Matthew had replied irritably, while Mark squealed, "Put that down! You're messing up our game!"

Now Luke almost trod on another boy's heel. The boy didn't even turn around. If everyone at the school were a chess piece, Luke realized, most of the boys were pawns. The hall monitors and the other ones Luke thought of as starers were the big, important pieces. The bishops. And the king. Luke remembered that Matthew and Mark had treasured those pieces, sacrificing pawns and knights and castles to protect them. But Luke hadn't understood why. And he didn't understand the hall monitor now.

But he knew how to find out about him.

CHAPTER *EIGHTEEN*

When dinner was over that night, Luke slipped out of the dining hall behind all of the other boys. Instead of going into the evening lecture room like everyone else, he ducked down a dark hall. It wasn't a direct route to the door that led outside, but if Luke turned three corners and backtracked a bit, he'd get there.

I know the school really well now, Luke marveled. *If I had a note I needed to read in private now, it wouldn't be a problem at all.*

Luke felt decades older than the scared little boy who'd worried so over the note from Jen's dad. And gotten so upset when he read it.

It was just a scrap of paper. What did I expect?

Luke wondered: Would he ever look back on this day and regret getting so upset about his ruined garden?

No.

Luke had told himself it didn't matter if he ran into hall monitors. He could just start asking them questions: *Why did you destroy my garden? What if I told the headmaster that you've been sneaking out?* But now, creeping down the deserted hallway, he was glad he didn't have to test his bravado. As far as he could tell, the hall monitors only guarded the main route to the door. He'd suspected as much. The monitors didn't have to be very cautious, because most of the boys at the school behaved like sheep, only going where they were told. And all of the teachers seemed to be gone in the evenings.

Luke reached the final corner before the doorway, and stopped. The sound of his watch ticking seemed to fill the entire hall. Luke pressed his wrist to his chest to muffle it. Then it was his heart pounding that seemed too loud. His ears roared with listening.

Was this how Jen had felt, the night she left for the rally? Brave, reckless, crazy, courageous, terrified—all at once?

It didn't seem right to compare. Jen had been going to the rally—leading it, in fact—in an effort to win rights for third children all over the nation. Even her parents didn't know what she was doing. But she had believed so strongly that nobody should have to hide that she'd died for it.

Luke was mad about a garden.

Thinking that way, Luke felt foolish. He wondered if he should turn around. But just because Jen's cause had been enormous, that didn't mean Luke's was unimportant. Like Jen, Luke wanted to right a wrong.

Just then he heard the sounds he'd been waiting for: someone whispering, a muffled laugh, the click of the door latching. Luke waited a full five minutes—it was too dark to see his watch, so he counted off the tics. Then he tiptoed out of the shadows and followed the others out the door.

CHAPTER *NINETEEN*

he moon was out.

It had been so long since Luke had seen the night sky that he'd forgotten how mystical it could look. The moon was full tonight, a beautiful orb hovering low over the woods. Luke also recognized the same pinpricks of starlight he'd been used to seeing back home. But the stars seemed dimmer here, overshadowed by a glow on the horizon beyond the woods. Luke puzzled over that glow— it was in the wrong part of the sky to be the sunset. What else was that bright?

Luke remembered that Jen's dad had said the school was near a city. Could a city have lights that bright, that shone this far?

"I don't know anything," Luke whispered to himself. He'd thought that coming out of hiding would expose him to the world, teach him everything. But being at Hendricks seemed like just another way to hide.

A light flashed in the woods just then, and Luke realized he didn't have time to hesitate. He'd planned to creep across the lawn, but the moonlight was so bright, he worried about being seen. He decided to take his chances with running.

Nobody yelled. Nobody hissed, "Get away from here!"

Luke reached the edge of the woods and hid behind a tree. Then he cautiously moved up to the next tree. And the next one. The light swung erratically, just ahead.

Luke wished he'd taken the time to explore the woods, to get his bearings. He was terrified of walking straight into a tree, stepping in some big hole or tripping over a stump. He banged his shin and had to bite his lip to keep from crying out. He stepped in something squishy and almost fell. He wondered if he was traveling in circles.

Then he heard voices.

"—hate nature—"

"Yeah, well, you find a better place to meet—"

Luke crept closer. And closer. A strangely familiar voice was giving a long explanation: "—it's just your fear of the outdoors cropping up again. You've got to overcome it, you know?"

"Easy for you to say," someone else grumbled.

Luke was close enough now to see the backs of several heads. He dared to edge up to the next tree and peek out. Eight boys were sitting in a semicircle around a small, dim, portable lantern. Suddenly another light flashed on the other side of the group of boys. A twig cracked. Luke ducked back behind the tree.

"So what's with the emergency meeting?"

It was a girl's voice.

Luke inhaled sharply.

Jen . . .

It wasn't Jen, of course. When Luke dared to look out again, he saw a tall, scrawny girl with two pale, thin braids hanging on either side of her face. Jen had been shorter, more muscular, her brown hair cut short as a boy's. But just to hear a girl's voice again made Luke feel strange. It kept him from doing any of the crazy things he'd half-planned: leaping from behind the tree and screaming accusations, pretending to be a ghost haunting the woods, finding some way to exact revenge.

All he could do now was listen.

"Sorry to disturb the princesses of Harlow," a male voice was answering mockingly.

Luke knew he knew that voice. He peered out. Yes. Of course.

Jackal boy.

"It's the new kid," jackal boy was saying. "He's acting weird."

I should have known jackal boy was involved, Luke thought. *He probably planned the whole thing, led the charge on my garden. . . .* He glowered. Then he realized what jackal boy had said. "The new kid"? As far as Luke knew, there was only one new kid at Hendricks: himself. They were talking about him.

"Weird?" the girl's voice replied. "He's a boy, right? Isn't weirdness just kind of required?"

There were giggles. Luke squinted into the darkness. He

thought there were three or four other girls beside the girl with braids.

"Quit being such an exnay," jackal boy said.

"Exnay and proud of it," the girl retorted.

Luke listened harder, as though that would help him make sense of their words. Who would be proud of being an "exnay"? If he'd learned anything at Hendricks, it was that "exnay" was one of the worst insults you could hurl at anybody.

"Yeah, yeah. I don't see you announcing it anywhere but in the dark, in the woods, when nobody's around," jackal boy taunted.

"So you're admitting you're nobody?" the girl said.

One of the boys beside jackal boy made a frustrated grunt. "Why do we bother talking to them?" he asked.

Luke saw jackal boy dig his elbow into the other boy's ribs.

"I'll be noble and ignore that," jackal boy said loftily to the girl. "Naturally, we don't expect you to offer us any assistance in this matter. But we thought it was in every-body's best interest to keep you informed."

The girl sat down, and the other girls followed her lead. "So inform us."

"The new boy—" jackal boy started.

"Has he got a name?" the girl interrupted.

"He's registered as Lee Grant," jackal boy said.

Luke noticed how he said that. "Registered as . . ." Not, "His name is . . ." Did jackal boy suspect?

"I looked him up," jackal boy continued. "His dad's in charge of National Gas and Electric. Filthy rich. And he's switched schools a lot."

"That could fit," the girl said.

"But he doesn't seem like he has autism or any of the other disorders. I don't think he's even agoraphobic."

Luke didn't even try to puzzle out the unfamiliar words. Jackal boy was still talking.

"Trey over there saw him coming in from outside this afternoon."

"He was outside?" the girl asked. She sounded amazed, maybe even impressed. "Out here? In the woods? During the day?"

"Don't know," jackal boy said. Luke felt almost triumphant at the note of misery in the boy's voice. But Luke was confused. Had jackal boy and his friends destroyed the garden without even knowing it belonged to Luke? Or was jackal boy lying?

"Trey didn't see him until he was back inside," jackal boy continued. "He—you know—he doesn't like looking right at the door."

"Great guard system you got going there," the girl said.

"Shut up, Nina!" one of the boys yelled. Luke guessed it was Trey.

"Don't call me that!" the girl—Nina?—yelled back. Why would she have a name she didn't want to be called?

And then Luke understood. He, too, had a name he hated. He hated it because it was fake. And so was hers.

"Nina" was another former shadow child. She had to be.

Luke looked with new eyes at the group sitting in front of him in the dark woods. They must all be illegal third children using false identities. Luke's heart gave a jump. At last, he'd found others like him. He'd found a place to belong.

Luke started to move out from behind the tree, to reveal himself. Finally he'd found other kids to talk to about how hard it was pretending to be someone else. Finally he'd found other kids who would know how tough it was to come out of hiding. Finally he'd found other kids he could trust, as he'd trusted Jen. They could grieve for Jen with him.

Then he remembered: He was almost certain these were the ones who'd destroyed his garden.

Luke stayed put.

"All right, all right," jackal boy was saying. "Calm down. The point is, this kid, this 'Lee,' doesn't fit any of the profiles."

"Did you give him the test?" Nina asked.

"Um, well, there was a little problem—" jackal boy said hesitantly.

"Go ahead and say it!" Trey burst out furiously. "I flubbed the whole thing! I don't know why you make me guard that spot!"

"Because you're the bravest one," jackal boy said. Luke recognized that tone: It was the same sort of wheedling voice that Luke's brothers had used on him when they wanted him to do something unpleasant, like clean out the hog pen or spread manure on the garden.

Trey turned and faced Nina directly. "I left the door open, but I couldn't stand to be that close to it. I walked down the hall. Just for a minute! When I got back, this Lee kid was nowhere in sight."

Left the door open . . . Suddenly Luke understood. That first time he'd noticed the door, when it was ajar, it had been a test set up by jackal boy's gang.

But what were they testing him for?

"Maybe he went outside then, too," Nina said.

All the boys seemed to be shaking their heads in disbelief.

"I waited for three hours," Trey said. "I stared at that door the whole time, honest. Nobody'd stay out that long."

Why not? Luke wondered.

"So is he one of us or not?" Nina asked.

The question seemed to hang in the dark woods. Luke wanted to know the answer, too.

"Who knows?" jackal boy said. "The problem is, he's getting bold. Weird, like I said. We're scared he's going to get the rest of us in trouble. Blow our cover. This afternoon, he just stared back at Trey like he didn't care what Trey saw, or what Trey did. He was—"

"Defiant," Trey said.

Even Luke could see the baffled look jackal boy gave Trey.

"Sorry!" Trey said. "All I had to do when I was hiding

was read, remember? I didn't have a TV like the rest of you. I learned too many big words. 'Defiant' means, um— he was defying me, he was—"

"Offering a challenge," Luke said aloud.

And then he stepped out from behind the tree.

CHAPTER *TWENTY*

uke felt twelve pairs of eyes on him. Nina's mouth was frozen in a little "o" of surprise. Jackal boy's jaw dropped in astonishment.

But nobody was more astonished than Luke. *Why did I do that?* he wondered. He remembered thinking that most of the boys at Hendricks acted like pawns. *I'm a pawn, too, remember? Just plain old Luke Garner, who doesn't know anything about anything, who cowers in the attic while his best friend dies for the cause. Stepping out from behind that tree was something Jen would have done. Not me.*

But he had done it. Now what?

Luke longed to slide back behind the tree again or, given that it wouldn't be much of a hiding place now, to turn tail and run. But his legs were trembling so much that just standing still took all his strength.

Everyone was so quiet that Luke could hear his watch ticking again.

All right. He'd gotten himself into this mess by acting like Jen. What would she do next?

Talk. Jen could always talk.

"You destroyed my garden," Luke accused. "You'll have to make restitution."

Luke could use big words, too. He thought he saw a glimmer of appreciation in Trey's eyes. Everyone else stared blankly.

Would Jen bother explaining, or would she prefer letting them feel dumb?

"Garden?" jackal boy asked. "What garden?"

That wasn't what Luke had expected.

"What garden?" he repeated. "*My* garden. Over there." He pointed into the dark. "Last night, somebody trampled the whole thing, kicked over my beans, broke off my raspberry plants. *You're* the only ones I see out in the woods." Luke tried to let his anger carry him through. But all the faces in front of him looked vacant. Had he made a big mistake? Could they possibly be innocent? He finished weakly, "So you owe me."

Jackal boy shook his head.

"We don't know what you're talking about."

He didn't *seem* to be lying. But how good was Luke at judging liars?

"I'll show you," Luke said impatiently. He suddenly had the notion that if he saw them looking at the destruction, he'd be able to tell by their expressions whether or not they were guilty. He turned hastily and started walking. He was surprised when he heard footsteps behind him. They'd actually listened to him? *Obeyed* him?

They made a strange procession through the woods, Luke leading the way, the other boys following with their lantern, then the girls with a dim flashlight. Luke made a few missteps, and even had to backtrack once, but he circled around, hoping none of the others would notice. Finally they reached Luke's clearing. In the moonlight it looked desolate, just a stump and scraggly plants. It didn't look like it had ever contained a garden.

"There!" Luke said, trying to sound wronged and indignant. His voice came out in a squeak. "See these broken-off raspberry plants? See the squashed beans? But why do I have to show you? You know what you did."

No guilt showed on their faces. They still looked puzzled.

"He *is* crazy," jackal boy hissed.

"Wait a minute," Nina said. "Did you guys walk back to school this way last night?"

Trey shrugged.

"We might have," he said.

One of the other guys spoke up.

"It's not like we can tell any of the trees apart."

"So maybe you stepped on his garden by mistake," Nina said. "And didn't even know it."

"*I* certainly wouldn't know what a garden looks like," one of the other girls said. "Like this? What were you growing?"

"Nothing," Luke muttered. He was suddenly overcome with shame. He'd felt so brave stepping out from behind that tree. Just to make a fool of himself. Looking around, he could see how the other boys could have missed noticing his efforts, and trampled his garden by mistake. This had been a pathetic excuse for a garden. He'd been pathetic for ever thinking it was anything, let alone anything worth taking a risk for. He wished he could go back and hide behind a tree forever.

Jackal boy started laughing first.

"You thought this was a *garden?* You were sneaking out here to make a *garden?*" he asked.

The others began to snicker, too. Luke's shame turned into anger.

"So?" he asked, defiant again.

"So you are a lecker," jackal boy said. He was laughing so hard, he doubled over in mirth. "A *real* lecker."

"You always say that," Luke grumbled. "I don't even know what a lecker is."

"Someone from the country," Trey explained helpfully. "Like a bumpkin. That's what it really means. But now the word's just kind of a general insult, like calling someone a moron or stupid."

Luke thought Trey almost sounded apologetic, but that only made things worse.

"What's wrong with being from the country?" Luke asked.

"If you have to ask . . . ," jackal boy said, laughing again. He had to sit down on the rotting stump to catch his breath. Luke hoped he got mold smears on his pants.

"Want to know something even funnier?" jackal boy continued. "I'm betting you're really an exnay, too. So all those insults—lecker, exnay, fonrol—they're all true. I don't know that I've ever met someone who's all three before. We'll have to come up with a new word, just for you. What'll it be?"

Luke stared at jackal boy and the others laughing behind him. His faced burned. How could he have thought, even for an instant, that these might be kids he could trust? That he might belong with them?

"Leave me alone!" he shouted, and turned and ran.

CHAPTER *TWENTY-ONE*

uke could hear someone crashing through the woods behind him, but he didn't look back. He'd run into the darkest part of the woods, and it took all his concentration to dodge the tree limbs that seemed to reach down out of nowhere. In fact, if Luke really wanted to terrify himself, he could think of those tree limbs as witches' arms, ghouls' fingers. He wasn't used to running through woods at night. Back home, when he'd gone outside after dark, it had mostly been for catching lightning bugs in the backyard, playing moonlight kick ball with his brothers—innocent fun.

He'd been so young, back then, back home.

He forced himself to run faster, but whoever was behind him seemed to be catching up. Luke zigzagged, because he'd read once that that was how rabbits escaped their predators. Then he slammed into a tree. He screamed in pain, and reeled backwards.

A dark shape pounced. Before he knew it, Luke was pinned to the ground.

Luke remembered another time he'd been tackled: the

first time he'd crept into Jen's house. He made a noise, and the next thing he knew, she had him facedown in the carpet. And they'd become friends.

This wasn't Jen.

"What do you think you're doing?" a voice hissed in his ear. Jackal boy's. "You go back now, during Indoctrination, and they'll catch you. They'll know. And then they'll come looking for the rest of us."

Indoctrination? Luke guessed that jackal boy meant the evening lecture. The name made sense—the lecture was always about how wonderful the Government was. But Luke hadn't even thought about what he was running toward. He was just running away.

"Who will catch me?" he asked. "The only ones who watch are the hall monitors. And they all report to you, right?"

"You got it," jackal boy said. He sounded pleased. "I worked hard setting up that system. The teachers didn't like hall duty, anyway. And now—"

"You can get away with anything, can't you?" Luke asked. "Unless I tell."

He didn't know what possessed him to make that threat. Maybe it was just habit—after twelve years of being the youngest brother, he knew the power of tattling.

And he knew how easily it could backfire.

"Make you a deal," Luke said quickly. "Let me up, and I won't go back now. Answer some questions for me, and I won't tell. I'll keep your secrets."

Jackal boy seemed to be considering. Finally, he said, "Okay."

Luke scrambled up and pulled away. He rubbed the side of his face. He wasn't sure if it was sore from hitting the tree or from being slammed against the ground. His hand came away wet.

"I'm bleeding," he said accusingly.

"You'll have to hide it," jackal boy said. "Are you good at hiding?"

Luke shrugged away the question. He knew jackal boy was really asking something else. But Luke wasn't ready to answer.

"What's your name, anyway?" Luke asked.

"Which one?" jackal boy asked. "If you look at the school records, I'm Scott Renault. Out here, I'm Jason."

"One of those names is fake," Luke said.

Somewhere in the woods, an owl hooted. Luke waited. Finally, jackal boy answered, softly, "Yes."

"Your friends all have fake names, too," Luke said.

"Yes." No hesitation.

"You're all third children who have come out of hiding with fake I.D. cards," Luke said.

"Exnays," jackal boy said.

"Is *that* what that means?" Luke asked.

"You didn't know?" jackal boy asked. "Where have you been all your life?"

Luke decided not to answer that question, either.

"And fonrols—" he started.

"—are any third children, hiding or not."

"Why does everyone at school call each other those names?" Luke asked. "Is everyone here an exnay?"

In the dark, Luke could barely see jackal boy shaking his head.

"Haven't kids called each other exnays and fonrols at the other schools you've been to? All the other places you've ever lived? Some say in the beginning the Government paid people to use 'fonrol' and 'exnay' as swear words. On TV, and stuff. Then those words were forbidden in public broadcast, which just meant that people used them more in private. They wanted to make sure that everyone thought of third children as terrible."

Luke wondered why Jen had never told him about that.

"Maybe I've never been to any other schools," Luke said cautiously. He'd said "maybe." He could still deny everything if he wanted.

Jackal boy laughed, openmouthed. His teeth glinted in the moonlight.

"Why don't you just come out and admit it?" he asked. "You're an exnay, too. I know it."

Luke dodged the question.

"Why do you harass me every night?" he asked. "When everyone else ignores me—"

"It's the procedure we developed for dealing with new boys," jackal boy said. "And new girls, over at Harlow School for Girls. We've discovered it's hard for shadow children when they first come out of hiding—they're overwhelmed, traumatized. Think about it. They've spent their whole lives thinking it's death to be seen, and suddenly they're expected to interact with others all day long, to sit through classes with dozens of other kids, behave normally. They freak out."

"Did you?" Luke asked, trying to picture jackal boy as the new kid, just come out of hiding, scared of everything. His imagination failed him.

"Me?" Jackal boy sounded surprised. "Sure. It was tough. The problem was, lots of exnays got so panicked, they'd do something really dumb—stand up and chant their real name, start screaming, 'Don't look at me! Don't look at me!'—you know, totally lose it. Now, Hendricks has a lot of disturbed kids, anyway—"

"It does?" Luke asked.

"Haven't you noticed?" Jackal boy sounded amazed. "The autistic kids—the ones who rock and won't look you in the eye—the phobic kids, we've got all sorts of troubled cases in there. Ever meet Rolly Sturgeon? *There's* a psycho for you. So exnays can get away with some pretty wacky behavior at Hendricks. But the Population Police still got in a few good raids. That's why a lot of us exnays got together and planned it all out. Every time a new kid arrives, we go into emergency mode until we can tell if he's an exnay or not. We watch. We protect." Luke remembered the hands pushing him down into the chair that first day, in his first class. "But we do it all in secret. We give the exnay plenty of breathing room. And we pick just one person to approach him. To be a friend."

Luke thought about having to chant, "I am a fonrol" fifty times, of having to do push-ups while everyone else laughed, of having to obey every single one of jackal boy's sarcastic commands.

"I thought friends were supposed to be nice to you," Luke said bitterly. "Maybe that's a word I don't understand, either."

"Being too nice to an exnay from the start only causes trouble," jackal boy said. "They break down. They get weepy. They're so happy to find a sympathetic ear that they tell everything, no matter who else can hear. No, exnays need the kind of friend who can toughen them up. Like I did for you."

Was that what had happened? Luke felt as over-whelmed and confused as he had his first day at Hendricks. Listening to jackal boy was like it used to be listening to Jen: They were both so sure of themselves, it was hard for Luke to figure out what he thought on his own.

"How can you tell if a new kid is an exnay or not?" Luke asked, stalling.

"We give them a test," jackal boy said. "When they're ready, we leave a door open and make sure they see it, we stare them right in the eye—we know exactly how an exnay would respond, compared with a typical agora-phobe, or a typical autistic kid."

"You've got everyone figured out, huh?" Luke said.

"Sure," jackal boy asked. "Can't you tell?"

Luke couldn't answer that question. He was feeling panicky again. In a minute, he was going to have to make a decision. With Jen, it had been easy—he'd trusted her right away. But he was older now, more suspicious. He knew that she had been betrayed.

And he could be, too.

"So you gave me the usual test," he said tentatively. "Did I pass?"

"Depends on what you call passing," jackal boy said. He sounded cagier now, like he wasn't sure whose side Luke was on.

Luke had run out of questions. Or—he had lots of questions, but none of them would help him decide whether to trust jackal boy and his friends with his secret. It would be so nice to be able to tell. But was it worth risking his life for?

Had he already risked his life by following them into the woods?

Luke didn't like thinking things like that. He missed Jen all of a sudden. She was always good at turning his fear into a joke.

"Did you know Jen?" he asked jackal boy abruptly.

"Jen?" jackal boy said, his voice suddenly exuberant. "Jen Talbot? You knew her, too?"

Luke nodded. "She was my, um, neighbor. I went over to her house whenever I could," he said.

"Wow," jackal boy breathed. "Come on!"

He grabbed Luke's arm and pulled him back through the woods, all the time marveling, "I can't believe you really met her. In person. It's incredible. She's legendary, you know—"

The low-hanging tree limbs didn't seem so frightening now. Luke and jackal boy simply ducked. Together. A couple times jackal boy held a branch out of the way so Luke could go first. A couple times Luke returned the favor. Jackal boy kept rushing Luke along. They burst back into the clearing where everyone else was still sitting, not even talking. They appeared to have nothing to do but wait for jackal boy.

"Listen, you all!" jackal boy announced. "This is unbelievable! He knew Jen. He went to her house and everything!"

There was a flurry of questions—"What was she like?" "Did she tell you about the rally?" "How did you know her?" Someone produced a bag of cookies and they all passed it around, like it was a party.

It was a party. It was a party where they were accepting Luke into their group. Just because he knew Jen.

Luke did his best to answer all the questions.

"Jen was—amazing," he said. "She wasn't scared of anything. Not the Population Police, not the Government, not anyone. Not even her parents." Luke thought about how strange it was that Jen's father worked for the Population Police. Mr. Talbot was like a double agent, trying to help third children instead of killing them. But he hadn't been able to prevent his own daughter's death. He'd just barely managed to keep the Population Police from finding out that she had been his daughter.

Luke didn't want to talk about Jen's death, just her life.

"She spent months planning the rally," he said. "It was her statement, 'I deserve to exist. We deserve to exist.' She wanted as many third children there as possible. Out of hiding. She thought the Government would have to listen. She took everyone to the steps of the president's house . . ." Luke remembered the fight they'd had when he'd refused to go. And how she'd forgiven him. He stopped talking, lost in grief.

"The Government killed everyone at the rally," Nina finished for him.

Luke nodded blindly. He couldn't ignore Jen's death. He choked out, "Jen was a true hero. She was the bravest person I'll ever know. And someday—someday everyone will know about her."

The others nodded solemnly. *They know how I feel,* Luke marveled. And then, in spite of his grief, he felt a shot of joy: I *am* one of them. I belong.

After that, somehow, he was able to tell happy stories about Jen. He had the whole crowd laughing when he described how Jen had dusted for his fingerprints the first time he'd gone to her house.

"She wanted to make sure I was . . ." Luke hesitated. He had been about to say "another shadow child, like her." But that wasn't how he wanted to reveal his secret, just letting it slip out like it didn't matter. He finished lamely, "She wanted to make sure I was who I said I was."

"So," jackal boy said, lounging against a tree. "Who are you, anyway? What's your real name, 'Lee'?"

Luke looked at the circle of faces surrounding him. Jackal boy's question had silenced the laughter. Or maybe it was Luke's sudden stammering. Now everyone was watching Luke expectantly. An owl hooted somewhere deeper in the woods, and it was like a signal. Finally. It was time to tell.

"L—" Luke started. But the word stuck in his throat. All those nights he'd whispered his name, all those times he'd longed to speak his name aloud—and now he couldn't.

Some of the dry cookie crumbs slid back on his tongue and he started coughing, choking. One of the other boys had to pound him on the back before Luke got his breath back.

"Lee Grant," Luke said, as soon as he could speak again. His urge to confess was gone. "My name is Lee Grant."

"Sure," jackal boy kidded him. "Whatever you say."

And then Luke felt foolish. Jackal boy had revealed his real name. Why couldn't Luke reveal his?

Because, Luke thought with a chill, *I didn't decide to belong. Jackal boy decided for me.*

CHAPTER *TWENTY-TWO*

Belonging to jackal boy's group made all the difference in the world. It began that night. Luke didn't have to creep back from the woods by himself, praying nobody noticed. He went with the others, as part of the crowd. They strutted down the hall, not even trying to be quiet.

"What if someone hears?" Luke ventured.

"Who cares?" jackal boy replied. "Indoctrination's almost over. If there are any teachers around, they'll just think we left early to man our hall monitor posts."

They were in a brighter end of the hall now. Jackal boy got a good look at Luke's face and whistled.

"You really did get all bloody. Come on. I'll take you to the nurse."

Jackal boy led Luke to an unfamiliar office, one he'd seen only once before, when he was searching for windows.

"My friend walked into the wall, coming out of Indoctrination," Jackal boy told the woman who answered the door. "Stupid, huh? Can you give him a bandage?"

"My, my, you boys. You never look where you're going,"

the woman fussed. She was old and wrinkled, like the pictures Luke had seen of grandmothers. She puttered around getting antiseptic and gauze and tape. Then she dabbed at Luke's cheek with a wet cloth. "This is an awfully rough abrasion. Which wall did you run into, dear?"

Jackal boy saved Luke from having to answer.

"Oh, he didn't get bloody from the wall," jackal boy explained. "He kind of bounced off the wall and fell down. Then he scraped his face on the carpet. Someone might have kicked him by mistake, too."

Luke's mother would have listened to an excuse like that and then said, "Okay. Now. What really happened?" But this woman only nodded and *tsk-tsked* a little more.

The antiseptic stung, and Luke had to bite his lip to keep from crying out. But the woman was quick, and his face was neatly bandaged before he knew it.

"Write your name and the time down in the log on your way out," the woman said. "And be more careful the next time, all right?"

Jackal boy even wrote Luke's name for him.

Up in their room, jackal boy stretched and yawned and proclaimed, "I don't feel like dealing with the new kid tonight. Let's just leave him alone. Okay, guys? He's getting boring, anyway."

Luke thought some of his other roommates looked disappointed, but nobody complained.

In the morning, jackal boy said, "You can have breakfast with us. We have our own table. Hall monitor privileges."

"But I'm not a hall monitor," Luke said.

"The teachers won't notice," jackal boy said. "And maybe you will be soon."

So Luke sat at a table with other boys. For once he didn't have to force himself to choke down his oatmeal. It practically tasted good. And for the first time, Luke got a good look around the dining hall without feeling like he had to glance quickly and furtively. With clean white walls and a peaked ceiling, it really wasn't such a bad place.

"Can I ask you some questions? Here, I mean," Luke said to jackal boy.

"As long as you're not acting like a real exnay," jackal boy said brusquely, as if he were truly swearing at Luke. But Luke caught the double meaning. It was a brilliant code.

"Why is this school like this?" Luke began. "I mean, with no windows, and the strange boys . . . and the teachers who don't seem to notice us unless we do something wrong. And even then, they just say, 'Two demerits.' I don't even know what that means."

Jackal boy pushed back his oatmeal and smirked.

"Confusing, huh?" he asked mockingly. But he started explaining, anyway. "Hendricks began as an educational experiment. Back when there were the famines, people had debates about whether the undesirables in society deserved food when so many were starving. They let all the criminals die, but a bunch of bleeding-heart, sympathetic types said it was cruel not to feed people with mental illnesses, physical disabilities, that kind of thing.

One man stepped forward and offered his family's estate to be two schools for troubled kids. Hendricks for boys and Harlow for girls. He said he'd feed them, too—you see how well he's doing." Jackal boy made a face at the oatmeal. "They built the schools without windows because Mr. Hendricks had the idea that kids with agoraphobia—the ones scared of wide-open spaces—would be better off not even seeing the outdoors. He thought they'd start longing for what they couldn't see. And he thought having windows would just overstimulate the autistic kids. But he also thought it'd be good to bring in some normal kids. Like role models."

Luke tried to absorb all of that. He thought about how differently jackal boy acted when he was explaining something, compared with how Jen had always been. Jen was always outraged, indignant over every little injustice. He could just hear her voice, rising in disgust: "Can you believe it? Isn't that terrible?"

Jackal boy just sounded secretly amused, almost haughty. Too bad. Poor kids. Who cares?

Luke swallowed another bite of lumpy oatmeal.

"And the teachers?" he prompted. "Why aren't they more ... um ..."

"Involved? Aware? Semi-intelligent?" jackal boy offered.

"Yeah. All the adults. Like, the nurse last night didn't seem very smart. And what's-her-name, in the office, when I was in there the first day, it was like all the students were just a pain to her."

"Think about it," jackal boy said. "If you were a grown-up, and you could get a job anywhere else, would you work here? We got the dregs, man, the real dregs."

Luke didn't know anything about grown-up jobs. He'd never thought he would be able to come out of hiding to have one.

Jackal boy was smirking again. "But it serves our purposes, all right, to have teachers who are just one step up from leckers. We can do just about anything we want. Got it?"

He looked around at his cohorts, the hall monitors, and soon they were all smirking, too.

Luke wanted to object to that word, "lecker." Just because someone came from the country, that didn't make him dumb. Did it?

Something else bothered Luke, too.

"But I wanted to learn a lot at Hendricks," he said. "Math and science and how to speak other languages. . . . I've been here a month and I haven't learned a thing. I don't even know if I'm going to the right classes. I wanted to—" he broke off at the last minute because he remembered he couldn't talk about being an exnay. He couldn't say that he wanted to learn everything he could to help make third children legal again.

Jackal boy was laughing anyway.

"Oh, right, we're all here to learn," he said, rolling his eyes. This made his friends laugh, too. "Just stick close to me," jackal boy continued. "That's how you learn what you need to know. Forget the classes. And if you're worried about grades—don't you think I know how to fix that, too? How do you think we all got on the honor roll?"

Luke didn't know. He didn't even know what the honor roll was.

But when the bell rang for the first class, he left the dining hall with jackal boy and his gang. He felt safe now, traveling in a pack. All the hall monitors he passed gave him knowing looks, with secret nods that nobody else could have noticed.

And when he hesitated between classrooms, jackal boy was quick to tell him where to go.

CHAPTER TWENTY-THREE

L uke didn't go back to his garden by himself anymore. But two or three times a week, jackal boy would whisper in his ear, "Tonight," and Luke's heart would jump. "Tonight" meant, "We're going to the woods. We're meeting the girls."

Each time he stepped outside, Luke would breathe in deeply, the same way a starving man gobbled down food. But he noticed that most of the others, all so brave and imposing indoors, positively cowered in the open air. They squeezed their eyes shut and took halting steps forward, like condemned men walking to their executions.

"You don't like the outdoors, do you?" Luke asked Trey once as they walked across the lawn to the woods.

Trey shook his head slowly, as if moving too quickly might make him throw up. He looked a little green already.

"It's better in the woods," he said through gritted teeth. "At least there we're covered."

"But—" Luke took another deep breath, savoring the smell of newly mowed grass and spring rain. He couldn't understand Trey. "Don't you hate being cooped up all the time?"

Trey gave him a sidelong glance.

"I spent thirteen years in the same room. I didn't step foot outside even once until I came here."

"Oh," Luke said. He suddenly saw that, for a third child, he'd been very lucky. Before the Government tore down the woods behind his house and built a neighborhood there instead, he'd spent most of his time outdoors. Except for not going to school, he hadn't lived that differently from his older brothers.

He couldn't imagine spending thirteen years in the same room.

"Jen went shopping on fake passes," he told Trey. "Her mother took her to play groups. I thought other third children lived like her."

"I wouldn't know," Trey said. "I—I wished—" He hesitated. "I miss my room."

Luke felt sorry for the other boy. How many of his other new friends had basically lived their entire lives in a box?

He watched jackal boy running ahead, then circling back to encourage the others.

"Jacka—I mean, Jason must have been like Jen," Luke said. "He must have gotten out a lot. He's not afraid of anything."

"No," Trey said. "He's not. He says he's overcome all his hiding-related phobias. And he's only been here a few weeks longer than you."

"He has?" Luke asked in surprise. He'd assumed jackal

boy was a long-timer, with years of experience at Hendricks.

"The rest of us only started last fall," Trey continued. "I think. No one talked much before Jason got here."

Before he could make sense of that, Luke had to remind himself all over again that "Jason" was really jackal boy. It was no wonder that Luke had been confused when he first started at Hendricks—the boys, at least the ones he hung out with now, did go by three or four different names. They might answer to the first or last part of their fake name at school, and the first or last part of their real name out in the woods. That was riskier. A few just went by initials.

Trey had explained that his name just meant "three." He wouldn't tell even jackal boy his real name.

They reached the woods, and what Trey had said finally sunk in.

"Wait a minute," Luke said. "You mean you weren't all friends before Jason came? You haven't been meeting in the woods all along?"

Trey flashed him a puzzled look.

"Just since April," he said.

Luke's mind was racing.

"The rally was in April," he said.

"Yeah," Trey said with a shrug.

The girls met them then, and they started the same kind of banter Luke had witnessed the first night. It sounded different to Luke now, not as if they were all worldly and experienced, but as if they were reading lines in a play, pretending to talk to each other the way normal boys and girls talked. Nina made jokes about how stupid boys were, and Jason made fun of the girls. Luke watched the faces of the ones who were quiet. They all looked scared.

"What's this meeting for?" Luke asked suddenly.

Jason turned to look at Luke in surprise.

"Why—we're planning ways to resist the Government over the Population Law. To follow up the rally."

"The rally," Nina echoed wistfully.

Luke's heart beat fast. This was what he'd wanted! He'd wanted to do something brave like Jen. It would be like apologizing to her for not going with her, for doubting her.

But could he be as brave as Jen?

Without dying, too?

"How?" he demanded. "How are we going to resist?"

Nina and Jason looked at each other.

"Well, that's what we're deciding," Nina said. "Just like a boy, asking dumb questions!"

But they didn't decide anything that night. They just joked around some more, made a game of guessing one boy's real name, and headed back to their schools.

Jason pulled Luke aside as they stepped back into the school building.

"Not everyone's as ready as you," he said. "You've got to give the others time. As long as they're trembling in their shoes every time they step outside, they'll never make good subversives."

Luke was flattered. It made sense.

"Okay," he said.

Jason playfully punched Luke's arm.

"Knew you'd understand. Hey—you ready for finals?"

"Finals?" Luke asked.

"You know, next week? End-of-term tests?" Jason said. "You pass, you get out of here, you fail, you're stuck for life?"

Luke stopped short.

"Oh, no . . . ," he breathed.

Jason laughed.

"Scared you, huh? Remember, you stay on my good side, I'll make sure your 'parents' get to look at a brilliant report!"

"I'm not even going to the right classes!" Luke said, panic coursing through his veins. "And I can't ask anyone now. It's been too long—"

"I'll find out for you!" Jason said, laughing again. He was already halfway down the hall.

CHAPTER *TWENTY-FOUR*

ason was as good as his word. The next morning at breakfast, he handed Luke a computer printout that said, at the top, CLASS SCHEDULE FOR LEE GRANT. It had times, room numbers, teachers' names.

"Where'd you get this?" Luke asked.

"You think your only computer hacker friend is dead?" Jason said.

He meant Jen. Luke had a flash of missing her all over again. He could picture her sitting at the computer, typing fast. She'd created a chat room for third children, with the password of "free." She'd connected hundreds of third children, so they weren't just sitting in their little rooms, all alone. She'd hacked into the records of the national police, to make sure none of the kids going to the third-child rally were caught before they got to the capital.

But what good had all her hacking done?

"Earth to Lee," Jason was saying. "Or whatever your name is. You should know, your schedule really doesn't matter. I can change all your grades on the computer, anyhow."

But after breakfast, Luke determinedly marched off to his first class, listened closely, and took detailed notes. By the end of the hour, he knew something he'd never known before: Prime numbers could be divided only by themselves and one.

In his second class, he boldly grabbed a textbook off the bookshelf and read the poem whose page number the teacher had written on the board. He could even make sense of the fancy language—two people were friends, and one of them died, and the other one felt sad.

Luke figured he had an unfair advantage, understanding that.

In science and technology class, the teacher was talking about gasoline motors. Luke could just picture one, all grease-covered, in Father's tractor. And now he knew how they worked.

By lunchtime, Luke was ready to brag to Jason, "I *am* learning something now." He was even confident enough to tease, "Maybe I won't need your help with my grades."

"You're going to learn a whole term's worth in just a week?" jackal boy mocked. "Right. Next week, Friday, at five o'clock, you'll come begging, 'Please, please, I need help! I'll do anything!'"

Luke only set his jaw and pulled out a book to study.

CHAPTER *TWENTY-FIVE*

B y the end of the week, all the teachers had test dates written in chalk on their blackboards. And Luke was spending every spare moment studying.

"Why?" Trey asked him one night as they were trudging out to the woods. "Jason can fix your grades. And it's not like your real parents are going to see them, anyway."

"When you were stuck in your room," Luke said, "didn't you ever want to know anything about the outside world? About whether other people were like you, or different, or whether grass grows the same way all over the world, or how a car runs?"

"Not really," Trey said.

Luke was sorry that he couldn't explain. It wasn't the grades themselves that mattered to him. But he felt like he had something to prove. Maybe that people from the country—leckers—weren't so dumb, after all. Maybe that Jen's dad hadn't risked his life for nothing, getting Luke a fake identity. Maybe that Luke wasn't wasting time just hanging out in the woods making jokes with the girls from Harlow while other third children still had to hide.

He was surprised that, with each day that passed, his classes made more sense to him. The teachers weren't really that bad, just distant. The history teacher, Mr. Dirk, could tell fascinating stories about kings and knights and battles, and they were all true. The literature teacher could recite whole poems from memory. Luke didn't always understand all the words, but he liked the cadence and rhyme. The math teacher said once, "Aren't numbers *friendly*?" and he really seemed to believe it. Luke wondered if the teachers were shy, too—if they had some of those phobias Trey and Jason had talked about, and were downright terrified of looking their students straight in the eye.

The night before his first test, Luke studied through dinner, and skipped going to the woods with all the others during Indoctrination so he could hunch over in a hallway, reading history. Jason mocked him—"What are you trying to do, bookworm? Learn as many big words as Trey?" and, "You could read all night and still not pass your tests. Come on."

"Leave me alone," Luke growled, eager to get back to the Trojan War.

Luke was surprised that Jason stepped back instead of insisting.

"Fine," he said. "Waste your time. See if I care."

The words sounded like the swaggering boy Luke was used to. But his tone seemed to say something else. So did the set of his shoulders as he walked away. He sounded wary, on edge.

Could Jason possibly be scared of Luke?

Luke was nobody. Jason was in charge. Luke decided he was imagining things, and went back to his book.

Still, after lights out, Luke couldn't sleep. He was too unsettled—worried about the test the next day, wondering what his family was doing back home, wishing Jen were there to figure out Jason for him. He even thought back to the advice Jen's dad had written for Luke: "Blend in." Who was Luke supposed to blend in with? The boys who trudged blindly through the halls each day? The ones who followed Jason? Or Jason himself?

Somewhere in the room, a bed creaked.

Luke thought it was just someone turning over in his sleep but he stiffened anyway, and listened hard.

There was a *pat-pat-pat* that could have been footsteps, or could have been Luke's imagination. And then, the hall light shone briefly into the room as the door was opened and closed.

Luke sat up. He crept over to the door and opened it a crack so he'd have light to see by.

All the beds were filled with sleeping boys except two. Luke's.

And Jason's.

CHAPTER TWENTY-SIX

L uke took time to grab one of his textbooks so he'd have an excuse if someone caught him out of his room after lights out. "I only wanted to study some more," he could say. "I'm worried about my tests."

But the only person who might catch him was Jason.

Out in the dimly lit hall Luke looked back and forth, not sure which way to go. Probably Jason had only needed to go to the bathroom, and Luke was foolish to follow him. Luke headed toward the bathroom first.

Why didn't I think to go to the bathroom after lights out, back when I was trying to find a place to read my note? Luke wondered. But Luke had been too terrified back then to think like that. He wouldn't have dared leave his bed. He had actually blended in quite well. *And if I'd read the note right away, I wouldn't have discovered the door to outdoors or the woods. I wouldn't have had those few days of setting up my garden.* He still missed his garden. He tried not to think about it. *And I never would have gotten to know anybody.*

But how well *did* he know his new friends? The only

friend he'd ever had before was Jen, and that friendship had been entirely different.

It wasn't fair to compare.

He sneaked quietly down the hall, feeling foolish. Of course Jason would be in the bathroom, and he'd only have rude comments and mockery for Luke when he saw him. "Can't even pee without your books, huh?" maybe, or even, "Hey, lecker, we've got toilet paper here and everything. You won't need to use that."

The bathroom was empty.

Luke backtracked, and glanced in his room again. Jason's bed was still empty. Luke went the opposite direction from the bathroom. All that lay down this hallway was the back stairs.

Maybe Luke wouldn't look for Jason anymore. What did he think he was going to do when he found him? But Luke was so thoroughly awake now that he decided he might as well study. The details of the Trojan War and the Peloponnesian War were blurring in his mind.

He went over to the stairwell and sat down on the top step. He leaned against the wall, opened his book, and began reading. "The Greeks fought battles for—"

Far below Luke, someone was murmuring.

Luke sat still for a minute, tempted to ignore it. It probably was Jason, but so what? If he was having a secret meeting without Luke, why should Luke care? It wasn't like Jason's gang ever planned anything real, anyway.

But Luke did care. If Jason's gang was going to help

third children, Luke owed it to himself—to his family, to Jen, to Jen's dad—to take part.

Luke eased down to the next step. And the next. And the next. He kept clutching his book because he didn't want to make any noise putting it down. Yet he wondered if he should be making noise, acting normal, so he could come upon the secret meeting casually, "Oh, hi, guys—didn't know you were down here. Can I help?"

There was nothing normal about walking around Hendricks in the middle of the night. Luke stayed quiet.

When he rounded the corner of the second flight of stairs, he could begin to distinguish words. The only person who seemed to be talking was Jason. Nothing new about that. Luke crouched behind the half-wall that surrounded the stairs. He listened closely.

"But it's too soon!" Jason was pleading.

Luke risked a peek over the banister. Maybe Trey was there, and would call out, "Hey, Lee! Glad you're here! I was hoping you would come!"

But Jason appeared to be alone.

He was talking into a small portable phone. At least, that's what Luke thought it was. He'd never seen one before, except in sketches in his science textbook.

Jason was facing the other way, so Luke kept watching and listening.

"I told you. There's no danger in waiting!" he exclaimed. "They're just sitting ducks!"

Jason was silent, listening. He turned slightly and Luke

caught a glimpse of the side of his face. Jason's expression was set, dead serious. Luke thought about all the times he'd seen Jason joking, joshing, prodding, mocking. Luke wouldn't have thought Jason could be 100 percent serious about anything. He seemed like a different boy.

Frightened, Luke ducked out of sight.

"I've got four and she's got two," Jason said. "But I could have more by the end of the week."

Four and two and more of what? Luke wondered.

"Well, I don't know about Nina," Jason said. "You'd have to ask her. But she says girls are harder to recruit."

Girls? Luke thought he'd solved his puzzle. Jason was making plans for some action against the Government—something like the rally, but safer, Luke hoped. He was telling someone how many boys and girls—how many exnays—were available to help. Except . . . the group that met in the woods had nine boys now, with Luke, and five girls.

Hadn't Jason told Luke once that the whole group wasn't brave enough yet to be subversives? Luke wondered whom Jason was counting and whom he was leaving out. Trey was pretty timid. So were several of the others.

What about Luke? What if Jason wasn't including Luke because Luke hadn't gone to the meeting in the woods that evening? Or because he knew that Luke was secretly the biggest chicken of all?

Luke started to stand up, to say, "Wait! Count me in!" His legs were quivering, but he could make himself be brave. He'd have to.

Jason had his back turned to Luke again. He was practically snarling into the phone now.

"You want names? All right, I'll give you the ones I have. Antonio Blanco, alias Samuel Irving. Denton Weathers, alias Travis Spencer. Sherman Kymanski, alias Ryan Mann. Patrick Kerrigan, alias Tyrone Janson."

Jason was saying the boys' real names. Luke was so thrilled, he couldn't speak. If only he'd told Jason his real name. He could just imagine hearing, "Luke Garner, subversive for the cause, coming to the aid of third children everywhere." Forget the alias. It didn't matter.

Jason shifted his portable phone in his hand, and Luke had a terrible thought. What if Jason's phone was bugged? Then Luke realized something even worse: Since it was a portable phone, the Population Police didn't even have to bug it. Luke had learned in science and technology class just last week that portable phones sent out messages indiscriminately. Didn't Jason know that? All the Population Police needed was a receiver.

And of course they had one. They had everything.

Luke rushed out from his hiding place and took the last flight of stairs in two leaps. He had to get the phone away from Jason before he accidentally betrayed another boy's identity. Jason still had his back to Luke. He was saying indignantly into the phone: "Of course I'll get the others to tell me their real names. They're just cagey. They do trust me. They don't have any idea I work for the Population Police."

CHAPTER *TWENTY-SEVEN*

L uke had his hand inches from the phone when Jason's words registered: " . . . I work for the Population Police." Luke's hand and arm kept going, even though his mind was suddenly frozen. He watched his hand as if it belonged to someone else. His fingers grasped the phone, jerked it out of Jason's grip, and threw it to the ground. Then someone's foot—no, Luke's foot, acting as independently as his hand—stomped on it.

Jason whirled around.

"You!" he spat.

Luke's frozen mind was struggling to thaw. Strange facts were emerging from the ice. Jason worked for the Population Police. That's why he hadn't cared about using a portable phone. He wasn't organizing subversive activity against the Government. He was turning in the exnays.

"You're an informer," Luke whispered.

Jason's eyes narrowed, calculatingly. Luke instantly saw his mistake. Why hadn't he played dumb? He could have pretended he hadn't heard Jason's last sentence. He could have acted hurt that Jason was leaving him out. He could have begged for a dangerous assignment.

It wouldn't have been too hard to act dumb. Until two seconds ago, he had been.

"Now, Lee," Jason said cautiously. He seemed to be trying to decide how to play things. Was Luke going to get, "Oh, don't be silly. What would make you think that? Why would I turn anybody in when I'm an exnay, too?" Or, "So you know the truth. That's it. You're dead"?

Jason took a step toward Luke. Luke clutched his history textbook like a shield. Jason came even closer.

And then, without thinking, Luke whipped the book out and swung it at Jason's head with all his might.

Jason crumpled. Knocked sideways, he tried desperately to regain his balance. Luke swung again.

This time, Jason fell backwards. His head hit the stairs with a loud *thunk*. His body rolled down to the landing.

He didn't move.

CHAPTER *TWENTY-EIGHT*

Luke hardly dared to breathe. He held his book high over his head.

Jason still didn't move.

What if Luke had killed him?

Luke knelt down and put his hand in front of Jason's nose. Very, very faintly, he felt bursts of air every few seconds. Jason wasn't dead, only knocked unconscious.

For how long?

Luke wasted time staring at Jason's motionless body. Luke wouldn't have wanted to be a murderer, but everything would be easier if Jason were dead.

Luke could kill him now.

Everything in Luke recoiled against that notion. Jason was the worst kind of fake—an informer, a traitor, someone who pretends to be a friend and then betrays. He probably had as good as killed four boys whose only crime was existing. Jason deserved to die.

But Luke couldn't kill him.

Luke was desperately trying to get his paralyzed brain to come up with another option, when the portable phone rang. The noise echoed in the stairwell as shrilly as a hundred roosters, all crowing at once. It sounded loud enough to wake the dead, not to mention the merely unconscious. Luke grabbed the phone, just to shut it up. It kept ringing. Luke stared at it stupidly. He'd never actually touched a phone before tonight. Didn't they stop ringing when you picked them up? He punched buttons on the phone at random. Finally, miraculously, the noise stopped.

Luke let out a sigh of relief. Why had the phone rung in the first place? Jason had been using it. Then when Luke pulled it away and stomped on it, that must have worked like hanging it up. But for it to start ringing again—

Someone was calling Jason.

Fearfully, Luke put the phone to his ear.

"Hello?" he whispered.

He had a sudden moment of hope. Maybe he'd misunderstood. Maybe Jason hadn't said that he worked for the Population Police, but that the exnays didn't trust him because they thought he *might* work for the Population Police. Or that the exnays didn't trust anyone, because of the Population Police. Maybe the person on the other end of the line was a good guy, working for the cause, worried that something had happened to poor, noble, misunderstood Jason.

"Hello?" Luke whispered again.

"Don't you ever pull that kind of a stunt on me again!" The angry voice on the other end came through the phone as forcefully as a tornado. "You hang up on the Population Police, you're a dead man. We'll kill you even before we kill those four exnays you just turned in."

Luke's hope dissolved. He struggled to keep his mind from dissolving, too. Think, think . . . He'd heard Jen's dad fool the Population Police once. Mr. Talbot had lied so smoothly that even Luke, who knew the truth, was practically convinced.

Luke put his hand over his mouth. He had to make the man on the other end of the line think he was Jason.

"I'm sorry," Luke muttered. "It was a mistake. I accidentally dropped the phone and it shut off by itself." With a little help from Luke's foot.

"What? I can't hear you!" the man yelled.

"It's a bad connection," Luke said, speaking louder. He'd heard Mother and Dad say that all the time. He hoped portable phones could have bad connections, too. "I said I was sorry. I dropped the phone by mistake. I didn't hang up on you. Why would I hang up on you when I'm trying to convince you to give me more time?"

"Whatever," the man growled. Luke could tell: The man didn't care what had happened. He just wanted Jason to grovel. And Luke had done it for him. Luke was good at groveling.

"Here's how it is," the man continued. "We'll give you another day. Then that's it. And, Jason? You get those other boys or else. We've got a quota to fill, you know."

The phone clicked. Luke realized the man on the other end had hung up.

Luke had fooled him. And he'd bought some time. He had another day.

Or until Jason woke up.

CHAPTER *TWENTY-NINE*

uke slid his hands under Jason's armpits and began dragging him down the stairs. Down was easier than up. And if Jason woke up and started screaming, he'd be less likely to wake somebody if he and Luke were on the first floor.

Of course, if Jason woke up and attacked Luke, there was also less chance Luke could get help on the first floor.

Luke made himself concentrate on pulling the bigger boy. Jason's feet slipped down the first step and hit hard. Jason moaned but didn't open his eyes.

Maybe he's just faking, Luke thought. *Maybe he's wide awake and he's just waiting for the right moment to attack.*

That thought made Luke sweat. But he pulled harder, and got Jason all the way to the bottom of the steps without waking him up.

Next, Luke dragged Jason down the hall. A right turn, a left turn, a right turn. Jason was heavy, and Luke's arms ached. His head ached, too, from trying to plan. He found the door he'd been looking for and forced himself to knock.

"Yes?" a sleepy voice responded.

Luke grimaced. He'd been half-hoping this idea would fail. *Be brave,* he told himself.

"Nurse!" he called out. "It's my—my friend. He's sick."

How could he have called Jason a friend?

Oh, well. He had a lot more lies ahead of him.

The door eased open. The nurse stood there in a ruffled dressing gown.

"Oh, my," she said dimly when she'd taken in the sight of Jason slumped on the floor. Luke tried to hold him up the way a concerned friend would, but it was hard. Luke would have enjoyed dropping him.

"He passed out," Luke said needlessly. "He was having a—a seizure, ranting and raving. He was . . . telling lies. Making up stories." That should help if Jason came to. "I think it's called delirium, what he had. I think staying unconscious is the best thing for him. Can you give him something that will keep him asleep?"

"Oh, my," the nurse repeated, frowning. "Usually, in these circumstances, we want to revive the patient."

It wasn't fair. Now the nurse seemed to know what she was talking about.

"Help me get him inside," she ordered Luke.

The nurse took Jason's legs, and Luke lifted. The strain on his muscles was terrible. Luke was panting by the time they got Jason to a bed in the nurse's office. She immediately began looking him over.

"Did he hit his head?" she asked Luke as she felt Jason's scalp.

Panic bubbled up in Luke's stomach.

"May-Maybe," he said. "He was, um, thrashing around a lot. In his sleep."

"I thought he was ranting and raving," the nurse said, fixing Luke with an unexpectedly sharp stare. "Was he doing that in his sleep, too?"

Luke gulped.

"No. He was thrashing about, and then he woke up, and acted delirious. And then he had a seizure and went unconscious. I think. It happened really fast. It was really scary."

Luke got another idea.

"You know, you should really strap him down in bed, so if he wakes up and starts acting weird again, he won't hurt himself."

"Thanks for the medical advice," the nurse said. She lifted one of Jason's eyelids and shone a flashlight into his eye. Luke held his breath. If Jason woke up now, he could tell the nurse anything he wanted, and she'd believe him. Jason was a much better liar than Luke. Jason's lips moved. Had he mumbled something that the nurse could hear but Luke couldn't? Luke tried to quell his panic. He watched with relief as Jason's eye rolled blindly back in his head. The nurse gently placed the eyelid back against the eye. Jason didn't move.

The nurse sat down at a desk and took up a pen.

"Now. What's your friend's name?" she asked.

"Ja—I mean, Scott Renault," Luke said.

The nurse peered at him doubtfully.

"And your name is—"

"Lee Grant," Luke mumbled.

The nurse was watching him carefully. Too carefully.

"Okay," she said. "Let me type your account of your friend's injury into the computer." She disappeared around a corner. Luke could hear the nurse muttering to herself. Then there was the *clickety-clack* of a keyboard. The sound made him miss Jen. He remembered Jason acting so excited when Luke had mentioned her name. But that had just been an act—an act contrived to get Luke to trust him, to reveal his real name, so Jason could betray him.

Luke's head spun. It was too hard to recast his memories with Jason as a traitor.

The nurse came back.

"Sign this," she said.

Disheartened, Luke signed without reading.

"Now. Why don't you go on back to bed?" the nurse said to Luke. "I'll take good care of your friend. I promise."

That's what Luke was afraid of.

But there was nothing else for him to do but back out of the door.

"Let me know how he is," Luke begged as he left. "And if he says anything crazy—"

"Don't worry," the nurse said. "I've heard plenty of crazy talk around here."

Out in the hallway, Luke wished he'd thought of another plan. Ropes! He could have tied Jason up, and gagged him, and . . . and put him where, exactly? Even the boys who stared at the ground all day would notice a bound and gagged boy lying around. And where was Luke supposed to get ropes and a gag? No, Luke had had to take his chances with the nurse. He just had to hurry even faster now. Who could tell what lies Jason might tell the nurse when he awoke? All Luke knew was, Jason wouldn't cast Luke as the heroic friend who'd carried Jason to help.

Actually, Jason wouldn't even have to lie. All he had to say was that Luke had hit him with a book and knocked him down. That was true, though not the whole truth. And if anyone wanted to investigate, they could examine Luke's book, and—

Luke's book. Stunned by his own stupidity, Luke realized: He'd left his book and Jason's portable phone back on the stairs.

Forgetting to go quietly, Luke raced down the hall, around corners, and back up the stairs. He saw the history textbook cast off in the corner of the landing, where he'd dropped it. He snatched it up and hugged it to his chest like a long-lost friend. Now, to find the phone—

The phone was nowhere in sight.

CHAPTER *THIRTY*

he landing was barely a four-by-four square, flat and empty. But Luke walked around it again and again, as if he'd just missed noticing the phone and it was right there, in plain sight.

It wasn't.

Luke looked on each stair below, and even the stairs above the landing—as if the phone could fly. It took forever for his stubborn brain to accept that the phone was missing. Then he sank down on one of the stair steps, puzzling out who might have taken it.

Did Jason have an accomplice?

Luke thought about all the hall monitors, all the boys who'd met in the woods. Now that Jason's true nature had been revealed, Luke couldn't be sure of anyone. Maybe they all worked for the Population Police.

Except for the four boys Jason had betrayed.

Luke was desperately confused, but he could figure out one thing: The missing phone meant those four were in more immediate danger.

And so was Luke.

Luke's first instinct was to hide, to get the other four to hide with him. The woods wouldn't be safe because Jason would lead the Population Police straight there. Was there a safe place in the kitchen? Somewhere in an unused classroom? Some dormitory room off by itself, and unlikely to be searched?

Hiding was no good. In the end, they'd only be found.

Luke had to do something to prevent the Population Police from ever searching. But he didn't even understand what was going on. He had to find someone who knew more than Luke, who could lie better than Luke, who knew how to handle the Population Police.

Jen's dad.

But how was Luke supposed to reach him?

CHAPTER *THIRTY-ONE*

uke crept back down to the first floor with only the vaguest plan in mind. He needed Mr. Talbot's phone number. He needed a phone. The school office should have both.

The school office was locked.

Luke stood before the ornate door for what felt like hours. The door had a glass panel at the top, so he could see in easily. He could make out the shape of a phone on Ms. Hawkins's desk. He could see old-fashioned file cabinets behind it. Surely there was a file in there with Luke's name on it—his fake name, anyway. Would Mr. Talbot's phone number be listed in there, because he was the one who'd brought Luke to the school? Luke thought so. But it did no good unless Luke could get into the files. And no matter how much he jiggled the knob of the office door, the door held firm.

Desperately, Luke kicked it. But the door was thick, solid maple wood. Nothing flimsy at Hendricks. Even the glass was probably—

Glass. Luke couldn't believe how stupid he was being.

He slammed the glass panel with his textbook, and a satis-fying spiderweb of cracks crept across it. He hit it again, a little lower, smashing that portion of the panel.

"And Jason thinks books are useless," Luke muttered to himself. "Take that!"

Luke covered his hand with part of his pajama sleeve and pushed through the bottom of the glass. Only a few shards fell to the ground. The rest of the panel stayed in place. It was high-quality glass. Anything cheap would have shattered completely, and fallen to the ground with an enormous clatter.

Luke reached on through, until he could touch the knob from inside. He turned it—slowly, slowly—until he heard the click he'd been waiting for. He eased the door open and raced to the filing cabinet.

With only the dim light from the hall, Luke couldn't read any of the labels on any of the files. He had to carry them out to the door to see whose they were.

The first batch he pulled had Jeremy Andrews through Luther Benton. He replaced them and moved further back in the file. Tanner Fitzgerald through—yes, there it was. Lee Grant.

Luke was surprised by the thickness of his file, consid-ering how short a time he'd been at Hendricks. The first set of papers were school transcripts from other schools— evidently the ones the real Lee Grant had attended, before he died and left his identity to Luke. There were pictures, too, seven of them, labeled, KINDERGARTEN, GRADE ONE, GRADE

TWO . . . all the way up to grade six. Strangely, the photos really did look like Luke. Same sandy hair, pale eyes, worried look. Luke blinked, thinking he'd been fooled. But when he opened his eyes, the resemblance was still there. Had the real Lee Grant looked that much like Luke?

Then Luke remembered something Jen had told him once, about changing photos on the computer.

"You can make people look older, younger, prettier, uglier—whatever you want. If I wanted to make my own fake I.D., I probably could," she'd bragged.

But Jen had wanted to come out of hiding with her identity intact. She hated the thought of fake I.D.'s.

Staring at the faked pictures, Luke could understand. It was all too strange. He knew he should be reassured by how thoroughly his records had been doctored. But it frightened him instead. There was no sign of the real Luke Garner. Probably even his family would forget him eventually.

Luke didn't have time for self-pity. He turned the page, hoping his admission papers would be next.

They weren't. Instead, there was some sort of a daily log. Luke read in horrified fascination:

April 28—Student withdrawn, surly during entrance interview. Refuses to look interviewer directly in eye. Refuses to answer questions. Sullen behavior. Hostility believed connected to dissociation with parents. Can assume high risk of repeated attempts at running away. Treatment to commence immediately.

April 29—Sullenness continues. Attempts at interaction
rebuffed. Teachers report disinterest, hostility.

The log continued in that vein, with an entry for every day Luke had been at Hendricks. There was repeated mention of therapy and treatment, and its success or failure. But Luke had had no entrance interview. He'd had no therapy, no treatment, no attention from the school officials at all. Obviously, this was another faked record.

But who had faked it? And why?

Thoroughly baffled, Luke turned the page. And there was the thick sheaf of his entrance papers.

Mr. Talbot was listed in the second column of the sixteenth page, as an emergency contact.

Luke grabbed the phone and started dialing.

CHAPTER *THIRTY-TWO*

A woman's sleepy voice answered.

"Is Mr. Talbot there?" Luke asked. "I need Mr. Talbot."

"It's three in the morning!" the woman hissed.

"Please," Luke begged. "It's an emergency. I'm a friend of—" He barely managed to stop himself from saying, "Jen's." Mr. Talbot's phone was probably bugged by the Population Police. Maybe the school's phone was now, too. Luke didn't know. But he tried again. "Mr. Talbot is a friend of my parents.'"

There was only dead air in response. Then a man's voice, just as sleepy as the woman's.

"Hello?"

It was Mr. Talbot.

Luke wanted to spill out everything, from his first confusing day at Hendricks, to Jason's treachery, to the oddness of the file Luke still held on his lap. If only he could explain all his problems, surely Mr. Talbot could solve them all. But Luke had to choose his words carefully.

"You told me to blend in," he accused, hoping Mr. Talbot

would remember. "I can't. You have to come get me." *And four other boys,* he added silently, as if Mr. Talbot were actually capable of telepathy. If only Luke could just say, flat out, "You need to get four more fake I.D.'s for these friends of mine. And you'll need to protect their families, too." But Luke couldn't think of any code that would clue in Mr. Talbot, without clueing in the Population Police as well.

"Now, now," Mr. Talbot said calmly, sounding like an elderly uncle dispensing wisdom. "Surely school isn't that bad. You need to give it more of a chance. Is this finals week or something?"

Luke couldn't tell whether Mr. Talbot really didn't understand, or whether he was acting for the sake of the bug.

"That's not the problem!" Luke almost screamed. "It's— it's like a problem I had before."

"Yes, problems do seem to repeat themselves," Mr. Talbot said, still sounding untroubled. "Usually, there's some root cause. You need to attack that first."

Was Mr. Talbot speaking in code? Luke hoped so.

"It's all very well to say that," he protested. "But the problems are multiplying. There are four others, now, I have to think about. And they can't wait until the, um, root cause is fixed. This is an emergency. You have to help."

Luke was proud of himself. He couldn't be any clearer than that, not using a potentially bugged phone. Surely Mr. Talbot would understand.

"You children can be so melodramatic," Mr. Talbot said irritably. Now he sounded like a man ripped from sleep at three in the morning for no good reason. "I have every confidence that you can deal with your problems by yourself. Now. Good night."

"Please!" Luke pleaded.

But Mr. Talbot had hung up.

CHAPTER *THIRTY-THREE*

uke stared at the phone. He'd tried so hard. It wasn't fair that he didn't even know if he'd succeeded or not.

No. He knew. He'd failed.

He'd heard the careless tone in Mr. Talbot's voice. Luke couldn't fool himself into thinking it was all an act, with each word carrying double meaning. It was three in the morning. He'd awakened Mr. Talbot out of a dead sleep. How could he possibly have understood what Luke needed?

Luke dropped the phone and put his face down on Ms. Hawkins's desk. The file he'd been holding on his lap spilled onto the floor, dumping out papers filled with lies. He didn't care. He didn't care that anyone walking by would catch him where he wasn't supposed to be. He was past caring about anything.

Had Jen ever reached this point, planning the rally?

Luke remembered the last time he'd seen her, the night she'd left for the capital. She'd seemed almost unearthly, as if she'd already passed out of the realm she shared with

Luke. And she had. He was still in hiding, and she was about to risk her life to be free.

It was simpler for you, Luke accused silently. *You weren't confused.*

It was hard having a dead hero for a best friend.

I just can't live up to you, Jen, he thought. *I'm not you.*

He wasn't Lee Grant, either. Slowly, just to get rid of them, he began picking up the faked papers and stuffing them back into the file. Moving like someone in a dream, he put the phone back on the desk and the file back in the filing cabinet, and shut the drawer. He walked out of the office and pulled the door closed behind him, making no effort whatsoever to hide the broken glass.

He'd have to run away, that's all there was to it. He could take the other four with him. They'd just have to take their chances. They could head to the city.

Luke had lost all track of time, now. Before he woke the others and terrified them out of their wits, he decided, he'd peek outside and see how much time they had left before daylight.

He went to the door they always used, the one that led to the woods and had once led to his garden. He tried to turn the knob, but his hand must have been weak with exhaustion. His fingers slipped right off. He gripped the knob again, and tried harder.

The door was locked. Locked from the outside.

Panicked, Luke ran to the front door, the one he'd come through with Mr. Talbot that first day.

It was locked, too.

What kind of a school kept its students locked in, at night?

No school. Just prisons.

Luke rushed around trying every door he could find, but it was hopeless. They were all locked. And none of them had glass panels for him to break.

Finally he sank to the floor outside his history classroom.

We're trapped, he thought. *Trapped like rats in a hole.*

Luke was not the least bit surprised when he heard footsteps coming down the hall. He hardly dared look up. But it wasn't Jason or someone from the Population Police standing over him. It was his history teacher, Mr. Dirk.

"Back to bed, young man," Mr. Dirk said. "I appreciate your dedication to history, but studying through the night is strictly prohibited. I'm afraid I'll have to give you—"

"I know, I know," Luke said. "Two demerits."

Under Mr. Dirk's stern gaze, Luke resignedly trudged back upstairs.

CHAPTER *THIRTY-FOUR*

Luke was overcome by guilt when he woke up the next morning. How could he have slept away so many hours? He'd had to come back to his room because Mr. Dirk was watching. But he could have sneaked out later. Why hadn't he at least warned the others?

Some rational side of his mind argued: What good would a warning do when they couldn't escape?

Around him, his other roommates were complaining about the exams they faced that day. One or two of them had books open on their beds and were studying as they got dressed. It seemed unreal that anyone could care about exams at a time like this.

Fearfully, Luke looked over at Jason's bed. It was empty. The sheets were rumpled the same way they'd been last night. The pillow still held an indentation. But Jason was nowhere in sight.

"Where's Scott?" Luke asked. His voice trembled despite his best efforts to sound casual.

His question was met with blank stares.

"Don't know," one boy finally mumbled, and went back to studying.

At breakfast, Luke sat with Jason's gang, but Jason was still missing. Luke peered around the table at the four boys Jason had betrayed: Antonio/Samuel, who had flashing dark eyes and a quick laugh; Denton/Travis, who knew hundreds of riddles; Sherman/Ryan, who talked with an accent Luke had never heard before; and Patrick/Tyrone, who had once claimed he got his fake I.D. by "the luck of the Irish." Luke couldn't have said he really knew any of them well. But it was agony to sit there watching them eat their Cream of Wheat, making jokes, totally unaware that they were doomed. Luke tried to lean over and whisper in Patrick's ear, "You're in danger—I need to tell you—" But Patrick only brushed him away with the words, "Quit it, lecker. You're bugging me." And then all the others stared at Luke. How many of them were on Jason's side, working for the Population Police?

Luke didn't dare give his warning out loud.

Breakfast time slipped away, with Luke's panic only growing. His thoughts ran in circles. He should go hide, by himself, if he couldn't save the others. But he couldn't just abandon the others. He had to save them. But how?

"If you're not going to eat your breakfast, I will," Patrick said when Luke's was the only bowl that wasn't empty.

Silently, Luke passed over his food.

"Hey, thanks," Patrick said, with a huge grin. "You're the greatest."

If only you knew . . . , Luke thought miserably.

Just then, the dining hall door banged open.

"Population Police!" a booming voice called out.

Luke froze. He'd known this was coming, but it still didn't seem possible. He tried to yell, "Run!" to Patrick and the others, but he opened his mouth and nothing came out. His legs were frozen, too. He could only sit and watch and listen in horror.

A huge man stepped into the room. Medals covered his olive green uniform. He clutched a sheaf of papers in his fist.

"I have a warrant here for the arrest of illegals who have compounded their crime by the use of falsified documents," he announced.

Luke closed his eyes, in agony. It was all over. He'd failed at everything. He hadn't saved the others, and he hadn't saved himself. He'd never done anything for the cause. He was going to die before he'd had a chance to accomplish a single thing.

The police officer peered at the papers in his hand. He cleared his throat.

"The sentence for those in violation of Population Law 3903 is death. The sentence for falsification of documents by an illegal citizen is death by torture, Government's choice."

One of the autistic boys was crying. Luke could hear him across the room. Everyone else sat in deathly silence. Luke hoped that he'd at least have the chance to apologize to the other four. The police officer continued.

"The first illegal I have come to arrest goes by the name of—"

"Relax, Stan. I found him," someone interrupted from behind.

Luke recognized the voice. A second later, Mr. Talbot came into the room.

And behind him, with his wrists in handcuffs and his ankles in leg-irons, was Jason.

CHAPTER *THIRTY-FIVE*

The entire dining hall full of boys gasped.

"He was hiding in the nurse's office," Mr. Talbot was saying. "And the other one's over at the girls' school. Come on. I don't want to miss my golf game this afternoon."

"No!" Jason roared. Even in chains, he had a commanding presence. The police officer with the chestful of medals turned to look at him with something like respect. "I told you! I'm not an exnay. I can show you the exnays!"

Jason stepped forward, chains rattling. Mr. Talbot reached out to grab his arm, but the officer stopped him.

"Maybe he's right," the officer said. "I always love it when they betray each other. And I wouldn't mind getting a bonus for exceeding my quota this month."

Mr. Talbot shrugged and looked at his watch, as if all that worried him was showing up late for his tee time.

Jason hobbled slowly across the room, until he reached Luke's table. Luke felt faint. Everyone around him seemed to be holding his breath, too.

Jason pointed.

"Him. Antonio Blanco is his real name, but he goes by Samuel Irving. Him. Denton Weathers, alias Travis Spencer. Him. Sherman Kymanski, alias Ryan Mann. Him. Patrick Kerrigan, alias Tyrone Janson." Now Jason pointed to Luke. "And him. I don't know his real name, but he's pretending to be Lee Grant." He turned back to the Population Police officer, beseechingly. "And I know there are more. Just give me some time—"

Mr. Talbot started laughing. His guffaws rang out in the silent dining hall like bells after a funeral.

"Lee Grant an imposter? Now, that's a good one. I've known Lee since he was a baby. His whole family used to celebrate Christmas with mine, back when we lived in the city. Come to think of it, I've got one or two of those Christmas pictures in my wallet right now. Want to see them?" Mr. Talbot asked the police officer. He was already pulling the wallet out of his back pocket. "Hey, Lee, good to see you. Come look. Remember the year your parents made you wear the Santa Claus hat?"

Somehow Luke managed to make his legs carry him over to Mr. Talbot. Once before, Mr. Talbot had lied and said that he was a close personal friend of Luke's father's cousin. That was dangerous enough. Mr. Talbot could never back up this lie.

But the picture Mr. Talbot thrust at him was crystal clear. There was Mr. Talbot and three other adults, standing by a fireplace. Two boys that Luke recognized as Jen's brothers—Mr. Talbot's stepsons—sat on the hearth. And there, right between them, was Luke, in a flannel shirt and a Santa hat.

Mr. Talbot even flashed the photo in front of Jason's face.

"But I know—" Jason fumed. "He—I mean, I'm sure of the others. I'm positive!"

"Um-hmm," Mr. Talbot said. "I bet you just made up those names, trying to save your own skin."

Suddenly Patrick/Tyrone spoke up.

"He is, sir. My name is really Robert Jones."

"I'm Michael Rystert," Sherman/Ryan added.

The other two gave different names, too—Joel Westing and John Abbott. All four boys spoke in calm, even voices. Luke was stunned. What was going on? How could they possibly pull this off?

"They're lying! Look at their records!" Jason screamed.

"Good idea," Mr. Talbot said. "Is there a teacher or administrator who would be so kind—?"

At a far table, Luke's history teacher, Mr. Dirk, stood up.

"Just give me a minute," he said. Luke wondered how he could have ever found the man intimidating. He scurried out of the room like a mouse. In no time at all, he returned with four thick files. He handed them to the police officer. "Mind, please don't let any of the boys see. We like to keep their records private—"

But everyone was craning his neck, straining to see. Luke had the advantage because he was still standing next to Mr. Talbot. The police officer flipped quickly through the top file—Luke could see MICHAEL written again and again on each page. And in the next file, it was ROBERT, over and over and over.

"They're fake!" Jason howled.

"Aw, who could have faked these? In the two minutes we were standing here?" the police officer said in disgust. He threw the files down on the table and jerked on Jason's arm. "Come on. Out of here. Enough of your lies. We'd better go make that other pickup quick, or Mr. Talbot here will make me reimburse him for his lost greens time."

"But—but—" Jason sputtered, all the way out of the dining room.

And then he, and Mr. Talbot, and the Population Police officer were gone.

CHAPTER *THIRTY-SIX*

t was strange, after everything that had happened, that the boys could shuffle off to their classes as usual. The hall monitors watched as usual. Once the bell rang, the teachers cleared their throats as dryly as ever and began lecturing about integral numbers or laws of thermodynamics or long-dead poets.

Luke took his history exam that afternoon, as scheduled. He was surprised that he could pencil in responses about Hercules and Achilles, Hannibal and Arthur, heroes of the distant past, even as his mind raced with questions about the present. He longed to ask Patrick/Tyrone—no, make that Robert now—for an explanation. Or any of the others. How had they known the right names to say? How had their records been changed? How was it that nobody in the entire dining room had stood up to challenge their stories? And—who had betrayed Jason?

But each time he saw the other boys, they only groaned about their exams, complained about the school food, told stupid jokes. They acted like their names had always been Michael, Robert, Joel, and John.

Nobody mentioned Jason.

"Are we going to the woods tonight?" Luke whispered to Trey as they were leaving dinner. "To talk about—you know."

Trey looked at him as though Luke was speaking a foreign language.

"Guess not, huh?" Luke said, unable to just let it go.

Luke felt an arm on his shoulder just then.

"I'd like a word with you, young man," a voice said.

With all his fears from breakfast-time rushing back, Luke had to force himself to turn around.

Mr. Dirk, his history teacher, stood there, looking stern.

"You are Lee Grant, are you not?" Mr. Dirk asked.

The other boys stepped past him. Luke watched the doors of the lecture hall close before he could bring himself to nod.

"Then come with me," Mr. Dirk said, and turned on his heel.

Luke followed a few paces behind. So Mr. Dirk was going to tell him how badly he'd failed the history exam. So what? Luke remembered that, with Jason gone, there was no one to doctor his grades. But Luke had never cared about the grades.

"I'll work harder next term," Luke started to say. "I didn't even start going to your class until last week—"

"Hush," Mr. Dirk said.

Luke fought the urge to giggle. It was so ridiculous that, after surviving the Population Police raid, he was getting in trouble because he had forgotten the names of a few dead guys most people had never heard of.

Mr. Dirk walked past his classroom. Luke started to protest, but Mr. Dirk was walking briskly now. Luke had to hurry to keep up. Mr. Dirk walked right up to the front door and turned the knob.

"Isn't it locked tonight?" Luke wanted to ask. But he was beginning to understand that Mr. Dirk wasn't going to scold him about ancient history. He kept his mouth shut.

The door opened easily. Luke and Mr. Dirk stepped outside together.

Tiers of steps lay before them in the twilight. Luke remembered his trepidation climbing these very stairs, his first day at Hendricks. They didn't seem quite so imposing now, probably because he was at the top looking down, instead of the bottom looking up.

"Where are we going?" Luke couldn't resist asking.

For an answer, Mr. Dirk put a finger to his lips.

They climbed down the steps and walked along the expansive driveway. June bugs sang, far off in the distance. They made Luke homesick. Back on the farm, his dad and brothers were probably just coming in for supper after a hard day of baling. Mother would just be getting home from the factory.

It didn't seem right that Luke had just had one of the most terrifying days of his life, and his own family would never know.

"Watch your step," Mr. Dirk said.

Luke had been so lost in thought, he hadn't even noticed that they had turned, and were now standing in front of a small cottage. No—not a cottage—the small scale had fooled him. This building had turrets and arches like a castle, but was nestled so neatly behind lilac bushes and rhododendron and forsythia that Luke could have walked right past without seeing it at all.

"Ring the bell," Mr. Dirk instructed. He turned to go.

Luke was swept with panic.

"Wait!" he cried. Mr. Dirk was hardly a comforting figure, but at least he was familiar. Luke didn't like being abandoned in a strange place, without explanation.

"I trust you can find your way back on your own, when you are finished," Mr. Dirk said, and disappeared into the shadows.

There was nothing for Luke to do but press the doorbell.

"Come in," a deep voice called from inside.

Luke gave the door a little push. It was made of the same kind of heavy wood as all the doors at Hendricks. It barely moved. Timidly, Luke edged it open and stepped inside.

A dim room lay before him. Prisms hung from old-fashioned lamps. Wood-framed couches curved between oddly shaped tables cluttered with dozens of framed pictures. Luke didn't even notice the man in the wheelchair until he cleared his throat.

"Welcome, young man," the man said. He was older than either Luke's parents or Mr. Talbot. He had thick white hair that swelled above his forehead like a snowbank. He wore crisp khaki pants and a pale blue shirt—the

same kind of Baron clothes Luke had almost become accustomed to wearing himself. "Would you care for a drink?
Bottled water, perhaps?"

Luke shook his head, baffled. Questions swarmed in his
mind.

"George," the man called.

Mr. Talbot stepped into the room from the back part of
the house.

Luke's knees went weak with relief. Finally! Someone
who could explain.

"Mr.—" Luke began.

But Mr. Talbot shook his head warningly. He waved a
long bar in front of Luke's chest and his legs, then behind
his back. Finally he leaned back and announced, "He's
clean. No bugs."

"I hate all this technology, don't you?" the man in the
wheelchair said, leaning back as though Mr. Talbot's
announcement had freed him to relax. He stirred a cup he
held in his hand. Luke thought he caught a whiff of something like the chicory coffee his parents had sometimes
drunk as a special treat. "But now I can introduce myself.
I'm Josiah Hendricks. You know my friend here, I presume."

Luke could only nod.

"Sit down, sit down," Mr. Hendricks said. "No need to
stand on ceremony."

Luke noticed that Mr. Talbot, always so much in charge
every other time Luke had seen him, obeyed instantly.
Luke quickly sank into an armchair as well.

Mr. Hendricks sipped his drink.

"You are an inquisitive young man," he said to Luke. "You wish some explanations. No?"

"Yes," Luke said eagerly. He looked over at Mr. Talbot, expectantly. But Mr. Talbot was staring pointedly at Mr. Hendricks.

"Once I was a very rich man," Mr. Hendricks said. "I spent my money foolishly—who doesn't when they have more money than they know what to do with? There is a long and not particularly attractive story about how I spent my younger days. But suffice it to say that I was given reason to develop compassion by the time of the Great Famines." He looked down quickly. Luke saw for the first time that both of his pants legs hung empty below the knee. "I am not disguising anything for you tonight," Mr. Hendricks said softly.

Luke shifted uncomfortably in his chair. What was he supposed to say? Evidently, nothing. Mr. Hendricks went on with his tale.

"You know the Government was considering letting the 'undesirables' starve, do you not?" Mr. Hendricks asked. "When there is not enough food, who deserves to eat? The blind girl? The deaf boy? The man missing his legs?"

The anger in his voice was unbearable. Luke stumbled over his own tongue, ready to say anything to move the story along.

"Jason—I mean, the one taken away this morning—he told me about that. At school."

"Indeed," Mr. Hendricks said. He seemed lost in thought, then roused himself to continue. "My family—and I—spent millions on bribes, to convince the Government to have a heart. They left the disabled alone. And passed the Population Law instead." He frowned, stirring his coffee. "And how compassionate had I been? I saved my own kind, knowing that others would likely be killed. So I set up the schools. As penance."

"Mr. Hendricks foresaw what others did not," Mr. Talbot said. "He understood that hundreds of illegal children would be born, and hidden. And he knew they'd need safe places to go if they were able to come out of hiding."

"But I thought your schools were for autistic kids, kids with phobias, the ones who—" Luke stopped. "Oh," he said.

Mr. Hendricks chuckled.

"So my charade fooled you?" he asked. "Who can tell if a child rocks because he has autism or because he is terrified out of his wits? Who can tell if agoraphobia is caused by oddities in the mind or lifelong warnings, 'Going outdoors is suicide'? In the beginning, yes, I accepted children whose problems stemmed from other causes. I nurtured a reputation as a schoolmaster who would take on any troubled child. And when the first illegal children began emerging, they came here, too."

Luke tried to grasp it all.

"So everyone's an exnay? And everyone knows?" he asked. "The teachers, Ms. Hawkins in the office, the nurse, all the other boys—"

"Oh, no." Mr. Hendricks shook his head emphatically. "My charade is complete. I don't even know for sure which boys are which. I don't want to know. There is the possibility of—"

"Torture," Mr. Talbot said grimly.

"Those I don't know, I can't betray," Mr. Hendricks said. "And I hire only employees who seem uniquely capable of ignorance. Teachers so enamored of their academic disciplines that they can't even recognize the students who sit before them for an entire year. Administrative staff whose incompetence is of such towering magnitude that they can't input records into computers, won't notice when files are faked or replaced. . . . There's a certain charm to my system, is there not?"

Luke remembered how Jason's portable phone had disappeared, how the doors had been locked, how the files under his four friends' new fake names had magically appeared.

"But *someone* knows," he insisted. "There has to be *someone* who oversees it all."

Mr. Hendricks shifted in his wheelchair.

"Oh, yes. I have my compatriots. Mr. Dirk, as you probably suspect, has been useful upon occasion, although his knowledge is limited. I will tell you no other names."

Luke should have felt relieved to finally get an explanation. For that matter, he should have been ecstatic to have an adult at Hendricks acknowledge his existence. But all he could think about, suddenly, was how lonely and isolated he'd felt his first few weeks at Hendricks, how invisible. How low he'd sunk, that he'd almost looked forward to Jason picking on him each evening. He felt a surge of anger.

"You think you're so great," he said before he could stop himself. "Don't you know how it feels to be an exnay? And then you just abandon us, among people who don't care. Or can't care. It's a wonder we don't all run back into hiding."

"Oh, no," Mr. Hendricks said, seeming totally unruffled by Luke's outburst. "You were never abandoned. I can assume you have never been deep-sea diving, correct?"

Luke shook his head, and resisted the urge to roll his eyes as well.

"But you understand the concept?" Mr. Hendricks didn't wait for a reply. "When a diver resurfaces, he has to go gradually, so his body can get accustomed to the change in pressure. Children coming out of hiding need that, too. They need places to adjust to the outside world. Somewhere that their extreme fear of the outdoors does not seem out of place. Somewhere that they can act antisocial and not stand out. Somewhere—well, like Hendricks. And then when they're ready, they move on."

"You mean—leave?" Luke asked, his voice squeaking in spite of himself.

"Yes," Mr. Talbot said. "And Mr. Hendricks and I agree: The events of the past twenty-four hours prove that your time has come. You're ready to go."

CHAPTER THIRTY-SEVEN

"**H** uh?" Luke said. He had not anticipated that turn in the conversation at all.

Mr. Hendricks leaned forward.

"My schools had never been infiltrated before," he said, with a sharp glance at Mr. Talbot.

Mr. Talbot frowned apologetically.

"The Population Police have always pretended that it's impossible for an illegal child to get a fake I.D.," Mr. Talbot added. "But after the rally—" His eyes clouded. Luke could see the effort he was making to continue without emotion. "After the rally, all the rules changed."

"So you see, we never expected betrayal," Mr. Hendricks said. "In the beginning, yes, we tiptoed and looked over our shoulders. And, fortunately, we kept habits of . . . strong security. But we were not prepared for the Population Police to plant impostors in our midst, to gather names, to encourage indiscretion."

Luke frowned.

"But Jason—he said there'd been raids before. He said—"

Mr. Talbot had a sarcastic smile on his face. Mr. Hendricks raised one eyebrow.

"My dear boy," Mr. Hendricks said. "He lied."

Luke grimaced. He didn't like them acting like he couldn't figure that out on his own. But he'd learned a lot from Jason. What was true and what was false? He remembered one of Jason's other explanations: *You can't be too nice to an exnay . . . exnays need the kind of friend who can toughen them up. Like I did for you.* Luke remembered how many times Jason had made him claim to be an idiot, do push-ups until his arms collapsed, make a total fool of himself. Jason hadn't been trying to toughen Luke up. He'd been trying to break him down.

But it hadn't worked.

Luke didn't know why. He felt breathless, thinking about what could have happened. Suddenly he was mad at Mr. Hendricks and Mr. Talbot, sitting there looking so condescending.

"Why didn't you know Jason was an impostor?" Luke said. "You should have. He acted so different from everyone else."

"Yes, and so did you," Mr. Hendricks replied quickly. "Should we have suspected you of working for the Population Police, just because you liked going outside?"

Luke blinked.

"Yes, we knew," Mr. Hendricks said. "Just as we knew Jason, as you call him, was forming a club of former hidden children. We'd never seen that happen before, and frankly, we viewed it as a positive development. Until you showed us the truth."

Luke remembered how frustrated and frightened and alone he'd felt, only the night before.

"I didn't do anything," he said. "I tried, but nothing worked. Mr. Talbot deserves all the credit."

"You stopped the infiltrator and knocked him out. Then you took him to the nurse who, under the school's protocol, had to alert me," Mr. Hendricks said. "She thought he was just another former hidden child, going through some very unusual trauma. But when he muttered, "my phone, my phone"—she got suspicious. We locked all the doors and made a search of the entire school building."

So that's what Jason had muttered to the nurse, Luke thought. He was kind of glad now that he hadn't heard. He had felt panicked enough, as it was.

"Once we confiscated his phone," Mr. Hendricks continued, "we found out that the last number he called was the Population Police. Meanwhile, your call made George here suspicious—"

"Without spilling everything for the bugs on my phone, thank you very much," Mr. Talbot said. "Because of your warning, I had time to double-cross the Population Police's efforts. So we arrested two traitors, instead of six former hidden children. A good trade, in my mind."

Luke felt dizzy. No matter how many explanations Mr. Talbot and Mr. Hendricks gave him, other questions sprang up in his mind like so many weeds. Both men were watching him.

"Nina," Luke said finally. "Nina was the other traitor."

"Yes," Mr. Talbot said.

Luke thought about how, just for a second, he'd mistaken Nina for Jen that first night out in the woods. He'd wanted to like Nina so badly. He'd liked the way she'd laughed. But she'd been a traitor, too.

"What will happen to them?" Luke asked. "Jason and Nina, I mean."

Mr. Talbot looked away.

"Sometimes it's better not to know," he murmured.

That meant they were going to be killed, Luke thought. Killed or tortured to death, which was even worse. He shivered. Was it his fault? Was there some way he could have saved the other exnays without destroying Jason and Nina? No—they were the ones who had chosen betrayal.

"This is a cruel business," Mr. Talbot said. "Don't dwell on it."

In a corner of the room, an old-fashioned clock ticked quietly. Luke gathered his thoughts for his next question.

"But why did the Population Police believe you instead of Jason? If he'd wanted to, that officer could have arrested us all," Luke said. He remembered how careful Mr. Talbot had had to be, ever since the rally, for fear that someone might connect him with Jen. "I thought you were out of favor at Population Police headquarters right now. No offense, of course," he added quickly.

Mr. Talbot shrugged, as though being out of favor was as insignificant as a mosquito bite.

"I had the evidence on my side," he said. "They like

evidence. And I have to say, it was a stroke of brilliance to computer-enhance that Christmas picture, to substitute your face over Jen's." He kept his voice even, saying Jen's name, but Luke noticed that Mr. Hendricks bowed his head, reverently, as though giving in to a moment of silent mourning. Had Mr. Hendricks ever even met Jen? Luke didn't know, but he found himself lowering his head as well.

"Jen would have liked that," Luke said. "Using her picture to fool the Population Police." He swallowed what might have been a giggle. Jen would have been very amused.

"And what better way to remember those we love than by doing what they like?" Mr. Hendricks asked.

Mr. Talbot nodded, silently. Mr. Hendricks took over the explanation.

"And, young man, you do not realize the power of the name you have been given. Lee Grant. Your father—the father listed on your school records—is a very important man in our society," he said.

"But he's not my father," Luke said, more forcefully than he intended. "I've never even met the man. And I'm not Lee Grant."

Mr. Hendricks and Mr. Talbot exchanged glances. Luke wondered if they were deciding he wasn't so ready, after all.

"But you know how to pretend to be Lee Grant," Mr. Hendricks said. "That is what matters."

Luke shook his head impatiently. He'd suddenly had it

with all this double-talk. None of this was real, not the way planting potatoes was, or growing beans. It was easier to be a farmer, to know by looking whether your crops were good or not. Still, another question teased at the back of his mind.

"Why did they do it?" he asked. "Jason and Nina—why did they betray their friends? Their fellow exnays?"

"They were never your friends," Mr. Hendricks said harshly. "They came to Hendricks and Harlow schools with one purpose, and one purpose only: to seek out and betray all the former hidden children they could. They preyed upon all the exnays' secret desire to speak their real name, because the Population Police needed the real names to complete the betrayal. Jason and Nina had never been hidden children. They were just plants. Impostors."

"But the Population Policeman said they were illegals with false documents—" Luke said.

"The Population Police can lie, too," Mr. Hendricks said grimly. "It suits the Government's purposes to say they are arresting third children rather than traitors."

Luke tried to absorb this. Nina, who spoke so passionately about the third children's cause; Jason, who talked about protecting exnays at Hendricks—they had never been in hiding themselves? They only wanted to harm the ones who trusted them most?

This was a level of evil Luke never could have imagined before, back on the farm.

And now Mr. Hendricks and Mr. Talbot wanted him to

go to another new place, someplace even more challenging than Hendricks?

"With all due respect to my friend here," Mr. Talbot nodded toward Mr. Hendricks, "we don't really know how Jason and Nina came to work for the Population Police, or why they came to these schools. We're mostly guessing. They're just kids, after all."

"'Just kids?'" Mr. Hendricks protested. "You think only adults are capable of such villainy? Naturally, adults must have put them up to it, but—"

"I'll be interrogating both of them tomorrow," Mr. Talbot interrupted quietly. "Let's just say I intend to discover facts that my Population Police colleagues probably don't want me to know. It's likely that those two kids were offered substantial bribes for their work. Or"—he laughed bitterly—"maybe they were true believers devoted to their cause. Who knows?"

Luke wondered about that. Long ago, when he'd first met Jen, he'd wondered if the Population Law *was* correct, if maybe he really didn't have any right to exist, to eat food that might go to others. But Jen had convinced him that wasn't so, that everyone had a right to live. No matter what. But what if Jason and Nina had truly believed in what they were doing, even among their enemies—just as Mr. Talbot believed in what he was doing, double-crossing the Population Police, even as he worked in their headquarters every day?

Luke rubbed his temples. This wore his brain out even

more than the history test had. He wished everyone could just be what they were, and not have to pretend.

The clock in the corner began donging, giving off distinguished, silvery peals. Luke read the time effortlessly, without having to count dongs: eight o'clock.

"Well," Mr. Talbot said, rising, "you'll need to get your things out of your room before the other boys come out of—what do you call it? Indoctrination? And then I can drive you to your next school tonight. I'll tell you about it on the way."

"No," Luke said.

Mr. Talbot and Mr. Hendricks looked at him in bafflement. Then Mr. Hendricks chuckled.

"Oh, so you boys have come up with another name for it besides Indoctrination?"

Luke understood the old man's confusion. He could go with that, make up some silly name for Indoctrination, pretend that that was all he'd been objecting to. But it wasn't.

"No," Luke said firmly. "I mean, I don't want to leave Hendricks."

Now Mr. Talbot and Mr. Hendricks absolutely gaped at him, thoroughly aghast. Luke could tell what they were thinking: *We gave him a new identity. We gave him a place to hide. We saved his skin today. And now he tells us "no"? How dare he?*

Luke gulped. He wasn't so sure how he dared, either. Only two months earlier, when he'd left home, he'd been a scared little kid afraid even to speak. He'd had a borrowed name and borrowed clothes—nothing but memories to call his own. But those memories were worth something, and so was he. He wasn't some pawn to be moved across a chessboard, according to other people's plans.

Luke thought about what he'd accomplished at Hendricks—not just what he'd done to help outsmart Jason, but what he'd done making his garden, trying to make friends, studying for his tests. *Jen, you'd be proud,* he thought. He tried to figure out how to explain to Mr. Hendricks and Mr. Talbot.

"I'm glad you want to help me," Luke started softly. "And I'm, um, honored that you think I'm ready to leave. But I don't think I'm done here. When I came out of hiding I told my parents that I wanted to help other third children. Only, I didn't know how. But now I do. I want to help them *here*."

Mr. Talbot and Mr. Hendricks exchanged glances. Then Mr. Talbot sat down.

"Tell us more," he said.

CHAPTER *THIRTY-EIGHT*

The sun was barely over the horizon, but it was already a steamy day. Luke brushed sweat out of his eyes and pushed another seed into the ground. It was late in the season to plant a garden, but they'd had to wait until after exams. Luke could only hope for a late frost in the fall.

Behind Luke, four other boys clutched a sturdy rope stretched across the garden rows. One boy dipped quickly toward the ground, dropping a seed before he straightened up.

"Good, Trey," Luke said, laughing. "But it's easier if you open your eyes."

"I might see something that way," Trey grumbled. "Everything's so bright out here."

"Just smell, then," Luke suggested.

Trey breathed deeply.

"It's so fresh," he said in a marveling voice.

"Wait until you taste the peas you're planting," Luke said.

Luke was still surprised that Mr. Hendricks and Mr. Talbot had agreed to his plan.

"I never intended to run an *agricultural* school," Mr. Hendricks had grumbled. "Some of these boys are from the richest families—or supposedly from the richest families—"

"Then they need to know how food grows, as much as anyone," Luke answered, surprised at his own tone of authority.

Sometimes Luke wondered if he was just taking the easy way out—staying at Hendricks because it was familiar, growing a garden because that's what he liked. But the Population Law had started over food, so nobody could say that growing food wasn't important. Or maybe that was the problem—that people had started believing it wasn't important.

Luke watched Trey plant another seed, this time with his eyes open.

"This little thing is really going to grow?" Trey asked incredulously.

Luke nodded.

"It ought to," he said. "And it'll be yours."

He hadn't been able to tell Mr. Hendricks and Mr. Talbot how much longer he wanted to stay at Hendricks school. Last week's exams had pointed out plenty of holes in his education, and he knew now that he could learn here. And, no matter what, he knew it had to be good for the other boys to get outside.

"Are you some kind of a teacher?" one of the boys behind Trey asked Luke. He spoke hesitantly, like a little kid just learning how to talk. "What's your name?"

"Just call me 'L,'" Luke said, without thinking.

Now, where had that come from? It wasn't Luke, it wasn't Lee—it was, somehow, both identities at once.

Just like Luke himself.

Turn the page for a chapter from the next book

in the chilling Shadow Children sequence

Among
the Betrayed

Nina stood beside Lee Grant, pulling corn from a row of stalks.

"Leave the small ears to grow," Lee cautioned. "We only need enough for the feast tonight."

"Only?" Nina laughed. "There'll be twenty people there!"

"Forty ears, then," Lee countered. "That's not much. Back home, when my mom was canning corn, we used to pick—"

"What? Forty million?" Nina teased.

In the days since she'd been caught, she'd been staying at Mr. Hendricks's house with Percy, Matthias, and Alia. But she'd spent a lot of time with Lee and already listened to dozens of "back home" stories. She didn't know what it was like at Harlow School for Girls, but at Hendricks, boys were not pretending so much to be their fake identities. They were telling the truth more.

Nina jerked another ear from a stalk.

"Anyway, forget forty ears," she said. "If you're figuring two per person, that's only thirty-eight. I don't think I'll ever be able to eat corn again, not after the way you scared me in the garden last week, midbite."

"More for me," Lee said, clowning a selfish grab around all the corn they'd picked so far.

Nina wondered if this was how normal children acted—children who'd never had to hide. She guessed she'd have a chance to find out now. She, Percy, Matthias, and Alia were being sent on to another school, one where third children with fake I.D.'s mixed with firstborns and secondborns. That was why they were having a feast tonight, a combination of a celebration and a farewell.

"Given how things happened, Harlow School is probably not the best place for you anymore," Mr. Hendricks had told Nina.

Nina had had another flash of remembering that horrific canyon of eyes, watching her walk to her doom.

"I . . . I think I can forgive the other girls," she had said. "Now."

"But are they ready to forgive you?" Mr. Hendricks asked. "No matter how much you reassure them, how much the officials reassure them, there will always be someone who suspects that you just got off, that you really were working with Jason. They haven't . . . grown up like you have."

And Nina understood. She wasn't the same lovesick, easily terrified child she'd been at Harlow School.

That was why she liked talking to Lee now. He'd grown up a lot, too. The other boys looked up to him. They didn't even call him Lee anymore. He was mostly L.G.—and they said it reverently.

Nina still called him Lee. She didn't like too many things changing.

"Nina," Lee said now, slowly peeling back the husk of an ear of corn to check for rot. "Before you leave tomorrow, there's something I've been wanting to tell you."

"What?"

Lee tossed the ear of corn onto the pile with the rest. It must have been okay.

"I've been thinking about Jason," he said.

Nina stiffened just hearing that name. She might be able to forgive her friends at Harlow, but she wasn't ready to forgive Jason.

"So?" she asked.

"Well, I was thinking about what I heard him say on the phone to the Population Police that night he was turning everyone in. He made it sound like you were working with him."

"I know," Nina said. "That's how I ended up in prison." She couldn't keep the bitterness out of her voice.

In one clean jerk Lee pulled another ear from another stalk.

"But I don't think Jason was saying that to get you in trouble. He didn't expect to be arrested, to have you arrested. He meant for the illegal third children with fake I.D.'s to be arrested. I think . . . I think he was actually trying to save you."

Nina reeled backward, stunned beyond words. Lee took one look at Nina's face and kept explaining.

"Don't you see?" he said. "It wouldn't have made any sense for Jason to say you were working with him if he wanted to get you in trouble. He thought he— and you—were going to be rewarded. He was . . . he was maybe trying to protect you from ever being turned in by anyone else. See, if years from now someone accused you of being illegal, he could pop up and say, 'Nina? How could Nina be an exnay? She helped turn them in!' "

Lee did such a good job of imitating Jason's voice that Nina could almost believe. But only almost.

"Jason was doing something wrong. Evil. He wanted innocent kids to die," she said harshly. She pulled so hard on an ear of corn that the whole stalk came out of the ground.

Lee frowned but didn't say anything about his precious cornstalk.

"Yeah. Believe me, I was pretty mad at Jason myself. But I'm just saying—I don't think he was all bad. I think he, um, really liked you. And that was why he was trying to save you."

Nina stood still, trying to make sense of Lee's words. It flip-flopped everything she'd thought for the past few months. How could she accept Lee's explanation? How could Jason have been so evil yet tried to save her?

For a minute she almost believed. Then she remembered.

"Mr. Talbot had a tape," she said dully. "Of Jason confessing. And he was lying and saying it was all my fault, that I was the one who wanted to turn in the exnays."

"Oh, Mr. Talbot could have faked that tape," Lee said. "I've seen him fake pictures."

"But it was Jason's voice," Nina said. "I heard him. I heard the tape!"

Lee turned back to the garden.

"Go ask him," he said with a shrug.

Nina stood still for a moment, then she dropped her corn and took off running. Hope swelled in her heart. She burst into Mr. Hendricks's cottage and dashed into the living room, where Mr. Hendricks and Mr. Talbot were conferring.

"The tape," she said. "Of Jason betraying me. Lying. Was it real?"

Mr. Talbot turned around slowly, looked at her blankly.

"You had a tape," she repeated breathlessly. "In prison. Of Jason saying it was my idea to betray exnays, my idea to turn them in to the Population Police. Did he really say that? Or did you fake the tape?"

Mr. Talbot blinked.

"Does it matter?" he asked.

"Of course it matters!" Nina shrieked.

Mr. Talbot raised one eyebrow. "Why?" he said.

Nina had so many reasons, they jumbled together.

"If he didn't betray me, if he was really trying to help me—then he really loved me. Then Aunty Zenka was right, and love is everything, and the world's a good place. And I can be happy remembering him. But if he betrayed me—how can I think about the time we had together without hating him? How can I ever trust anyone, ever again?"

"You've believed for months that he betrayed you," Mr. Talbot said. "And you still trusted Percy, Matthias, and Alia. You've been acting like you trust Lee and Trey and Mr. Hendricks and me. Don't you?"

"Yes, but . . ." Nina couldn't explain. "Maybe I shouldn't trust you. You've lied to me a lot."

Nina was surprised when both Mr. Talbot and Mr. Hendricks burst out laughing.

"It's not funny," she protested.

Mr. Talbot stopped laughing, and sighed. "Nina, we

live in complicated times. I would have loved it if that first time I talked to you in your prison cell, I could have come straight out and said, 'Here's the deal. I hate the Population Police. What about you?' And it would have been great if I could have been sure that you would give me an honest answer. But—can you really see that happening? Don't you see how muddy everyone's intentions get, how people end up doing the wrong things for the right reasons, and the right things for the wrong reasons —and all any of us can do is try our hardest and have faith that somehow, someday, it will all work out?"

Nina looked down at her hands, still splotched with mud from the garden. She looked back up.

"Was the tape fake or not?" she asked again.

Mr. Talbot looked straight back at her.

"It was fake," he said quietly. "Some of our tech people spliced it together."

A grin burst out over Nina's face. "So Lee was right. Jason did love me," she whispered in wonderment.

Mr. Talbot and Mr. Hendricks exchanged glances in such a way that Nina felt like she was back with Percy, Matthias, and Alia.

"So that's enough for you?" Mr. Talbot asked. "It doesn't matter that Jason was trying to get other kids killed? You don't care about the evil he did as long as he loved you?"

Nina's smile slipped. Why did Mr. Talbot have to confuse everything again?

"No, no," she said. "That's not what I believe. This just means—he wasn't all bad. He's dead anyway. So I can . . . hold on to the good memories and let go of being mad at him." She wondered what had made Jason the way he was. She remembered how desperate she'd felt in the jail cell when she'd been so tempted to betray Percy, Matthias, and Alia. What if Jason had been even more desperate? What if he hadn't wanted to betray anyone, either, but had been too weak to resist?

It was odd to think of Jason as weak. She could actually feel sorry for him now. She could hold on to that forever, the way she held on to memories of Gran and the aunties.

"Nina," Mr. Talbot said. "Jason isn't dead. I thought they had executed him, but . . . it turns out that another faction of the Population Police thought he might still be useful. I've only recently found out that he's working for the Population Police in some top secret project. Something we who oppose the Government are very concerned about." He paused for a second, as if waiting for the news to sink in. "So, what does that information do for you? Are you going to rush to his side, to help him, because he loves you?"

Nina stared at Mr. Talbot in amazement. "He's alive?" she whimpered. "He's alive?"

Strangely, this seemed like bad news. If Jason were dead, she could go all misty-eyed remembering him, day-dreaming about what might have been, just like Aunty Zenka mooning over one of her books. But with him alive and working for the Population Police—"I have to stay mad," she said aloud. "I can't ever forgive him."

"Bitter is a bad way to live," Mr. Talbot said.

Nina remembered that he had lost Jen, that he had reason to stay angry at the Government forever. She sank down onto one of Mr. Hendricks's couches. This was all going to overwhelm her. She was just a little girl who'd spent most of her life hiding, listening to old ladies' foolish stories. Or had they been foolish? All the fairy tales Gran and the aunties had told her were about people staying true to what was right in the face of great adversity. She'd heard the wrong part of the stories if she thought she was just supposed to sit around like a princess, waiting for some prince to fall in love with her.

She looked straight at Mr. Talbot.

"I don't want to stay bitter. But I want to help you—what can I do to make sure Jason's project fails?"

Mr. Talbot almost smiled. Nina felt like she'd passed another test.

"We'll see," he said. "We'll see."

Nina went back out toward Lee's garden to finish picking corn. The sun was setting now, casting long shadows over the path. Just about every step Nina took alternated between sunlight and dark. Nina's thoughts bounced back and forth just as dramatically. Jason did love me. That's what really matters. . . . But he was still evil. . . . Why did I say I'd help Mr. Talbot oppose the Government? . . . How could I not have said that, after everything Mr. Talbot did for me? . . . What can I possibly do, anyway?

As Nina approached the garden she saw Lee waiting for her there. Whatever she did for Mr. Talbot, she realized, she would not be alone. Lee would probably be involved, and so would Percy and Matthias and Alia.

Nina remembered how alone she'd felt in her jail cell, all those months ago. Feeling abandoned and betrayed was worse than hunger, worse than cold, worse than the handcuffs on her wrists. But she hadn't been abandoned; she had only accidentally been betrayed.

"Well?" Lee said as soon as she got close enough to hear. "Was I right?"

It took Nina a moment to remember what he was talking about: the tape. Jason's betrayal.

"It's a long story," Nina said. "And it's not over yet."

But part of her story was over—the part where she was innocent and stupid and useless. She'd been so worried before that people might not remember her as Elodie—sweet, loving, little-girl Elodie. But she'd outgrown Elodie. She'd outgrown Nina the ninny, too. She was ready now to make whatever name she carried one that people could respect and revere.

Like Jen Talbot's.

"I think . . . I think I just volunteered to help Mr. Talbot and Mr. Hendricks fight the Population Police," she said.

Lee's gaze was steady and unfailing.

"Good," he said. "Welcome to the club."

—— THE MISSING ——

"Fans of Haddix's Shadow Children books will want to jump on this time travel adventure. . . . An exciting trip through history." —*Kirkus Reviews*

MARGARET PETERSON
HADDIX

FOUND
978-1-4169-5421-7
Available now

SENT
978-1-4169-5422-4
Coming August 2009

**FROM SIMON & SCHUSTER
BOOKS FOR YOUNG READERS**

ENTER THE WORLD OF

EREC REX

Books 1 and 2 in stores now

THE DRAGON'S EYE   THE MONSTERS OF OTHERNESS

And Book 3 coming in June 2009

THE SEARCH FOR TRUTH

Travel into magical new worlds with

The Chronicles of the Imaginarium Geographica!

HERE, THERE BE DRAGONS

THE SEARCH FOR THE RED DRAGON

THE INDIGO KING

THE SHADOW DRAGONS

Among
the Betrayed

If you purchased this book without a cover, you should be aware that this book is stolen property. It was reported as "unsold and destroyed" to the publisher, and neither the author nor the publisher has received any payment for this "stripped book."

This book is a work of fiction. Any references to historical events, real people, or real locales are used fictitiously. Other names, characters, places, and incidents are the product of the author's imagination, and any resemblance to actual events or locales or persons, living or dead, is entirely coincidental.

First Aladdin Paperbacks edition August 2003

Copyright © 2002 by Margaret Peterson Haddix

Simon & Schuster Books for Young Readers
An imprint of Simon & Schuster
Children's Publishing Division
1230 Avenue of the Americas
New York, NY 10020

All rights reserved, including the right of
reproduction in whole or in part in any form.

Also available in a Simon & Schuster Books for Young Readers hardcover edition.
Designed by Greg Stadnyk
The text of this book was set in Elysium.

Manufactured in the United States of America
30 29 28 27 26

The Library of Congress has cataloged the hardcover edition as follows:
Haddix, Margaret Peterson.
Among the betrayed / by Margaret Peterson Haddix.
p. cm.
Sequel to: Among the imposters.
Summary: Thirteen-year-old Nina is imprisoned by the Population Police, who give her the option of helping them identify illegal "third-born" children, or facing death.
ISBN-13: 978-0-689-83905-4 (hc.)
ISBN-10: 0-689-83905-7 (hc.)
[1. Betrayal—Fiction. 2. Conduct of life—Fiction. 3. Science fiction.] I. Title.

PZ7.H1164 Ak 2002
[Fic]—dc21
2001032214
ISBN-13: 978-0-689-83909-2
ISBN-10: 0-689-83909-X
0410 OFF

among the betrayed

MARGARET
PETERSON
HADDIX

SIMON & SCHUSTER
BOOKS FOR YOUNG READERS

NEW YORK   LONDON   TORONTO   SYDNEY   SINGAPORE

CHAPTER *ONE*

You were supposed to wake up from nightmares.

That's what Nina kept telling herself as she cowered on the floor of her concrete cell. All her life she'd had horrible dreams about being captured by the Population Police. Sometimes they carried shovels and scooped her up like trash on the street. Sometimes they carried guns and prodded her in the back or pointed at her head.

But she always woke up before anyone pulled a trigger.

Once she'd even dreamed that the Population Policeman who came for her was wearing Aunty Zenka's ruffled lace nightie, complete with a nightcap. For months after that dream Nina refused to give Aunty Zenka a good-night kiss, and nobody understood why. Nina wouldn't say, because then everyone would laugh, and it wasn't funny.

Nina knew she was right to be terrified of the Population Police. They were the bogeyman and the Big Bad Wolf and the Wicked Witch and the creep-show monster and every other villain she'd ever heard of, all rolled into one.

But like the bogeyman and the Big Bad Wolf and the Wicked Witch and the creep-show monster, the Population Police belonged in stories and nightmares, not real life.

Now Nina banged her head against the cement wall beside her.

"Wake up!" she ordered herself desperately. "Wake up!"

The banging made her head ache, and that didn't happen in dreams, did it? In dreams nothing hurt. They could flog you until your back bled, and you didn't feel a thing. They could tie your feet together so you couldn't run, and the ropes didn't burn at all.

Nina's wrists and ankles were rubbed raw from the handcuffs and ankle cuffs that chained her to the wall. The skin had been whipped from her back; even the slightest touch of her shirt against her spine sent pain shrieking through her body. One of her eyes seemed to be swollen shut from the beating.

Everything hurt.

But it had felt like a nightmare, being arrested, Nina told herself stubbornly.

She savored the dreamy quality of her memories, as if her arrest had been something good—not the worst moment of her life. She couldn't even remember the Population Policemen coming into the dining hall or calling her name. See? See? Didn't that prove it hadn't really happened? She had just been sitting there eating breakfast, rejoicing over the fact that she'd gotten three whole raisins in her oatmeal. And then suddenly the entire room was deathly quiet, and everyone was looking at Nina. She could feel all those eyes on her; she dropped her spoon. Oatmeal splashed on the girl beside Nina, but Lisle didn't complain, just kept staring like everyone else. And it was those stares, not the sound of her name, that had made Nina rise, and go forward, holding out her wrists to be handcuffed.

Which name did they call? Nina wondered. *Nina or . . . or—*

No, she wouldn't even think it. Sometimes in dreams the Population Police could read your mind.

Nina went back to remembering, remembering how the other girls sat like dolls on a shelf while Nina walked down the endless aisle between the tables. The familiar dining hall had somehow turned into a canyon of eyes. Nina did not turn to the right or to the left, but she could feel all those eyes following her, in silence. Those eyes were like dolls' eyes, as blank as marbles.

Why didn't anyone defend me? Nina wondered. *Why didn't anyone speak out, plead, beg, refuse to let me go?*

She knew. Even if it was just a nightmare—it was, wasn't it?—she knew that everyone would have been too terrified to make a peep. Nina knew she would have been too terrified to speak, too, if it had been someone else dazedly gliding toward the man with the medals on his chest. Someone else being arrested. (Why was it her? How had they found out? Why was she the only one they knew about? *Stop,* she chided herself. *Nightmares never make sense.*)

She remembered how hard it had been to keep her feet moving—up, down, right, left, closer, closer. . . . She couldn't protest or defend herself, either. Opening her mouth, even just enough to let out a whimper, would have released hysterics.

Please don't kill me! I'm only a kid. I didn't want to break any laws. It's not my fault. Oh, and please don't take Jason. . . .

Now, in her jail cell, Nina clenched her teeth, afraid that she might still let those words spill out. And she couldn't. Someone might be listening. Someone might hear his name. Whatever she did, she had to protect Jason. Jason and Gran and the aunties. And her parents, of course. But she could hold her tongue about all the others. It was Jason's name she wanted to wail, Jason she wanted to call out to.

Jason, do you know where I am? Did you worry when I didn't show up at our meeting place in the woods? You're so brave. Can you . . . can you rescue me?

She was being so silly. This was just a dream. In a few minutes the morning bells would chime, and she'd open her eyes in her swaying top bunk at Harlow School for Girls. Then she'd brush her teeth and wash her face and change her clothes and maybe, just maybe, get four raisins in her oatmeal at breakfast. . . .

She remembered her arrest again. She remembered

reaching the front of the dining hall, facing the policeman. At the last moment, right before the policeman snapped the metal cuffs on Nina's wrists, she had noticed another man standing behind him, watching Nina just as intently as all her classmates were. But all her classmates had gone glassy-eyed with fear, their gazes as vacant as dolls'. This man's dark eyes said everything.

He was furious. He hated her. He wanted her to die.

Nina gasped. She couldn't pretend anymore. She remembered too much. She couldn't have dreamed or imagined or made up that look. It was real. Everything that had happened to Nina was real. She had real handcuffs on her wrists, real scars on her back, real fear flooding her mind.

"They're going to kill me," Nina whispered, and it was almost a relief to finally, finally give up hope.

CHAPTER TWO

"**W**hy?"

The word exploded in Nina's ears, and she jerked awake. Then she jerked back because a man's face was just inches from hers, yelling at her.

"Why did you betray your country?" the man demanded.

Nina blinked. She was doomed anyway—why not argue? "Betray my country?" she could sneer. "What kind of a country thinks it's a betrayal just to be born? Was I supposed to kill myself out of loyalty? Out of patriotism? How is it my fault that my parents had two babies before me?"

But anything she said would betray her mother and Gran and the aunties—everyone who'd kept her hidden, everyone who'd kept her alive.

She didn't speak.

The man sat back on his heels. It was dark in Nina's prison cell; she thought it was probably the middle of the night. The man's silhouette was just a dim shadow in front of her. *He's a shadow and so am I,* Nina thought. She was still groggy enough that that seemed funny.

Then the man turned his head and murmured, "Now." Instantly the entire cell was flooded with harsh, too bright light from the one bare electric bulb overhead. Nina squeezed her eyes shut.

"I know you're awake," the man said softly. "You can't hide."

Nina stiffened at that word, "hide." He knew. Of course he knew. Why else had she been arrested? She thought she'd resigned herself to dying, but suddenly she was drowning in panic. Was this it? Was the man about to shoot her? Or was he going to take her somewhere else to die? How did the Population Police kill illegal children?

Nina opened her eyes a crack because it was better to see her killer than to cower sightlessly, expecting a gunshot at any moment. But seeing gave her another jolt: She recognized the man. He was the one who'd been there when she was arrested, staring at her with those hate-filled eyes.

Weakly Nina closed her eyes again. It didn't matter. She still had the man's image imprinted in her mind. He was tall and muscular and richly dressed, like someone on TV. His dark hair waved back from a high forehead. He looked powerful, just as Jason always looked powerful. But Jason had never once looked at her with such hatred.

Nina remembered something Gran always said: "If looks could kill . . ." *Looks can kill, Gran,* Nina wanted to say. *That look's going to kill me.*

The man chuckled.

"I don't care if you talk or not," he said. "Your cohort already told us everything. *He* cracked like an egg. I just thought you'd like the chance to tell us *your* version. Maybe your friend lied a little to save his own skin. To make himself look a little better and you, well, a lot worse. Guiltier. You know?"

The man was practically crooning in Nina's ear; his face was so close to hers that she could feel his breath on her cheek. Nina could barely think. What was the man talking about?

For a minute Nina didn't even understand the words he'd used—"cohort"? What was that? Then she remembered all the mystery novels Aunty Lystra had read aloud back home, on nights when the TV wasn't working. The detectives in those books were always accusing people of being "cohorts in crime." Cohorts were partners, helpers. Did he mean Gran and the aunties, who were cohorts in hiding her?

Nina barely managed to keep herself from gasping. *No!* she wanted to scream. *You didn't catch them. You couldn't have!* Tears began streaming down her face, silently.

But the man hadn't said "cohorts" and "they" and "them." He'd said "cohort." "He." "Him."

Nina knew only one him.

No, she corrected herself desperately. *I met other boys from Hendricks School. Just because I didn't really know them, that doesn't mean they didn't betray me. In fact, it makes it more likely that they turned me in.*

Nina thought about the guys she and her friends had sneaked out to meet in the woods at night. As a group, they were as skittish and timid as rabbits. She couldn't imagine any of them having the nerve to speak to the Population Police.

Except one.

No! The denial slammed through her brain. Maybe she even screamed it aloud. Even if you forgot that Jason loved her, even if you forgot that he'd kissed her, secretly, by moonlight—he was an illegal third child, too. All of them were, all the kids who met in the woods. Even if they wanted to, it would be too risky for any of them to betray her.

Maybe it's my father, Nina thought bitterly. *Maybe Gran was wrong and he did know I was born, did know I exist. Maybe he thought he'd get a reward for turning me in.*

Nina opened her eyes, angry enough now to face the hating man without flinching.

The man was smiling.

"Oh, Scott—or should I say *Jason*—had some very interesting tales for us," the man said cheerfully. "He made you out to be quite the operator."

Nina screamed. The sound echoed in her tiny concrete cell, one long wordless howl of rage and pain.

When she stopped screaming, the man was gone.

CHAPTER *THREE*

If morning came, Nina had no way of knowing it. She sat for hours, stiff and sore and heartbroken, huddled under the harsh light of the one bare bulb.

People always say that death's the worst thing that can happen to you, she thought. *It's not.*

She wished the man had just killed her and been done with it. She could have died—well, not happily, but at least with something to clutch on to, something to believe in: *Jason loves me. Oh, Jason, my beloved, good-bye!* In the time since her arrest, she realized, she'd begun picturing herself and Jason as the kind of tragic, star-crossed lovers who inhabited Aunty Zenka's favorite books and TV shows.

Gran and the other aunties always made fun of Aunty Zenka for liking those books and shows.

"Oh, give me a break!" Nina could remember Aunty Lystra complaining one evening when Aunty Zenka was reading aloud by candlelight. "Why doesn't the beautiful, vivacious heroine just tell Jacques, 'Hey, you've got incurable TB. Life's too short to hang around watching you die. Ciao!' "

"Because they're in love!" Aunty Zenka had protested. "And love is—"

"A load of garbage," Aunty Lystra finished for her. Aunty Lystra worked for the sanitation department. She was always comparing things to garbage.

Nina had felt sorry for poor, sentimental Aunty Zenka, who could get misty-eyed in the first seconds of one of her shows, with the first sentence of one of her books. But now Nina thought Aunty Lystra must be right. Aunty Lystra would think Nina had been a fool to trust Jason in the first place.

But he was so nice to me, Nina defended herself. *And he was so strong and handsome, and he knew so much. . . .*

For the first time Nina thought to wonder: *How* had he known so much? He'd known that the woods were a safe place to meet. He'd known about Harlow School for Girls. He'd known the exact right time of day to slip a note under the front door of the school, when the girls were walking to class. So a girl, not a teacher, would find his note.

Nina had been that girl. She lost herself, remembering. Two months ago, in the hallway at Harlow School, she'd scooped up a folded-over page that other girls had walked right past. She'd held the cream-colored, heavy-weight paper in her hand for a long moment, daydreaming about what it might be. She'd known it was probably nothing interesting, nothing that concerned her: a notice about electric rates, maybe, or a government edict about the size of spoons in the school kitchen. But as long as she didn't open it, she could imagine it was something exciting—like Cinderella's invitation to the prince's ball, perhaps. And since *she* was the one who'd picked it up . . .

The suspense had been too much. Nina had slid her finger between the edges of paper, breaking the seal. Carefully she'd unfolded the page and read:

> *To all Harlow girls*
> *who are concerned about shadows:*
> *Please join the like-minded students of Hendricks School for Boys*
> *for a meeting at 8 P.M., April 16,*
> *halfway into the woods between our schools.*

Nina had never heard of Hendricks School. She had never been in the woods—any woods. Except for the day she came to the school, she'd never been outdoors at all. She was a little worried about the word "shadows." Did it mean what she thought it meant? Was this dangerous?

But Nina didn't really care. She knew instantly that she was going to that meeting. She would have gone if the note had said, "To all Harlow girls who are concerned about hammers." Or "fruit flies." Or "pencils." Or "prehistoric civilizations' development of canals and aqueducts"—the subject she'd just ignored in her last class. Nina felt like she'd been waiting her entire thirteen years to receive this invitation.

Convincing her friends was a little harder.

"We're not supposed to go outside," Sally said timidly when Nina whispered her secret after lights-out that night.

"Nobody ever *said* that," Nina argued, trying to keep her own panic out of her voice. If her friends refused to go, would she have the nerve to go alone?

"They never said, 'Don't brush your teeth with toilet water,' either, but that doesn't mean I'm going to do it," Nina's other roommate, Bonner, argued.

Sally was tiny and golden haired, and Bonner was tall and dark and big boned, practically burly. Since Nina was medium height and medium weight, with medium brown hair, she always felt like the link between the other two. When they walked down the hall together, Nina was always in the middle. When the other two disagreed, Nina was always the one who suggested a compromise. Having both the other two oppose her made Nina feel a little desperate.

"Look, they want to talk about shadows," Nina said. Even in the dark she could tell that both of her friends froze at the sound of that one word. Harlow School was full of secrets that everyone knew but almost never discussed. At the beginning of the school year, when Nina was still horribly homesick, she'd amused herself by imagining Aunty Rhoda, her most practical aunt, materializing in the dining hall at breakfast or lunch or dinner, and marching up to the front of the room to lay out the truth for everybody:

"Fact: Every single one of you girls is a 'shadow child'—

a third or fourth or maybe even fifth child whose very birth was illegal because the Government doesn't allow people to have more than two kids.

"Fact: All of you came here with fake I.D.'s certifying that you are somebody else, somebody the Government thinks has a right to exist.

"Fact: Anyone with half a brain could see you're all pretending. Half the time the blond, Swedish-looking girl forgets to answer to the name, Uthant Mogadishu. And she's not the only one. All of you cower at any mention of the Government. All of you tremble any time the door opens.

"Conclusion: So why don't you all just drop the little charade and talk about it? Tell one another your real names. Talk about your real families, not the pretend brothers and sisters and parents you've probably never even met. Compare notes on how you managed to hide, all these years, before you got a fake I.D. Console one another about the difficulties of coming out of hiding, instead of lying in bed each night sobbing silently, pretending you don't hear your roommates crying, too."

But of course Aunty Rhoda was miles away, and Nina wasn't brave enough to stand up and make that speech herself. Still, with Sally and Bonner, in the dark of their room at night, she'd dropped hints, and they'd dropped hints, too. All school year it'd been like following the trail of bread crumbs in the fairy tale—Nina had never learned very much at any one time, but by spring she knew that

Sally had two older sisters and a house by the seashore and parents who were working with the Underground, attempting to overthrow the Government. And Bonner had a brother and a sister and a huge extended family of aunts and uncles who all lived in the same apartment building and took turns taking care of Bonner.

"They want to talk about shadows," Bonner repeated. "Right. So do the Population Police. What if it's a trap?"

"What if it isn't?" Nina hissed. "What if this is our only chance?" She prayed the other two wouldn't ask what it was a chance *for*—she'd never be able to explain. Maybe Sally and Bonner had never gotten to the point, in hiding, where they wanted to scream at the four walls around them. Maybe they hadn't read and reread and re-reread all the fairy tales where princesses were released from magic spells and evil enchantments. Maybe they'd never thought, even at Harlow, *Oh, please, there's got to be more. This can't be all my life is.*

"Look, you can take your I.D. card with you into the woods," Nina said. "The Population Police can't do anything to you if you have your I.D. card. And we don't even have to talk to these boys. We can just hide behind the trees and watch them. Just come with me. Please?"

"Oh, all right," Bonner said grimly.

"Sally?" Nina asked.

"Okay," Sally said in her smallest voice. Nina knew that if there'd been even a glimmer of light in the room, she would have been able to see absolute terror in Sally's eyes.

For once Nina was glad for darkness.

So they'd gone into the woods, clutching their fake I.D.'s like lifelines. But they hadn't just hidden and watched. They'd met Jason and his friends. And Jason had told them a wonderful story about a girl not any older than them, Jen Talbot, who'd led a rally demanding rights for third children like them. Jen had been brave enough to tell the Government that third children shouldn't have to hide. Jen had died for her beliefs, but still, listening to Jason's wonderfully deep voice praise Jen, Nina had wanted to be just like her.

But now that Nina had been arrested, it looked like Sally and Bonner had been right. The woods had been dangerous. The three of them shouldn't have stepped foot outside Harlow School. Nina should never have met Jason, never have kissed him, never have fallen in love.

"No!" Nina found herself screaming again. "No, no, no, no, no . . ."

CHAPTER *FOUR*

T he hating man came back. Nina stared at him coldly, her eyes like slits, her chin held high.

"You're the one who lied," she said. "Why should I believe you? You can say anything you like. But I know. Jason wouldn't betray me."

The hating man wouldn't meet her gaze. He glanced to the other side of her jail cell.

"Why haven't you eaten?" he asked.

For the first time Nina noticed a tray of food just beyond her feet. Two thick crusts of black bread, a smear of synthetic butter on each, were stacked on a plate with a small, wormy-looking apple. It was no worse than the food she'd eaten at Harlow, or at home.

"I wasn't hungry," Nina said defiantly, and it was true. But now that she looked at the food, her stomach rumbled.

"Right," the man said with a disbelieving snort. "Hunger strikes aren't terribly effective when you're condemned to die anyway."

He spoke so casually that it was all Nina could do not to gasp. So it was true. They were going to kill her. Fine.

But they couldn't make her die hating Jason.

The man rocked back on his heels and squinted at Nina, like a naturalist studying an interesting bug. For a while the Government had been big on the idea that everyone should eat insects, so they'd shown a lot of bug shows on TV. Nina had never thought to feel sorry for the bugs being studied.

"So," the man said. "Is Nina Idi your real name?"

No! Nina wanted to scream. It would feel so good to tell the truth now, at the end. Nina had always loved her real name, Elodie. Elodie Luria. When she was really little, Aunty Zenka had even made up a song about Nina's name: "You're just like a melody . . . Our little Elodie." Elodie was a fairy-tale name, a princess's name. When Gran and the aunties had scrimped and saved and finally gotten enough money to buy Nina a fake I.D. on the black market, Gran had come home and laid out the I.D. card on the table like a golden prize. Nina had tiptoed over and read the name, with all the aunties and Gran circled around like the good fairy godmothers at Sleeping Beauty's christening. Then Nina had begun screaming.

"Nina Idi? That's my name now? That's like . . . like Ninny Idiot! You want me to be a Ninny Idiot?" Even screaming, Nina had felt ashamed. That little rectangle of plastic was her ticket to freedom. It represented twelve years of Aunty Lystra wearing glasses she couldn't see through anymore, twelve years of Aunty Rhoda wearing the same coat, twelve years of Gran darning socks so many times the socks were more darn than sock. Twelve years of all of them living on stale bread and thin broth. Still, Nina couldn't help feeling that the precious card was her death sentence instead of her reprieve. If she wasn't Elodie anymore, if she was supposed to be this strange new person, Nina Idi, then she wasn't Aunty Zenka's little melody, she wasn't Gran's little sweetiekins, she wasn't the one beloved ray of sunshine in an apartment full of tired old women. She wasn't anybody at all.

Somehow, amazingly, Gran and the aunties had recognized Nina's screaming as fear, not brattiness. They'd all crowded around her, hugging her, comforting her, "You'll always be our special girl, no matter what. Even when you're away at that school. . . ."

And just hearing that word, "school," Nina had understood that Nina Idi really was killing Elodie Luria. Elodie could exist only in Gran's apartment. Nina was the one who was going to leave.

But now if Nina Idi was about to die, wouldn't she rather die as Elodie?

It was so tempting.

"That's not a tough question," the man chided her. "Are you Nina Idi or not?"

"You're the one who arrested me," Nina snapped, just to buy some time. "Don't *you* know my name? Maybe you didn't even arrest the right person!"

The man turned around.

"Guard?" he called toward the door. "A chair?"

Minutes later a guard appeared with a solid wood chair that the man slid into. He leaned back in it, obviously enjoying the greater comfort. Nina still huddled on the cold concrete floor. The guard left, locking the door behind him.

"I decided this conversation might be worth continuing longer than I wanted to spend squatting on your putrid floor," the hating man said, as if it were Nina's fault her jail cell was dirty. He leaned toward her, resting his chin on his hands, his elbows on his knees. "Now. Surely you realize my question wasn't as stupid as you imply. After all, the other criminal we arrested yesterday morning, Scott Renault, was masquerading as Jason Barstow, pretending to be an illegal third child who'd gotten ahold of a fake I.D. *Supposedly* he was trying to trick other illegals with fake I.D.'s into revealing their true identity so he could report them to the Population Police. Got all that? His story, of course, is ludicrous. Everyone knows that in this great country of ours it's impossible for an illegal to get a fake I.D. No law-abiding citizen would defy our beloved Government so flagrantly."

Nina stared back at the man in confusion.

"What . . . what was I arrested for?" she asked quietly.

"Treason, of course," the man said, almost cheerfully. "You betrayed your country."

"How?" Nina asked again.

"Hey, who's supposed to be asking the questions here?" the man protested. He answered her anyway: "You and this Jason—Scott?—what should I call him?"

"Jason," Nina whispered. "He's Jason."

"Okay. Whatever. You and this Jason tried to trick the Population Police into paying you for turning in a bunch of so-called exnays—illegals trying to pass themselves off as legitimate citizens. Just what I said before. Except all the supposed 'exnays' actually *were* legitimate citizens, some of them with very powerful and well-connected families. Just think if the Population Police had fallen for your little ploy . . ."

Nina stopped listening. She had never felt so thick-headed and stupid before in her life. None of this made sense.

"You don't think *I'm* an illegal third child with a fake I.D.?" she asked cautiously.

"Of course not," the man said. "There's no evidence of that. And if you were an exnay yourself, why would you betray your own comrades?"

Nina closed her eyes, afraid the man might see how relieved she was. She felt like turning cartwheels right there in her jail cell. *They don't know!* she wanted to scream. They wouldn't be tracking down Gran and the aunties, and her mother, to arrest all of them for hiding her. No one at Harlow School would get in trouble for harboring a fugitive. The Population Police wouldn't kill Nina for being illegal.

No. They'd just kill her for something she hadn't done. Treason? Turning in exnays?

Nina opened her eyes, gave the hating man her most indignant stare.

"There's been a mistake," she said firmly. "I never tried to turn in any exnays. I never tried to get the Population Police to pay me."

The man whipped out a little notebook and began to write.

"Ah, now you're talking," he murmured. "I knew you'd come to your senses and try to blame Jason, just like he tried to blame you. No honor among thieves, I suppose." He stopped writing but kept his pen poised over the paper. "So, what's your story? You gonna be the poor, innocent little girl who just did what Jason told you? It always helps if you cry during that one."

Nina felt like he'd slapped her.

"No, really," she protested. "I didn't do anything. And Jason didn't, either. I'm sure of it."

"So you can vouch for Jason?" the man asked. "His whereabouts and his actions, every minute of every day?"

"No, but—"

"But what?" The man was smirking now.

"But I *know* Jason. I know he'd never do anything like that."

"Just like you know he'd never betray you," the man said.

"Right! Exactly!" Nina said eagerly.

The man pulled a rectangular plastic case out of the inside pocket of his jacket. He twisted around again and yelled, "Guard?" Moments later the guard appeared and passed a metal box through the bars.

"Ever seen a tape recorder before?" the man asked Nina.

"No," Nina said.

"Well, that's what this is. We can record anything any-one says. On a tape." He held up the plastic case he'd taken out of his pocket. He slipped the tape into the recorder. "And once we've recorded something, we can play it back as many times as we want." He pushed a button.

Nina heard a whirring sound, then a voice. The tape was a little crackly and hard to hear, like TV on brownout days. But Nina still recognized the voice: Jason's. She leaned forward eagerly, as if Jason were really there and she could throw herself in his arms.

"And Nina said to me, 'Did you ever see those commer-cials on TV? About third kids and how the Population Police want to hunt them down?' She said, 'I bet they'd pay good money if we turned somebody in.' And I said, 'I don't know any third kids.' And she laughed and said, 'So what? All we have to do is pretend. We can turn in any-body we want. And we'll get a reward.' And I said, 'But that's *lying!* That's wrong! We can't do that.' But then she made me—you know how girls are."

Nina reached out and grabbed the tape recorder. She hurled it at the opposite wall as hard as she could. It cracked hitting the concrete; the tape crashed out when it fell to the floor. Nina strained to reach for the tape because she wanted to destroy it, too. But the man was quicker than she was. His hand closed around the tape as Nina's handcuffs bit into her wrists, holding her back. He put the tape back in his pocket.

"Now, now," he said. "What a temper." He pulled his notebook out again. "So can I put you on record as saying exactly what Jason said, only with the names reversed? 'And *Jason* said to me, "I bet they'd pay good money if we turned somebody in." . . . And I said, "But that's *lying!* It's wrong! We can't do that!" ' " He made his imitation of Nina's voice prissy and falsetto and incredibly childish.

Nina didn't answer. She turned her face toward the wall so the man couldn't see that she was crying. Vaguely a thought flickered in her mind, *This isn't a nightmare. Even nightmares are never this bad.*

"Do I take your silence for agreement?" the man goaded her. "But what are you agreeing to? That you want to betray this Jason you knew so well, the way he betrayed you? Or that what he said was right, and you're to blame for everything? Which is it?"

Nina forced herself to look back at the man.

"I," she said fiercely, "will never agree with anything you say."

"Hmm," the man said. "That's interesting. Because I was about to make you an offer that could save your life. But it appears you're not in the greatest of moods at the moment. Guess my offer will have to wait."

He stood up and took his chair and the pieces of the broken tape recorder and let himself out of her cell. Nina kept her head turned away from him so she could sob facing the wall.

But when Nina was sure he was gone, she looked back and saw that he'd left behind a white handkerchief, neatly folded, perfectly pressed. Nina grabbed the handkerchief and crumpled it into a ball, ready to hurl it at the wall as well. But a handkerchief wouldn't hit with as much satisfying force as the tape recorder had. A handkerchief would only float gently to the ground, like a bird finding a safe perch.

Nina looked around to make sure no one was watching, then loudly blew her nose.

CHAPTER FIVE

Nina ate the bread, too. She was disgusted with herself, that she could gobble up every crumb and eat the wormy apple down to its seeds. She should be pining for Jason, sobbing endlessly like some poor spurned heroine in one of Aunty Zenka's books. But Nina wasn't heartbroken anymore. She was mad. The food just gave her more energy for fury.

"I was a Ninny Idiot," she muttered to herself. "I deserve my name."

How could he? How could Jason have stood there in the moonlight, night after night, gazing into her eyes so lovingly, then turn around and do this? Had he been planning to betray her even a month ago, the first time he'd whispered in her ear, "Why don't we let the others go on back? We still have a few more minutes, just for us"? And then he'd held her hand and nuzzled her neck, and Nina had felt weak clear down to her toes. Even now she could still feel the sensation of his hand against hers, the pressure of his lips on hers. She had relived every kiss, every touch, so many times. Her ears could still bring back the sound of his voice, whispering, "I love you."

But he hadn't loved her. He'd told the Population Police she'd done something evil, and they were going to kill her for it.

Nina spit out an apple seed with such force that it bounced across the floor.

She'd made a total fool of herself over Jason. She could remember all those meetings they'd held out in the woods, when she'd stared at him adoringly and said stupid things. Flirting. She could remember one time when a new boy, Lee Grant, had started coming outside, too. Jason was telling Lee about the rally that Jen Talbot had held, to demonstrate for the rights of third children. And Nina hadn't contributed a thing to the conversation except to echo Jason, "The rally . . ." She wasn't capable of saying anything intelligent, because she wasn't really listening to the conversation, just watching the dim light on Jason's face, admiring his strong profile. Studying the perfect slope of his nose.

Idiotic.

Even before that, before the first time she and Jason kissed, she'd flirted in a different way, acting big, making fun of males. "Well, isn't that just like a boy!" she'd said probably a hundred times, with a simpering, stupid look on her face. She'd felt like she was acting in one of Aunty Zenka's TV dramas. All she needed was a ball gown and one of those dainty little fold-up fans to wave in front of her face whenever she said something particularly precious.

Ridiculous. That's how she'd really looked—ridiculous. How had she forgotten? She was a gawky thirteen-year-old with thin braids hanging down on either side of her face. Even if she'd had the ball gown and the fold-up fan, they would only have made her look sillier.

No wonder Jason had betrayed her. No wonder Sally and Bonner had inched away from her in the woods, like they didn't want to be seen with her.

Nina wanted to cry again, but the tears didn't come. Her heart felt like a rock inside her chest. Everything around her was cold and hard and merciless: the concrete walls, the cement floor, the iron bars of her door. She had thought she could wrap herself in her memories of being loved—by Jason, by her friends at Harlow, by Gran and the aunties. But Jason's love was fake. Her friends hadn't defended her. And Gran and the aunties seemed so far away and long ago that it seemed like it was some other little girl they had loved. Some little Elodie that Nina could barely remember.

Nina fell asleep, dry-eyed and hard-hearted, just one more cold thing in the jail.

CHAPTER SIX

"**H**ere's the deal," the man said.

It was the middle of the night again, Nina thought, blinking stupidly and trying to wake up. The overhead light was blinding again. She felt dizzy from lack of food. Two crusts of bread and one small apple—in what, a day and a half?—did almost nothing to stave off hunger.

"We think you can be useful to us," the man was saying smoothly. He was holding out his hand to her. Nina blinked a few more times and made her eyes focus. What the man had in his hand was too incredible to be believed: a sandwich. And it wasn't black bread and moldy cheese, the kind of sandwich Nina was used to, but a towering bun, thick and golden brown, with pale pink curls of—was that ham?—*ham* overflowing the sides. Nina had seen such a thing only on TV, on the forbidden channels that showed life before the famines.

"Here. Take it," the man said, waving the sandwich carelessly before Nina's eyes.

Nina had half the sandwich shoved in her mouth before she was even conscious of reaching for it.

"I see nobody ever bothered to teach you manners," the man said in disgust.

Nina ignored him. The sandwich was divine. The bun was light and airy and hid a slice of pungent cheese along with the ham. There were other flavors, too—the words from an ancient commercial flowed through Nina's mind: "Lettuce, tomato, pickle, onion . . ." Nina wasn't sure if that was actually what she was eating, but the sandwich was wonderful, absolutely perfect. She slowed down her chewing, just to savor it longer.

"That's better," the man said huffily. Nina had almost forgotten he was there. He handed her a bottle to drink from, and the liquid it contained was delicious, too, sweet and lemony. Nina drank deeply, thinking of nothing but her thirst.

When the sandwich was gone and the bottle was empty, she finally looked back at the man.

"A . . . a deal?" she said hesitantly.

"By law, we could have executed you the day we arrested you," the man said. "But sometimes even the Population Police can benefit from ignoring certain aspects of the law."

Nina waited, frozen in her spot.

"Oh, not that we would *break* the law," the man said. "Given the importance of our mission, there are loopholes written specifically for us. Say we have a criminal in front of us who might be rejuvenated to serve our needs. What purpose is there in executing her?"

"What," Nina asked through clenched teeth, "do you want me to do?"

The man shrugged. "Nothing that you and your buddy Jason weren't pretending to do anyway."

The words flew out of Nina's mouth before she could stop them: "Would Jason help me?"

"Jason, alas, did not seem as useful as you," the man said with an even more careless shrug.

"So he's—"

"Dead? Of course," the man said. "Swift and efficient justice, that's our motto."

Nina felt like everything was falling apart inside her. Her lips trembled.

"Now, now," the man said. "Don't give me any of that fake grief. He betrayed you, remember? Didn't hesitate an instant to stab you in the back when he thought it would save his own neck. Which it didn't, naturally. But I guess someone who would betray his own country wouldn't care in the least about betraying a mere girl."

Nina tried not to listen, but it was impossible. Jason had betrayed her. She remembered his voice on the tape, cold and calculating. She felt her anger coming back, and it was a relief, something to hold on to.

"Why did you think I could be useful and not him?" she asked, doing her best to hold her voice steady.

"I dunno. Maybe I can't see a little girl with braids as a hardened criminal," the man said carelessly. "Maybe I think the ones you need to trick would be more likely to trust a girl. Maybe I just didn't like Jason."

Nina longed to defend Jason, to yell and scream at this man that he was a fine one to be calling Jason unlikable. But it was impossible to defend Jason. Surely he had known that betraying Nina would lead to her death. *Why* had he done it? Why had he tried to trick the Population Police himself?

Nina didn't have time to lose herself in such questions. The man was talking again, explaining what he meant for her to do.

"We have a group of illegals that we've arrested," he said. "Shadow children with fake I.D.'s—"

"I thought you said that was impossible. Shadow children can't get fake I.D.'s," Nina interrupted.

"Well, not *good* ones. Not ones that would fool anyone in authority," the man said. "That's why these kids got caught. I wouldn't be surprised if these kids made the fake I.D.'s themselves. But they're not talking. I have a duty, to the Population Police, to find out who made those I.D.'s, if there's anyone else involved in this evil. And we need to know who's been harboring these illegal children all these years. They were all found out in the street, and they refuse to reveal their parents' names or addresses. You see our dilemma? If we execute the children immediately, other criminals—the ones who hid them, the ones who made their I.D.'s—will never be caught. But if we put you in the same prison cell as these kids, and you get them to trust you and tell you the truth, then you can tell me, and we can get rid of all the criminals. And society's needs will be served. Do you understand?"

Nina understood, all right. That was why she was shivering violently. Even her braids were shaking.

"And if I refuse?" she asked. Her voice shook, too.

The man raised his eyebrows. "You would dare even to think of that as an option?" he thundered. "If you refuse, you join your wonderful friend Jason. You die."

The sandwich that had tasted so good only a few minutes ago was now churning in Nina's stomach. How could she possibly agree to do what the man was asking of her?

But how could she *not* agree, and let them kill her?

Jason had betrayed her. Her friends had not defended her. It was the way of the world to look out only for yourself.

"Why would any of these shadow children trust me, anyway?" Nina asked.

"Because," the man said, "we'll make them think you're an exnay, too. Surely you can act the part."

Oh, yes. I can do that, Nina thought. *But can I live with myself if I get these kids to trust me, and then I betray them?*

The man was already standing up, brushing crumbs off his pants.

"So, it's settled," he said, as though the conversation was over and Nina had agreed to help. "We'll move you into their cell in the morning."

He turned around and walked slowly toward the door.

It seemed to take him a good five minutes to get his key out, put it in the lock, turn the key so the door sprang open. Nina kept telling herself to call out to him, *Wait! I won't do it! I'd rather die than work for the Population Police! I am an exnay! My name is Elodie and I'm proud of it. . . .* But Nina couldn't get her mouth to open, her tongue to move.

And then the man was out the door. He flipped a switch and Nina's cell was plunged into darkness again. She heard his footsteps echo down the hall, a lonely sound in the bleak prison.

I belong here now, Nina thought. *I am a betrayer. I am evil.*

CHAPTER *SEVEN*

By morning Nina was thinking about a fairy tale. But this time it wasn't one about a beautiful princess falling in love with a handsome prince. It was "Rumpelstiltskin."

I'm like the miller's daughter, Nina told herself. *The king told her she had to spin straw into gold or die. Given that choice, of course she didn't speak up and say, "Oops, sorry, I can't do it. Kill me." I'm not going to say that, either.* But the miller's daughter wasn't supposed to hurt anyone else. She was just supposed to do something impossible, not wrong.

What Nina was going to do was definitely wrong.

Maybe these other kids will be horrible and nasty, and I'll be glad to betray them, Nina thought. *Maybe they deserve it.*

She couldn't make herself believe that.

Nina was still sitting wide awake in the dark when she heard the door of her jail cell scrape open. A guard came over and yanked on her arm.

"Come on with you," he snarled.

"The handcuffs—I'm chained," Nina protested. "I'm chained to the wall."

The guard swore and kicked her in the stomach. Nina doubled over in pain. *This* was how the Population Police treated people who worked for them?

The guard stalked out of the jail cell and came back moments later with a key. He unlocked the chains on the wall, then jerked Nina to her feet. Nina hadn't stood in two days. Her legs felt stiff and useless beneath her.

"Come *on*!" the guard commanded, pulling on her arm.

Nina stumbled after him. They went down stairs and through long corridors, past dozens of barred doors. Nina wanted to peek in some of them, but it was too dark, and the guard was rushing her too fast. They descended a final set of stairs, and the air got clammier. Nina tripped and fell, and her bare knee touched standing water before she could right herself. She ran her fingers along the stone wall, and it was moist, too.

They were in the basement. Maybe it was even a cave.

They reached yet another door—this one solid wood— and the guard gripped her arm tighter. With his free hand he unlocked the door, then propelled her forward.

"And if you make any more trouble, you'll get even worse!" he yelled as he released his grip on her arm. Nina flew forward, landing in a heap. The door slammed shut behind her.

"Hello?" Nina called tentatively. She peered into the darkness around her but couldn't make out anything. For all she knew, the walls could be inches from her nose, or miles away. "Hello?" she called again. "Is anyone there?"

There was a rustling off to her right. Nina wondered if it was just rats or mice, and this was all a cruel trick. But in the next second a match flared in the darkness, and someone whispered, "No, I've got it. . . ."

And then a candle glowed. In the dim light Nina could make out two—no, three—faces. These were the kids Nina was supposed to betray. In horror she cried out, "Are any of you older than five?"

CHAPTER EIGHT

A ll three faces stared resentfully back at Nina. She had never seen such filthy, ragged children in all her life. After two days in prison—with her dress torn and blood-soaked, her face streaked with tears and dirt, her braid ties lost—Nina knew she wasn't exactly a fashion plate herself. But these kids looked—and smelled, come to think of it—like they'd been born in one of Aunty Lystra's precious garbage dumps. They had dirt caked on their cheeks. They had smears of who knows what dribbled down their patched, baggy clothes. Their matted hair hung in ragged clumps into their eyes. It was impossible to tell if they were boys or girls. Nina wouldn't even have been sur-prised to discover that they were neither, but some sort of strange humanlike animal she'd never heard of.

Then they started talking.

"We're *all* older than five," the one in the middle said. "We're just small for our ages."

The smallest one nodded vigorously. "Matthias is ten, Percy is nine, and I'm six."

"And what's your name?" Nina asked gently.

"Alia," the child answered.

Alia. So the littlest one was a girl. *How can I betray a little girl?* Nina asked herself. When Nina was six, her aunties had taken turns holding her on their lap, teaching her to read. Gran herself was in charge of math lessons, and Aunty Rhoda taught her how to spell. Nina could still remember how it felt to snuggle so cozily in an aunty's lap, in the big armchair, with a book balanced on her knees. No matter how cold it got in their apartment, Nina always felt warm, when she was six.

And this six-year-old girl was huddled in a damp jail cell, waiting to die.

"If you don't mind," the biggest one—Matthias?—asked, "I think we'll put out the candle now. We only have the one. But we wanted to get a good look at you."

"Oh, go ahead," Nina said, though she longed for light. Two days in darkness had been much too long.

"My turn!" Alia said joyfully. She leaned over and blew. The flame vanished. Nina longed for it to come back.

But in the darkness I can trick them more easily. They won't be able to tell from my face when I am lying.

Was Nina going to lie to them? She couldn't decide.

"So. Who are you?" an unfamiliar voice—Percy's?—asked in the darkness.

And Nina was already lost. Which name should she say? Which names had they told her—real or fake? She had trouble imagining anyone wanting to name their kid Percy. So they were probably still pretending to be the people their fake I.D.'s said they were.

"You can call me Nina," she said cagily. "But my real name is—"

"No! Don't say it!" Alia screamed.

"We think they might be listening," Matthias explained in a whisper.

"So what?" Nina said recklessly. "They're going to kill us anyway."

Somehow Nina could feel the shocked silence on the other side of the room. Even in the dark she could picture those three grimy faces agape with horror.

"No, they're not," Alia said. "They're going to find out we're innocent, and then they're going to release us."

Alia's voice was buoyant with hope, calm and confident. Did she really believe what she was saying? Was she that stupid? Just from the way the three kids had huddled together, in the brief moments that the candle had been lit, Nina could tell that Matthias and Percy watched out for Alia. Maybe the boys, not wanting a hysterical six-year-old on their hands, had filled her head with lies: "Everything's okay. They won't hurt us. We'll get out soon."

Or was Alia acting, for the sake of the Population Police they thought were listening? Maybe one of the boys had told Alia, "Act like you think we're innocent, and maybe they'll believe it." But could a six-year-old act so convincingly?

Anyway, how could they possibly think the Population

Police were listening? (Or *know*—if Nina told the Population Police everything, wasn't it like they were listening through Nina's ears?)

Nina rubbed her forehead. Everything was a muddle. How could she ever get these kids to trust her and spill all their secrets now? Did she really want them to tell her all their secrets?

I could find out their secrets and just not tell the Population Police, she told herself.

"How long have you been here?" she asked, trying to keep her voice casual, like she didn't really care but didn't have anything else to do but ask questions.

Nobody answered right away. Nina thought maybe they were whispering together on the other side of the room. Then Percy spoke up.

"We don't really know. It's hard to tell day from night down here."

"They've only brought us food three times," Alia said helpfully.

"How were you arrested?" Nina asked.

Again, it was a while before anyone answered. Nina wished so badly that she could see them.

"We were standing in line to buy cabbage. All three of us," Matthias finally said. "The Population Police came through the market, checking I.D.'s. They said ours were fake. So they arrested us—"

"But they're not fake!" Alia interrupted. "They're real, and the Population Police should know that. DO YOU

HEAR ME?" Alia's voice was directed not at Nina, but at the door. Her words echoed so loudly, Nina could barely hear the two boys shushing her.

Nina decided to pretend she didn't notice.

"Why haven't your parents come to get you out?" Nina asked.

"Don't got any parents," Alia said.

Nina noticed the way she'd said that—"Don't got any,"—not "Our parents are dead," or "We live with our grandparents," or "It'd be our aunt coming for us."

"Who takes care of you?" Nina asked cautiously.

"We take care of ourselves," Alia said hotly.

And this time Nina was sure the boys were whispering to Alia, telling her not to say anything else. A miserable lump filled Nina's throat. Filthy as they were, at least those three kids had one another. Nina wanted someone to huddle with, too. *If Jason were here*—

No, not Jason. He was dead now, and anyway, he had betrayed her. How could she forget? Remembering his hugs made her skin crawl; thinking about his kisses made her wish she'd punched him in the nose instead of kissing back. Why hadn't she challenged him: "You keep saying we ought to do something about third children's rights, something like the famous Jen Talbot's rally. So why don't we?" Nina could have exposed him as a fake, right then and there. She could have been a hero, like Jen.

Instead, she was about to become a traitor.

CHAPTER *NINE*

Nina fell into a miserable sleep because that was the only way to escape. Let the other three whisper together all they wanted.

She woke when a light flashed over her—someone was shining a flashlight in through the open door.

"Nina Idi," a bored voice called.

Nina stumbled to her feet. She glanced around and saw that the other three had fallen asleep as well, in one giant heap. Alia was cuddled in Matthias's lap; Matthias's head was on Percy's shoulder. The light didn't seem to awaken any of them. Alia turned so her face was against Matthias's leg instead of his arm. But her eyes stayed shut.

Nina squinted back toward the light. The person holding it lowered it toward the floor, and Nina could see better without the glare directly in her eyes. It was a guard behind the light, in the shadows.

"Come on now," he said irritably.

Nina thought it might be the same guard as before, but it was hard to tell. Maybe all the guards looked and sounded alike, so grim in their dark uniforms. Nina took a step toward the door, her chains clanking against the stone floor. She turned around, and all three of the other kids were wide awake now.

Nina hated the sight of all those terrified, round eyes.

"You're wanted for questioning," the guard said.

Nina took another step forward, but she watched the other kids exchanging glances. *As soon as I'm gone,* she thought bitterly, *Matthias is going to tell Alia, "See, that's why we can't tell her anything. She's not trustworthy."* Nina would have liked it if even one of the kids had mouthed a "Good luck" at her or flashed her a look of pity. But they all sat as still and silent as statues.

The guard grabbed Nina's arm and pulled her on out the door. But once the door was shut and they were down the hall a bit, the guard bent over and unlocked the chains from her ankles. When he straightened up, he took the cuffs off her wrists.

"You're setting me free?" Nina asked in disbelief.

The man snorted. "Are you crazy?"

But he let her walk on her own, beside him, down the rest of the hall and up the stairs. He turned to the left at the top of the stairs and unlocked a metal door. On the other side of the door there was carpet and soft light and cream-colored walls. It seemed like a different universe than the rest of the prison. It seemed like a different universe than any place she'd ever been. Harlow School for Girls had been nice, especially compared with Gran's apartment. But there had still been cracks in the plaster walls, scuff marks on the tile floor. Here Nina couldn't see so much as a tuft of carpet that wasn't perfect.

The guard must have noticed her awestruck stares, because he snorted again. "Officers' suites," he explained. "Nothing but the best for the top brass."

He led her into a room with a long wooden table, beautifully carved with grapes and apples and other designs Nina couldn't even identify. Nina sat down in a chair, and it was a kind she would have expected the president to use.

"Your interrogator will be here shortly," the guard said, and left.

Nina kept gazing around, blinking in amazement. On each wall portraits hung in elegant gold frames. And at the front of the room two windows stared back at Nina like giant eyes.

Nina didn't know much about windows. Harlow hadn't had any, for some strange reason. And in the apartment with Gran and the aunties they'd had to keep the blinds pulled all the time, for fear that someone outside might see in and get a glimpse of Nina, then report her to the Population Police. ("We're not missing anything, believe me," Aunty Zenka had assured Nina once. "Those windows just look out on an alley and a trash Dumpster. You've done us a favor, actually. How much better it is to look at those blinds and pretend that beautiful scenes lie just beyond—flowing rivers and glorious mountains, rose gardens and towering forests. . . . That's what *I* prefer to think is out there.")

But being seen presented no danger to Nina now. The Population Police had already caught her. Nothing worse could happen. Daringly, she stood up and walked over to one of the windows. Shrubs curled against the glass on the other side. It was bright daylight—something Nina had never seen for real, since it had been raining the day she traveled to Harlow and the day she left it. The sky was a deep, beautiful blue that made something ache in Nina's chest. Wispy white clouds sailed high overhead. And beyond the row of shrubs an expanse of grass sloped down to a lake and, just at the horizon's edge, a small woods.

It was a scene worthy of Aunty Zenka's imagination.

"Enjoying the view?" a voice said behind Nina.

Nina gasped and turned—it was the hating man. She stepped back from the window.

But the man didn't seem upset. He stepped forward and looked out, too.

"Not exactly what you'd expect near a prison, huh?" he mused. Nina wondered if he was just talking to himself. "You'd think, with a prison, there'd be high fences, lots of barbed wire, guards patrolling with guns. . . . And there are, back there, where all the prisoners are. But for this section, well, we officers like to see beauty occasionally. So much of our work is . . . brutal and ugly. You know?"

Nina didn't know if she was supposed to answer or not. After a moment the hating man moved away from the window. "Thank you," he said over his shoulder. He turned back to Nina. "Shall we dine?" he asked her.

Nina saw that while she'd been staring out the window, the guard had silently placed a tray on the table—a tray containing a feast. Roast chicken, platters of potatoes and peas, a basket of airy rolls . . . The man pulled out a chair for Nina. Nina remembered suddenly how grimy she looked—not at all the sort of person who should have a chair pulled out for her. Self-consciously she pushed hair out of her eyes.

"Now, now," the man said. "I'm sure you're longing for a good, long shower, but we do need to keep you in character."

Nina sat down. As if in a dream, she reached for a roll, ate the chicken the man placed on her plate, spooned peas into her mouth, swallowed rich, creamy milk. "This," she heard herself say, "is the best meal I've ever had."

"Well, there are perks to assisting the Population Police," the man replied with a chuckle.

Nina stopped eating.

"Full?" the man said.

"Um, kind of," Nina said, though it wasn't true. Nina could have eaten another huge serving of everything.

"Just a minute," the man said. He stood up and walked toward the door, and seemed to be conferring with the guard about something. Nina stared at the basket of rolls in front of her. The image of Alia's thin, hungry face swam before her eyes. She remembered Alia saying, bravely, "They've only brought us food three times." The man wasn't looking. What would it hurt if Nina swiped just a roll for Alia? She could grab three, even, one for each kid, and hide them in the sleeve of her dress. Nobody would know.

Nina remembered the way the three kids had stared at her when the guard came for her. She remembered how they hadn't said a single word of comfort or encouragement. She didn't reach for a roll.

Moments later the guard came in and took all the food away. The hating man settled into his chair across from Nina. He leaned back and put his feet on the table.

"Well," he said casually. "I understand that you haven't exactly been winning friends and influencing people. I'd wager that you don't have a single thing to tell me."

"You've been listening!" Nina accused.

The man gave a little snort of amusement. "Now, now. Mighty paranoid, aren't we? Of course we haven't been listening. That's what *you're* in there for. I'm just interpreting body language. Mack—that's the guard; you weren't properly introduced, were you?—Mack tells me that when he came to get you, you were sleeping on one side of the cell, and the other three were huddled together as far from you as possible. Doesn't exactly sound like you've all been palling around together."

"They're all friends together," Nina protested. "They knew one another before they were arrested. I'm just a stranger to them."

"Well, get unstrange, then," the man said. "Don't you want to live?"

Nina gulped.

"They're hungry and cold and terrified. They don't *feel* like talking," Nina said. Even to her own ears she sounded like a whiny child. "And they do think you are listening. They won't talk about . . . certain things because they think the Population Police can hear everything. It's hopeless!"

The man clicked his tongue in disapproval.

"I thought you were smarter than that," he said, shaking his head. "You have to make them tell you things. You work for the Population Police now. Act like it!"

CHAPTER **TEN**

Nina stumbled back into her jail cell to find the other three huddled around a burning candle.

"Alia got scared," Matthias explained. "She thought you might have been . . . you know."

Nina glanced over her shoulder, afraid that the guard might see the candle and take it away. But he was already slamming the door, locking it. He hadn't even looked into the cell.

"You were . . . worried about me?" Nina asked.

Matthias only shrugged, but Alia nodded, her eyes huge and solemn in her skinny face. Nina suddenly felt horrible that she hadn't snatched any rolls for the other kids.

"What did they want?" Percy asked.

"They just asked some questions."

"They did that to us, too, when we first came," Alia said. "They took us away, one at a time. But none of us said anything dangerous. Sa—I mean, we knew just what to say."

Nina heard that one slip of the tongue, "Sa—," and because the candle was still burning, she saw Matthias dig his elbow into Alia's side. To warn her? To silence her?

MARGARET PETERSON HADDIX

What had she almost said? "Sa—" Was it the beginning of someone's name?

Nina struggled to keep from showing the others how curious she was about that one little syllable, "Sa—".

"How did you know what to say, and what not to say?" Nina asked, hoping to make it sound like she just wanted to be able to avoid problems herself. "Did someone tell you?"

"Oh, we just knew," Alia said. "We're all pretty smart. Like, say you're a shadow child. Just pretend. If you're a shadow child, you're safe as long as you never ever tell the Population Police your real name."

"Of course," Nina said. "If I were a shadow child, and I had a fake I.D., I sure wouldn't tell anybody my real name. Besides my family, I mean."

But she had. She could remember one night when Jason had kissed her under the trees. He'd whispered in her ear, "You're so beautiful, and I don't even know who you really are. . . ." And the words had slipped out: "Elodie . . . I'm Elodie. . . ." It was her gift to him.

And look what he had done with it.

"Did you tell the Population Police anything about us?" Percy was asking. His question brought Nina back to the present, back to the cold, dripping jail cell and the six eyes staring at her and the horrible choice she was going to have to make.

"Just that you were hungry and cold down here," Nina said. It really wasn't even a lie. "And I told the man who was asking questions that you all thought they were listening to everything we said down here. He laughed and said that was ridiculous."

"Why did you say that?" Matthias asked furiously. "If they know we know, now we can't say anything to trick them."

Nina was getting confused, but she thought she knew what he meant.

"Well, it hasn't done any good so far, has it?" she challenged. "You're still stuck down here, and they haven't fed you, and they haven't even given you soap to wash your face!"

"They haven't killed us, either," Alia said softly. Nina stared at the younger girl. *When I was six, I wouldn't have known to say something like that,* she thought. *I was still a baby, playing with dolls and dressing up in the aunties' old clothes, pretending to be a princess. And I had four old ladies treating me like a princess.*

"I'm sorry," Nina said. "I didn't mean to do anything wrong."

But she'd let the hating man think she was going to spy for him. She'd eaten his food, and that was like . . . like taking blood money or something. She hadn't refused anything. She hadn't screamed and hollered and told him that the Population Police were wrong. She hadn't demanded that he set Matthias and Percy and Alia—and herself—free.

Nina bent her head down, too ashamed to look at the others.

A scraping sound behind her saved her from having to say anything else.

"Food!" Alia said delightedly.

The guard was opening the door. He tossed in a dark bundle, then shut the door and retreated.

Alia reached the bundle first. She grabbed it up and took it over to the boys. Matthias held the candle so they could all see in.

"Ooh, Nina, look!" Alia squealed. "There's one, two, three, four, five . . . eight slices of bread! They've never brought more than six before!"

"There's one more of us now, silly," Percy said. "We still get two each."

"Oh," Alia said.

Nina moved over with the other kids, feeling like she'd crossed some invisible line. She squatted down with them and peered into the bag. It held the same kind of hard black bread she'd had for her first meal in prison. There wasn't even any butter or apples to go with it. After her feast with the hating man she couldn't pretend to want this bread.

"You know what?" she said with studied casualness. "I'm not really hungry. Why don't you all take my slices, too?"

They all stared at her.

"Are you sure?" Alia asked. "I don't think they feed us every day."

"That's okay. You take it," Nina said.

They didn't need any extra urging. In seconds the three kids had gobbled up all the bread. Nina did notice, though, that Matthias had a strange way of dividing up Nina's share of the food: Alia got a whole slice, and Matthias and Percy split the other one. Nina's full stomach ached, watching the others eat so hungrily.

When they were done, they searched for any dropped crumbs and ate those as well. Nina hovered beside them, pretending to look for crumbs, too. Then they all sat back, happily sated. Nina sat down beside Alia, and Alia leaned over and gave her a big hug.

"Thanks, Nina. I hope you don't get hungry later. I think that was the best meal I ever had."

Nina could have brought Alia fresh, beautiful rolls, but she hadn't. Instead, she'd let the little girl have old, moldy, practically inedible black bread just because Nina herself was too full of the Population Police's fine meal to pretend to want it. And now Alia was thanking her.

Nina felt guiltier than ever.

CHAPTER *ELEVEN*

Days passed. Nina had no idea how many, because nothing happened with any regularity. Sometimes the guard brought food; sometimes the guard pulled one of them out for questioning. Sometimes Matthias decided they could light the candle for a few minutes—but only for Alia, only when he thought she needed it.

Nobody knew when any of those things would happen.

Other than that, they could measure their time in the prison-cave only by how many times they got sleepy or thirsty or needed to go to the bathroom.

None of those needs were easily satisfied.

Their "bathroom" was just a corner of the cave they all avoided as much as they could. It stank mightily.

They had no bedding at all, not a single pillow or blanket. Sleeping on wet rock only left Nina damp and stiff and more tired than ever.

And when they were thirsty, they had to go to the dampest part of the cave and lick the wall. The guard never brought water. Matthias got the idea to keep one of the cloth bags the food had come in, in order to soak up as much water as possible. (He told the guard they'd dropped the bag over in the bathroom corner. "He won't come in here and check," he argued in a barely audible whisper. And he was right.) Matthias put the bag at the bottom of the damp wall, where the water dripped constantly. When the bag was saturated, he carefully squeezed the water from the wet cloth into Alia's waiting mouth, and then Percy's, and then a few precious drops into Nina's. Nina choked and spit it out.

"Yu-uck!" she screamed.

"What?" Alia asked.

"It tastes terrible," Nina complained. The water was unpleasant enough licked straight from the wall—it tasted like rock and sulfur and, distantly, some kind of chemical Nina couldn't identify. But from the cloth bag the water tasted like rock and moldy bread and old, rotting, dirty bag. Maybe even somebody else's vomit as well.

"It's water," Matthias said. "It'll keep us alive."

Nina didn't say anything else. But after that, she went back to getting her water straight from the wall, a drop or two at a time, and let the others squeeze all the water from the cloth for themselves.

Nina suspected that the other three kids had had a much rougher life than she before they were captured by the Population Police. They didn't seem to mind the darkness like she did; they didn't seem to mind the lack of food. They didn't complain about the stench of the bathroom corner. (Well, they all smelled bad themselves anyway. So did Nina.)

Nina tried as much as possible to sit close to the other kids—for body warmth and to keep the guard from tattling on her again. And maybe to learn something. But several times she woke up from a deep sleep and found that they'd moved to another side of the room and were whispering together.

"There was a draft over there," Alia would say. "We got cold, but you looked comfortable. We didn't want to wake you."

It sounded so innocent. Maybe it was innocent. But it still made Nina mad.

I will betray them, *she'd think.* That'll show them. And I won't care at all.

That was when she'd moan something like, "Oh, I miss my family so bad. Who do you miss?"

Even Alia wouldn't answer a question like that.

And later, facing the hating man, Nina would be glad for the other kids' silence. Because, with his piercing blue eyes glaring at her, she knew she wouldn't be able to keep any secrets. She felt like he knew she really was an exnay. She felt like, if he asked, she'd be forced to tell him Gran's full name and address. Whether she wanted to or not, she'd describe every single one of her aunties down to their last gray hair, and give their civil service ranks and departments.

Fortunately, he never asked about who had hidden her.

He just asked about Alia, about Percy, about Matthias.

"Give me more time," Nina would beg. "I don't know them yet." (Though, secretly, Nina thought she could spend centuries in the prison-cave with them and still not know anything about them. Percy was like a rock, hard and unyielding, revealing nothing. Matthias was no more talkative than a tree. Even Alia, who looked like the weak spot on their team of three, was quiet more and more, polite and nothing else.)

"Time? You've been in there for days," the hating man ranted back during one interrogation session in the middle of the night. "How long does it take to say, 'My parents are so-and-so. What are your parents' names?'"

For one terrifying instant Nina thought he really was asking her her parents' names. Against her will her lips began to pucker together to form the first syllable of her mother's name. *Rita. My mother's name is Rita. My father's name is Lou. Gran's name is Ethel. And I am . . .*

Nina bit down hard, trapping all those words in her mouth. The hating man didn't seem to notice. He was pacing, facing away from her. He continued fuming.

"Even first names would help. Even initials. You've got to give me something."

He hadn't been asking her her parents' names. He'd merely been telling her the question she was supposed to ask the others. Nina's heart pounded out a panicky rhythm that made it hard for her to think.

What if . . . what if he doesn't care about my parents'

names because he already knows them? What if he already knows about Gran and the aunties? Is that why he never asks?

Nina frantically tried to remember if she'd ever breathed a word about any of her family to Jason. She hadn't, had she? Talking to Jason, she'd wanted to seem exotic and desirable. A grandmother and a bunch of old-maid aunts didn't really fit that image.

The hating man was done pacing. He whirled on his heel, put his face right up against Nina's. They were eye to eye, nose to nose.

"You cannot play around with the Population Police, little girl," he said. "That's how people die."

Nina quivered.

The man stalked out and slammed the door behind him.

Nina sat alone, terrified, in the luxurious interrogation room. The table in front of her was loaded down with bowls of food. She'd been eating ravenously during their conversation. Perhaps because it was the middle of the night, instead of midday, the foods were snacks, not a real meal, mostly things Nina had never tasted before: popcorn, peanuts in their salty shells, orange cheese crackers, raisins in delicate little boxes. Nina was still starving—she was always starving, she couldn't think of a single time in her entire life when she'd had her belly completely full. But she couldn't bring herself to eat another bite, not with the hating man's threat echoing in her ears. Still, she found herself reaching out for the bowl of peanuts. She watched her own hands lift the bowl and pour its contents down the front of her dress, making a bag of her bodice. She cinched her belt tighter, holding the peanuts in at her waist. She'd barely finished when the guard opened the door.

"He's done with you early, I hear," the guard growled. "Back to the cell with you."

Nina stood slowly. None of the peanuts fell out. She crossed her arms and held them tightly at her waist, keeping the belt in place. She took a step, and then another, and nothing happened. The peanut shells tickled, but Nina didn't care.

I'm stealing food from the Population Police! Nina thought. *I'm getting away with it!*

Walking back to her cell, Nina did not feel like a girl who'd nearly betrayed her parents, whose beloved Gran and aunties might be in danger. She did not feel like an illegal child, with no right to live. She did not feel like a lovesick, silly teenager who'd been betrayed by the boy she'd fallen for. She did not feel like a potential traitor to her own kind.

She felt giddy and hopeful, crafty and capable. All because of the rustle of peanut shells under her dress.

CHAPTER TWELVE

Nina kept stealing food.

Invariably, during every meeting with the hating man there came a time when he'd leave the room briefly—to confer with the guard, to go to the bathroom, to get a new pen. And then Nina would grab whatever food was nearest and stuff it down her dress, in her socks, wherever she could. She took apples, oranges, biscuits, raisins. She took dried bananas, unshelled walnuts, cereal boxes, oatmeal bars still in their wrappers. She stole another of the bags the guard brought black bread in, and took to carrying it around with her, tied under her dress, so she could swipe even more food each time.

The problem was, she didn't know what to do with the food she stole.

She was hungry. She could easily have eaten it all herself. But once she was back in her jail cell with the other three, her stomach squeezed together at the thought of eating so much as a crumb of the stolen food. What if they heard her chewing? How could she eat such delicacies while they were starving, right there beside her? (How could she eat any of the Population Police's food when the other three were starving?)

She did think about sharing. That was probably why she'd reached for the bowl of peanuts in the first place, because she felt so guilty about not taking the rolls for Alia. But how could she explain where she'd gotten all that food?

An evil thought crept into her mind one night when the guard shoved her back into her cell and she saw the other three cuddled together. Nina sat down beside them and leaned into Alia, and Alia squirmed away in her sleep, closer to Matthias. The ground was wet and hard, and Nina was freezing. Everything seemed hopeless; Nina didn't care what happened to anyone else as long as *she* got warm, as long as *she* got dry clothes, as long as *she* got out of jail. *I could use the food,* she thought. *Like a bribe. I could tell them they can have as much as they want to eat, as long as they tell me their secrets. No—I'd dole it out, a peanut at a time, a raisin at a time, with every one of my questions. Who's "Sa-"? Where'd you get your I.D.'s? Who else should have been arrested with you?*

Nina didn't do it. She just kept stealing food she couldn't eat, couldn't give away, couldn't use. She felt like she'd been in prison forever and she would stay in prison forever. She saw nothing ahead of her but more nights sleeping in damp, filthy clothes on cold, hard rock, more days trying to overhear the others' whispers, more randomly spaced trips to the hating man's room, where he yelled at her and gave her food she could not eat, only steal.

Then one day he cut her off.

"You have twenty-four hours," the hating man barked at her. "That's it."

Nina stared back at him, her brain struggling to comprehend. She'd practically forgotten that twenty-four hours made a day—that there were things such as numbers and counted-off hours in the world.

"You mean . . . ," she said, more puzzled than terrified.

"If you do not tell me everything I need to know by"— he looked at the watch on his wrist—"by ten-oh-five tomorrow night, you will be executed. You and the three exnays."

Nina waited for the terror to come, but she was too numb. And then she was too distracted. Mack, the guard, was pounding at the door to their meeting room. The hating man opened it, and Mack stumbled in, slumping against the table. Nina saw he still clutched the ring of keys he always used to get her in and out of her cell. His long arms hit the wood hard. Then his fingers released, and the keys went sliding across the table and onto the floor.

"Poi—," Mack gulped. "Poisoned . . ."

The hating man sprang up and grabbed a phone, punching numbers with amazing speed. "Ambulance to the Population Police headquarters immediately!" he demanded. "One of our guards has been poisoned."

He dragged Mack out into the hall, Mack's feet bouncing against the floor. "Stay with me, Mack," the hating man muttered. "They're coming to help you."

"Unnhh," Mack groaned.

Both of them seemed to have forgotten Nina. Nina looked down and saw the guard's key ring on the floor, just to the left of her chair. All the keys stuck out at odd angles. Slowly, carelessly, as if it were nothing more than just another stray peanut shell, Nina bent down and picked up the whole ring.

CHAPTER *THIRTEEN*

ina slipped the ring of keys around her left wrist and pushed it up her arm—farther, farther—until the ring stayed in place on its own. The points of the keys bit into her arm, but it wasn't an entirely unpleasant sensation. It woke her up.

I have keys.

I have food.

I have twenty-four hours.

I need a plan.

The hating man strode back into the room. Nina didn't have the slightest idea how long he'd been gone. Maybe she'd been sitting there fingering the keys through her sleeve for hours.

"I can't believe this!" the man fumed. "Mack's—I've got someone else with Mack now. I'll take you back to your cell. Come on! I want to get back here as soon as I can. . . ."

Nina stood up, feeling the full weight of the food bag tied around her waist, the pinch of every individual key around her arm. As slowly as she dared, she circled the table toward the hating man. He grabbed her arm—her right one, fortunately—and pulled.

"Don't know what this world's coming to," the man muttered as they came to the door from the luxurious hallway into the rest of the prison. Nina held her breath. Would he realize now that he needed Mack's keys?

No—he was pulling keys of his own out of his jacket pocket, jamming a key into the lock, jerking the key around, jabbering the whole time. "Mack's a good, honest man, got kids of his own—I don't know why . . ."

They were at another door. The man unlocked this one, too, with barely a pause.

Down the stairs, through another door—the man hustled Nina all the way. Nina was daring to breathe again. Then they reached the door of Nina's cell.

The hating man stopped, stared at his key ring.

"Wouldn't you know it!" he grumbled. "I'm missing this key. I'll have to go back for it."

He glanced around toward the door they'd just come through. The disgust and impatience played over his face so clearly, Nina felt like she could read his mind: *Now I'll have to go all the way back upstairs, take this nasty girl with me, then come back down here into this muck.* Yes, that had to be what he was thinking. He even raised his foot distastefully to look at the mud on the bottom of his polished shoe. *And I don't want to have to think about this useless kid anymore, I just want to go check on poor Mack—*

"Tell you what," the hating man said. "I'm not even going to put you in the cell. I'll just leave you in this hall. There isn't anyone else in this wing right now anyway, and that door will be locked tight. . . ." He spoke as though it were Nina, not he, who might worry that she wouldn't be imprisoned well enough. "The morning guard can put you back in your cell when he comes through on his eight A.M. rounds."

He was already going back through the other door. "Can't be helped," he muttered, and shut the door in Nina's face.

Nina stood beside the solid metal door and put her finger over the keyhole. One of the keys on Mack's key ring fit into that hole. She was sure of it. If the hating man had put her back in her cell, the keys would have done her no good; the door of the prison cell couldn't be unlocked from the inside.

But she had keys to all the doors between her and the interrogation room, with its windows to the outside.

She had keys, she had food—she could escape.

CHAPTER *FOURTEEN*

Nina blindly poked keys into the keyhole, searching for the right one. The only light in the hallway was a dim, dirty bulb, several yards away, so she had trouble just keeping track of which keys she'd already tried and which keys she hadn't. It was also hard trying to keep the rest of the key ring from banging on the metal door while she was turning each individual key. She was sure she had to work silently. But why? Surely the hating man was already upstairs, hovering over the poisoned Mack. And he'd said there were no other prisoners down here. Except Percy, Matthias, and Alia, of course.

Percy, Matthias, and Alia.

It was strange, but Nina had not thought about them even once since that first moment her fingers closed around the guard's key ring. She'd forgotten they existed. All she'd thought about were the keys, the keyholes, her own life.

Percy, Matthias, and Alia.

Thinking about them now made Nina drop the whole ring of keys. It clattered to the stone floor and slid several inches. The sound seemed to bounce all around in Nina's ears, as though she'd dropped a thousand keys on a thousand floors. She half wished one of the three kids—Percy, Matthias, or Alia—would pound on their cell door, yell out, "Hey! What's going on out there?"

Because then Nina would have to talk to them, have to face them, have to look into their eyes while she decided, *Should I ask them to come with me?*

But none of them pounded on the door, none of them called out to her. She shouldn't have expected them to. If they had even heard the noise of the keys through the heavy wood door, they probably just assumed it was a guard making a little more racket than usual. Whether they heard the noise or not, they would have stayed cowering together in their little corner of the cell. In prison it was foolish to call attention to yourself.

In prison it was foolish to think about anyone but yourself.

Nina still didn't bend over to pick up the keys. Not yet.

Ever since the hating man had told her, days ago, "Here's the deal," she'd been avoiding any decisions. She'd lain down in filth, she'd stumbled along behind the guard, she'd sat with her head bowed while the hating man harangued her. But she hadn't done anything to harm Percy, Matthias, and Alia. She hadn't exactly done anything to help them, either—she'd sat precisely in the middle of a perfectly balanced scale.

But now it was time to tip the scale. She had to choose.

If Nina left on her own, without a single look back,

she'd be sending Percy, Matthias, and Alia to their death. Hadn't the hating man said he was going to kill them all if he didn't get the information he needed by ten o'clock the next night? In her heart of hearts Nina knew that that "if" helped only her—if Percy, Matthias, and Alia were still in their jail cell tomorrow, he'd kill them.

But I don't have that much food, Nina thought. *It'd be harder for four kids to hide out, traveling to safety, than just one. And Alia's so little. She probably can't walk very fast at all, and I need to walk as far as possible tonight, before anyone discovers I'm gone. One way or another, those kids are going to die. Taking them with me would just mean that I die, too.*

Nina thought about Jason betraying her, about all her friends just staring when the Population Police came to arrest her. *Nobody helped me!* she wanted to yell at that small, stubborn part of herself that refused just to pick up the keys and go. But then she thought about Gran, Aunty Zenka, Aunty Lystra, and Aunty Rhoda, four old ladies who could have enjoyed the few small luxuries they could afford on their old-age pensions. They'd kept working instead, at mindless, drudgery-filled jobs, and diapered and coddled a small child in their off hours. She thought about her own mother, a woman she'd barely met, hiding her pregnancy, traveling secretly to Gran's house, sending money whenever she could. It would have been easier for everyone if they'd gotten rid of Nina right from the start.

But it would have been wrong.

Nina sighed, letting out all the damp, unhealthy prison air she'd been breathing. Then she bent down and scooped up the keys. She turned around and walked to a different door, fumbled for a different key. Amazingly, she found this one on the first try. The solid wood door creaked open.

"Alia? Percy? Matthias?" she called. "Come on. Let's get out of here."

CHAPTER *FIFTEEN*

Six eyes bugged out at Nina. She had thought she'd lost all awareness of time, but she could feel seconds ticking away—useful, possibly lifesaving seconds—while the others stared speechlessly at her.

"Huh?" Percy finally said.

"I stole a lot of food," Nina said. "Then somebody poisoned the guard, and he dropped his keys, and the hating man didn't see me pick them up, and he was in a hurry, so he didn't bring me all the way back to the cell, he just wanted to get back to Mack as soon as possible. Mack's the guard. Anyway, I have the keys, and nobody knows it, so we can escape. Come on!"

Another long pause. They didn't seem to understand.

"Did you poison the guard?" Alia asked in a small voice.

"No—I don't know who poisoned him. I don't care. All that matters is that it made him drop his keys, and now I have them, and I'm running away. And you guys can come, too, if you come *now*."

"Maybe it's a trick," Percy muttered.

"Maybe it's a test," Matthias muttered back. He stood up

and walked over to Nina. "Why should we trust you?" he asked.

Nina's jaw dropped. She'd expected them to be delighted, grateful, eager to leave immediately. She'd never dreamed that they might question her offer.

"Why should you trust me?" she repeated numbly. "Because . . . because you're sitting in this horrible prison cell, licking water off the wall and peeing in a corner. And tomorrow, if you're still here, the Population Police are going to execute you. You don't exactly have tons of choices here. I'm your only chance."

Percy and Alia came to stand beside Matthias, like reinforcements.

"She has a point," Percy whispered to Matthias. "But . . ."

Nina was losing patience. This was entirely backward. They should be pleading with her, not her with them.

"And I'm a nice person," she argued. "Really I am. You don't really know me because I haven't been myself here in prison, because . . ." She couldn't say "because I was trying to decide whether or not to betray you." "Never mind. But you can trust me. I promise."

Percy looked at Alia. Alia looked at Matthias, who looked back at Percy.

"Okay. We're coming," Matthias announced.

"Well, *good,*" Nina said, unable to resist a hint of sarcasm. "Glad that's decided." She turned back toward the other door, rattling the key ring in her hand.

"What's your plan?" Percy asked.

"Plan?" Nina repeated.

"Didn't you say some guard had been poisoned?" Percy asked. "How are you going to avoid all the other guards, who'll be scared and angry and looking for someone to blame?"

"Um—," Nina said.

"And where are we running away to?"

Nina felt stupid. Just as the keys had made her forget Percy, Matthias, and Alia, they'd also made her forget all logic. She couldn't just run away from prison. She had to run *to* someplace else.

She thought about Gran and the aunties', but it was too dangerous. And at Harlow School—everyone there knew she'd been arrested. Nobody would dare to help hide her. She swallowed hard.

"Do you know any place safe?" she asked quietly.

Again the other kids did their three-way look, this time Alia peering at Percy, Percy peering at Matthias, Matthias peering at Alia. It was probably a good thing that most of the time Nina had spent with the other kids had been in darkness, because that look would have driven her crazy.

Maybe it still would.

"We don't know any place safe," Matthias said. "Not anymore."

"Well, this is just great," Nina raged, slumping against the wall. "We have food, we have keys, we have everything we need to escape—except a place to go."

"It's not an easy thing, surviving. Out there," Percy said,

jerking his head toward the metal door, as if the entire world lay just on the other side. "You need food, you need shelter, you need heat—well, not this time of year, but come winter—"

"You need to be safe from other people," Alia chimed in.

"Away from the Population Police, or anyone who might report you to the Population Police," Matthias agreed.

Nina was beginning to regret her decision. The last thing she needed right now was to be lectured by three little kids about how dangerous the world was. Didn't they think she knew that? As if there was any place away from people.

An idea tickled Nina's brain. *Away from people . . .* Like a slide show, her mind flashed on image after image of trees, just trees—a woods going on for miles, between vast yards that led up to two schools without windows. Schools whose students probably never went out into the woods anymore, after Nina and Jason were arrested. . . .

"I think I know a place," Nina said slowly, still thinking.

"Does it have lots of food?" Alia said eagerly.

"No, but . . ." Nina gave the bag at her waist a little tug through the material of her dress. She was being foolish again, though, because the four of them would probably eat all her stolen food before they even got to the woods. And it wasn't like there'd be food lying around in the woods—or would there? Nina remembered the new boy in Jason's group of friends from Hendricks School. He'd called himself Lee Grant, though Jason had told Nina more than once that he was sure that was a fake name. The first time Nina met Lee, he was furious because he'd been making a garden in the woods, and the other kids had trampled on it.

Food grew in gardens. Nina was a city kid, but she knew that much. If Lee Grant could make a garden in the woods, so could Nina and Percy and Matthias and Alia.

"This place I'm thinking of—we can grow our own food there," Nina said, then explained quickly. She was careful not to say Jason's name, not to give away too much about why she'd been at Harlow School or why she'd had to leave.

Once again Percy, Matthias, and Alia exchanged glances.

"I think growing food's harder than you're making it sound," Percy said.

"But"—Matthias looked around at the prison walls—"it beats being here."

"I like trees," Alia said softly.

And with those words it was settled. Nina found herself giving the other three a genuine, full-blown smile for the very first time. She was delighted that she didn't have to dodge their gaze anymore, didn't have to try to eavesdrop on them, didn't have to worry that they knew she was supposed to betray them. There wasn't a chance anymore that she might betray them.

She was saving their lives instead.

CHAPTER SIXTEEN

The four of them decided, after much debate, to wait before they unlocked all the doors and slipped out of the prison.

"If someone got poisoned, everything will be topsy-turvy for a while," Percy said. "We should probably wait until the middle of the night."

"But the hating man—that's the guy who was interrogating me—he said no one would come to put me in the cell until eight A.M. That's, uh, ten hours away. We can get a long way away from the prison if they don't discover us missing for ten hours."

"An hour," Matthias said, as though the decision was his and his alone. "We'll wait an hour. That'll give the guards time to settle down. And"—he glanced back at the door to the jail cell—"in case someone comes to check, the three of us ought to go back in there for now."

Nina could tell from his face—and Alia's and Percy's—how much they all hated that idea. With freedom only an hour away, going back into the jail cell seemed like an unbearable punishment. Just peering into the dark beyond the door made Nina shiver. She was glad she, at least, got to stay in the hall under the glow of a lightbulb, even a weak one.

"Lock us in," Percy said quietly.

The three kids stepped over the threshold of the cell and pulled the door shut. Nina turned the key in the lock. The bolt slid into place with a permanent-sounding *thud*.

Not me, Nina thought. *I wouldn't have gone back in there. I couldn't have.* If it'd been her, she would have taken her chances, ready to risk losing all possibility of escape just to avoid sitting in the dark, damp, miserable cell for one more hour. But none of the others had murmured so much as a word of protest.

Nina spent the next hour pacing—from the door of the jail cell to the metal door that led out to the stairs, and back again. Again and again and again. It would have made sense to conserve her energy, to save her muscles and her shoe leather for the hours of walking that lay ahead. But Nina couldn't sit still, couldn't rest for a second. When she felt sure that an hour had passed, she knocked at the door of the jail cell.

"Now?" she called through the wood.

"Not yet," Matthias's muffled voice came back.

Nina paced some more. She sat down and looked through her food bag. (She kept her back toward the metal door, figuring she'd have to hide everything quickly if she heard anyone opening the door from the other side.) The biscuits were crumbled now, the apples were bruised, the oranges were starting to go soft. Was this really enough food for all four of them?

You can still leave without the others, an evil voice whispered in her head. *It's not too late to change your mind.*

No, Nina told herself firmly. She went back and knocked on the wood door again.

"Nobody's come," she said. "Nobody's going to come. It's time to go."

"Okay," one of the boys answered. She couldn't even tell which one.

She unlocked the door, and the others came out. They looked calm and unworried, as if they were off to a picnic, instead of escaping from the Population Police. Nina began trying keys in the outer door again.

"Can I?" Percy asked.

Nina hesitated. She'd been so worried about getting the others to trust her, she hadn't even thought that she might not be able to trust them. What if Percy grabbed the keys, pushed Nina back, escaped without her?

He was a nine-year-old kid. Nina handed the key ring over. Percy looked at the keyhole, sorted through the keys, then held up a dull silver one.

"Try this one next," he said.

Nina stabbed it into the hole. It fit. The lock clicked and the door gave way. The stairs lay right ahead of them, deserted and dim.

"Should one of us go up to make sure it's safe?" Nina whispered.

"Me," Alia said.

Nina waited for one of the boys to say, "Oh, no, not you." How could they send the youngest out first? But no one said anything, so Nina didn't, either. Alia tiptoed forward, as graceful and silent as the cats Nina had seen on TV. When Alia got to the top, she turned around, waved back at them, and mouthed the words, "All clear." Percy and Matthias stepped forward, and Nina followed.

"She's done that before," Nina whispered. "She's used to being the lookout."

"Shh," Matthias said over his shoulder.

By the time they reached the door to the officers' suite, Nina was convinced she was hanging out with a bunch of professional thieves. Maybe she was. What did she know about the other three kids, anyway?

I knew they were going to die if I didn't help them, Nina told herself. *That's what matters.* And anyhow, it was wonderful to have Percy, at every door, select the exact right key, without any hesitation, any noisy fumbling. It was wonderful to have Alia slipping forward, always watching, always ready to warn them. Nina felt safer with the other kids.

But at the door to the officers' suite Matthias held Nina back.

"Isn't there another way out?" he asked.

"Not that I know of," she answered. "Why?"

He pointed to gray wires running along the doorframe, so thin and nondescript Nina would never have noticed them on her own.

"Security system," Matthias muttered.

Panic welled in Nina's chest. How could they turn back now, when they were so close?

But how could they get past a security system?

CHAPTER SEVENTEEN

Nina blinked hard, trying to hold back tears.

"That's it, then," she said in a voice clotted with disappointment.

But the others weren't turning around. They didn't even look upset.

"How many more doors are there before we're out?" Matthias asked.

"Just one," Nina said. "Into the interrogation room. Then we can go out the window. I mean, we could have." She looked down, scuffing the toe of her boot against the filthy floor.

When she looked up again, Alia was scrambling up onto Matthias's shoulders. She swayed, raising her arms toward the security system wire.

"Steady," Percy said.

"What are you doing?" Nina asked.

"Cutting the wire," Alia said. She reached into the pocket of her skirt and pulled out a knife.

"Isn't that dangerous?" Nina asked. She didn't know much about security systems, but Gran and the aunties had always warned her to stay away from outlets and wires.

"Yeah," Alia said. "That's why I'm being careful."

It didn't look like she was being careful. It looked like she was sawing at the wire, making the cut as jagged and rough as possible. Alia had scraped the plastic coating off a wide section of the wire. Some of the gray coating was even floating down to the floor.

"They'll notice that right away," Nina said.

"They'll notice as soon as their monitors go black," Percy answered. "But this way, it'll look like some mice chewed on the wire, not like some prisoners were trying to escape."

"Got the key ready?" Alia asked through her clenched teeth.

"Ready," Percy said, standing as close to the door as possible. He glanced back over his shoulder at Nina. "As soon as she makes the final cut, we run. Got it?"

Nina nodded and moved over to stand behind Percy.

Alia jerked the knife one last time, letting out a stifled "Ooh!" of pain. Percy stabbed a key into the lock and turned. Alia jumped down from Matthias's shoulders and rushed through the door beside Nina. Percy was already attacking the door into the interrogation room.

"It's our lucky day," he breathed. "It's unlocked."

Nina ran through the door and shoved open the window. All four of the kids tumbled out together. The branches of the shrubs scratched Nina's arms and pulled at her dress, but she kept moving, rolling on down the hill.

The food sack bumped against her legs. Out of the corner of her eye she saw that Matthias stayed behind, pulling the window down behind him.

"Come on!" Percy hissed in Nina's ear. "Head for the trees."

Half running, half falling, Nina dashed blindly behind Percy and Alia. They were fast. In the darkness Nina was terrified that she'd lose them. She found herself navigating more by sound than by sight. As long as she could hear the other kids panting, she was okay.

The grass she was running through grew thicker, pulled more at her ankles. No, it wasn't grass—it was scrub brush on the floor of the woods. They were surrounded by trees now.

"All right," Matthias said softly, right behind her. Somehow he'd caught up. "Let's stop and watch now."

Nina wanted to keep running, but Percy put his hand on her shoulder, held her in place. The other kids crouched down, so Nina did, too, peering back at the prison.

Now that she was away from the prison, Nina could see that what the hating man had told her was true—the prison did have high barbed-wire fences and guard stations and bright lights at the back. The officers' quarters, where they'd escaped from, was just a small, one-story addition on an unprotected side. It was swathed in darkness. Nina had to squint to see it against the glare of the rest of the prison.

"They're not looking for us yet," Matthias mumbled.

"No—there! Look!" Percy breathed, pointing.

A dim light—a flashlight?—shone briefly through the window they'd climbed out of. Then the light disappeared, and reappeared in another window of the officers' quarters.

"Nobody's coming outside," Matthias muttered. "We fooled them."

Nina shivered, thinking about what might have happened if Matthias had left the window open; if Alia had cut the security system wire straight out, instead of making it look like the work of an animal's teeth.

"What would we have done if they'd come looking for us?" Nina asked.

"Hidden," Percy said matter-of-factly. "We're good at hiding."

"You're good at a lot of things," Nina said wonderingly. "I . . ." She wanted to thank them, to admit that she wouldn't have been able to escape without them. But the other three were already standing up, getting ready to move on.

"Moon's coming up over there, so that's east," Percy said. "Which direction is this safe place you were telling us about?"

Nina looked around, from the full moon's glow to the glare of the prison lights to the darkness of the woods beyond. The panic that had been threatening all night finally overwhelmed her.

"I don't know!" she wailed. "I don't know how to get there!"

CHAPTER *EIGHTEEN*

The other three kids didn't even look surprised. Nina felt more ashamed than ever, that they had expected her not to know, expected her to be stupid and ignorant.

"Calm down," Matthias said, none too gently. "We can think this through." He looked over at Percy expectantly.

"The place you think is safe, it's by the school you used to go to, right?" Percy asked.

Nina nodded.

"And the Population Police brought you to prison from your school, right?"

Nina nodded again.

"What time of day was it when they brought you here?"

For a minute Nina was afraid she wasn't even going to be able to answer that question. But she recovered quickly, her mind supplying a frightening jumble of images.

"Morning," she said. "They arrested me at breakfast." She could still smell the oatmeal, could still see those three lonely raisins hiding among the oats. The memory made her want to gag.

"Okay. Good," Percy said encouragingly, like he was talking to a really little kid, even younger than Alia. "Now, think carefully. When they were driving you here, what side of the car was the sun on?"

"The sun?" Nina wasn't sure she'd heard the question right. Then she wasn't sure she could answer it. She'd just been arrested by the Population Police, she'd been terrified out of her wits—who in their right mind would pay attention to the sun at a time like that? Then she remembered the splat of water on the car window beside her, the flow of drops on the glass. "The sun wasn't even out," she said triumphantly. "It was raining."

Percy and Matthias exchanged glances. Nina got an inkling that she shouldn't be feeling so triumphant.

"Why does it matter?" she asked.

"If we knew what side of the car the sun was on," Matthias explained, "we'd know which direction you were traveling. The sun is on the east side of the sky in the morning. If it was raining and the sun wasn't out, we don't know where you were coming from."

"Oh," Nina said. Though she couldn't see clearly enough, Nina had the distinct feeling that Matthias had spoken through gritted teeth.

It wasn't fair to expect Nina to know about the sun and the sky. She'd seen so little of either of them in her lifetime. What made Percy and Matthias such experts?

"Can you think hard?" Percy was asking patiently. "Was there any part of the sky that was brighter than the rest of the sky that morning?"

This was like Aunty Lystra's detective shows. The detectives were always saying things like, "I know it's a strain, ma'am, but it's important for you to remember—are you sure you heard Mr. X leave his room before midnight?" But in Aunty Lystra's shows the witnesses were always sure of themselves: "Oh, yes. I heard his door open just before the midnight train went through, just before the clock chimed." Nina hadn't been looking at the sky when the Population Police brought her to prison. She'd been looking down, at the cuffs on her wrists, the chains on her ankles. But if she'd looked out long enough to see the rain . . .

"It was still dark when we left the school," Nina said slowly. "But then, I think . . . I think there was kind of a glow in the sky, through the rain, out my window."

"Sunrise," Matthias muttered.

"The sun rises?" Nina asked. She'd never thought about how it got up into the sky. In pictures and on TV it was just there, overhead.

Percy ignored her question and asked one of his own: "Which side of the car were you on?"

"Left side. In the back," Nina said.

"So the left side's east—you were going south," Percy announced.

"If you say so," Nina said.

"Her school's probably right off Route One," Matthias said. "North of the city. Do we dare walk alongside the road?"

"If we don't, we'll be lost for sure," Percy said.

Nina noticed how they didn't even pretend to ask her opinion. At least both boys glanced quickly at Alia, long enough for her to nod her agreement.

Nina told herself she didn't care. She just hoped she was right about the direction of the sunrise.

CHAPTER NINETEEN

The four of them trudged through the woods for hours. Nina got so tired that she stopped paying attention to where she was going, what the others said, or anything else. All that mattered was forcing herself to pick up one foot after the other, putting each foot down a little farther ahead of the other. She remembered how she'd told herself the other kids might slow her down—what a joke. *She* was the slow one. *She* was the one the others turned around and waited for, impatiently.

Finally Alia danced back to Nina and took her hand and said, "You can sit down now. We're going to wait while . . . while Percy and Matthias do something."

Nina sank down to the ground and let her head flop back against a tree trunk. It felt better than any pillow.

"Do you want something to eat?" she said drowsily.

"Oh, yes!" Alia said. "Can I?"

Nina untied the food bag from around her waist and opened it toward the little girl.

"Take whatever you want," Nina said.

"I think—just something small," Alia decided. "Until

the boys come back. They'll know how to make the food stretch out."

Nina didn't even bother staying awake to see what Alia chose. The next thing she knew, Alia was gently sliding an orange slice into Nina's mouth.

"This will give you energy," Alia said.

Nina chewed and swallowed. She hadn't had oranges much. This one was sweet and juicy. And one slice wasn't nearly enough. All it did was remind Nina how ravenous she was. She pawed through the food bag and pulled out a box of cereal. She ripped off the top and began pouring it into her mouth. She'd never gobbled anything down so quickly before in her life.

"It's your food, not ours," Alia said. "But shouldn't you save some to make sure we have enough for our trip?"

In the dark Nina hadn't even realized that Alia could see what she was doing. Nina blushed and stopped chewing. She'd been eating so greedily that some of the cereal flakes had bounced off her face and fallen to the ground, ruined.

"Did Percy and Matthias say you were my boss while they were gone?" Nina grumbled.

"No," Alia said.

Nina began picking cereal out of the box, one flake at a time, and carefully placing each flake on her tongue.

"Where are they, anyway?"

"Um, they can tell you when they get back," Alia said uncertainly.

This was maddening. Nina felt like throwing the whole box of cereal at the little girl. But just then she saw a glimmer of light bobbing through the woods. Coming toward them.

"Alia, look!" Nina whispered. "It's the Population Police. They're following our trail! We've got to run. . . ." She jumped up, only barely managing not to spill the rest of the cereal.

"Nina, relax. It's Percy and Matthias," Alia answered.

"How do you know?"

"That's our signal. The way the light jumps."

Nina looked again, and it did seem like the light was bobbing in a particular pattern: twice to the right, once to the left. Then twice to the right, once to the left again.

"Where'd they get a flashlight?" Nina asked.

Alia didn't answer.

A few minutes later the light went out. A twig crackled behind Nina and she stiffened, but it was only Percy and Matthias, sneaking closer.

"Safe?" Alia asked.

"Yep," Percy said.

"Where were you? Where'd you get the flashlight?" Nina asked.

"We found it. Wasn't that lucky?" Matthias said.

Nina noticed he had answered only one of her questions. And she didn't entirely believe that answer. Flashlights were valuable, especially if they had batteries. She'd never even seen one until she went away to school.

Who would leave a flashlight just lying around out in the woods?

"Nina offered us food," Alia said.

Nina fought down her irritation. She hadn't offered *them* food—she'd shared it with Alia. And why did she get the feeling that Alia was mostly trying to change the subject? But she couldn't think of anything to do but hold out the food bag with an ungracious, "Here."

Percy and Matthias each pulled out a box of raisins.

"It's almost dawn," Percy said. "I think it's safe for us to rest for a while. We can take turns sitting sentry."

"Sentry?" Nina asked. "You mean—"

"One person watches while the others sleep," Alia said.

Nina narrowed her eyes, thinking. Alia sounded like she knew all about sitting sentry.

"I can go first," Nina said. "I got some sleep already, while you were out 'finding' things." She hoped they would notice the ironic twist she put on those words, but nobody said anything.

Within minutes, it seemed, the others were sound asleep, curled up together in a heap on the ground. Nina stared out into half darkness that seemed to be filled with mysteries. She wanted to turn on the flashlight, as if light could be company for her. But it was too dangerous—the light would only advertise their location to anyone who might be nearby. And the flashlight was too much of a mystery itself. Just thinking about it scared Nina.

Nina turned around and looked at the other three kids.

As the darkness faded, Nina watched the other kids' features emerge from the shadows. She'd spent so much time with them without light, she'd never had a chance to really study their faces. In sleep, Alia looked sweet and cute and cuddly. Even though she had a streak of dirt across her cheek, her light hair was neatly pulled back into a ponytail at the nape of her neck. Her dress was ragged and dirty, but the rips in the skirt had been mended with tiny, meticulous stitches. Nina wondered who had sewn those stitches, who had done Alia's hair. Had Percy and Matthias been sitting in the darkness of the jail cell every day carefully combing Alia's hair? Where had they learned to do that?

Maybe Alia had done it all herself. Nina remembered how confidently she'd climbed the stairs back at the prison, how confidently she'd turned back and mouthed the words, "All clear." Where had Alia learned to be a lookout?

Nina looked out into the woods again—after all, *she* was supposed to be the lookout now—but nothing stirred. Not so much as a fern frond moved in the wind. She turned her gaze back to the other kids, settling this time on Percy. Everything about Percy was sharp—his nose, the set of his mouth, the bony elbows jutting out of his oversized, rolled-up shirtsleeves. His dark hair was longish and tangled. If he was the one who served as Alia's hairstylist, he used up all his effort on her and didn't do a thing for himself.

Huddled against Percy's back, Matthias looked worried, even in his sleep. His eyes squinted together and he moaned softly, as if he was having a bad dream. He turned his head from side to side, and his brown hair flopped down over his eyes.

What did Matthias dream about? What did he think about? Who was he, anyhow? She wondered, vaguely, if he'd killed someone to get the flashlight. For a minute, she could almost imagine it. It didn't seem impossible. So now the Population Police wouldn't be looking just for escaped prisoners, but murderers as well.

Nina shivered. Any way she looked at it, she was lost in a strange woods, in danger, with three kids she didn't trust. For all she knew, they could be like Jason—ready to betray her at any second. Crazy ideas sprouted in her mind: Maybe they were planning to kill her and steal her food. Maybe they were trying to figure out a way to turn her in to the Population Police and get a reward, without getting caught themselves. Maybe Nina should be running away from them right now, as fast as she could.

Alia sighed softly in her sleep, and that sound was enough to stop Nina's panic. Nina wasn't sure what to make of Percy and Matthias—after all, the last boy she'd trusted had betrayed her. But surely sweet, lovable Alia couldn't be in on a plot to hurt Nina.

Could she?

Nina stared back into the woods again, a strange, wild place with branches jutting out at odd angles and vines hanging down like curtains. Nina couldn't have said if this woods looked like the one by her school or not. She'd never seen the other woods by daylight, only groped through it in the dark, clinging to Jason's hand. This sunlit woods was a terrifying place. The leaves on the trees seemed to hide eyes; the underbrush was probably crawling with snakes. Worse yet, Nina had no idea which way she was supposed to go to get to safety. But Percy did. Matthias did. Probably even Alia did.

Whether Nina wanted to trust the other kids or not, she had to.

She couldn't survive without them.

CHAPTER *TWENTY*

Nina fell asleep.

She didn't mean to, but it was too hard to fight after walking all night. She kept telling herself to keep her eyes open—just a little longer, just until someone else woke up—but even her own eyes tricked her. They slid shut while she wasn't paying attention, and the next thing she knew, she was jerking awake, panicked.

"What? Who?" she sputtered senselessly.

Birds sang overhead. The day was hot now. Even in the shade of the woods Nina could feel sweat trickling down her back. But no Population Police officer stared down at her, no vicious snake hissed at her feet, no nightmare-come-to-life stood before her.

And everyone else was still asleep.

Alia's eyelids fluttered.

"Is it my turn?" she said drowsily.

"No, no, go back to sleep," Nina managed to reply.

But Percy was stirring now, too; Matthias was stretching and yawning. He squinted up at the sky.

"It's after noon now. Were you sentry the whole time?"

he asked Nina. "Thanks for letting the rest of us sleep."

"No problem," Nina said uncomfortably. She couldn't bring herself to admit that she'd been sleeping, too. Nothing had happened, so it didn't really matter. Did it?

Percy was looking up at the sun, too. You'd think it was a clock and a map, the way they acted.

"I bet we can make it to your safe place by nightfall," he told Nina.

Nina shrugged, not wanting to ask how he knew that.

"Can we have some breakfast?" Alia asked in her sweet, little-girl voice.

"Lunch, you mean," Matthias corrected her.

Reluctantly Nina hauled out her food sack. By daylight it looked ragged and gross. But she was too hungry to care. She pulled an oatmeal bar out for herself and handed the sack on to Matthias. He selected a crumbly biscuit.

"These will go moldy if we don't eat them first," he said, and Nina heard the criticism in his voice, that Nina had picked something else.

Percy and Alia also chose biscuits. The oatmeal stuck in Nina's throat.

"We're going to need water," she mumbled. "I'm so thirsty. Can people die without water?"

It was amazing what she didn't know, what she'd never needed to know before. Being raised by Gran and the aunties—doted over, cosseted, her every need anticipated and met—wasn't exactly good training for surviving in

the woods. Harlow School hadn't taught her anything useful, either.

"There's a river up ahead," Percy said.

This time Nina did ask, "How do you know?"

"I can hear it," he answered.

And then Nina heard it, too, a distant hum, barely
audible over the chirping of birds and the sound of the
wind in the trees. Was that how water sounded?

"Let's go, then," Nina said. She was afraid suddenly that
her throat might close over, that she might die of thirst
right then and there.

"We have to clean up first," Matthias said.

Nina had her mouth open to ask what he meant—there
was dirt everywhere, how did he expect to clean up a
woods? But he and Percy and Alia had already gone to
work, picking up crumbs, ruffling up the grass they'd slept
on and flattened, erasing all signs of their presence.

"How did you know to do that?" Nina asked.

Percy shrugged. "We're not stupid," he answered. Nina
heard the words he didn't say: "Not like you."

Nina turned away so no one could see how hurt she
was. The others began walking toward the sound of the
river, and she followed at a distance, her throat aching.

The hum of the water got louder the closer they got. It
was like the buzz of traffic Nina had been able to hear in
the summer, when they kept the windows open, at the
apartment she'd shared with Gran and the aunties. The
sound made Nina strangely homesick. *If Gran could see*

me now, she thought. *Filthy, ragged, disgusting. Desperate.* Gran used to scrub Nina's whole face if she had so much as a speck of jam by her mouth. No matter how much heating oil cost, Gran insisted on heating Nina's bathwater until Nina felt parboiled every time she bathed. "Kills germs," Gran always said.

The memories stuck in Nina's mind as she fell to her knees before the river and, like the others, scooped water into her hands to drink and drink and drink. When she'd slaked her thirst, she announced to the others, "I'm taking a bath here, too."

They stared at her.

"We're filthy," Nina said. "I haven't had a bath since they arrested me. You guys should wash up, too."

"Do you know how to swim?" Percy asked.

"No," Nina admitted. She stared out across the wide river. Was it deep, too? "I'll stay close to the edge."

She untied the food bag from around her waist and hung it on a branch high over the others' heads. She hoped they wouldn't notice that she didn't trust them. Then she took off her boots and stockings and, still in her dress, eased into the water.

Mud squished between her toes, and she hesitated. Could she get clean, or would the muddy water only make her dirtier? But the water felt cool and wonderful against her skin. She took another step forward, bent down, and scooped water onto her arms, rubbing off the prison grime. She splashed water up against her face and into her hair.

She unbraided her hair and dipped her whole head in. She lifted her feet from the river bottom, and the current carried her downstream a little. She put her feet down again.

"Come on in," she urged the others. "It's great!"

She saw Alia glance questioningly back at Matthias. Matthias shrugged. Alia began taking off her heavy boots.

"Look! I'm swimming!" Nina shouted, moving her arms the way she'd seen swimmers do on TV. She lowered her head and felt her hair stream out behind her, floating on the water. She felt happier than she'd felt since she'd been arrested, since she'd found out that Jason had betrayed her, since the hating man had asked her to betray Percy, Matthias, and Alia. Water flowed past her, and the current seemed almost strong enough to carry away all her hurt and anger and suspicions. Behind her, she could hear Alia giggling.

"I'm a fish!" Nina said, and ducked underwater. Her dress weighed her down and the skirt tangled in her legs, but it didn't matter. She floated with the water bugs, then surfaced to let the sun warm her skin again.

"Don't go out too far," Percy warned from the side.

"I'm fine!" Nina yelled back. "It's not over my head. The bottom's right . . . right . . ." She reached her foot down— and down—and down. No friendly mud touched her toes. The next thing she knew, her head slipped underwater.

She flailed her arms and thrust her head up long enough to gulp in some air. Her clothes felt even heavier now, pulling her down, down, down. The current pushed at her, faster and faster, carrying her away from Percy, Matthias, and Alia. Frantically Nina shoved at the water, trying to fight her way back to the shore.

And then she put her foot down again, and miraculously, there was solid ground there again.

"I'm okay!" Nina called back to the others. "Don't worry!"

She stood still, savoring the feel of mud squishing through her toes—lifesaving mud. Everything had happened so fast, her mind hadn't had time fully to grasp what might have happened, but she could have drowned, fooling around. How silly it would have been, to survive Jason's betrayal, to survive the Population Police's jail, only to die taking a bath.

She looked around, appreciating every safe, wonderful breath she drew into her lungs, every chirp of birdsong she heard in the trees around her. And then her eyes began to register the view in slow motion. It wasn't just trees and river and sky around her. The river had carried her around a bend. Right in front of her was a bridge, a huge, ugly Government-made concrete bridge. And on the bridge, leaning over the edge, were two men in uniform. Two men in uniform, leaning over, opening their mouths, yelling.

Nina seemed to hear their words at a slower than normal speed, too.

"You there! In the river! That's not allowed! Come out and show us your I.D.!"

CHAPTER *TWENTY-ONE*

If only Nina could swim. She wanted to dive back into the water, swim for miles without surfacing once. Escape.

Failing that, she needed to jump out of the water, run through the woods, hope she could disappear into the trees. But the Population Police would only start a manhunt here, comb through the whole area. She didn't have a chance.

All those images—swimming, running, being caught—flashed through Nina's mind in an instant. She even saw Percy and Matthias and Alia being caught with her. It would be all Nina's fault. She had betrayed them after all.

Nina froze in agony. Her mind wouldn't supply a single response she could give to the uniformed men, a single method of buying even a second more to think.

Then she heard Alia's voice behind her.

"Just a minute," the little girl said. "My sister and I left our I.D.'s with our shoes on the shore."

Okay, Nina thought, a part of her mind surprisingly lucid despite her terror. *That gives me an extra minute or two. I should have thought of that. But won't it make the policemen angrier when they discover she's lying?*

"Get your I.D.'s, then," one of the men on the bridge growled.

Nina looked back over her shoulder. Alia disappeared around the bend.

It's not fair, Nina thought. *Now Alia and the boys are going to be safe, and I'm not.* She could just imagine Alia and Percy and Matthias running now, getting as far away from the river as possible. Sure, Alia had given Nina a little extra time—but what good was that? How long before the Population Policemen on the bridge realized Alia wasn't coming back? What would they do to Nina then?

But there was Alia, wading back toward Nina, carrying two plastic cards in her hand. Nina gaped, strained her neck to see what Alia was holding. Alia drew even with Nina, slipped her fingers into Nina's hand, and pulled her along.

"Don't look so surprised," Alia hissed out of the side of her mouth. "Let me do all the talking."

That wouldn't be hard. Nina was so stunned, she didn't think she even had a voice anymore. For she'd glimpsed the cards in Alia's hand, and they looked like ordinary I.D.'s. One was stamped, SUSAN BROWN. The other said, JANICE BROWN.

And they contained Alia's and Nina's pictures.

No—Nina looked again—it wasn't really their pictures. But the resemblance was so close, Nina was sure the policemen would be fooled. As long as she and Alia didn't make any mistakes.

Alia held the I.D.'s as carelessly as if they were just some pretty leaves she'd picked up off the ground.

They reached the shore, and still Alia marched forward, Nina trailing by a few steps. The brush growing at the water's edge poked her ankles and pricked her feet. She stepped gingerly, half stumbling. Alia's strong grip held her up.

"It's illegal to swim in that river," one of the men said sternly. "That's Government property. We could arrest you for trespassing."

Alia held out the I.D.'s for his inspection. He took them, glanced at them quickly, then handed them to the other man.

"Well?" the first man said. "Aren't you scared of being arrested?"

"Oh, please don't arrest us," Alia said, her little-girl voice sounding even more sweet and childish than ever. "We're going to visit our grandmother, and we slipped in the mud. We couldn't let her see us like that. We thought we could just wash off quickly—we didn't know we were breaking any laws. We're sorry."

"Where does your grandmother live?"

"Terrazzine," Alia said confidently. Nina had never heard of the place.

"Doesn't your sister talk?" the second man said, handing the I.D. cards back to Alia. Alia stuffed them in her pocket.

"No, sir," Alia said, just as Nina was opening her mouth to answer. Nina closed her mouth and hoped nobody had noticed. "My sister's mute, sir. And not quite right in the head, if you know what I mean. I have to take care of her, my mother says."

"Well, you're a brave little thing," the first man said. "We'll let you off, this time. But you be careful, and stay on the road from now on, you hear? We're not far from the Population Police prison, you know. I've been saying for years, if any of those prisoners escaped—"

"I know, sir," Alia said, seeming to quell a shiver of fear. "My mother has told us about the prison."

The policemen turned in one direction, and Alia and Nina went the other way. Nina noticed for the first time that Alia had her boots and Nina's looped around her neck, tied together by the shoelaces.

"Here. Let's put our shoes back on, Janice dear," Alia said, a little too loudly.

Dumbly Nina stuck out first one foot and then the other, and let Alia cram her stockings and boots on. She heard a car roaring away behind her. The policemen were gone.

Nina sagged against a tree in relief.

"What . . . how did you—"

"Shh," Alia said. "Sometimes they come back and check out your story. It's not safe for you to talk yet. But keep walking."

She tugged on Nina's hand, and Nina obediently kept

pace beside the younger girl. They were walking down the middle of the road now, in plain sight, for anyone to see.

"Can't you explain as we walk?" Nina grumbled, trying not to move her lips.

"Nope," Alia said.

The sun beat down from overhead. The woods fell away alongside the road, and they walked past scattered houses and scraggly fields. This was countryside Nina had seen twice before—coming to school and then leaving it—but she'd been inside a car and numb with fear both times. She was beyond numbness now. Her mind kept replaying her moments of terror—the water pulling her under, the policeman yelling, "Come out and show us your I.D.!" And Alia coming to her rescue.

"When it's safe to talk," Nina said quietly, "when we meet up with Percy and Matthias again, the three of you are going to tell me everything. And . . . and I'm going to tell you everything, too."

Alia flashed her a look that Nina couldn't read. It might have meant, "Quit talking." It might have meant, "You're crazy if you think we're telling you anything."

But it also might have meant, "All right. It's time to share."

CHAPTER TWENTY-TWO

Alia and Nina had reached the driveway to Harlow School for Girls before Alia deemed it safe to talk.

"Is that your school over there?" Alia asked quietly when they rounded a bend in the road.

Nina stared out at the expanse of grass and the imposing three-story brick building. The school had no windows—that had seemed so natural from the inside, when Nina wasn't used to seeing out windows anyhow. But from the outside the lack of windows looked odd, as if the building were supposed to be a monument or a memorial, not any place that people could live.

"That's it," Nina said. "And the woods are behind the school."

She pointed. Alia nodded and detoured around the school, skulking behind bushes and shrubs.

"What about Percy and Matthias? And . . . and our food?" Nina didn't want to seem more concerned about her food sack than the two boys. But it was hard not to be, what with her stomach growling.

"They'll find us," Alia said confidently.

A few minutes later they entered the coolness of the woods. Alia sat down on a stump, and Nina sank onto the ground beside her. She took off her boots and rubbed her sore feet.

"How far do you think we walked?" Nina asked.

"Couple of miles," Alia said.

"How did you know how to get here?"

"There aren't that many roads in use anymore," Alia said. "Percy thought this would be the right way." She looked around the woods and said cheerfully, "This is a nice place."

"I guess," Nina said doubtfully. She watched a spider climb into her boot. Were spiders poisonous? Would she survive the Population Police prison, a near drowning, and the long escape only to die of a spider bite?

Alia reached over and shook the spider out of Nina's boot. The spider scampered away.

"Thanks," Nina muttered. She wondered if she'd ever get used to being outdoors. It didn't seem natural not to have four walls around her, a ceiling above her head, and a solid floor beneath her feet. Jason had always teased the kids who were scared of the woods. *No, no,* she chided herself, *don't think about Jason ever again.* Still. The woods were unpleasant enough now, in the warm sunshine. What would they be like when it was raining, or when winter came?

Alia obviously didn't care. She began whistling, sounding as carefree as a bird. Her whistle evidently tricked birds, too, because one called back to her, "Tweet-tweet," in answer to her "Tweet-tweet-tweet."

And then Nina realized it wasn't another bird, but Percy and Matthias. They stepped up quietly behind her.

"Safe?" Alia asked.

"Safe," Matthias answered.

The boys sat down beside Nina. As if they'd all agreed ahead of time, Percy opened the food bag and handed out what seemed to be a feast: a box of cereal, a box of raisins, and an apple for everyone. Nina didn't object. Matthias raised his apple like he was making a toast: "To our new home," he said.

"To roughing it," Percy said.

"To Nina's idea," Alia said.

Nina looked from face to face, then raised her own apple and said, "To my new friends getting us here safely."

Eating required full concentration. Chewing and swallowing was such a joy that no one spoke until they were down to the cores of their apples, picking out the last bits of flesh from among the seeds. Then Nina said what she'd worked out during her long, silent walk with Alia.

"The three of you are used to roughing it," she said. "I don't know where you lived before you were arrested, but it was outdoors. And I don't know how, but you made fake I.D.'s for third children. That's what Percy and Matthias went to get last night when we were running away. When you brought back the flashlight."

Nina waited while the other three exchanged glances. Alia nodded, ever so slightly at the other two.

"Yes," Percy said softly. "You're right."

"Why didn't you tell me we had I.D.'s?" Nina asked. "We could have gone somewhere else if we didn't have to hide. Somewhere with walls and a roof and a floor."

"Where?" Matthias asked. "I.D.'s aren't food. They aren't rent money. They aren't adults to answer nosy questions from the Government. I.D. cards are just pieces of plastic."

Nina shrugged. Before she was arrested, she'd never lacked for food or shelter or adult care. All she'd ever missed was a legal identity. She tried a different tack.

"I could have given everything away when the Population Police saw me," she said. "Since I didn't know you'd made an I.D. card for me, I was about to scream and run. Then they would have known—"

"You thought those guys were Population Policemen?" Percy asked incredulously. "Population Police would have known to look for runaways. Those guys were just local cops. Minor league. They probably hate the Population Police as much as we do."

Nina tried to absorb this news. "But—"

"Look, the Population Police wouldn't tell anyone else that someone had escaped from their prison. It'd be like . . . like a blow to their pride. They like everyone to think that they're invincible, impossible to beat. So it's just Population Policemen looking for us. And if they ask the local cops, the local cops won't tell them about seeing two girls on the northbound road out of the city. That's why we're safe," Matthias said.

Nina wondered how he could sound so sure.

"We lived on the streets before," Alia said softly. "In the city. We know how things work."

Nina tried to imagine it. No wonder the other three had always looked so grubby. But how had they managed it? How had they gotten food? How had they avoided being arrested years ago?

"Who took care of you?" Nina asked.

"God took care of us," Alia said. "We prayed to him and he took care of us. Just like we prayed in prison and he sent us you to get us out."

Nina had heard of God before. Gran, for one, had prayed back home, even though Aunty Lystra made fun of her for it.

"That's one thing the Government's right about," Aunty Lystra had said. "If there were a God out there who really cared about us, do you think we'd be living like this?" "This" seemed to encompass everything from the leaky roof to the weevils in the flour to the long line at the store for cabbage.

"You believe what you want to believe, and I'll believe what I want to believe," Gran always answered. "I, for one, see a few miracles around here."

Nina had liked the way Gran's eyes rested on her when she said that. Even when Nina was too tiny to understand the word "miracle," she'd liked it, liked the way Gran talked about God.

But she didn't understand how God could take care of three little kids alone on the streets.

"I'm thirsty," Percy announced, with a warning glance toward Alia. "Let's go find some water and explore a little."

The other three scrambled up. Nina pulled her boots back on and followed, thinking hard.

They hadn't told her everything, after all. And so she hadn't said a word about her past, either.

CHAPTER *TWENTY-THREE*

The days that followed the kids' arrival in the woods were strangely like a holiday. The sun shone down on them—just warm enough, not too hot—and they had fun hiking around, exploring. They slept under the stars each balmy night. Nina did not exactly forget Jason's betrayal and the nightmare of prison, but all the horrors she'd experienced seemed far in the past. She worried less and less about being caught again. When she opened her eyes each morning to see gently waving branches and a mosaic of maple leaves against the sky, it didn't seem possible that she could be imprisoned in a dark underground room ever again.

For their part, Percy, Matthias, and Alia seemed perfectly happy to treat their time in the woods as one long vacation. They didn't talk about prison; they didn't talk about their lives before prison. They climbed trees; they skipped rocks in the stream; they drew pictures in the dirt with twigs.

Then one morning Nina reached her hand into the food bag for breakfast and closed her fingers on—nothing. She reached farther down, her stomach suddenly queasy with hunger. She brought up a small, battered box of cereal and an empty peanut shell. She laid those on her knees and reached in again.

Nothing. Truly nothing. Not even a moldy biscuit crumb remained in the sack.

"We don't have any more food!" Nina gasped.

The others paused in the midst of their own meals. Percy held a half-eaten oatmeal bar up to his mouth; Alia froze with an apple against her lips. Matthias kept chewing his cereal.

"What?" he said, his mouth full.

"We're out of food!" Nina repeated. "What you're eating now—that's all we have!"

"So is your garden ready?" Percy asked casually. "You said you could grow a garden here."

Nina gaped at him.

"I didn't . . . I meant . . ." What had she promised, in desperation, back in prison when they were planning their escape? Were the others really counting on her to provide all their food? Why hadn't they mentioned it before now? "I—Alia, give me the seeds from that apple."

Obediently Alia dug her fingernails into the middle of the apple and handed Nina three grimy brown seeds. Nina scratched in the dirt by her feet and dug three holes, side by side. She placed a seed in each hole. Then she patted dirt back over the seeds until they were hidden from sight.

"There," she said. "At least we'll have more apples."

"How long does it take?" Percy asked.

Nina stared down at the dirt, hoping something might happen right away. She suspected it took longer than a few minutes for an apple tree to grow. Probably a lot longer. And for an apple tree actually to produce apples . . .

"I don't know," she said miserably. She had a feeling it might take days, weeks, months. Years. "I don't know anything about growing food," she confessed. "I just thought we could . . . figure something out once we got here. This *is* better than being in prison, isn't it?"

"They fed us in prison," Alia said in a small voice.

"And they were going to kill us," Nina countered harshly.

Alia looked down at the ground. Percy and Matthias looked at each other. Nina couldn't stand to see them exchanging glances once again.

"Look, I'm just a kid," she pleaded. "I don't know anything about anything. My gran and the aunties—they always took care of me. Then when I got to school—well, it wasn't like they really wanted us to think for ourselves there. There was always food, three times a day. We didn't have to know where it came from."

The other three didn't say anything for a moment. In the silence, Nina could hear the wind shifting direction in the trees.

"You never told us about your gran and the . . . the aunties?" Alia finally said. "You didn't tell us about your school."

"I didn't know if I could trust you," Nina admitted. "I'm a third child. An illegal."

"We thought so," Percy said.

Silence again. Then Matthias added softly, "So are we."

Nina held her breath. The last time she'd confessed to being an illegal child, and heard someone else confess the same to her, it had led to Population Police arresting her at breakfast. She stared hard at the trees around her, as though any one of them might be hiding a Population Police officer, just waiting for the right moment to grab her. But nothing happened. No one moved.

"It's funny, isn't it," Nina said. "The reason they made third children illegal was because of food. There wasn't enough after the drought and the famines. But someone always found food for me when I was illegal. Now I've gone through two different fake I.D.'s, and I've run out of food. I'm legal now—I've got a card to prove that I'm legal—and I'm going to starve to death. We're all going to starve."

She knew now why the last few days had seemed like such a vacation. It *had* been a vacation—from reality. None of them had wanted to face the truth: It wasn't enough to escape from the Population Police. It wasn't enough to have fake I.D.'s. They were still doomed. It was easier to swing in the trees and skip rocks than to think about the fact that they had nothing to keep them alive once the food sack was empty.

"Nobody's going to starve," Percy said. "We'll figure out something. Don't you know any way to find out how to grow a garden?"

Nina started to say no, but then she remembered how she'd thought of a garden in the first place.

"There's a kid," she said. "At the boys' school. Lee Grant. He was the one who knew about gardens. If we could find him . . ."

Nina explained how she and her friends had met with the group from the boys' school. Somehow the whole story came tumbling out this time—how she and Bonner and Sally had thought they were so big, meeting guys in the woods. How she'd fallen in love with Jason. How he'd betrayed her.

The other three were silent for a long time after she finished.

"So can you trust this Lee Grant or not?" Percy asked. "Was he working with Jason?"

"I don't know," Nina said, miserable again. "He seemed okay. But . . ." She didn't finish the sentence: *Jason seemed okay, too. I thought he was a lot better than okay. How can I trust my own judgment ever again?*

"One of us will have to sneak into the school and find this Lee, and see if we can trust him," Matthias said.

"Maybe he could even give us some food from his school," Nina said. "Maybe they feed the boys better than they feed the girls."

She felt more cheerful now. Everything could work out. She waited for Percy or Matthias to volunteer to be the one to sneak into the boys' school. Matthias was closer to Lee Grant's age—if Matthias pretended to be a new student, he'd be more likely to get placed in the same classes as Lee. But Nina thought Percy was smarter—he would know what to do, how to trick Lee into telling him everything.

But neither Percy nor Matthias spoke up. Surprised, Nina looked from one boy to the other—and discovered they were both staring at her.

"Well?" she said. "Which one of you is going to do it?"

Percy waited a while longer, then shook his head in disgust, as if he couldn't believe Nina hadn't figured everything out.

"You're the only one who knows what this Lee Grant looks like. You're the only one he knows, the only one he'd be likely to trust. It's got to be you," he said.

"But I'm a girl!" Nina said. "It's a *boys'* school!"

"You can tuck your hair up in my cap," Percy said. "You can wear Matthias's clothes. You can pretend."

Nina gawked at him. She imagined herself in Matthias's ragged shirt and patched jeans, standing amidst the Hendricks boys in their fancy clothes. She'd be noticed in an instant, thrown out in a flash.

"You don't understand," she said. "I'm not like all of you. I've never had to . . . to live by my wits. If anyone stops me, I won't know what to say. That's why . . ." At the last minute, she managed to stop herself from spilling everything. *That's why I didn't know what to do when the hating man asked me to betray you. That's why I almost did betray you.* Instead she finished lamely, "That's why someone else should go instead of me. You can't trust me."

"We trust you," Alia said softly.

How could Nina disagree with that?

CHAPTER *TWENTY-FOUR*

It was dusk. The way the shadows slanted through the trees reminded Nina of a dozen other dusks she'd spent in the woods, when she and her friends had sneaked out to meet Jason and his buddies. Once again she was crouched behind a tree, watching and waiting. Once again she was listening for the snap of a twig, the approach of danger. Once again her heart was pounding in her chest, her every nerve ending was alert with the thrill of the risk she was about to take.

But this time she was preparing to sneak out of the woods, not into it. She pulled Matthias's cap a little lower over her eyes and peeked around the tree. She had picked dusk as the safest time for her mission. She was hoping that the boys' school, like the girls' school, had dull indoctrination sessions in the evening, which students slept through or sneaked out of. Surely she could spy on the indoctrination session, locate Lee Grant, and pull him aside as everyone was leaving. She hoped. She'd been making plans all day long.

What she hadn't counted on was how much the shad-

120   MARGARET PETERSON HADDIX

ows spooked her. Not just the shadows in the trees, but the shadows that stretched across the long, long lawn between the woods and Hendricks School for Boys. If she was going to find Lee Grant, she'd have to run across those shadows, out in the open, out where someone might see.

It had been one thing to walk across the Harlow School lawn to the woods with Sally and Bonner on either side of her, giggling nervously all the way. She knew now that they had not actually expected to face real danger—only some pale imitation of it, nothing that couldn't be waved away with an I.D. card.

Nina knew she had been frightened, too, walking out in the open with Alia after they were questioned by the two policemen on the bridge. But Alia had rescued her so magically from the policemen that Nina knew she had a false sense of confidence—no matter what happened, Alia or Percy or Matthias could save her.

But the other three weren't going into Hendricks School with her now. She was completely alone.

Now I know why Gran believed in God, Nina thought. *God? Can you help me, too?*

Nina inched forward, to the edge of the woods, then threw herself into a desperate run across the lawn.

She reached the side of the building more quickly than she'd expected. She realized she'd kept her eyes squeezed shut for most of her run. She was lucky she hadn't smashed into the building. She turned around and looked back and couldn't believe she'd come all that distance, through all those shadows. She took a deep breath and clutched her fingers on to one of the bricks in the wall of the school, as if that could hold her steady.

"A door," she whispered to herself. "I need to find a door."

Sliding the palms of her hands along the wall, she moved forward, looking ahead. By the time she reached the corner, her fingertips felt ragged from the rough bricks. She didn't seem to be thinking very well. Had she missed noticing a door? Or was there one entire side of the school without any entrance at all?

Rather than turning around, she turned the corner. And there was solid metal, with a metal knob sticking out. A door and a doorknob. Just what she'd been looking for.

Without giving herself time to lose her nerve, she grabbed the knob, turned, and pulled.

A dark hallway gaped before her. She stepped into the school. The door slid shut behind her.

If Nina's heart had been pounding before, it was beating away at triple time now. Every nerve ending in her body seemed to be screaming, "Alert! Alert! Danger! Danger! Turn around and go back to safety!"

Nina was surprised her brain could still override the warning, could still make her feet slide forward. She stumbled but didn't fall, and kept moving.

The dark hall ended in a T with another dark hall. Nina turned right at first, hesitated, then turned around. Over the pounding in her ears she could hear shrieks and screams coming from the opposite direction. Somewhere down that hall boys were laughing and yelling at the top of their lungs.

It didn't sound at all like the indoctrination lectures Nina was familiar with—some dry, dusty old teacher droning on uselessly at the front of the room. This sounded like . . . like fun.

Nina crept back toward the noise, picking up speed when she realized there was no way anyone could hear her footsteps over all that commotion. Finally she reached a lit doorway that was obviously the source of all the noise. She peeked cautiously around the corner, sticking her head out just far enough to see past the doorframe.

It was a huge room, like the dining area back at Harlow School for Girls. Nina saw tables and chairs stacked against the wall—this probably was the dining room for the boys' school, but it'd been converted tonight, with boys running around chasing dozens of rubber balls across the floor.

"Kick it here!"

"No, no, I'm open!"

"Throw me the ball!"

Nina closed her eyes and slipped back out of sight around the corner of the doorframe. The boys' game had thrown her back into a memory from years before:

It was summertime. The apartment was stifling, so Aunty Lystra yanked up the windows behind the blinds, letting in little, useless whispers of breeze. But the open

windows also made the noise from the street below distinct for the first time in Nina's memory. She heard
little-kid voices chanting, "One potato, two potato, three
potato, four . . ." She heard the thud of something—a
rope?—and jumping feet hitting pavement, and voices
singing, "Mama called the doctor and the doctor said . . ."
Nina stood in the middle of her hot little apartment, and
an expression of wonder broke over her face. "There . . .
there are other kids out there," she stammered in amazement. "And they're playing. They're being loud, and it's
okay. Nobody's yelling at them. Can I . . ." But the question
died in her throat, because she saw the answer in Gran's
eyes, in the eyes of every single one of her aunties. Other
kids could play outside together and be loud. Nina couldn't.
Nina would never be allowed to be like other kids.

Nina slid weakly to the floor.

How was it that the boys at Hendricks School were
allowed to have fun? Nina remembered how the Harlow
girls had sat like little mice through all their classes, squeaking down the hall in terror, ready to dart back into hiding
at the slightest threat. It had taken Nina days to get up the
nerve to whisper to Sally and Bonner in the dark of their
room at night. She couldn't imagine *yelling* with them,
throwing her voice across a crowded, brightly lit room.

But that was what the boys were doing.

Nina turned her head and looked again. This time she
held back her sense of astonishment enough to peer at
faces. Was Lee Grant in that group of wild, screaming boys?

Nina's eyes skipped from boy to boy—too small, too tall, too dark, too fair. . . . Was she even capable of remembering what Lee looked like?

Then someone yelled, "Good, good, just pick it up faster," and she recognized the voice. Maybe. She snapped her gaze over to the boy who had yelled. He was standing off to the side, swinging his arms and directing the other boys. He looked taller than Nina remembered Lee being, but maybe he had grown in the past few months. Something else was different about him, too—she couldn't quite tell what it was, but the difference was great enough that she hesitated, wondering if she'd made a mistake. Maybe this boy looked more relaxed than the Lee she remembered, maybe he grinned more confidently.

She didn't remember ever seeing Lee grin before. She couldn't imagine the Lee she'd known cheering so proudly, "That's it! That's it! You scored!"

Or slapping another boy's back so triumphantly.

Nina drew back from the door, shaken. She sat still for a long while, letting the noise from the boys' games spill over her.

She couldn't do it.

She couldn't go up to this strange boy to ask for help. He wasn't the boy she remembered—even if he was Lee Grant, she hadn't known him well enough, or he'd changed too much for her to trust him. This boy positively swaggered—he seemed as overconfident as the hating man.

Or Jason.

Nina moved farther from the door, creeping backward down the hall. She reached the other hall she'd come down and practically crawled to the door to the outside. She raised her body only high enough to turn the knob, and dropped out to the ground.

The last light of dusk was slipping away now. The woods were one huge shadow off to the left. Nina couldn't bear the thought of facing Percy, Matthias, and Alia now. Blindly she inched straight out from the school, toward another clump of shadowy plants. Maybe she could hide there, tell the others about her cowardice in the morning.

Nina reached the edge of the shadows. Something squished beneath her feet, and she wrinkled her nose in disgust. Then she sniffed.

Tomato. Suddenly the air around her smelled like tomato.

Nina reached down, groping in the dark. She felt prickly stems, delicate flowers, pointy leaves. And then she felt small, round balls. She jerked on one of the balls, pulling it off the plant. She brought the round ball up to her mouth, bit into it cautiously.

The taste of fresh tomato exploded in her mouth. Nina dropped the tomato in amazement. She took off running for the woods, forgetting all caution in her delight.

"Alia! Percy! Matthias!" she yelled. "I found a garden! We're saved!"

CHAPTER *TWENTY-FIVE*

They came back with the flashlight, all four of them. None of them was cautious. They shone the light from plant to plant—"Look at all the tomatoes!" "And cabbages—" "Are those green beans?" Matthias made a wondrous discovery when he tripped over a root and accidentally upended a leafy plant. A huge potato hung from the bottom of it, pulled from its hiding place in the dirt. After that, Nina pulled up other plants and found more potatoes. They gobbled them raw and didn't care. They also found underground carrots, which they ate without even cleaning.

When they'd feasted until they were full, Percy shone the light around at the toppled plants, the discarded stems, the footprints in the dirt.

"Someone's going to know," he said.

Nina raked her fingers through the soil, erasing a footprint.

"We'll cover our tracks," she said. "Like we did in the woods."

They went back and forth, carrying all the uprooted

plants out to the woods to hide. They buried the smashed tomatoes they'd carelessly knocked to the ground; they picked up every stray leaf and discarded stem.

"There," Percy said, letting one last clod of dirt filter through his fingers, covering one last trampled plant. "Is this how it looked before?"

Nina shone the flashlight back and forth. The globes of red and green looked eerie on the tomato vines. The leaves of the remaining potato plants cast shadows over the holes they'd covered so carefully.

"I don't know," she said doubtfully. It was hard to remember what the garden had looked like in the beginning; she'd been so hungry and so overjoyed at the prospect of eating. "I think next time we'll have to be more careful."

She traipsed back to the woods with the other three kids. All of them were subdued suddenly, worn out after their burst of excitement.

After that, one of them went to the garden every night and picked a day's worth of food. They tried to pick no more than one tomato from each plant and dig up no more than one potato from each row. They stayed away from the cabbages because picking a huge cabbage head would leave a gaping hole that anyone might notice. But there was still plenty of food to eat. Nina just wished some of the plants grew bread or fruit—she was getting sick of vegetables.

"If we could even cook the potatoes—," she complained one evening over raw green beans.

"Someone would see the fire," Matthias said. "They'd find us."

Percy shrugged. "At least we have food."

Nina sighed. She wished one of the others would gripe even once—about the discomfort of sleeping on roots and itchy leaves, about the rain that had fallen on them half of one night, about the muddy taste of the water they drank from the stream. But the way they acted, you'd think the woods was a palace, you'd think the raw vegetables were gourmet food. She wondered yet again about their lives before the Population Police had captured them.

"What did you eat in the city, when you were living on the streets?" she asked.

"Same kind of food as everyone else," Percy said, brushing dirt from a carrot.

"Sometimes we'd find doughnuts in the garbage outside a bakery," Alia said dreamily, as if that were one of her dearest memories.

Nina shuddered. "Didn't you make any money from selling fake I.D.'s?" she asked. "How did you manage to do that, anyway?"

"Let's just say it was a nonprofit operation," Matthias said. "Anybody mind if I have the last potato?"

Nina could tell when she'd had a door slammed in her face. Matthias had as good as said, "Don't ask any more questions." She did, anyway.

"Do you think you could start doing that again?" she asked. "And I could help you. Why didn't you think you could go back to the city and live on the streets again? I could come with you—we could work together. . . . Maybe we could even find doughnuts again." She grinned a little at Alia. Suddenly it all seemed possible—even eating doughnuts out of the garbage. The woods and the raw vegetables were only temporary. They had to make some plans beyond the next day. When the garden died . . . when winter came . . . they had to be ready.

"We were arrested when we lived in the city, remember?" Percy said harshly. "Someone betrayed us. We don't know who. So—we can't go back. We wouldn't know who to trust."

Nina blinked back tears she didn't want the others to see. She stood up.

"I'll go to the garden tonight," she mumbled. "It's my turn."

Listlessly she threaded her way between trees, stepped out onto the lawn that led to the garden. She'd forgotten the flashlight, but it didn't matter. It was still early for a trip to the garden. The shadow from the boys' school was only beginning to stretch across the lawn. The red tomatoes gleamed in the last glow of twilight.

"Tomatoes, potatoes, beans, and carrots," Nina muttered to herself. By comparison, even doughnuts plucked from a trash Dumpster sounded good. She reached the edge of the garden and picked her first vegetable: a cucumber, just for variety's sake.

Knowing that someone had betrayed the other three

kids made her feel worse than ever. Even if their story came out only in bits and pieces, she felt more like she understood them now. No wonder they hadn't wanted to trust her in the beginning, when the hating man first put her in the prison cell with them. Maybe she should tell them about the rest of her story, after Jason betrayed her. Maybe she should tell them about the hating man wanting her to betray them. Maybe then . . .

Nina didn't know what would happen if she told the others everything. Maybe it would just give them something to betray her with.

The world seemed to contain entirely too many betrayals.

Nina pulled an ear of corn from one of the stalks at the edge of the garden. She pulled back the husks, wondering if the cob inside actually contained something worth eating. None of the corn so far had been edible, but Nina still had hope. She brought the tiny nubs of grain up to her mouth, bit, and chewed thoughtfully. Not bad. She looked toward the next row of cornstalks, hoping for bigger ears.

Then she froze.

There in the cornstalks, his face distorted with anger, a boy stood glowering at her.

"You!" he hissed. "You're the one who's been stealing from my garden!"

"No, wait, I can explain—"

But the boy rushed forward, grabbed her by her wrists. Another boy joined him from behind and clutched Nina's right arm. Nina looked from one to the other. She recognized them both now.

"Lee! Trey!" she screamed. "Don't you remember me? I'm Nina. I used to meet you in the woods—"

"Yeah. And then you helped Jason try to betray us," Lee snarled back.

"I didn't! I didn't!" Nina screamed.

But it was no use. They were dragging her away.

CHAPTER *TWENTY-SIX*

Nina tried to dig her heels in, to hold back. She tried to yank her arms out of the boys' grasp. She remembered them both as skinny, wimpy kids—like little rabbits beside Jason's brawn. But somehow they'd developed muscles. Even squirming was useless.

Lee and Trey half pulled, half carried Nina past the school and down a driveway. Then they turned down a path. A stone cottage loomed ahead of them. Nina made one last attempt to jerk away from the boys, but they only tightened their grip.

"Where are you taking me?" Nina demanded.

"To Mr. Hendricks," Lee said abruptly.

Nina wondered who Mr. Hendricks was. It had never occurred to her that Hendricks School might have been named after a real person. Was there a Mr. Harlow, too? A Mrs. Harlow?

Nina didn't know how she could wonder such things at a time like this. They were in front of the cottage now, and Lee was pounding on the door.

"Mr. Hendricks! Mr. Hendricks! We found the thief!"

The door opened. Nina, looking straight ahead, didn't see anyone there. Then she looked down, like the boys were doing.

A man in a wheelchair sat before them.

"Indeed," he said.

Lee jerked on Nina's arm, drew her into the house.

"And what do you have to say for yourself, young lady?" Mr. Hendricks asked when all three kids stood before him in the foyer.

Nina opened her mouth, but nothing came out.

"Surely you have something to say, some defense to give," Mr. Hendricks said.

"I don't know what to tell you," Nina blurted. "I don't know whose side you're on."

Mr. Hendricks chuckled.

"Then I guess you'll have to tell me the truth," he said.

Everyone waited. Nina kept her teeth clenched firmly together. It was all over now. This Mr. Hendricks would undoubtedly call the Population Police, and she'd be arrested all over again. This time, she was sure, the hating man wouldn't give her any more chances to prove herself. The only thing Nina could hope for now was that somehow Percy, Matthias, and Alia could avoid being caught, too. Somehow she'd have to warn them. . . .

"So, you're not talking?" Mr. Hendricks said. "Perhaps my young friends here might tell me what they observed, and we'll go from there."

"Sir," Lee began. "We caught her eating our corn. And

134   MARGARET PETERSON HADDIX

she was putting lots of our vegetables into her bag there."

Nina realized she still had the old, smelly burlap bag slung around her neck. Quickly, before anyone might ask how one girl could possibly eat all that food, she said, "I was hungry. Very hungry."

"Ah," Mr. Hendricks said. "Now we hear an excuse." He squinted, seeming to look far off into the distance. He shook his head, ever so slightly, his thick white hair barely moving. "Boys, I believe I can handle this situation by myself now. Why don't you take her into the living room and then go resume your posts?"

Nina wondered what "resume your posts" meant. Both boys nodded. Lee tugged on Nina's arm and muttered, "Come on."

Once they were in the living room—the fanciest place Nina had ever seen, crowded with heavy wood furniture— Lee half shoved Nina toward a couch. Nina realized she'd probably never see Lee again.

"Lee," she whispered. "You probably won't believe me, but . . . I didn't try to betray you. I didn't know what Jason was doing. Would you . . . would you tell the others? So they can remember me the right way?"

Lee didn't say yes or no, only backed away. Nina couldn't even be sure that he'd heard her. She didn't expect anyone to think too highly of her—she wasn't Jen Talbot, hero for the cause of third children everywhere. But she hoped that Sally and Bonner, at least, wouldn't live the rest of their lives thinking of her as a traitor. She hoped that if the

Hendricks School boys and the Harlow School girls ever started meeting in the woods again, they wouldn't pass down stories of Jason and Nina, equally deceptive, equally evil.

After Lee and Trey left, Mr. Hendricks rolled into the living room. He pulled the wooden door mostly shut behind him.

"Now," he said. "Perhaps you'll be a bit more forthcoming without an audience."

Nina's gaze darted around the room, taking in the unlatched door, the thick glass in the windows, the picture frames and heavy knickknacks on the tables. She was looking for an escape. Maybe a weapon, too. What would happen if she threw a ceramic bird at a man in a wheelchair? Could she hit him? Would it do any good?

Nina looked Mr. Hendricks over carefully. Despite the white hair, he was hardly old and decrepit. She even suspected the wheelchair was just a fake, meant to deceive her into thinking she could overpower him easily. Probably he was as strong and muscular as Lee and Trey. Probably . . .

Nina's glance reached Mr. Hendricks's feet—or rather, the empty space where his feet should have been. He didn't have any feet.

He can't chase me, Nina thought. *If I can escape . . .*

But he would call for help. He'd have a search party ready in a matter of minutes.

But minutes are all I need to warn Percy, Matthias, and Alia. . . .

"Well?" Mr. Hendricks said.

Nina sprang up from the couch, grabbed the back of the wheelchair, and dumped it forward, spilling Mr. Hendricks to the floor. She dashed out the living room door, out the front door, down the front steps. She worried about running into Lee and Trey—where were their "posts," by the garden?—but her feet flew so quickly, everything was a blur. She couldn't watch for them or anyone else.

Before she knew it, she was crashing into the woods, toward the glade where she'd left the others waiting for food.

"Percy! Matthias! Alia!" she called. "I have to warn you. . . ." The words wouldn't come quickly enough between her gasps for air.

Alia popped out from behind a tree.

"Nina!" she scolded. "You're making too much noise. Someone will hear you!"

"It . . . doesn't . . . matter," she panted. She stopped running, caught her breath. She saw that Matthias and Percy were staring out at her from the shadows behind a bush. "They caught me. I escaped again, but they'll probably be looking for me soon. I had to warn you. . . ." She took another deep breath. Her brain still felt starved for oxygen. "This isn't a safe place anymore. You'll have to go somewhere else. But you can. You guys are smart."

"Nina," Alia protested. "Come with us, then—"

"No," Nina said. "I'd be . . . dangerous to you. They know to look for me now. I probably don't have much time. But

I wanted to tell you . . . the hating man. In prison. He put me in your cell to betray you. He wanted me to tell him all your secrets. And I might have. If we hadn't escaped, I—"

"But you didn't," Matthias said. "You didn't tell the Population Police anything."

"I wanted to," Nina said. "Jason betrayed me, and I wanted to hurt someone else. And I wanted to save my life. . . ."

"It's all right," Alia said, stepping closer.

"And I don't blame you for never trusting me," Nina continued. "I wasn't trustworthy. Even that first night in the woods, when I was supposed to be sitting sentry, I fell asleep." It was such a relief to confess that, even that. "I never really trusted you, either. The last time I had friends, they didn't help me at all when I was arrested. So I thought . . ."

Nina was crying. Between being caught and running away—and, probably, because of having nothing to eat in days but vegetables—she felt dizzy and light-headed. But it was important for her to tell the others everything. All her stories spilled out. Probably the others could make no sense of what she said. Tales of playing dolls with Aunty Zenka were all mixed up with tales of meeting the Hendricks School boys in the woods with Sally and Bonner.

"I want you to know my real name, too," Nina said. "It's Elodie. When you remember me, remember Elodie."

The woods were dark when Nina finished talking. She

was just lucky she hadn't been found immediately. She couldn't see the others' faces, couldn't tell what they thought of her stream of words. But for practically the first time since she'd been arrested, Nina was sure she'd done the exact right thing. The others were going to be safe now. And she'd told them the truth.

"You should go now," she said. "Oh—here." She pulled the grungy food bag from around her neck and handed it to Alia. "There's not much in it because . . . well, something's better than nothing, isn't it?"

The tears flowed down her face. She reached down and drew Alia into a hug. Percy and Matthias stepped forward, too, and threw their arms around both girls. All four kids stood together, swaying slightly, holding one another up.

Nina had her eyes shut, squeezing out the tears. But through her tears she suddenly saw a glimmer of light off to the right. She pulled away from the hug, stared off toward a flashlight bobbing in the woods. Then she saw other flashlights, circling closer and closer.

"They're looking for me!" she hissed. "Go on! Hide somewhere far away from me."

Nina didn't have time to make sure that the others had moved out of sight. For, seconds later, a flashlight shone right in her face and a booming voice cried out, "Nina Idi! Fancy meeting you here!"

It was the hating man.

CHAPTER *TWENTY-SEVEN*

Terrified, Nina turned to run. But something clawed at her arm, something held on to her leg. She tumbled forward, sprawled across the ground.

"Let go of me!" she roared, though it must have been a vine tangled around her ankle, must have been a branch scratching against her arm. Nina tried to scramble up, but it was too late. The flashlight shone in her eyes; when the hating man's voice came again, it was practically in her ear.

"Nina, Nina, Nina," he said. "It's all over now."

Nina struggled to sit up. It was Percy who was holding onto her arm, Matthias who was holding onto her leg.

They had betrayed her, too. They were turning her in to the hating man.

Alia stepped up beside the boys, smiling at Nina. Nina's eyes swam with tears. Not Alia, too. Nina couldn't take the thought that Alia had betrayed her as well.

"No," Nina moaned. Then she screamed, "No!"

Nina didn't care who heard. Behind the hating man she could see the shapes of perhaps a dozen people, all with flashlights shining right at her. Their faces were com-

MARGARET PETERSON HADDIX

pletely in shadow, impossible to make out.

Alia leaned into the circle of light with Nina.

"You're safe now," she said happily. "You passed the test."

Nina shook her head violently, not wanting to believe the evidence in front of her eyes.

"Alia, run," Nina whispered. She wasn't sure which she wanted more—for the little girl to be safe, or for Alia merely to prove that she was scared, too, and hadn't helped betraying Nina. Alia didn't move. Nina hoped she just hadn't heard. "Alia, you have to escape. That man is from the Population Police. He's the hating man!"

"No, he's not," a familiar voice called out from the shadows. "He only pretends to work for the Population Police. He's Mr. Talbot. Jen Talbot's dad." Lee Grant stepped forward and bent down beside Nina. "Remember who Jen Talbot is?"

"Of course I do," Nina snapped. "She's the hero for the cause of third children everywhere. Jason used to tell us about her all the time. But . . ."

She wondered suddenly if that was a lie, too, if there'd never been a Jen Talbot, or if she hadn't been a hero. Dazedly Nina looked around at the faces circling her. Everyone came forward, crowding close. Percy and Matthias lifted Nina up to see, instead of holding her back. Lee and Trey and a few other Hendricks School boys stood in a clump off to the right.

The hating man—Mr. Talbot?—cleared his throat.

"It's true, what Lee said," he began. "I am a double agent working for the Population Police, but only in order to double-cross them. Back in the spring I faced a dilemma. A boy at Hendricks School for Boys told the Population Police he knew of several shadow children at the school who were using fake identities and pretending to be legitimate. If this boy managed to convince the Population Police that he was telling the truth, I knew several children would die. Thanks to young Lee Grant over there, as well as some quick-thinking administrators, we managed to foil his plan.

"But this boy—Jason, as you all know—said he had an accomplice at the girls' school. Nina Idi. You. We arrested you as well. But the longer I spent interrogating you, the more convinced I became that you were truly innocent and actually knew nothing of Jason's plan. But I couldn't be entirely sure, and it was a matter of life and death that I be absolutely, one hundred percent certain."

"Yeah. My life. My death," Nina grumbled, still too dazed to think straight.

"And many others," Mr. Talbot said. "You knew the truth about dozens of kids."

Every girl at Harlow School, Nina thought. *And lots of boys at Hendricks. I knew they were all former shadow children. Did everyone really think that I might betray them?*

"About the same time, a Population Police informer in the capital had turned in three kids who were involved in manufacturing fake I.D.'s,—Percy, Matthias, and Alia. I figured they were safer in prison than out on the streets, for the time being. Their protector, Samuel Jones, had been killed in the rally for third-children rights in April."

"That's who 'Sa—' was. You almost said his name once," Nina said, almost to herself.

"He took in third children," Alia whispered. "When our parents abandoned us. He raised us. He took care of us."

"I thought you said God took care of you," Nina scoffed. She sounded just like Aunty Lystra at her most skeptical.

"Who do you think Samuel was working for?" Alia said.

Nina kept shaking her head, as if she could deny everything she heard.

"Percy and Matthias had promised Samuel to stay away from the rally to protect Alia," Mr. Talbot said. "So they alone were spared, and they alone were still around to be betrayed. Then later, in prison, they agreed to help me give you a test, to see which side you were really on. If you had betrayed them, we would have known you couldn't be trusted. If you protected them . . . we'd save you."

Nina gasped, finally beginning to make sense of his words. If the hating man didn't really believe in the Population Police's cause—if he was a double agent working against them—then everything was backward.

"So, if I'd double-crossed them, trying to save my own life . . . you would have killed me?" Nina asked.

"Yes," Mr. Talbot said.

Nina thought about how close she'd come to betraying

the others, how miserable she'd been in prison, how willing she'd been to do almost anything to save herself.

"I didn't do it," she said. "I could have, but I didn't."

"But you didn't refuse to betray them, either," Mr. Talbot said. "You weren't committing yourself either way. We had to add a more dangerous part to the test."

Nina couldn't figure out what he meant. Then she remembered the guard, Mack, sprawling across the table, his ring of keys sliding right toward Nina.

"You let us escape," Nina accused, as if it were a crime. "You let me get the keys and have a way out, and made me think I was figuring out everything on my own. Why, I bet . . . I bet Mack wasn't even sick."

Mr. Talbot chuckled. "No, but he put on a good act, didn't he?"

"And then"—Nina was still putting everything together—"the other three kids knew that I might offer to help them escape. Why wasn't that enough? Why didn't you trust me then?"

She thought about the past—was it weeks?—of sleeping outside, of living on stale, moldy food or dirty raw vegetables. Could she have avoided all that?

"We still weren't sure about you," Percy said in his usual logical tone. "It was possible that you were only taking us along because you were scared to go on your own. You might have just been using us."

Nina remembered how unconcerned the others had been when they ran out of food, how little they had cared about making plans for the future. No wonder. They were waiting on her. Waiting on her to prove herself.

"When we met the policemen by the river—," she said.

"That was part of the test," Mr. Talbot said. "Those weren't policemen. They were people working with our cause."

"And I passed that test?" Nina asked.

"Sort of," Mr. Talbot said. "You didn't try to turn the others in. But we still weren't sure of your motives."

Nina shivered, thinking about how closely she'd been watched all along. Every time she complained about their rocky, uneven "beds" in the woods. Every time she griped about the dirty vegetables.

"I bet the rest of you were getting food somewhere else," she said.

"Not much," Alia said in a small voice, looking down. She looked back up at Nina, her eyes flashing. "*I* thought you were good. I wanted to tell. But these guys"—she pointed at Percy, Matthias, and Mr. Talbot—"they said I had to wait until you told us everything. Until you told us that you were supposed to betray us to the Population Police."

"I did that tonight," Nina said wonderingly. She looked around again at the circle of people, the circle of light in the dark woods.

She remembered how panicked she'd been, running out to the woods only minutes earlier. She hadn't been thinking at all of saving her own life. She'd only wanted to save Percy, Matthias, and Alia.

But she hadn't cared that much about them back when she first met them, when she offered them a chance to escape, when she saw the fake policemen by the river.

"You gave me a lot of chances," she said to Mr. Talbot.

"I thought you deserved them," he said. "You didn't deserve what happened to you before."

Nina remembered the day she was arrested, how nobody had spoken out on her behalf as she glided forward in the dining hall. She remembered how much she'd trusted Jason, and then he had betrayed her. No, she hadn't deserved that. Nobody did. What she deserved was the way Gran and the aunties had loved her, the way they'd hidden her even though they might have been killed for it. But Alia, Percy, and Matthias hadn't deserved being betrayed, either. They hadn't deserved weeks in a dark prison cell, weeks sleeping outdoors on rocks and twigs and itchy leaves. But they'd endured all of that, willingly, for her. They'd agreed to endure all of that before they even knew if she was good or bad.

Nina's eyes filled up with tears, but they weren't tears of fear or panic or sorrow now. They were tears of joy.

"Thank you," she whispered, and the words seemed to encompass everyone in front of her—Percy, Matthias, and Alia, Mr. Talbot, even Lee and Trey. But the words were more powerful than that. Her whisper seemed to fly through the night, through the dark. Somewhere, far away, she could even imagine Gran and the aunties hearing her, too.

CHAPTER TWENTY-EIGHT

Nina stood beside Lee Grant, pulling corn from a row of stalks.

"Leave the small ears to grow," Lee cautioned. "We only need enough for the feast tonight."

"Only?" Nina laughed. "There'll be twenty people there!"

"Forty ears, then," Lee countered. "That's not much. Back home, when my mom was canning corn, we used to pick—"

"What? Forty million?" Nina teased.

In the days since she'd been caught, she'd been staying at Mr. Hendricks's house with Percy, Matthias, and Alia. But she'd spent a lot of time with Lee and already listened to dozens of "back home" stories. She didn't know what it was like at Harlow School for Girls, but at Hendricks, boys were not pretending so much to be their fake identities. They were telling the truth more.

Nina jerked another ear from a stalk.

"Anyway, forget forty ears," she said. "If you're figuring two per person, that's only thirty-eight. I don't think I'll ever be able to eat corn again, not after the way you scared me in the garden last week, midbite."

"More for me," Lee said, clowning a selfish grab around all the corn they'd picked so far.

Nina wondered if this was how normal children acted—children who'd never had to hide. She guessed she'd have a chance to find out now. She, Percy, Matthias, and Alia were being sent on to another school, one where third children with fake I.D.'s mixed with firstborns and secondborns. That was why they were having a feast tonight, a combination of a celebration and a farewell.

"Given how things happened, Harlow School is probably not the best place for you anymore," Mr. Hendricks had told Nina.

Nina had had another flash of remembering that horrific canyon of eyes, watching her walk to her doom.

"I . . . I think I can forgive the other girls," she had said. "Now."

"But are they ready to forgive you?" Mr. Hendricks asked. "No matter how much you reassure them, how much the officials reassure them, there will always be someone who suspects that you just got off, that you really were working with Jason. They haven't . . . grown up like you have."

And Nina understood. She wasn't the same lovesick, easily terrified child she'd been at Harlow School. That was why she liked talking to Lee now. He'd grown up a lot, too. The other boys looked up to him. They didn't even call him Lee anymore. He was mostly L.G.—and they said it reverently.

Nina still called him Lee. She didn't like too many things changing.

"Nina," Lee said now, slowly peeling back the husk of an ear of corn to check for rot. "Before you leave tomorrow, there's something I've been wanting to tell you."

"What?"

Lee tossed the ear of corn onto the pile with the rest. It must have been okay.

"I've been thinking about Jason," he said.

Nina stiffened just hearing that name. She might be able to forgive her friends at Harlow, but she wasn't ready to forgive Jason.

"So?" she asked.

"Well, I was thinking about what I heard him say on the phone to the Population Police that night he was turning everyone in. He made it sound like you were working with him."

"I know," Nina said. "That's how I ended up in prison." She couldn't keep the bitterness out of her voice.

In one clean jerk Lee pulled another ear from another stalk.

"But I don't think Jason was saying that to get you in trouble. He didn't expect to be arrested, to have you arrested. He meant for the illegal third children with fake I.D.'s to be arrested. I think . . . I think he was actually trying to save you."

Nina reeled backward, stunned beyond words. Lee took one look at Nina's face and kept explaining.

"Don't you see?" he said. "It wouldn't have made any sense for Jason to say you were working with him if he wanted to get you in trouble. He thought he—and you—were going to be rewarded. He was . . . he was maybe trying to protect you from ever being turned in by anyone else. See, if years from now someone accused you of being illegal, he could pop up and say, 'Nina? How could Nina be an exnay? She helped turn them in!'"

Lee did such a good job of imitating Jason's voice that Nina could almost believe. But only almost.

"Jason was doing something wrong. Evil. He wanted innocent kids to die," she said harshly. She pulled so hard on an ear of corn that the whole stalk came out of the ground.

Lee frowned but didn't say anything about his precious cornstalk.

"Yeah. Believe me, I was pretty mad at Jason myself. But I'm just saying—I don't think he was all bad. I think he, um, really liked you. And that was why he was trying to save you."

Nina stood still, trying to make sense of Lee's words. It flip-flopped everything she'd thought for the past few months. How could she accept Lee's explanation? How could Jason have been so evil yet tried to save her?

For a minute she almost believed. Then she remembered.

"Mr. Talbot had a tape," she said dully. "Of Jason confessing. And he was lying and saying it was all my fault, that I was the one who wanted to turn in the exnays."

"Oh, Mr. Talbot could have faked that tape," Lee said. "I've seen him fake pictures."

"But it was Jason's voice," Nina said. "I heard him. I heard the tape!"

Lee turned back to the garden.

"Go ask him," he said with a shrug.

Nina stood still for a moment, then she dropped her corn and took off running. Hope swelled in her heart. She burst into Mr. Hendricks's cottage and dashed into the living room, where Mr. Hendricks and Mr. Talbot were conferring.

"The tape," she said. "Of Jason betraying me. Lying. Was it real?"

Mr. Talbot turned around slowly, looked at her blankly.

"You had a tape," she repeated breathlessly. "In prison. Of Jason saying it was my idea to betray exnays, my idea to turn them in to the Population Police. Did he really say that? Or did you fake the tape?"

Mr. Talbot blinked.

"Does it matter?" he asked.

"Of course it matters!" Nina shrieked.

Mr. Talbot raised one eyebrow.

"Why?" he said.

Nina had so many reasons, they jumbled together.

"If he didn't betray me, if he was really trying to help

me—then he really loved me. Then Aunty Zenka was right, and love is everything, and the world's a good place. And I can be happy remembering him. But if he betrayed me—how can I think about the time we had together without hating him? How can I ever trust anyone, ever again?"

"You've believed for months that he betrayed you," Mr. Talbot said. "And you still trusted Percy, Matthias, and Alia. You've been acting like you trust Lee and Trey and Mr. Hendricks and me. Don't you?"

"Yes, but . . ." Nina couldn't explain. "Maybe I shouldn't trust you. You've lied to me a lot."

Nina was surprised when both Mr. Talbot and Mr. Hendricks burst out laughing.

"It's not funny," she protested.

Mr. Talbot stopped laughing, and sighed. "Nina, we live in complicated times. I would have loved it if that first time I talked to you in your prison cell, I could have come straight out and said, 'Here's the deal. I hate the Population Police. What about you?' And it would have been great if I could have been sure that you would give me an honest answer. But—can you really see that happening? Don't you see how muddy everyone's intentions get, how people end up doing the wrong things for the right reasons, and the right things for the wrong reasons—and all any of us can do is try our hardest and have faith that somehow, someday, it will all work out?"

Nina looked down at her hands, still splotched with mud from the garden. She looked back up.

"Was the tape fake or not?" she asked again.

Mr. Talbot looked straight back at her.

"It was fake," he said quietly. "Some of our tech people spliced it together."

A grin burst out over Nina's face. "So Lee was right. Jason did love me," she whispered in wonderment.

Mr. Talbot and Mr. Hendricks exchanged glances in such a way that Nina felt like she was back with Percy, Matthias, and Alia.

"So that's enough for you?" Mr. Talbot asked. "It doesn't matter that Jason was trying to get other kids killed? You don't care about the evil he did as long as he loved *you*?"

Nina's smile slipped. Why did Mr. Talbot have to confuse everything again?

"No, no," she said. "That's not what I believe. This just means—he wasn't all bad. He's dead anyway. So I can . . . hold on to the good memories and let go of being mad at him." She wondered what had made Jason the way he was. She remembered how desperate she'd felt in the jail cell when she'd been so tempted to betray Percy, Matthias, and Alia. What if Jason had been even more desperate? What if he hadn't wanted to betray anyone, either, but had been too weak to resist?

It was odd to think of Jason as weak. She could actually feel sorry for him now. She could hold on to that forever, the way she held on to memories of Gran and the aunties.

"Nina," Mr. Talbot said. "Jason isn't dead. I thought they had executed him, but . . . it turns out that another faction of the Population Police thought he might still be useful. I've only recently found out that he's working for the Population Police in some top secret project. Something we who oppose the Government are very concerned about." He paused for a second, as if waiting for the news to sink in. "So, what does that information do for you? Are you going to rush to his side, to help him, because he *loves* you?"

Nina stared at Mr. Talbot in amazement.

"He's alive?" she whimpered. "He's alive?"

Strangely, this seemed like bad news. If Jason were dead, she could go all misty-eyed remembering him, daydreaming about what might have been, just like Aunty Zenka mooning over one of her books. But with him alive and working for the Population Police—"I have to stay mad," she said aloud. "I can't ever forgive him."

"Bitter is a bad way to live," Mr. Talbot said.

Nina remembered that he had lost Jen, that he had reason to stay angry at the Government forever. She sank down onto one of Mr. Hendricks's couches. This was all going to overwhelm her. She was just a little girl who'd spent most of her life hiding, listening to old ladies' foolish stories. Or had they been foolish? All the fairy tales Gran and the aunties had told her were about people staying true to what was right in the face of great adversity. She'd heard the wrong part of the stories if she thought she was just supposed to sit around like a princess, waiting for some prince to fall in love with her.

She looked straight at Mr. Talbot.

"I don't want to stay bitter. But I want to help you—what can I do to make sure Jason's project fails?"

Mr. Talbot almost smiled. Nina felt like she'd passed another test.

"We'll see," he said. "We'll see."

Nina went back out toward Lee's garden to finish picking corn. The sun was setting now, casting long shadows over the path. Just about every step Nina took alternated between sunlight and dark. Nina's thoughts bounced back and forth just as dramatically. *Jason* did *love me. That's what really matters. . . . But he was still evil. . . . Why did I say I'd help Mr. Talbot oppose the Government? . . . How could I not have said that, after everything Mr. Talbot did for me? . . . What can I possibly do, anyway?*

As Nina approached the garden she saw Lee waiting for her there. Whatever she did for Mr. Talbot, she realized, she would not be alone. Lee would probably be involved, and so would Percy and Matthias and Alia.

Nina remembered how alone she'd felt in her jail cell, all those months ago. Feeling abandoned and betrayed was worse than hunger, worse than cold, worse than the handcuffs on her wrists. But she hadn't been abandoned; she had only accidentally been betrayed.

"Well?" Lee said as soon as she got close enough to hear. "Was I right?"

It took Nina a moment to remember what he was talking about: the tape. Jason's betrayal.

"It's a long story," Nina said. "And it's not over yet."

But part of her story was over—the part where she was innocent and stupid and useless. She'd been so worried before that people might not remember her as Elodie—sweet, loving, little-girl Elodie. But she'd outgrown Elodie. She'd outgrown Nina the ninny, too. She was ready now to make whatever name she carried one that people could respect and revere.

Like Jen Talbot's.

"I think . . . I think I just volunteered to help Mr. Talbot and Mr. Hendricks fight the Population Police," she said.

Lee's gaze was steady and unfailing.

"Good," he said. "Welcome to the club."

Turn the page to read an excerpt from the
fourth book in Shadow Children sequence

Among
the Barons

MARGARET PETERSON HADDIX

Hey, L.! Mr. Hendricks wants to see you!"

Such a summons would have terrified Luke Garner only a few months earlier. When he'd first come to Hendricks School for Boys, the thought of having to talk to any grown-up, let alone the headmaster, would have turned him into a stammering, quaking fool desperately longing for a place to hide.

But that was back in April, and this was August. A lot had happened between April and August.

Now Luke just waved off the rising tide of "ooh's" from his friends in math class.

"What'd you do, L.? Have you been sneaking out to the woods again?" his friend John taunted him.

"Settle down, class," the teacher, Mr. Rees, said mildly. "You may be excused, Mr., uh, Mr. . . ."

Luke didn't wait for Mr. Rees to try to remember his name. Names were slippery things at Hendricks School anyway. Luke, like all his friends, was registered under a different name from what he had grown up with. So it was always hard to know what to call people.

Luke edged his way past his classmates' desks and slipped out the door. His friend Trey, who had delivered the message from Mr. Hendricks, was waiting for him.

"What's this about?" Luke asked as the two fell into step together, walking down the hall.

"I don't know. I just do what he tells me," Trey said with a dispirited shrug.

Sometimes Luke wanted to take Trey by the shoulders, shake him, and yell, "Think for yourself! Open your eyes! Live a little!" Twelve years of hiding in a tiny room had turned Trey into a human turtle, always ready to pull back into his shell at the slightest hint of danger.

But Mr. Hendricks had taken a liking to Trey and was working with him privately. That was why Trey was running errands for him today.

Trey looked furtively over at Luke. His dark hair hung down into his eyes. "Do you suppose it's—you know—time?"

Luke didn't have to ask what Trey meant. Sometimes it seemed like everyone at Hendricks School was just holding his breath, waiting. Waiting for a day when none of the boys would be illegal anymore, when they could all reclaim their rightful names, when they could go back to their rightful families without fear that the Population Police would catch them. But both Luke and

Trey knew that that day wouldn't come easily. And Luke, at least, had promised to do everything he could to bring it about.

His stomach churned. The fear he thought he'd outgrown reached him at last.

"Did he say . . . did Mr. Hendricks say . . . ," he stammered. What if Mr. Hendricks had a plan for Luke to help with? What if that plan required more courage than Luke had?

Trey went back to looking down at the polished tile floor.

"Mr. Hendricks didn't say anything except, 'Go get your buddy L. out of math class and tell him to come see me,'" Trey said.

"Oh," Luke said.

They reached the end of the hall, and Luke pushed open the heavy wood door to the outside. Trey winced, as he always did anytime he was exposed to sunshine, fresh air, or anything else outdoors. But Luke breathed in gratefully. Luke had spent his first twelve years on his family's farm; some of his fondest memories involved the feeling of warm dirt on his bare feet, sunshine on the back of his neck, a hoe in his hand—and his parents and brothers around him.

But it didn't do to think much about his parents and brothers anymore. When he'd accepted his fake identity, he'd had to leave them and the farm behind. And even when he'd been with them, he'd had to live like a shadow or a ghost, something no one else outside the family knew about.

Once when his middle brother, Mark, was in first grade, he'd accidentally slipped and mentioned Luke's name at school.

"I had to tell the teacher that Mark just had an imaginary friend named Luke," Luke's mother had told him. "But I worried about that for months afterward. I was so scared the teacher would report you, and the Population Police would come and take you away. I'm just glad that a lot of little kids do have imaginary friends."

She'd bitten her lip telling Luke that story. Luke could still see the strained expression on her face. She hadn't even told him about that episode until the day before he left the farm and his family for good. By then she'd meant the story as assurance, he knew—assurance that he was doing the right thing by leaving.

At the time, Luke hadn't known what to make of that story. It just added to the jumble of confused thoughts and fears in his head. But now—now that story made him angry. It wasn't fair that he'd had to be invisible. It wasn't fair that his brother couldn't talk about him. It wasn't fair that the Government had made him illegal simply because he was a third child and the Government thought families should have no more than two.

Luke stepped out into the sunshine feeling strangely happy to be so angry. It felt good to be so sure about what he thought, so totally convinced that he was right and the Government was wrong. And if Mr. Hendricks really did have a plan for Luke, it'd be good to hang on to this righteous anger.

The two boys climbed down an imposing number of marble steps. Luke noticed that Trey glanced back longingly at the school more than once. Not Luke. Hendricks had no windows—to accommodate the fears of kids like Trey—and Luke always felt slightly caged anytime he was inside.

They walked on down the lane to a house half hidden in bushes. Mr. Hendricks was waiting for them at the door.

"Come on in," he said heartily to Luke. "Trey, you can go on back to school and see about learning something for once." That was a joke—Trey had done nothing but read while he'd been in hiding, so he knew as much about some subjects as the teachers did.

Luke opened the door, and Mr. Hendricks rolled back in his wheelchair to give Luke room to pass. When he'd first met Mr. Hendricks, Luke had been awkward around him, particularly because of the wheelchair. But now Luke practically forgot that Mr. Hendricks's lower legs were missing. Going into the living room, Luke automatically stepped out of the way of Mr. Hendricks's wheels.

"The other boys will find this out soon enough," Mr. Hendricks said. "But I wanted to tell you first, to give you time to adjust."

"Adjust to what?" Luke asked, sitting down on a couch.

"Having your brother here at school with you."

"My brother?" Luke repeated. "You mean Matthew or Mark . . ." He tried to picture either of his rough, wild older brothers in their faded jeans and flannel shirts walking up the marble stairs at Hendricks. If he felt caged at the windowless school, his brothers would feel handcuffed, pinned down, thoroughly imprisoned. And how could Mother and Dad possibly afford to send them here? Why would they want to?

"No, *Lee,*" Mr. Hendricks said, stressing the fake name that Luke had adopted when he'd come out of hiding. Luke knew that he should be grateful that the parents of a boy named Lee Grant had donated his name and identity after the real Lee died in a skiing accident. The Grants were Barons—really rich people—so Luke's new identity was an impressive one indeed. But Luke didn't like to be called Lee, didn't like even to be reminded that he was supposed to be somebody else.

Mr. Hendricks was peering straight at Luke, waiting for Luke to catch on.

"I said your brother," Mr. Hendricks repeated. "Smithfield William Grant. *You* call him Smits. And he's coming here tomorrow."

THE MISSING

"Fans of Haddix's Shadow Children books will want to jump on this time travel adventure. . . . An exciting trip through history." —*Kirkus Reviews*

MARGARET PETERSON HADDIX

 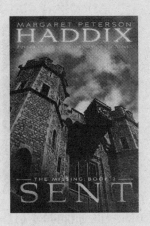

FOUND
978-1-4169-5421-7
Available now

SENT
978-1-4169-5422-4
Coming August 2009

FROM SIMON & SCHUSTER
BOOKS FOR YOUNG READERS

ENTER THE WORLD OF

EREC REX

Books 1 and 2 in stores now

THE DRAGON'S EYE   THE MONSTERS
OF OTHERNESS

And Book 3 coming in June 2009

THE SEARCH FOR TRUTH

Travel into magical new worlds with

The Chronicles of the Imaginarium Geographica!

HERE, THERE BE DRAGONS

THE SEARCH FOR THE RED DRAGON

THE INDIGO KING

THE SHADOW DRAGONS

Imagine a world where families are allowed only two children.

Illegal third children—shadow children—must live in hiding,

for if they are discovered, there is only one punishment:

Death.

Read the Shadow Children series by

MARGARET PETERSON HADDIX

Simon & Schuster • www.SimonSaysKids.com

Among
the Barons

Among
the Barons

MARGARET PETERSON HADDIX

SIMON & SCHUSTER
BOOKS FOR YOUNG READERS
NEW YORK LONDON TORONTO SYDNEY

If you purchased this book without a cover, you should be aware that this book is stolen property. It was reported as "unsold and destroyed" to the publisher, and neither the author nor the publisher has received any payment for this "stripped book."

This book is a work of fiction. Any references to historical events, real people, or real locales are used fictitiously. Other names, characters, places, and incidents are the product of the author's imagination, and any resemblance to actual events or locales or persons, living or dead, is entirely coincidental.

First Aladdin Paperbacks edition September 2004

Text copyright © 2003 by Margaret Peterson Haddix

SIMON & SCHUSTER BOOKS FOR YOUNG READERS
An imprint of Simon & Schuster
Children's Publishing Division
1230 Avenue of the Americas
New York, NY 10020

All rights reserved, including the right of
reproduction in whole or in part in any form.

Also available in a Simon & Schuster Books for Young Readers hardcover edition.
Designed by Greg Stadnyk
The text of this book was set in Elysium.

Printed in the United States of America
30 29 28 27 26 25 24 23 22

The Library of Congress has cataloged the hardcover edition as follows:
Haddix, Margaret Peterson.
Among the Barons / Margaret Peterson Haddix.
p. cm.
Sequel to: Among the betrayed.
Summary: In a future world of false identities, government lies, and death threats, Luke feels drawn to the younger brother of a boy whose name Luke has taken.
ISBN 0-689-83906-5
[1. Brothers—Fiction. 2. Science fiction.] I. Title.
PZ7.H11135 Am 2003
[Fic]—dc21
2002004534
ISBN 978-0-689-83910-8 (pbk.)
0410 OFF

For my father

CHAPTER ONE

Hey, L.! Mr. Hendricks wants to see you!"

Such a summons would have terrified Luke Garner only a few months earlier. When he'd first come to Hendricks School for Boys, the thought of having to talk to any grown-up, let alone the headmaster, would have turned him into a stammering, quaking fool desperately longing for a place to hide.

But that was back in April, and this was August. A lot had happened between April and August.

Now Luke just waved off the rising tide of "ooh's" from his friends in math class.

"What'd you do, L.? Have you been sneaking out to the woods again?" his friend John taunted him.

"Settle down, class," the teacher, Mr. Rees, said mildly. "You may be excused, Mr., uh, Mr. . . ."

Luke didn't wait for Mr. Rees to try to remember his name. Names were slippery things at Hendricks School anyway. Luke, like all his friends, was registered under a different name from what he had grown up with. So it was always hard to know what to call people.

Luke edged his way past his classmates' desks and slipped out the door. His friend Trey, who had delivered the message from Mr. Hendricks, was waiting for him.

"What's this about?" Luke asked as the two fell into step together, walking down the hall.

"I don't know. I just do what he tells me," Trey said with a dispirited shrug.

Sometimes Luke wanted to take Trey by the shoulders, shake him, and yell, "Think for yourself! Open your eyes! Live a little!" Twelve years of hiding in a tiny room had turned Trey into a human turtle, always ready to pull back into his shell at the slightest hint of danger.

But Mr. Hendricks had taken a liking to Trey and was working with him privately. That was why Trey was running errands for him today.

Trey looked furtively over at Luke. His dark hair hung down into his eyes. "Do you suppose it's—you know—time?"

Luke didn't have to ask what Trey meant. Sometimes it seemed like everyone at Hendricks School was just holding his breath, waiting. Waiting for a day when none of the boys would be illegal anymore, when they could all reclaim their rightful names, when they could go back to their rightful families without fear that the Population Police would catch them. But both Luke and

Trey knew that that day wouldn't come easily. And Luke, at least, had promised to do everything he could to bring it about.

His stomach churned. The fear he thought he'd outgrown reached him at last.

"Did he say ... did Mr. Hendricks say ... ," he stammered. What if Mr. Hendricks had a plan for Luke to help with? What if that plan required more courage than Luke had?

Trey went back to looking down at the polished tile floor.

"Mr. Hendricks didn't say anything except, 'Go get your buddy L. out of math class and tell him to come see me,'" Trey said.

"Oh," Luke said.

They reached the end of the hall, and Luke pushed open the heavy wood door to the outside. Trey winced, as he always did anytime he was exposed to sunshine, fresh air, or anything else outdoors. But Luke breathed in gratefully. Luke had spent his first twelve years on his family's farm; some of his fondest memories involved the feeling of warm dirt on his bare feet, sunshine on the back of his neck, a hoe in his hand—and his parents and brothers around him.

But it didn't do to think much about his parents and brothers anymore. When he'd accepted his fake identity, he'd had to leave them and the farm behind. And even when he'd been with them, he'd had to live like a shadow or a ghost, something no one else outside the family knew about.

Once when his middle brother, Mark, was in first grade, he'd accidentally slipped and mentioned Luke's name at school.

"I had to tell the teacher that Mark just had an imaginary friend named Luke," Luke's mother had told him. "But I worried about that for months afterward. I was so scared the teacher would report you, and the Population Police would come and take you away. I'm just glad that a lot of little kids do have imaginary friends."

She'd bitten her lip telling Luke that story. Luke could still see the strained expression on her face. She hadn't even told him about that episode until the day before he left the farm and his family for good. By then she'd meant the story as assurance, he knew—assurance that he was doing the right thing by leaving.

At the time, Luke hadn't known what to make of that story. It just added to the jumble of confused thoughts and fears in his head. But now—now that story made him angry. It wasn't fair that he'd had to be invisible. It wasn't fair that his brother couldn't talk about him. It wasn't fair that the Government had made him illegal simply because he was a third child and the Government thought families should have no more than two.

Luke stepped out into the sunshine feeling strangely happy to be so angry. It felt good to be so sure about what he thought, so totally convinced that he was right and the Government was wrong. And if Mr. Hendricks really did have a plan for Luke, it'd be good to hang on to this righteous anger.

The two boys climbed down an imposing number of marble steps. Luke noticed that Trey glanced back longingly at the school more than once. Not Luke. Hendricks had no windows—to accommodate the fears of kids like Trey—and Luke always felt slightly caged anytime he was inside.

They walked on down the lane to a house half hidden in bushes. Mr. Hendricks was waiting for them at the door.

"Come on in," he said heartily to Luke. "Trey, you can go on back to school and see about learning something for once." That was a joke—Trey had done nothing but read while he'd been in hiding, so he knew as much about some subjects as the teachers did.

Luke opened the door, and Mr. Hendricks rolled back in his wheelchair to give Luke room to pass. When he'd first met Mr. Hendricks, Luke had been awkward around him, particularly because of the wheelchair. But now Luke practically forgot that Mr. Hendricks's lower legs were missing. Going into the living room, Luke automatically stepped out of the way of Mr. Hendricks's wheels.

"The other boys will find this out soon enough," Mr. Hendricks said. "But I wanted to tell you first, to give you time to adjust."

"Adjust to what?" Luke asked, sitting down on a couch.

"Having your brother here at school with you."

"My brother?" Luke repeated. "You mean Matthew or Mark . . ." He tried to picture either of his rough, wild older brothers in their faded jeans and flannel shirts walking up the marble stairs at Hendricks. If he felt caged at the windowless school, his brothers would feel handcuffed, pinned down, thoroughly imprisoned. And how could Mother and Dad possibly afford to send them here? Why would they want to?

"No, *Lee*," Mr. Hendricks said, stressing the fake name that Luke had adopted when he'd come out of hiding. Luke knew that he should be grateful that the parents of a boy named Lee Grant had donated his name and identity after the real Lee died in a skiing accident. The Grants were Barons—really rich people—so Luke's new identity was an impressive one indeed. But Luke didn't like to be called Lee, didn't like even to be reminded that he was supposed to be somebody else.

Mr. Hendricks was peering straight at Luke, waiting for Luke to catch on.

"I said your brother," Mr. Hendricks repeated. "Smithfield William Grant. *You* call him Smits. And he's coming here tomorrow."

CHAPTER TWO

Mr. Hendricks handed Luke a picture, but Luke was too shocked to look at it yet.

"Lee's brother," he finally said quietly. "Lee's brother is coming to school here. Tomorrow."

"Yes, your brother," Mr. Hendricks repeated. "*You* are Lee."

"Aw, Mr. Hendricks," Luke protested. "It's just you and me. We don't have to pretend, do we? And the other kids—they *know* I'm not really Lee Grant. This Smits kid is going to know I'm not his brother. So we don't have to act like it, do we?"

Mr. Hendricks just looked at Luke. Luke couldn't stop the flow of questions. "Why's he coming here, anyway?"

"He misses his older brother," Mr. Hendricks said. "He misses you."

The "older" was a surprise. Luke felt even stranger now.

"Mr. Hendricks, I never even knew Lee had a brother. This kid couldn't miss me. He's never met me. What's really going on here?"

Mr. Hendricks seemed to sag a bit against the back of his chair.

"I'm only repeating what his parents told me over the phone this morning," he said.

"Well, of course," Luke said. "They know it's not safe to say anything real over the phone. They know the Population Police tap phone lines all the time. This is all some . . . some mix-up or something."

"Luke—Lee, I mean—I don't really know what's going on here. But I think it's best to proceed with caution. You do need to begin acting like Lee. You do need to pretend that you know Smits well, as a brother. For the sake of everyone involved."

Usually Luke had a lot of respect for Mr. Hendricks, but now he couldn't resist making a face.

"That's crazy," Luke said. "Why pretend when nobody's going to be fooled?"

"Nobody?" Mr. Hendricks countered. "Nobody? Don't be so sure. Actors can't always know who's in the audience."

Luke shook his head disdainfully.

"This is Hendricks School," he said. "This isn't Population Police headquarters. This isn't some Government convention. We're safe here. Everyone knows we're almost all third children with fake I.D.'s. Nobody's going to report us."

"Really," Mr. Hendricks said. "Is your memory that short? What about Jason?"

Jason had been a Population Police spy who'd infiltrated

the school. Just hearing his name could still send a shiver of fear through Luke's body, but he held it back, tried not to let Mr. Hendricks see.

"Jason's gone now," Luke said. He was proud of the way he kept his voice level and calm. "And you said yourself, you're screening new applicants better, you're not going to let that happen again. And we're all so . . . comfortable here now. We're talking to one another about being illegal, about having fake I.D.'s. We're all friends."

Mr. Hendricks rolled over to the window and stared out at a cascade of forsythia that hid his house from the lane.

"I worry that you've all become too comfortable. That we're not preparing you for . . ." He let his voice trail off. Then he looked back at Luke. "For reality. What if this Smits is another Jason?"

The question hung in the air. To escape Mr. Hendricks's gaze, Luke glanced down at the photo of Smits. He saw cold gray eyes, a patrician nose, light hair, a sneer. Smits Grant was probably only eleven or twelve years old, but he might as well have been a miniature adult. The look he had given the camera—and now seemed to be giving Luke—made Luke feel like a poor, dumb country kid again. Never mind that Luke himself was wearing leather shoes, tailored pants, and a fancy shirt and tie. He felt barefoot, snotty-nosed, and ignorant beyond words, compared with the photo of Smits.

"Can't you tell him not to come?" Luke asked Mr.

Hendricks. "Say he's not allowed at your school? If you're worried, I mean."

"He's Smithfield *Grant*," Mr. Hendricks said. "His father—your father—is one of the most powerful men in the country. I'd have a better chance of stopping the wind than stopping a Grant from doing what he wants."

"I'm a Grant, too," Luke said. He wasn't sure whether he was trying to make a joke or trying out the words, trying to make them sound true. His voice came out limp and uncertain, failing on all accounts.

But Mr. Hendricks nodded.

"Good," he said. "Remember that."

CHAPTER THREE

Luke sat at the top of the steps that led to Hendricks School. Smits Grant was due to arrive any minute, and Luke had already begun his charade.

My brother's on his way, Luke told himself. *I'm so excited, I couldn't wait inside. I couldn't stand it if I weren't the first one to see him.*

Nothing could have been further from the truth. Mr. Hendricks had all but threatened Luke with a firing squad just to get him outside. As far as Luke was concerned, he'd be happy if he *never* saw Smits.

Could that happen? What if Luke turned around now, hid inside, and somehow managed to stay out of Smits's way forever? They ought to have different classes. Luke could find out the other boy's schedule and make sure their paths never crossed. Luke had plenty of experience hiding.

Of course, to avoid Smits he'd also have to go without eating. All the boys always ate together, in the dining hall.

Luke just couldn't see Mr. Hendricks agreeing to let Luke eat somewhere else.

And he didn't want to. *His* friends would all be eating in the dining hall. What he really wanted was for Smits to be the one set apart, hidden. That is, if he had to be at Hendricks at all.

For perhaps the billionth time since he'd learned about Smits, Luke wondered, *Why in the world would he want to come here?*

Luke kept his eyes on the long, curving driveway. A dark car turned in at the Hendricks School gates, disappeared behind a clump of trees, reappeared, and sped on toward the school. Luke's stomach churned.

The car pulled up in front of the school. It seemed about as long as a tractor and a hay wagon combined. The windows—all ten of them—were tinted black, so Luke couldn't tell if there was a boy inside staring out just as intently as Luke was staring in.

Oh, no. What if Smits's parents had come, too?

Luke hadn't thought of that before. Now panic coursed through his veins. He couldn't meet all three Grants at once. He just couldn't.

The driver's door glided open—smoothly, like it was on oiled hinges. Luke held his breath, waiting to see who would appear. A polished boot stepped out, followed by a second one that seemed even shinier. Then a tall, aristocratic-looking man in a dark blue uniform and stiff cap stood up. The uniform had gold braid around the cuffs and collar, and at the rim of the cap. Luke could even have believed it was real gold, pure metal.

The man turned and practically marched, soldierlike, to the other side of the car. He opened a second door, held out his hand, and said, "Sir?"

So this wasn't Mr. Grant. This was a servant. A chauffeur.

Luke could see a very pale hand thrust out of the car and clasp the chauffeur's. Then a boy stepped out. Luke recognized him from the picture of Smits Grant.

Somehow Luke managed to make his feet maneuver down the stairs, toward the car. Mr. Hendricks had made it quite clear: Luke *had* to act eager to see Smits. He had to rush over to him right away. But Luke's mind was racing faster than his feet.

What am I supposed to do when I get there? Shake his hand? Or—oh, no. What if the Grants are the type of family who hug one another?

Luke stumbled at the bottom of the stairs but caught his balance again quickly. He didn't think the chauffeur or Smits even noticed. They weren't looking toward Luke. Luke planted his feet a mere yard from the younger boy, but he had to clear his throat before Smits turned his head toward Luke.

"Hi, uh, Brother," Luke said awkwardly.

He lifted his right arm tentatively, to shake hands if that's what Smits wanted to do. Or if Smits stepped close enough and reached out, Luke could probably force his arms to wrap around Smits in something like a hug. If he had to.

Smits didn't move.

His cold gray eyes looked straight at Luke—straight through him, it almost seemed. For a horrible second Luke was afraid that Smits was going to refuse to acknowledge him, maybe even yell out, "This boy's a fraud! He stole my real brother's name!" Then Smits's gaze flickered away, and he mumbled, "Hey, Lee."

Luke exhaled, only barely managing not to let out an audible sigh of relief.

Smits looked at the chauffeur.

"My luggage?" he asked.

"Of course, sir," the chauffeur said, and walked to the back of the car.

Luke let his half-extended right arm fall back to his side. It was clear that Smits didn't want Luke to touch him. While Smits was watching the chauffeur, Luke got the nerve to peer past him, into the car. If Mr. and Mrs. Grant were in there, he wanted to be prepared.

"They didn't come," Smits said.

Luke jumped. "Huh?"

"Mom and Dad," Smits said. "They had no interest in accompanying me here." He sounded so smug saying that, Luke wanted to punch him.

"Oh," Luke said. "Well, why would they?" He was

trying to sound casual, the way he would with his own brothers. His real brothers.

"Because of *me*," Smits said. "Because they might have wanted to say good-bye to *me*."

CHAPTER *FOUR*

By dinnertime the rumors were flying through the school. The new boy had brought four suitcases, his own computer, and a giant TV. The new boy had taken one look at the room he was supposed to share with five other boys, stalked down to the office, and demanded a room of his own. A big one even. The new boy had wandered into the dining hall, gotten one whiff of the evening meal, and instantly ordered that all *his* meals be privately catered, brought in from the city, an hour away.

Luke was willing to believe any of those rumors. But as far as he knew, he was the only boy in the school who had actually met Smits.

"What's he really like?" Trey asked as he poked his fork at the tasteless heap of boiled greens on his plate. "Is he truly awful?"

Luke chewed for a minute and swallowed, glad for once that the food was so stringy and tough. It gave him time to think. He shrugged, trying for nonchalance.

"Well, he's my brother," Luke said. "Aren't most brothers awful?"

Trey snorted. "Your brother—right. So why didn't *you* bring a computer and a TV? Why don't *you* have a private room? Why are you eating this slop when you could be having—I don't know—caviar? Foie gras?"

Luke didn't have the slightest idea what caviar or foie gras was, but he wasn't about to admit it. He could feel the whole tableful of boys watching him, waiting for his response. He shrugged again.

"Guess I'm just not as picky as he is," Luke said. "Guess I'm a nicer person."

Luke was relieved that the other boys had stopped staring at him. Instead, their gaze was trained just beyond him, right over his head.

"Lee," someone said.

Luke whirled around and saw what the others were looking at. It was Smits. Luke felt his face go red. How much had Smits heard?

"Aren't you going to introduce me?" Smits asked coldly. He slid into a seat beside Luke. The other boys scrambled to make room for him, as if the table actually belonged to Smits and they were just grateful that he wasn't ordering them away entirely.

"Um, sure," Luke said. "Everybody, this is my brother, Smits." He was proud of himself that he could get the words of that colossal lie out of his mouth so smoothly. "Uh, Smits, this is Trey and, um, Robert and Joel and John. . . ."

Smits nodded after each name and reached out his hand for each boy to shake. After some fumbling, Luke's friends managed to think to stick their hands out as well. Luke wasn't surprised by his friends' awkwardness, but he felt strangely ashamed. Why couldn't Trey have remembered to put down his fork before he reached out his hand? He'd splashed some of the slimy greens right onto Smits's shirt. And Smits only made it worse, pretending not to notice, just shaking hands right and left, smooth as a politician.

"Nice to meet you," Smits said again and again. "Nice to meet you."

Luke remembered what he'd thought when he'd first seen the picture of Smits—that Smits looked like a miniature grown-up. He acted like one, too. Or like a little robot, programmed to say what some stiff, formal grown-up would want a kid to say. Luke had half a mind to yell at him, "Oh, knock it off. Tell us all the truth. Why are you here?"

But of course he didn't.

"So," Smits said when the introductions were finally over. "Is this a decent place? Lee here hasn't told me a whole lot. Doesn't write home as much as Mom wants him to." He gave Luke a playful punch on the arm and sort of winked at the rest of the boys. "I must say, I've found the staff quite accommodating."

Luke figured Trey was the only one at the table who knew what "accommodating" meant. That had to be the reason Trey actually opened his mouth.

"So they did let you have a private room," Trey said. "And get the food you want."

Smits looked down at the other boys' meals.

"Sure," he said. "Nobody could possibly be expected to eat *that*."

Luke saw Joel and John silently put their forks down.

"It's not so bad," Luke said. "You should give it a try before you make up your mind."

Smits laughed.

"No, thanks," he said. "Mom always did say you had an undiscriminating palate. Dad used to joke, 'Lee'll eat anything that doesn't eat him first.' *I'm* not like that."

"Nothing but the best for Smits, right?" Luke said quietly.

Smits clapped him on the back.

"You remembered!" he said. He shoved away from the table. "Well, I'll be off now. Just wanted to meet Lee's friends. See you all later."

And, in total defiance of school rules, he strolled out of the dining hall.

Nobody stopped him. Luke and his friends stared off after him for a full minute.

"What was that all about?" Trey said finally.

"I haven't the slightest clue," Luke said.

CHAPTER *FIVE*

They had games after dinner.

This was something that Luke was very proud of. It had been his idea to ask Mr. Hendricks for a time to run and play. Most of his friends, in hiding, had been in small spaces. They'd been trained from birth to be quiet and still, to whisper, not yell, to tiptoe, not run. Their lives had depended on it. Luke didn't know how many shadow children had ever been discovered because of a poorly timed squeal of joy or a scamper across a creaky floor. He didn't want to know. But his friends were so good at not moving, at not talking, that they sometimes seemed hidden even now.

"They need a chance to be kids," Luke had argued with Mr. Hendricks back at the beginning of the summer. "They need a time to run as fast as they can, to scream at the top of their lungs, to . . ." Luke hadn't been able to finish his sentence. He'd been overcome with the memory of all the games he'd played with his brothers—his real brothers.

MARGARET PETERSON HADDIX

Football, baseball, kickball, spud. Dodgeball, volleyball, kick the can, tag . . .

"All right," Mr. Hendricks had said. "You're in charge."

At first Luke's idea had seemed like a disaster. Boys who had sat still all their lives had no idea how to run. They cowered at the sight of a ball rolling toward them, collapsed in fear to see a football spiraling their way. But Luke had been patient, throwing the balls so slowly they barely seemed to move, applauding anyone who managed even to walk fast. And now, after three months, Trey had a pretty good pitching arm on him, and John was a master at dodgeball, and there was a little kid in the eight-year-old class who could run so fast, he could even beat some of the teachers who occasionally stayed for races.

Luke thought he had every right to be proud. They still mostly played in the dining hall, with all the tables and chairs cleared away, because the idea of going outside was too much for most of the boys. But Luke had hopes. By next summer, he thought, they'd all be outdoors climbing trees, maybe even making up games of their own.

That was what Luke dreamed of, when he wasn't dreaming of the Population Law being changed.

But tonight, as he began folding up chairs and tables after dinner, Ms. Hawkins, the school secretary, stopped him.

"No games for you tonight, young man," she said.

Luke gaped at her. Ms. Hawkins never stayed around school until dinnertime, let alone afterward. She was a shadowy figure herself—Luke couldn't remember her saying two words to him even once since the first day he'd arrived at school.

Ms. Hawkins went on talking, as if she was used to boys not answering. She probably was.

"You're to meet your brother in the front hallway instead," she said. When Luke didn't move, she snapped, "Now! Get on with you!"

Luke handed her the chair he was holding. She managed to grasp it but looked puzzled, as if she could no longer understand what it was just because it was folded up.

Except for Mr. Hendricks, all the staff at the school were a little strange. If Luke hadn't known better, he would have wondered if they'd all spent their childhood in hiding as well. But the Population Law had been in effect for only fourteen years; Luke was among the oldest kids to come out of hiding. Mr. Hendricks had just hired odd people on purpose.

"If Ms. Hawkins ever tried to turn any of you in," he'd told Luke once, "who would believe her?"

That was true of the teachers, too, and the school nurse. It was even true of the school janitor. Luke understood Mr. Hendricks's reasoning, but sometimes he longed to be around normal adults. He wasn't sure now what to believe of Ms. Hawkins's instructions. What if she was just confused? Shouldn't Smits be here playing games with the other boys, instead of pulling Luke away, too?

"Didn't you hear me?" Ms. Hawkins said threateningly.

"Um, sure," Luke said. "I mean, yes, ma'am."

He turned and walked toward the door.

"Trey, can you organize the games tonight?" he called to his friend on his way out.

"Wha—how do I do that?" Trey asked. He sounded as panicked as if Luke had asked him to attack Population Police headquarters.

"Get John to help. And Joel," Luke said.

Joel and John glanced up from the table they were folding. They looked every bit as stricken as Trey.

Luke had no confidence that they'd manage without him. But he pushed his way out the door anyhow.

The hall outside the dining room was quiet and dimly lit. Luke rushed past dark classrooms and offices. He'd just tell Smits to get lost—that's what he'd do. Smits had no right to order him around.

But when Luke got to the front hallway—an echoey place with ancient-looking portraits on the walls—his resolve vanished. Smits was standing there alone. He had his back to Luke, and for the first time Luke realized what a small boy Smits really was. From behind he looked like the kind of kid you'd pick last for a baseball team.

Then Smits turned around.

"Hey, bro," he said heartily. "I thought you might give me a tour of the school grounds. Let me see what this place is really like."

"Okay," Luke said hesitantly.

Smits was already pushing open the front door, as if he, not Luke, were the one who knew Hendricks School. They walked down the stairs in silence, then Smits turned around and regarded the building with narrowed eyes.

"Why aren't there any windows?" he asked.

Luke wondered how much Smits had been told about Hendricks, about third children, about the needs of kids coming out of hiding. Surely Smits knew the truth. Surely he didn't need to ask a question like that.

Luke opted for the safest answer possible anyhow.

"Some of the kids here have agoraphobia. Do you know what that is? It means they're afraid of wide-open spaces. Not having windows is part of the way Mr. Hendricks is trying to cure them," he said. "He thinks that if they can't see the outdoors, they'll start longing for it."

"But that's pretty much torture for the rest of us, isn't it?" Smits countered. "It's like cruel and unusual punishment. And it's a fire hazard." He shook his head, flipping hair out of his eyes. "I'm going to have a window installed in my room. Maybe in every room I'd ever be in. It wouldn't do to have the heir to the Grant fortune killed in a fire or something."

Luke noticed he said "heir," not "one of the heirs." Was that a clue? Was that why Smits had come—to warn Luke away from the family money? Was this Luke's cue to say, "Hey, I don't want a dime of your fortune. I don't want anything from your family. Just an identity. Just the right to exist"?

Luke didn't say anything. It was true, he didn't care about the Grants' money. But he couldn't bring himself to speak sincerely to this strange, overconfident kid. It was easier to keep pretending the lie between them was reality.

They started strolling down the driveway. In different company this would have been a pleasant walk. Crickets sang in the bushes; the sunset glowed on the horizon. But Luke was too tense to enjoy any of it.

"That's the headmaster's house over there," he said, pointing. He was just talking to break the silence. "It's where Mr. Hendricks lives. You won't see him around the school much. He kind of lets it run on its own."

"I've already talked to him four times today," Smits said.

"Oh," Luke said. A few months ago he wouldn't have had the nerve to say anything else. But now he ventured, "What about?"

"Important matters," Smits said. They walked on. Luke could tell Smits wasn't really paying attention to anything around them. Not the weeping willows draping gently toward the driveway, not the sound of the brook gurgling just beyond the school grounds.

"I already saw all this, driving in," Smits said impatiently. "Isn't there anything else?"

"There's the back of the school," Luke said. "That's where we have our garden. And the woods—"

"Show me," Smits said.

They turned around. Luke struggled to hide his reluctance. If he was proud of the school's nightly games, he was even prouder of the school garden. Under his direction the Hendricks students had planted it, weeded it, and coaxed it into its full glory all summer long. Luke could just imagine

Smits barely glancing at it, then sniffing disdainfully, "So?"

And the woods—the woods were a special place, too. Back in the spring, when Luke had first arrived at Hendricks, he'd found refuge in the woods. He'd made his first attempt at a garden in a clearing there. He'd dared to stand up to the impostor Jason there. He'd met girls from the neighboring Harlow School for Girls there—including his friend Nina, who, he was sure, would also someday help in ending the Population Law.

Luke knew he could never explain all of that to Smits. Smits had no right to hear any of it. He probably wouldn't even care. So the woods, to Smits, would just look like a scraggly collection of scrub brush and untended trees.

Silently seething, Luke led Smits off the driveway and along an overgrown path winding down toward the woods. Darkness was falling now. Maybe Smits would be satisfied if they just rushed by the woods and the garden, and Luke wouldn't have to listen to any of Smits's comments.

At the edge of the woods Luke turned around. "Here. This is it. The woods. Now you've seen it."

Smits didn't answer, just ducked under a low branch. He reached out and touched a tree trunk hesitantly, as if he were afraid it would bite.

"Do you come here a lot?" Smits asked.

"I used to," Luke said brusquely.

"I don't know anything about nature," Smits admitted. "Sometimes I wonder . . ."

"What?" Luke asked.

Smits shook his head, as if unwilling or unable to say more. His fingers traced a pattern on the bark. He looked back toward Luke. In the twilight his face seemed paler than ever.

"Can you help me?" he whispered. "Can you be Lee?"

CHAPTER SIX

L uke stared at the younger boy.

"I—I don't know," he admitted. It was probably the first honest thing he'd said to Smits. "I can try."

Smits dropped his gaze.

"There's something wrong with the way he died," he whispered. Luke had to lean in close to hear.

"He was skiing, wasn't he?" Luke asked. Luke had only the faintest idea of what skiing was. "Did he run into a tree or something?"

Smits shook his head impatiently.

"You don't understand," he said. "He—" Smits broke off, his gaze suddenly riveted on something far beyond Luke. Then he snapped his attention down to the ground and raised his voice. "Ugh! Why did you bring me here! Now my shoes are all muddy!"

Baffled, Luke glanced over his shoulder. A burly man Luke had never seen before was running down the hill toward them.

"I see you, Smithfield," the man yelled. "Your game is up."

The man came closer. It was like seeing a tree run, or a mountain—the man was that imposing. Luke could only watch in awe. The man had muscles bulging from his arms and legs. His neck looked thicker than Luke's midsection. He had his fists clenched, as if he was ready to fight. Luke felt instant pity for any opponent this man might face.

"Hello, Oscar," Smits said, his voice as casual as it had been back in the dining room, greeting all of Luke's friends. He suddenly seemed like the little robot again.

"It is not funny, what you did," the man—Oscar—raged. "I have fully informed your parents. They are not amused, either."

Smits shrugged.

"Having a bodyguard is very tiresome, you know," Smits said.

For a minute Luke was afraid that Oscar was going to slug Smits. The huge man stepped closer, but he did nothing more threatening than narrowing his eyes.

"It is necessary," Oscar huffed. "It is not safe for you to go anywhere without protection. Especially"—he gazed distastefully around him, taking in the scrubby trees, the tall, untrimmed grass at the edge of the woods—"especially someplace unsecured like this."

"Well," Smits said. "Here's Lee. Why aren't you protecting Lee, too?"

Oscar's gaze flickered toward Luke, then back to Smits. His glare intensified.

"Your parents hired me solely to protect you," Oscar said. "I do my job with honor and dignity and pride." He spoke so pompously, Luke almost expected Oscar to snap into a military salute.

Smits was rolling his eyes.

"So you say. 'Honor and dignity and pride,'" he repeated, making a total mockery of the words. "You must have had a hard time explaining why you woke up hours late this morning, locked in your closet, when I had already left."

"I blame you!" Oscar exploded. "Your parents blame you! I told them the whole story. You drugged me and dragged me into that closet."

Luke decided he'd totally underestimated Smits if Smits had managed to drag Oscar so much as an inch. Smits would not be the last kid picked for a baseball team. He'd be the kid who could trample every other player, even without teammates.

"Me?" Smits said innocently. "I'm just a little kid. Where would I get anything to drug you with? How could I drag you anywhere?"

"You had help." Oscar growled. "The chauffeur—"

"Hey"—Smits shrugged again—"it's your word against his. And mine."

"But your parents believe me," Oscar retorted. He grabbed Smits's arm and jerked him practically off his feet.

"Come along. Let's get you somewhere safe."

"Fine," Smits said. "You can wipe the mud off my shoes when we get back to my room."

Oscar grunted.

Luke followed the other two up the hill. He kept a few paces behind. Smits seemed to have forgotten about him; Oscar had barely noticed him in the first place. Smits was now keeping up a running banter, making fun of Oscar for being muscle-bound and stupid and easily tricked.

What kind of a game was Smits playing? And—was it really a game?

Luke remembered the urgency in the other boy's voice. "Can you help me? Can you be Lee?" And, "There's something wrong with the way he died." What had Smits meant?

Luke thought he'd been escaping danger when he took Lee Grant's identity. Why did he suddenly feel like he'd only traded one peril for another?

CHAPTER SEVEN

I t turned out that Smits did have classes with Luke—
every single one of them.

"See, this is what happens when the big brother goofs off, runs away from school, and gets left behind a grade," Smits said, slipping into a desk beside Luke the next morning. "He gets stuck with his younger brother every minute of the day."

Luke could feel all his friends watching them. Smits beamed happily back at everyone.

"*I'm* the smart one in the family, in case you couldn't tell," Smits said.

Luke glowered. "Knock it off," he muttered under his breath.

"Someone's listening," Smits hissed back.

Luke half turned. At the back of the classsroom, barely two feet away, a hulking presence towered over all the boys still scurrying into the room.

Oscar.

Luke wasn't the only one staring. The huge man was enough of a sight to attract attention just by himself. But he stood out even more today because of what he held in his massive fists: a sledgehammer.

"Hey, everyone. Meet my bodyguard," Smits said.

"Is he always, um"—Trey gulped—"*armed* like that?"

"You mean the hammer?" Smits asked. He made a mocking face. "That's my parents' idea of a compromise. He'll be carrying that around until Mr. Hendricks installs a few windows." Smits looked around at blank expressions. "Didn't any of you ever think about what would happen if there was a fire here? How trapped you'd all be? You won't have to worry now. Hey, *your* parents should be chipping in on Oscar's wages, too. He'd be saving you guys, too, knocking down walls."

Smits pretended to swing an imaginary hammer himself.

From the front of the room Mr. Dirk, the teacher, said mildly, "Boys, we've always had plans in place for emergency evacuation procedures."

Everyone turned to stare in amazement at Mr. Dirk. Luke wondered if any of his friends had ever thought to worry about a fire before. The danger outside the walls of Hendricks School had always seemed so great, he was sure no one had ever feared being trapped inside. He felt like standing up and asking everyone, "Does it make you feel any better to have more to be scared of?"

Instead, he slid lower in his seat and kept quiet as Mr.

Dirk started lecturing about ancient history.

The rest of the day went about the same way. Smits made a spectacle of himself, Luke's classmates gaped at Oscar, and Luke could only slump lower and lower in his chair in each successive class. Meals should have been a relief, because Smits didn't show up for them. At least, not physically. But everyone in the dining hall seemed to be talking about him.

"What do you suppose *he's* eating right now?" Joel asked at dinner as thin gruel dribbled from his spoon.

"Roasted wild duck—illegally, I might add—garlic pota-toes, French-cut green beans, and chocolate mousse," Trey said gloomily. "He told me."

"Maybe he was lying," Luke said.

"No," Trey said. "I believe him."

Luke did, too—about that. But he wasn't going to admit it.

"Hey, how much do you think his bodyguard has to eat to keep all those muscles?" John asked. "Did you see him? I couldn't do a bit of homework at study hour. All I could think about was what would happen if he swung that hammer at me. He was standing right behind me, you know."

"You never do any homework at study hour anyhow," Luke said. But nobody seemed to hear him.

By bedtime Luke just wanted the day to be over. But he'd barely fallen asleep before he woke to someone shak-ing him. It was a thick hand with muscular fingers. He'd never known before that people could have highly developed muscles in their fingers.

"Your brother needs you," a deep voice whispered. "Come on."

It was Oscar. Luke stifled a yelp of terror.

"Don't wake your roommates," Oscar warned.

Luke wondered if any of them were awake already but pretending to sleep. Seven other boys slept in his room. How many had their eyelids open, just a crack, just enough to watch Luke leave? If Oscar was luring Luke away to hurt him—to kill him, even—how many boys would be able to tell Mr. Hendricks, "Oscar came into our room at midnight to get Luke. It's Oscar's fault. Oscar's dangerous"?

Luke told himself Oscar had no reason to want to hurt Luke, let alone kill him. Luke had no reason to fear Oscar.

But he did anyway.

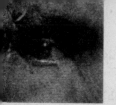

CHAPTER *EIGHT*

Luke forced himself to slide out of bed. Oscar kept a warning hand on Luke's shoulder, and it was all Luke could do not to grab Trey, who slept in the bunk bed above Luke, or Joel, who slept in the bed across from him, and beg, "Come with me! Protect me!" Luke suddenly felt like he needed a bodyguard, too.

But Luke kept silent, as if what mattered most was denying his own fear. Oscar propelled him out the door, into the hallway, and up a set of back stairs. Luke couldn't help remembering another time he'd been out of his room at night, and terrified. Then, he'd been desperate to thwart the plot of Jason, the Population Police spy who'd pretended to be another third child with a fake I.D. Now—did Oscar have a plot? Did Smits?

Luke reminded himself that, back then, he hadn't known if he could trust anybody at Hendricks. Now he could trust his friends, if he had to. He could trust Mr. Hendricks. He could run to any of the adults in the school, and even if they were strange, they would do their best to help him.

At the top of the stairs Oscar turned Luke toward a carved wooden door. Before Oscar even opened the door, Luke could hear someone crying behind it. As the door gave way Smits sat up in bed and stared resentfully at Luke.

"I miss . . ." he began. Whatever else he intended to say was lost in a wail of sorrow.

"Home," Oscar finished for him. "He's homesick. Acting like a stupid little kid."

Oscar sank into a chair at the end of the bed. He pushed Luke toward Smits. Smits's wail turned into keening. As Luke eased down onto the bed beside Smits he suddenly understood what Smits had intended to say. *Lee.* Smits missed Lee, the real Lee, the real older brother he must have looked up to and admired. And loved. For the first time Luke felt sorry for the younger boy. He couldn't imagine what it would be like to know that one of his real brothers, Matthew or Mark, was dead. It was bad enough that Luke would probably never see either of them again, but at least he could still think of them back home, playing pranks and baling hay, making fun of each other. Missing Luke. He could imagine their lives going on, even without him.

But Smits—Smits had nothing left of his brother. He was gone.

And Luke had taken his name.

Luke glanced fearfully back at Oscar. How could anyone hear Smits sobbing and think he was merely a foolish, homesick kid? Luke knew what grief was like. He could hear all the pain in Smits's wordless wails: *My brother is dead. I loved him and now he's gone, and I hurt more than I thought it was possible to hurt. . . .* What if Oscar suddenly understood, too?

Smits's grief was dangerous. Smits's grief could kill Luke.

Luke reached out and awkwardly patted Smits's shoulder.

"There, there," he said. His voice sounded wooden even to his own ears. "You're okay."

Smits stiffened. He looked at Luke in bewilderment, as if he'd never seen him before.

"Are you really homesick?" Luke asked. "Or did you just have a bad dream?"

Behind them Oscar turned on the overhead light. The harsh glare hurt Luke's eyes. Smits blinked rapidly.

"I guess I just had a bad dream," he said. "I—I dreamed you died."

"Well, I should hope you were crying, then," Luke said, trying to make his words sound like a joke between brothers, not a warning between strangers. "Go back to acting," Luke wanted to tell Smits. "Don't let Oscar know the truth. Don't you know what's at risk here?" But he wasn't sure that Smits did know. He wasn't sure that Smits cared.

Smits sniffed.

MARGARET PETERSON HADDIX

"Can I tell you the dream?" he asked.

Luke stole another quick glance at Oscar, who was now practically reclining in his chair, his eyes half closed. His very posture seemed to say, "Hey, I'm just supposed to guard the kid's body. Bad dreams aren't my problem."

"Sure," Luke said. "Tell me your dream."

"Y-you were skiing," Smits said. He stopped and gulped. He wouldn't look at Luke. He kept his head down, his eyes trained on his blanket. "You were skiing and you were in danger. You knew you were in danger—"

"What, were you skiing behind me?" Luke asked. "Was I scared you'd fall on me?" He was determined to keep this light, to keep Smits from descending back into that mad grief.

Smits flashed Luke a look of sheer fury. And Luke understood. Smits wasn't describing a dream. He was describing what had really happened to Lee. He thought Luke needed to know, and this was the only way Smits could tell him.

"I wasn't there," Smits said quietly. Luke wanted to protest, to say Smits was giving away too much now. But dreams sometimes had that kind of logic, that the dreamer could know things that happened far away.

"Did L—I mean, did I know what the danger was?" Luke asked.

Smits tilted his head thoughtfully.

"I don't know," he said. "Probably. You were carrying something. You weren't just skiing for fun. You were trying to get somewhere, to deliver something. And then a soldier shot you."

"A soldier?" Luke asked. He was used to fearing the Population Police. He'd never thought about soldiers hurting ordinary people.

Of course, the real Lee Grant had never been an ordinary person. He'd been the son of one of the richest men in the country.

"Why would a soldier want to shoot me?" Luke asked.

"I don't know," Smits said. He was crying again, but quietly. "He wanted to stop you from going wherever you were going. From delivering whatever you were delivering."

"And you don't know what that was? Or where I was going?"

Silently Smits shook his head.

Behind them Oscar suddenly released a giant snore. Luke jumped. Oscar's snores subsided into gentler rumblings. Smits giggled.

"Guess we don't have to worry about—," Luke started to say.

But Smits stopped giggling and clapped his hand over Luke's mouth. Then he leaned over and whispered in Luke's ear, "He might be faking. He's not as stupid as you'd think. He's always watching. . . ."

Smits backed away from Luke. The two boys stared at each other, trying to fit back into the roles they'd been playing.

"So that's all there was to your dream?" Luke said.

Smits nodded.

"So, see, it was just a nightmare. It wasn't real. I'm right here. Nothing happened to me. No soldier shot me. I wouldn't be skiing anyhow, this time of year."

With every word Luke spoke, he could see more tears welling up in Smits's eyes. Because, Luke knew, it was no comfort to Smits to have Luke there. It wasn't reassuring to know that Luke was alive. The real Lee was still dead.

"Here," Luke said roughly, patting Smits's pillow. "Just go back to sleep. You'll feel better in the morning."

Smits obediently slid down lower in the bed. But he didn't close his eyes.

"What's your favorite memory from when we were little kids?" Smits asked.

Luke hesitated. Then he said, honestly, "Having Mother tuck me into bed at night." He knew the real Lee had probably called his mother Mom, not Mother. But that didn't matter. This was one time when telling the truth wouldn't hurt.

Smits smiled drowsily. "Know what I remember? I remember when we got that big red wagon, and our nanny would pull us around in it, both of us together. Hour after hour. And then we got a little older, and you'd pull me in the wagon alone. Around and around the playroom. And I'd scream, 'Again! Again!' But I never pulled you. I should have pulled you, at least once . . ."

"You weren't big enough, stupid," Luke said. Smits

wasn't his real brother; Luke had never even seen that red wagon Smits was talking about. But Luke still had chills listening to him. "Tell you what. Next time we're anywhere near a wagon, you're welcome to pull me in it."

"It wouldn't be the same," Smits murmured. "It wouldn't be the same."

CHAPTER *NINE*

Mr. Talbot showed up the next day.

Mr. Talbot was the person who had helped Luke get his fake I.D. in the first place. Back when Luke was still in hiding, the Government had forced Luke's family to sell the woods behind their farm to build fancy houses for rich people. When the houses were finished, Mr. Talbot and his family had moved into the one closest to Luke's. Having other people so close by had terrified Luke's family; they were afraid that someone would discover Luke's existence. But instead Luke had discovered another third child in hiding: Mr. Talbot's daughter, Jen.

For several wonderful months Luke had secretly sneaked back and forth between his house and the Talbots'. Jen became his friend, and through an Internet chat room she introduced him to other third children in hiding. She also shared her dream with him, of a day when all third children could be free.

And then Jen was killed during a rally seeking that freedom.

Mr. Talbot had rescued Luke, given him Lee Grant's identity, and brought him to Hendricks School. Luke had seen him only twice since then—both times when there was danger.

And now he was back again. Just seeing him made Luke worry.

But the way Mr. Talbot acted, Luke could have believed that Mr. Talbot didn't have a care in the world. He breezed into Luke's science class and boomed out, "I'm sorry to interrupt—so sorry. I certainly believe that science is important, of course. But would anyone in here want to skip class to have lunch with me?"

In another classroom, at another school, Luke could imagine such an invitation causing kids to wave their arms in the air, screaming out, "Ooh! Ooh! I will! Pick me!"

But in Luke's class the boys froze. They stared warily at Mr. Talbot. Luke noticed that Smits was the only one who didn't look terrified. He narrowed his eyes and tilted his head thoughtfully. But even he didn't answer Mr. Talbot's question.

Mr. Talbot laughed heartily.

"Don't all jump at once," he joked. He turned to the teacher and said, "I see you have them all so entranced with science that they don't want to leave. I compliment you on the brilliance of your teaching."

The teacher, Mr. Nimms, looked every bit as frightened as his students.

"Well, I'm taking up too much of your time," Mr. Talbot said. "Mr. Hendricks really only has room for two boys at his table, and I promised the Grants I'd check up on their sons while I was here. Come on, Lee. Come on, Smits. Let's go have some gourmet food."

Luke heard somebody mumble resentfully, "Smits has that every day." Luke had to hide a grin as he, Smits, and Oscar stood up to leave.

"Oh, wait a minute," Mr. Talbot said. "You don't need to come." He was speaking to Oscar. "Mr. Hendricks has an excellent security system in his house, I assure you. Both of the Grant boys will be safe with me. You can take an hour off. I'm sure you'd be happy to have a break."

"My orders are to go wherever the boy goes," Oscar growled. "Always."

Luke had seen Mr. Talbot outsmart Population Police officers—not just once, but twice. He was sure Mr. Talbot would manage to twist Oscar's words around, twist his plans around, so that Oscar suddenly found himself agreeing, "Oh yes, yes, right. I will stay here. You go with the boys. I trust you."

But Mr. Talbot only shrugged.

"Your loss," he said. "I'll be sure to let your employers know how dedicated you are."

Luke was acutely aware of the presence of Oscar and Smits behind him as he walked beside Mr. Talbot out of the classroom, down the hall, then out the door toward Mr. Hendricks's house. Without them he could have been asking Mr. Talbot question after question: *Do you know why Smits is here? What are the Grants thinking? Is Smits dangerous? Can I trust him? And how did the real Lee die?* Mr. Talbot always had all the answers.

But today Mr. Talbot didn't seem to care about the questions in Luke's mind. He turned around and began talking to Smits.

"Have you adjusted to your new school yet?" Mr. Talbot asked. "Are you letting your parents know that every-thing's okay?"

"Why would they care?" Smits asked.

"Well, you are their son," Mr. Talbot said, still jovial.

"They liked Lee better," Smits said.

Oh, no. Had he really said "liked"—past tense? Luke's heart pounded as he panicked over what Oscar might have heard. He glanced over his shoulder. Oscar was trudging silently beside Smits, giving no sign that he'd heard any-thing at all.

"Oh, surely not," Mr. Talbot said quickly. "Surely they *love* you equally." Luke was grateful for the emphasis Mr. Talbot put on the present tense. "It must just seem like they prefer Lee right now, because Lee has done such a great job of turning his life around since he came to Hendricks. No more skipped classes, no more flunked courses—he's really applying himself. As I'm sure you'll apply yourself here, too."

"Whatever," Smits said.

They arrived at Mr. Hendricks's house, and Mr. Hendricks let them in.

"We're having a fine vegetable pot pie," Mr. Hendricks said. "With some of the peas and carrots and beans grown right here at the school, thanks to Lee."

Luke hoped that Smits heard the pride in Mr. Hendricks's voice, that Smits knew what Lee had accomplished. But Smits seemed to be off in his own little sullen world.

With Oscar standing guard behind them, they sat down at the dining-room table. At first there was a flurry of passing plates and dishing out servings. Then an uncomfortable silence fell over the table. Everybody seemed to be waiting for somebody else to speak. Finally Smits put down his fork.

"If you're here as my parents' messenger," Smits said, staring right at Mr. Talbot, "you can tell them they can't make me do anything."

"Ah," Mr. Talbot said. "And should I glare at them, just so, when I tell them that? I think the glare is an important part of the message, don't you?"

Smits glowered down at his plate and didn't reply.

"They're your parents," Mr. Hendricks said gently. "They care about you."

"They don't," Smits muttered.

"You know, I was once a boy like you," Mr. Hendricks said. "Selfish, only concerned with my own desires—"

"Selfish?" Smits exploded. "Selfish? Is it selfish to want to—" He broke off suddenly, looking from Oscar to Luke. Then he shoved his chair back from the table and turned and ran out of the room. Oscar was after him in a flash. Seconds later Luke glimpsed both of them outdoors. Oscar was chasing Smits, and Smits had enough of a head start that it might take Oscar a while to catch him.

"What was that all about?" Luke asked.

Mr. Talbot went over to the window, keeping a close eye on the huge man chasing the boy.

"Your brother," he said grimly, "is in danger of being confined to a mental institution."

"A mental institution?" Luke repeated. "Like where they put crazy people? But he's not crazy. A little strange, a little rude—but not crazy."

"He's told people that his older brother, Lee, is dead," Mr. Talbot said, still watching out the window. "Back at his old school he told classmates that his brother was killed by the Government."

Luke gasped. "But—"

Mr. Talbot turned around. "They didn't believe him," he said. "Fortunately, Smits had established quite a reputation as a liar before that. But he is dangerous. In this country a twelve-year-old boy armed with the truth can be very dangerous indeed."

Luke shook his head, trying to make sense of what he'd heard.

"Would the Grants really do that?" Luke asked. "Put

Smits in some insane asylum because he can't keep his mouth shut? They'd send their real son away to—to protect me?"

"The Grants don't care about you," Mr. Talbot said harshly. "They're trying to protect themselves."

Luke shook his head again, but by now he'd given up on anything making sense. If Smits was a liar, how much had he lied to Luke?

"Was Lee Grant really killed by the Government?" Luke asked.

Mr. Talbot looked straight at Luke. He had his eyebrows lowered, his eyes narrowed, his lips pursed. He seemed to be judging what he could and could not safely tell Luke. Finally he said, "Probably."

Oscar and Smits burst back into Mr. Hendricks's house. Oscar had one huge fist gripped around Smits's right arm; Smits was breathing hard but kept glaring resentfully at the man towering over him. When they came to stand at the threshold of the dining room, Luke saw Smits jerk back his leg and give Oscar a sharp kick on the shin. Oscar didn't even flinch.

"I will take Smithfield to his room," Oscar said. "If he cannot show his manners, he does not deserve to eat with civilized people. Lee, you will bring him his homework for the rest of the day."

It was the first time Oscar had ever addressed Luke by name. Was it possible that Oscar still believed the lie?

"Um, sure," Luke said.

And Oscar carried Smits out the door, Smits squirming the whole way.

When they were gone, Luke realized that he finally had what he'd longed for before: Mr. Talbot and Mr. Hendricks to himself. But he was almost too stunned to come up with any more questions. And Mr. Talbot and Mr. Hendricks looked too worried to give him the patient explanations he wanted.

"What do you think will happen to Smits now? And—and to me?" he finally managed to say.

And Mr. Talbot, who always had all the answers, said, "I don't know."

CHAPTER *TEN*

What happened next was—nothing.

Mr. Talbot left and Luke went back to class. He took notes on plant life and musical compositions. Right before dinner he went up to Smits's room to deliver Smits's homework assignments, but Oscar just took them at the door. Luke didn't even catch a glimpse of Smits.

The next day Smits was back in class, as arrogant as ever, with Oscar as menacing as ever standing behind him with his sledgehammer. Just having the two of them there killed all conversation and forced everyone to cast fearful glances over his shoulder, all the time. Luke even caught some of the boys sending resentful stares his way, as if it was his fault that Smits and Oscar were there.

And in some strange way he knew it was. Though he now realized that even Mr. Talbot wasn't sure why the Grants had sent Smits to Hendricks.

A week passed, two weeks, three. Luke kept expecting some dramatic event—maybe another explosion from

Smits. But all he had was math, science, literature. History, music, games. And, every now and then, a summons from Smits after everyone else was asleep.

Smits didn't talk anymore about Lee's death, either as it had really happened or as he pretended it'd happened in a dream. Instead, he'd talk about his memories of Lee, late into the night while Oscar slept—or pretended to sleep.

"Remember that time we played the trick on the butler?" Smits would say. "When he put on his shoes and those firecrackers went off—remember how high he jumped?"

Or, "Remember that nanny who smelled like bananas? And we couldn't figure out why, because she was certainly never allowed to eat any. And then the housekeeper caught her washing her *hair* with banana paste because she'd heard somewhere that that would make it thicker, and she was in love with the chauffeur we had then, and you and I walked in on them once, kissing in the garage. . . ."

Or, "Remember how we kept stealing the maids' feather dusters? You told me they were real birds, and I was scared they'd come to life and fly around the house in the middle of the night. . . ."

Smits's memories didn't always make sense because he'd jump from story to story. And Luke could never tell how old he and Smits were supposed to have been during any of the tales. Had Smits and the real Lee flushed entire rolls of toilet paper down the toilet when they were two and three or when they were eleven and twelve? Luke could hardly ask questions. After all, the stories Smits told were supposed to be Luke's memories, too. He shouldn't need Smits to tell him, for example, how many cooks had gotten seared eyelashes when the flaming dessert exploded at that fancy dinner party their parents had had.

Smits didn't seem to care if Luke understood his ramblings or not. But strangely, after just a few nights, Luke found he could join in the reminiscing, as Smits began to repeat stories Luke had already heard.

"Oh, yeah, the feather dusters!" Luke exclaimed. "I'd almost forgotten about that. Now, why in the world were you so scared of them? You didn't *really* think they could come back to life, did you?"

Smits fixed Luke with a curious look.

"Yes," he said. "I did. I didn't know what death was." And he launched into another tale.

At first Luke only acted—pretending to listen, pretending to care. But slowly he was drawn into Smits's hypnotic unreeling of the lives that he and Lee had once lived. It was all a foreign world to Luke. Luke had grown up on hard work and fear; life for his family had been a constant struggle. Smits and Lee had each had a miniature car they drove around the paths of their estate. Smits had once had a birthday party where an actual circus had come and performed for his thirty-five guests.

But Luke had had a mother who tucked him into bed every night, and a father who would play checkers with him on those dreary winter days when there was no farmwork to be done. Smits and Lee seemed to have had only servants.

One night, at the beginning of Smits's fourth week of storytelling, Luke ventured to ask in the middle of a long, involved tale about a missing teddy bear, "I forget. Where was Mom then?"

Smits stopped and squinted in confusion at Luke.

"I forget, too," he said. "Probably at a party. Entertaining. Like always."

And he went on, telling in outraged terms about the nanny who'd refused to step out onto the roof to retrieve the teddy bear from the rain gutter, where Smits had thrown it.

It wasn't long after that night that Smits said at the very end of a long session of reminiscing, "I'm sorry. I know you've been trying to help. At least you've stayed awake." He rolled his eyes toward the huge, snoring form of Oscar. Luke stifled a yawn of his own and almost missed seeing the stern set of Smits's jaw. Smits looked like a miniature grown-up once again.

"Whatever happens," Smits said, "you can tell people I told you: None of this is because of you. It won't be your fault. I even . . . I even kind of like you."

He sounded surprised.

CHAPTER *ELEVEN*

Luke stumbled back down to his own room, so drowsy that he almost considered just lying down on the stairs and going to sleep there. In the back of his mind he suspected that he needed to figure out exactly what Smits had meant. "Whatever happens . . . it won't be your fault. . . ." But Luke had missed so much sleep staying up with Smits. He felt like his brain was functioning amazingly well just to be able to command his feet: down the stairs, left, right, down, and down again. He knew he wouldn't be capable of thinking about anything important until morning.

And Smits himself was probably already asleep. Whatever Smits thought was going to happen surely wouldn't occur until morning.

Luke reached his room, fell into his bed, and was asleep almost instantly.

Loud, clanging alarms woke him only minutes later, it seemed. He opened his eyes to flashing lights and a voice booming throughout the room: "Evacuate immediately! Evacuate immediately!"

Around him his roommates were sitting up dazedly in their beds, holding their hands over their ears. The voice on the loudspeaker was so intense, Luke could barely think. He saw Trey slip down from the bunk above. Trey's lips were moving, and Luke could tell he was asking Luke a question, but Luke had no hope of hearing Trey over the blaring alarm. Luke gave Trey a confused look and held up his hands helplessly.

Trey leaned in close and screamed directly into Luke's ear: "What if it's a trick? I think we should hide."

Luke shook his head. For the first time something else registered with his brain. He cupped his hand over Trey's ear and yelled as loudly as he could: "No! I smell smoke!"

The loudspeaker voice announced, "You are in danger! The school is on fire! Evacuate immediately! Go through the secret door in your room!"

Secret door? Luke had no idea what that meant. Then suddenly a crack appeared in a blank portion of a wall Luke had never paid much attention to before. Seconds later a door sprang open in the wall, revealing a corridor with dim lights.

Luke looked suspiciously at the door. Trey was worried about tricks—what if the voice was directing them into danger, not away from it? Cautiously Luke stuck his head through the mysterious door. At the end of a dimly lit corridor he could see stairs leading down. Could this be the best way out? He went back to the regular door of his room and jerked on the handle: The door didn't budge. It was locked or stuck. Either way he couldn't open that door. If he and his friends didn't go through the secret door, they'd be trapped.

Luke inhaled sharply. He was sure now. He did smell smoke. The scent was stronger than ever.

"Come on!" Luke yelled, though no one could hear him. He began shoving boys toward the secret door. No one wanted to go. They seemed to prefer to cower in their beds. Luke had to drag Robert across the room, and even then Robert just huddled at the entrance to the secret corridor. Would Luke have to carry him down all those stairs?

Suddenly, out of nowhere, Mr. Dirk, their history teacher, appeared in the doorway to the secret corridor. He grabbed Robert by the arms and pulled him to his feet. Together, Luke and Mr. Dirk shepherded the boys down the steps.

At the bottom Mr. Dirk pressed on a door and it opened, revealing a clear view of the night sky. They were outdoors.

Gratefully Luke gulped in fresh air and rushed out. But around him the other boys balked.

"No!" Luke yelled. "Out!"

Joel and John and Trey slipped fearfully out the door, but Luke had to peel Robert's fingers off the railing of the stairs, had to propel him inch by inch toward the outdoors.

Luke was just ready to step outside himself when Mr. Dirk said into his ear, "Now help me get the rest."

The rest?

In a daze, Luke followed Mr. Dirk back up the stairs. From the secret corridor they entered room after room, pulling boys out of beds and from closets where they were crouched and trembling. Luke lost track of time. He lost track of how many kids he prodded and pulled. Some he even carried. After about the second room he didn't look at faces anymore. He just knew he had to get everyone out.

Finally, finally, Luke and Mr. Dirk reached the bottom of the stairs and Mr. Dirk didn't immediately head back up again. Luke started to—his legs seemed to move on their own.

"No, no," Mr. Dirk said. "Everyone's safe now. We've evacuated everyone on the second and third floors."

He gently pulled Luke back from the stairs. Gratefully Luke finally stepped outside. The cool night air rushed at him. He hadn't realized how sweaty he'd gotten; his pajamas were drenched. His muscles ached. Behind him the alarms didn't seem so blaring, the loudspeaker voice didn't sound so urgent. Everyone was safe now. Everyone from the second and third floor. And nobody would have been on the first floor, because nobody would have been in the classrooms in the middle of the night. As for the fourth floor . . .

Luke whirled around.

"Smits!" he yelled desperately.

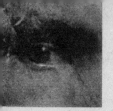

CHAPTER *TWELVE*

Luke was ready to race back up the stairs, but Mr. Dirk grabbed his arm.

"The evacuation corridor network doesn't go up to the fourth floor," he said. "I'm sure Smits got out by other means. He doesn't have the same, uh, fears as the rest of you boys."

Frantically Luke looked up, toward the top of the school. He wanted so badly to see a gaping hole made by Oscar's precious sledgehammer. Instead, he saw only smooth brick, all the way to the roof, seemingly unmarred by either fire or escape. A few last tendrils of smoke rose toward the moon.

"Looks like the fire's out," Mr. Dirk said cheerfully. "I'm not sure how serious it was to begin with, but it's good we had such a successful test of our evacuation procedure. It was my idea, you know. We figured you boys would naturally be inclined to want to hide in an emergency, so we thought we'd have to work around that tendency. Don't you think the secret doors and corridors and stairs worked great?"

Luke had never heard Mr. Dirk talk so much about any event that hadn't happened centuries ago.

"You were a wonderful help, I must say," Mr. Dirk rambled on.

"I have to find Smits," Luke said rudely, and walked away.

All the other boys were standing or sitting numbly in clusters around the yard. Luke went from group to group, asking again and again, "Have you seen Smits? Have you seen Smits?"

Nobody had.

Even in his desperate search for Smits, Luke couldn't help but notice how stricken all his friends and classmates were. Luke wasn't sure if they were traumatized by being pulled from their beds in the middle of the night because of a fire—or if they were simply terrified of being outdoors. But several of the boys were shaking uncontrollably. Some were even crying.

"There, there, everything's okay," someone said soothingly.

Luke turned around. It was Mr. Hendricks. He had rolled his wheelchair across the rough lawn and was patting one of the younger boys on the back. Luke rushed to his side.

"Is everyone safe?" Luke demanded. "Is Smits?"

Mr. Hendricks gave Luke a measuring look.

"Yes, everyone's safe," he said. "Smits and Oscar are at my house right now, locked in separate rooms."

"Why?" Luke asked, bewildered.

"Smits is accusing Oscar of setting the fire, of trying to kill him," Mr. Hendricks said. "And Oscar is accusing Smits."

MARGARET PETERSON HADDIX

CHAPTER THIRTEEN

Luke wanted to ask questions; he wanted Mr. Hendricks to solve every mystery right then and there. But Mr. Hendricks was already turning to other boys, repeating again and again, "It's all right. You're safe."

"They need to be indoors," Luke muttered. He looked around at the forlorn clusters of boys scattered across the shadowy lawn. "Is there room for everyone in your house, Mr. Hendricks?"

"An excellent idea," Mr. Hendricks said. He raised his voice. "Hot apple cider and biscuits will be served at the headmaster's house in five minutes."

Fearfully the boys began moving through the darkness. Once again Luke got stuck herding the others.

"It's safe on the path, really," he had to assure one boy after another. "You're not going anywhere dangerous."

He had thought his classmates had made so much progress, had become so much braver. All that seemed to have been erased tonight.

Once everyone got to Mr. Hendricks's house, they all crowded in eagerly. Nobody wanted to be left out on the porch, even if it meant standing shoulder to shoulder, elbow to elbow. Someone started a brigade of biscuits and cups of cider. The cider sloshed on the floor and crumbs dropped everywhere, but no one seemed to care. They were all coming back to life.

"When that door opened in my room, I couldn't believe my eyes," Joel said.

"Did anybody know those doors were there?" John asked.

"Why didn't they just let us go out the regular doors?" Robert asked.

"Because they knew we'd all be too scared," Trey said glumly. "They knew we were cowards."

Trey seemed thoroughly disgusted with himself. He wouldn't meet Luke's eyes. Luke thought about how he'd feel now if he'd been one of the boys cowering in their beds or trembling in their closets. He felt a surge of pride; he, at least, had been brave. This time.

"Hey, maybe there wasn't a fire at all. Maybe this was just a drill," Joel said. "Maybe it was just a test Luke and the teachers cooked up to see how we'd react. They probably got the idea from Smits, talking about needing a sledgehammer to escape."

He and several other boys turned almost accusingly toward Luke.

"No, there was a fire," Trey said dully. "Didn't you smell the smoke?"

"Hey, where is Smits?" John asked. "Why isn't he here bragging about how *his* bodyguard got him out, because he's so rich and *his* life is so much more valuable than any of ours?"

Now everyone looked expectantly toward Luke, waiting for him to explain. Smits wasn't even Luke's real brother, and Luke was still supposed to be Smits's keeper.

"He's here in Mr. Hendricks's house, too," Luke said. "He's just in a different room."

"*He's* probably got a room to himself," Joel said resentfully.

Luke didn't answer this time. He was still trying to make sense of what Mr. Hendricks had told him. The last thing he wanted to do was try to explain everything to the others, who didn't think much of Smits anyway. But they didn't like Oscar, either. They'd probably want to blame both of them for setting the fire.

Luke was pretty sure he knew which one was guilty. But why?

The conversation seemed to swirl away from Luke as the other boys moved from the dining room to the kitchen. Only Trey stayed by Luke's side.

"Weren't you scared at all?" Trey asked softly. "Why didn't you want to hide, too?"

Luke thought back. It was hard to remember what he had been thinking when that first alarm went off, when that first order came over the loudspeaker: "Evacuate immediately!" He wasn't even sure if he had been thinking.

"I probably did want to hide," he told Trey. "I just knew that I couldn't. And I was worried about everyone else."

"Of course," Trey said. "That's because you're brave. You're a hero. And I'm not. I never will be."

Luke remembered how miserable he'd been when he found out that his friend Jen had died at the rally for third children's rights, when Luke hadn't even had the courage to go to it. But Luke, at least, had had the comfort of knowing that his cowardice—if that's what it was—had probably saved his life. Trey's cowardice could have led to his death.

"I'll make you a deal," Luke said lightly. "Next time, you're welcome to be the hero instead of me."

Trey shook his head. "I'm not joking," he said. "It's not that easy. When I'm terrified, I can't just stand up and say, 'Well, it's hero time!' I can't. And you—you went back into a burning building, what—six, seven, eight times? You risked your life."

Luke didn't like thinking about what he had done in those terms.

"There wasn't that much danger," Luke said. "I never even saw any flames."

"That's because the escape corridors are sealed," Trey said. "Mr. Dirk explained everything. They sealed off our dormitory rooms and the escape route as soon as the first alarm went off. It really is an ingenious system. None of us deserve it. Except you."

Luke had never seen Trey like this before. Trey had never

seemed to mind being easily frightened; he'd never seemed to long for courage. What had the fire done to him?

"All right, everyone," Mr. Hendricks announced at the front of the room. "We've now checked the entire school thoroughly. It's safe for all of you to go back to your rooms. I realize this has been a disruptive experience—all morning classes are canceled, so you all may sleep late."

The boys had recovered enough of their spirit that they managed to raise a feeble cheer. But the exuberance died as soon as they began moving out into the darkness once more, facing their fears of the outdoors yet again.

Luke moved around the edges of the crowd, thinking he'd need to guide the others along the path to the school. But Mr. Hendricks stopped him at the door.

"Not you," he said, laying a cautioning hand on Luke's arm. "I need your help."

"With Smits?" Luke asked.

Mr. Hendricks nodded. "And Oscar."

CHAPTER *FOURTEEN*

Luke waited on the couch until all the other boys were gone. When Mr. Hendricks finally shut the front door and rolled his wheelchair back toward Luke, Luke started to blurt out, "Mr. Hendricks, it had to have been Smits who set the fire. He told me—"

Mr. Hendricks held up his hand, stopping Luke.

"Now, now," he said. "The last thing I need right now is to hear any more wild accusations. Think very carefully before you tell me anything."

What would it hurt to tell Mr. Hendricks the truth? Luke wondered. He slumped on the couch in confusion.

"One of the few things that Oscar and Smits agree on is that you were the last one in Smits's room last evening," Mr. Hendricks said. "Besides the two of them, of course. What I would like you to do for me right now is to go up to Smits's room and tell me if you see anything amiss. Apart from the fire damage, that is."

"The fire was in Smits's room?" Luke asked.

Mr. Hendricks nodded.

"Entirely," he said. "We were able to contain it quite successfully."

Luke's certainty ebbed a bit. No matter what Smits had said, why would Smits want to burn his own room?

But for that matter, why would Oscar want to injure the boy he was supposed to be protecting?

Luke could easily understand why Mr. Hendricks looked so troubled. Luke stood up.

"All right," he said. "I'll be back in a few minutes."

He went out the front door. The night air that had felt like such a relief only an hour or so ago seemed cold now. Threatening. Luke felt like he'd caught the other boys' fear.

But none of the other boys were going to have to inspect a charred room all by themselves. Only Luke.

In his head Luke carried on an imaginary conversation with Mr. Hendricks and Mr. Talbot: *Guess what? When I said I was willing to be brave for the cause of helping to free all the third children, this isn't what I meant. This is scaring me—this is danger, for no reason. This has nothing to do with the cause. Smits isn't my concern. Smits shouldn't be my problem.*

But he couldn't imagine what Mr. Hendricks's or Mr. Talbot's response would be if he actually spoke those words to either of them.

Luke slipped in the front door of the school and lightly raced up the stairs. He saw none of the other boys, but some of the teachers seemed to be patrolling the halls. No one stopped Luke.

On the fourth floor the smell of smoke was overpowering. Luke longed for an open window to lean his head out. But except for the smell, Luke found no other evidence of fire until he reached the door of Smits's room. The door was pulled shut, but burn marks spiked out from the frame. Gently Luke pushed the door open.

The room he'd stood in only hours before was transformed. The carpet was covered with wet ash; the comforter on the bed was burned away. Luke thought about what little Mr. Hendricks had told him about Oscar's and Smits's differing versions of how the fire had started. Could Oscar possibly have set Smits's bed on fire while Smits was in it?

To still the terrifying questions growing in his mind, Luke moved over to Smits's desk, which seemed relatively untouched. His schoolbooks were stacked neatly off to the side, only slightly charred but, like much of the rest of the room, soaking wet. The computer everyone had been so impressed by when Smits arrived was now only a sad heap of melted plastic.

Luke wanted to run away, to rush back to Mr. Hendricks and report, "I didn't see anything strange." And then maybe he could wiggle out of any obligation Mr. Hendricks thought he had to Smits and Oscar; he could go back to bed like all the other boys. He could fall asleep and tell himself that everything frightening him was just a nightmare.

But something made Luke keep looking, methodically,

with a sort of horrified fascination. He pulled out drawers, examined papers that had managed to escape all flame. But they were just ordinary homework—musical scales and conjugated verbs. Luke moved away from the desk. In the closet, totally unscathed, he found the folded-up cot that Oscar evidently slept on when he wasn't sleeping in the chair.

And then, tucked under the sheet, inside a split seam of the cot's mattress, Luke found something rigid and plastic and rectangular. Luke dug into the mattress and pulled out two identification cards.

Fake ones.

Or were they?

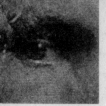

CHAPTER *FIFTEEN*

One of the I.D. cards showed Smits's face but a different name: Peter Goodard. The other I.D. showed no picture, just a name: Stanley Goodard. Why was the picture missing? Had the fire prevented Oscar from gluing his picture on—or from taking Smits's picture off? Were Oscar and Smits really not Oscar and Smits, but Peter and Stanley? Or were they really Oscar and Smits, planning to go undercover as other people? Why would they want to do that? And whose plan was it? Oscar/Stanley's or Smits/Peter's?

Luke felt so overwhelmed that he sank to the floor, neither remembering nor caring that he'd get ash all over his clothes. He stared at the fake I.D.'s in his trembling hands.

"Are you finding everything satisfactorily?" a voice said behind him, from the doorway of the room. It was Mr. Dirk.

Luke scrambled to hide the I.D.'s. He slid his hand toward his pant pocket, forgetting he was still wearing pajamas. And even fancy Baron pajamas lacked pockets in the pants. The only pocket was on the pajama shirt.

Desperately he cupped the I.D.'s in his hand, trying to keep them out of sight.

"Mr. Hendricks sent me to check on you because you were taking so long," Mr. Dirk said.

"Oh—I was just being thorough," Luke said. "Like you tell us to be on essay tests."

Mr. Dirk laughed, without any humor.

Would there be any harm in telling Mr. Dirk the secret Luke had just discovered? Luke certainly intended to tell Mr. Hendricks, and Mr. Hendricks trusted Mr. Dirk. Then Luke remembered what Mr. Hendricks had said: "Think very carefully before you tell me anything." What was Mr. Hendricks so afraid of? Shouldn't Luke pass the burden of this secret to a trustworthy grown-up as soon as possible?

He wanted to. But something made him keep quiet.

"So, thorough or not—are you almost done? Mr. Hendricks is waiting, you know," Mr. Dirk said.

"Um, sure," Luke said.

He turned slowly, trying to slip the I.D. cards up his sleeve as he moved. And because he stayed low to the floor, for the first time he saw what lay under Smits's bed.

"Oscar's sledgehammer," Luke said, and pointed with the hand that wasn't hiding the I.D. cards.

Mr. Dirk walked into the room, his shoes squishing on the wet, burned carpet. He bent down and pulled the sledgehammer out from under the bed. It was near the head of the bed, directly below the pillows that Smits had been lying on the last time Luke had seen him.

"Is that a clue?" Luke asked. "Is it important where we found it?"

"Perhaps," Mr. Dirk said. "I'm not a forensics expert. This is why I like history. With the advantage of hindsight you can almost always tell what's important."

Luke tried to remember whether Oscar had been holding the sledgehammer the last time Luke had been in Smits's room. But Luke hadn't been paying attention to Oscar then.

"I'll take it to Mr. Hendricks," Luke said. "He'll know what to do with it."

Grasping the sledgehammer in one hand and holding the I.D.'s inside his pajama sleeve with the other, Luke left Mr. Dirk looking perplexed, standing in the middle of Smits's ruined room.

Back at Mr. Hendricks's house, Luke silently laid the sledgehammer and the two I.D.'s on the dining-room table. Mr. Hendricks's eyes widened in surprise when he saw the I.D.'s, but he quickly swept them from the table and thrust them back at Luke.

"Keep these out of sight," he said. "Did anyone else see them?"

Luke was relieved that he could shake his head no. Still, he carefully slipped the I.D.'s into the pocket of the pajama shirt.

"This is an interesting development indeed," Mr. Hendricks muttered, seemingly to himself.

"What if this is who Smits and Oscar really are?" Luke asked, tapping the pocket. "What if they've been lying about their identities all along?"

"Smits is Smits, all right," Mr. Hendricks said. "I've no doubt of that. But Oscar could be anyone. That's why he's dangerous."

Luke shook his head, trying to clear it. Outside Mr. Hendricks's windows Luke could see the first tinge of dawn creeping over the horizon. And Luke had had barely five minutes of sleep all night. That must be the reason it took so long for Mr. Hendricks's words to register. When they did, he jumped back in panic.

"Oscar could be anyone?" he repeated. "Do you think he's from the Population Police?"

"No," Mr. Hendricks said, "but you might want to act as though he is."

Luke squinted at Mr. Hendricks in total confusion. Mr. Hendricks sighed and handed Luke a set of keys.

"Smits is in the back bedroom," he said. "Why don't you go get him and bring him to me?"

Luke half expected Smits to be asleep, but he sprang out of the room the instant Luke got the door open.

"Am I safe now? Have you sent that murdering scum off to jail where he belongs?" Smits yelled. Then he slumped against the doorframe as soon as he saw it was only Luke. "Oh, Lee. Hi."

"Are you out of your mind?" Luke asked.

The younger boy didn't answer, only followed Luke down the hall. When they reached the dining room and he saw the sledgehammer lying on the table, Smits resumed his hysteria.

"So you found Oscar's weapon," Smits raged. "Under the bed, right? He never meant to use that to save me, you know. I'm lucky he never bludgeoned me to death in my sleep."

"Smits," Mr. Hendricks said patiently, "how did you know where Oscar hid the sledgehammer, to avoid saving you, if, as you told me before, you were asleep when he supposedly set the fire?"

Smits visibly wilted.

Mr. Hendricks shook his head. "Smits, with as many untruths as you've been accused of telling, I'd think you'd be a more accomplished liar by now."

"That's my problem," Smits said sulkily. "I've never been a good liar. Haven't you ever noticed? The people who are good at it never get caught. If I could lie well, I wouldn't be here right now."

Luke wondered exactly what Smits meant by that.

"Smits," Mr. Hendricks said gently, "why did you set the fire?"

Smits looked down. "I wanted you to send Oscar away," he mumbled. Then he peered earnestly at Mr. Hendricks. "Couldn't you still do that? Couldn't you tell my parents that he was to blame, and then they'd fire him and he'd go away? And you could tell them that I'm doing really well here, so I don't need another bodyguard. . . ."

"And what would that accomplish?" Mr. Hendricks asked.

Smits looked from Mr. Hendricks to Luke.

"Then I could act the way I want to act. I wouldn't be . . . spied on. I could find out . . ." He broke off and looked back at the floor.

"Find out what?" Mr. Hendricks asked.

But Smits only shook his head. He kept his face down. Luke wondered if he'd started crying.

"Sit down, Smits," Mr. Hendricks said. "Lee, could you go open Oscar's door now?"

So Luke took another key and went to another door at the back of the house. Like Smits, Oscar was waiting close to the door. But when Oscar saw Luke, he said nothing, only rushed past him, out to Mr. Hendricks.

"I must call my employers," Oscar announced. "I demand to be given a phone this instant!"

Mr. Hendricks gave Oscar an amused look.

"I believe, as headmaster of this school, that I shall be the one calling the Grants," he said. "If they ask to speak to you, I shall, of course, let them. Now, sit!"

Oscar sat. Luke hid a smile at the sight of the huge, muscular man obeying the command of an old man in a wheelchair. Oscar could easily have overpowered Mr. Hendricks and grabbed as many phones as he wanted. But Mr. Hendricks had such an aura of control about him, Luke bet that it didn't even occur to Oscar to disobey.

Mr. Hendricks rolled into his office to use the phone. Oscar, Luke, and Smits sat silently around the dining-room table. After a few moments Oscar reached out and grabbed his sledgehammer. Luke saw Smits flinch beside him. But Oscar didn't do anything with the hammer, only cradled it in his arms.

Then Mr. Hendricks returned.

"The Grants have been informed now that we had a minor fire at our school, possibly electrical in nature," he said. He looked directly at Smits. "They want you to come home as soon as possible, until our wiring can be thoroughly checked. For safety's sake."

"But—," Smits protested.

Luke noticed that Oscar looked ready to complain, too, but he kept his mouth shut.

"They were adamant," Mr. Hendricks said. "I don't believe that anything you might say would change their minds. Now, why don't you and Oscar go and pack up whatever can be salvaged from your room?"

Astonished, Luke watched Smits and his bodyguard leave.

"You trust the two of them alone together?" Luke asked as soon as they were out the door.

"Yes," Mr. Hendricks said. "As long as Oscar stays awake. And I don't believe he'll be sleeping anytime soon."

The notion of sleep sounded mighty good to Luke. But he still had one more question before he left, too.

"Why didn't you tell the Grants the truth about how the fire started?" Luke asked.

"In a country as full of lies as ours," Mr. Hendricks said, "sometimes the truth doesn't matter as much as what people like the Grants believe."

Luke frowned, trying to understand. "You're giving Smits another chance," he said.

Mr. Hendricks nodded. "You could look at it that way. Though I'm not sure how much of a chance I've given him.

I'm sure Oscar will be eager to tell them his version of events. Anyway, as you're always reminding me, the phone lines aren't secure. No need to alert any eavesdroppers to problems here."

Luke shrugged. What Mr. Hendricks said made sense. It occurred to Luke that with Smits and Oscar leaving, all his problems were over. He just couldn't imagine Smits ever returning, not if his parents found out the truth. Luke wouldn't even need to worry about the mystery of the fake I.D.'s now. He could have his old life back. He and his friends could talk about being shadow children again. They wouldn't have to pretend for the sake of the spoiled rich kid and the hulking bodyguard in their midst.

Luke felt like a massive burden had just been lifted from his shoulders. He turned to go, certain that, for the first time in more than a month, he'd finally get some good sleep.

"Luke," Mr. Hendricks said behind him. "The Grants didn't want just Smits and Oscar to come home."

"Huh?" Luke said.

"They're worried about the safety of both their sons."

Luke whirled around. "You don't mean—"

"Yes, Luke," Mr. Hendricks said. "When the chauffeur returns to pick up Smits tomorrow, they want him to bring you home, too."

CHAPTER *SIXTEEN*

L uke gaped at Mr. Hendricks.

"You told them no, didn't you? You told them I was fine here, right?" he said.

Mr. Hendricks sighed. "Luke, your father is a very powerful man. Some would say he has as much control over our country as the president. Nobody tells him no."

"But—"

"And, legally, you are his son. You're underage. He can order you to go anywhere he wants."

Luke was practically shaking now. He fought to keep his fears under control.

"What do they want from me?" he asked.

Mr. Hendricks grimaced.

"I don't know," he said. "I'm sorry. I really wish I did. There's something going on here that I don't understand. The best thing I can do is get Smits and Oscar away from my school. I have to protect my students."

Now Luke wondered whose idea it had been to send Smits and Oscar home.

"*I'm* one of your students, too," he said. "Don't you want to protect me?" He didn't wait for an answer. "I know. Why don't you call Mr. Talbot, have him come and give me a different fake I.D. I'm not Lee Grant. I don't have to be. Let me be somebody else. Somebody who can stay here."

But Mr. Hendricks was shaking his head. "Don't you know how hard it was to get this identity for you? Don't you know how many kids are still in hiding, still waiting for what you already have?"

Luke squirmed, trying to avoid Mr. Hendricks's gaze. The fake I.D.'s in his shirt pocket poked his chest, giving him an idea.

"What about one of these identities?" he asked, tapping the pocket. "I could be Peter or Stanley. I've got my choice."

"Do you really think it could be that easy?" Mr. Hendricks asked. "You've got no idea what baggage those identities carry. What if the real Stanley Goodard, whoever he is, is wanted for murder? What if—"

"Okay, okay. I get the point," Luke grumbled.

Mr. Hendricks's expression softened. "I'm sorry. But you can't swap identities just like that. Even if it were easy to fake being someone else, you can't cast off Lee Grant. Not now. Because, for some reason, *they* want you to be Lee now."

Luke remembered what Smits had said to him on

Smits's first night at Hendricks: "Can you be Lee?" Why would Smits or his parents care?

And did they care for the same reasons?

Luke couldn't sort out his feelings. What did he really think would happen to him at the Grants'? He didn't know. That was the problem.

Luke thought about what Trey had said to him barely an hour ago: "You're a hero. . . ." Trey thought Luke was so brave. Luke wanted Mr. Hendricks to think that, too. Luke wished he could pull off an unconcerned act, could shrug casually and say something like, "Well, if I've got to go, I've got to go. If Mr. Grant's so powerful, how about if I talk him into freeing all the third children while I'm there?" But Luke wasn't brave. He was terrified. Rushing into a burning building and convincing cowering boys to leave seemed like nothing compared with going to the Grants' house with Smits and Oscar.

A new thought occurred to him.

"The servants will know I'm not really Lee," he said. "Mr. and Mrs. Grant's friends will see me. . . ."

"The Grants don't seem worried about that," Mr. Hendricks said. "We'll have to have faith that that won't be a problem."

Luke bit his lip, trying to think of another obstacle.

"Luke, I don't know if this helps, but . . . I do wish I could protect you, too," Mr. Hendricks said gently. "I just can't. But I will tell you—of all the boys at Hendricks, you're the one I'd trust the most to come out of this safely.

Just use your common sense. You'll be all right."

And so those were the words Luke repeated to himself, over and over again, a mere two hours later as he climbed into a limousine behind Smits to go to a home that wasn't his.

You'll be all right, you'll be all right, you'll be all right. . . .

Luke just wished he could believe it.

CHAPTER *SEVENTEEN*

"**D**id you notice, Lee? It's a new chauffeur," Smits said after he pulled a panel of glass shut between the driver and the space where he, Oscar, and Luke reclined on luxurious leather seats. Luke thought Hendricks School was formal and fancy, but just the interior of this car made Hendricks look like a hovel. Luke had a feeling he'd better get over being awestruck right now—the Grants' house was likely to be even more ostentatious.

He wasn't sure how to deal with Smits, so he only shrugged and kept looking out the window. They had driven past Mr. Hendricks's cottage already; they were turning out onto the main road.

"Our parents never keep servants for very long," Smits continued.

Was Smits trying to tell Luke something? Like, maybe Luke would be safe at the Grants', since there would be no old servants to remember what the real Lee had looked like?

M A R G A R E T   P E T E R S O N   H A D D I X

No, Smits was talking to Oscar now.

"Did you hear me?" he demanded. "I said our parents never keep servants around for very long. They must have fired the last chauffeur. And as soon as they hear what happened at Hendricks, they'll fire you, too."

"Smits, the last chauffeur was fired because of you," Oscar said. "He was fired because you bribed him into tricking me."

"So?" Smits taunted. "And you'll be dismissed because of me, too. Because you didn't protect me during the fire."

"You set it yourself!" Oscar roared.

Smits gave a so-what shrug. For once Luke could sympathize with Oscar's rage. Whenever he closed his eyes, Luke could still see the fear in the faces of his friends—friends he hadn't even had a chance to say good-bye to.

"Smits, lots of other boys could have died because of you," Luke said. "That fire could have burned down the whole school."

"Aw, there were sprinklers in every room," Smits said. "There wasn't any danger."

Was that true? Had Luke's heroism been for little more than a fire drill? Strangely, he felt as though Smits had taken something away from him.

Luke turned his face back to the window, hoping Smits would get the message that he wasn't in the mood to talk. The limousine was driving down a road Luke had never seen before—which wasn't terribly surprising. Luke had been in a car only once before, when Mr. Talbot had driven him from his family's farm to Hendricks School. Luke had felt so overwhelmed then, he'd barely been able to take in anything he saw. Now he forced himself to pay attention. What kind of people lived in those tiny houses by the road? Was anyone tending the derelict fields? It was nearly October now—why wasn't the countryside full of farmers busy with harvest? Luke was sure that, back home, his father and brothers were working frantically. His mother had probably taken time off from the chicken factory to help out. Did they still miss Luke as much as he missed them?

Luke swallowed a lump in his throat and closed his eyes. Sometimes it was better not to pay attention. It would be better not to think about where he was going, either, or what he might face there. . . .

The next thing Luke knew, the car had stopped and the chauffeur was peering in through the open door.

"Please, sirs," he said timidly. "Please? You are home now, no? Your parents will be wanting me to help you out. Sirs?"

Groggily Luke forced himself to open his eyes. He had been so soundly asleep that for a long moment he had trouble remembering where he was. Why wasn't he in his bed at Hendricks, staring up at the bottom of Trey's bunk? Why was his face stuck to his pillow? Or no, it wasn't his pillow. Why was he sleeping on a leather seat?

Outdoors, behind the chauffeur, Luke could see what looked like thousands of diamonds hanging from the sky.

Even when Luke peeled his face away from the seat and shook his head to clear his mind a little, the diamonds didn't disappear. Except now he could tell that they were cascading from a roof covering the driveway.

The chauffeur saw where Luke was looking.

"You like your mother's new chandelier, no?" he said. "That is new since you were home last, no?"

And Luke didn't know how to answer. Already an innocent question had stumped him.

On the opposite seat Smits and Oscar were also waking and stretching. Smits scowled at the chauffeur.

"It's ugly, you idiot," Smits said. "That's the ugliest chandelier we've ever had."

Sure, Smits was rude. But at least he'd saved Luke from having to answer.

Dazed, Luke stepped out of the car onto a driveway that was paved with thousands of tiny tiles, all intricately connected. Above him the chandelier swayed in the breeze. Luke stared at it in disbelief. A huge gold globe hung from the portico, with bars reaching out to a dozen smaller globes, all in a circle. The diamonds dangled in ropes from each of the smaller globes, twisting together and coming to a point in a huge crystal directly beneath the largest gold globe. Each of the diamonds threw out rainbows of light all over the portico. Really, Luke decided, the chandelier couldn't be diamonds; there couldn't be that many huge diamonds in the whole world. The chandelier was probably just glass, and Luke couldn't tell the difference.

Either way, it was breathtaking, stunning beyond words.

Everything was. The walls of the Grant mansion rose before him like a sheer cliff; he really couldn't tell where the mansion ended and the rest of the world began. Luke wouldn't have been terribly surprised if the mansion *didn't* end. Unlike Hendricks School, the Grant mansion had windows, dozens and dozens of them, all split into intricate panes of heavy leaded glass. Each pane of each window shone as though the glass was polished on an hourly basis. For all Luke knew, maybe it was.

On the other side of the limousine a velvet green yard stretched out to a row of perfectly trimmed trees. Luke could see no other houses in any direction. The Grants' estate seemed every bit as secluded as Luke's family's farm had been.

"You missed your home?" the chauffeur said to Luke. "You are glad to be home now, no?"

Imitating Smits's rudeness, Luke only shrugged this time.

"Oh, oh, allow me to announce you," the chauffeur said.

He stepped up to the double front doors and threw them open.

"Your sons are home!" he said, his voice taking on a regal rumble.

Smits stepped over the threshold first, onto a gleaming white floor. Luke hesitantly followed him.

"They're probably not even home," Smits said bitterly. "Dad's at work. And Mom's at a party, of course."

But footsteps were coming down the long, curving hallway. Just from the way they sounded—authoritative, commanding—Luke could tell it wasn't servants headed toward him. A man and a woman came into sight. They were probably as old as or older than Luke's parents, but their faces didn't have lines and sags like Luke's father's, their eyes didn't look frightened and defeated like Luke's mother's. The woman had blond hair, styled into a helmet of perfect curls. She wore a brilliant red sweater and dark pants. The man had dark hair, dark eyes, and a dark suit. Luke didn't need to see any price tags to know that everything they wore was very, very expensive. He decided the couple didn't look the least bit like parents. Luke couldn't imagine either one of them bandaging a scraped knee, burping a crying baby, kissing a child's forehead. Of course, if Smits's stories about all the servants were true, they probably never had.

"My boys!" the woman shrieked in a dignified kind of way. "We've been counting the minutes until you got home!"

Luke braced himself to be ignored. He'd have to act normal, somehow, for the sake of the servants—the chauffeur and what looked like three maids peeking in from a nearby room. Luke just wasn't sure what passed for normal behavior in a house like this. He watched Smits for clues, but Smits had gone all stiff, waiting for his parents to finish rushing down the hall.

And then Mrs. Grant brushed right past Smits and

grabbed up Luke in a dizzying embrace. Luke got a whiff of elegant perfume, and then she released him. She stood back, looking him up and down.

"Oh, Lee, you have grown so much while you were away," she exclaimed. "Why, last fall you barely came up to my shoulder. And now . . ." Now Luke could look her straight in the face, eyeball to eyeball, if only he had the nerve. "Oh, I've missed you! Why did you have to stay away for a whole year?"

She wrapped him in another hug. Over her shoulder Luke caught a glimpse of Smits's face. His whole expression had crumpled in pain.

"Smits," Mr. Grant said, quite formally, and offered his son a hand to shake.

Luke expected the two parents to trade off—with Mrs. Grant hugging Smits and Mr. Grant thrusting a stiff hand at Luke. But when Mrs. Grant released Luke a second time, the two grown-ups only stood there, staring awkwardly at the two boys. Smits made no move toward his mother, and he might as well have been invisible, for all the attention she paid him. At least Mr. Grant managed a curt nod toward Luke.

"Well, you'll want to get settled in your rooms," Mrs. Grant said at last. "You must be tired after your journey. Oscar, could you . . ."

Mrs. Grant didn't even have to finish her request. Oscar stepped forward, practically standing on Smits's heels.

"I'm going, I'm going," Smits muttered.

Luke felt like saying, "Don't you want to know what happened at school? Don't you know that those two are dangerous together?" He was used to his own parents, who would have been curious. Who would have been concerned.

He watched Smits step past his mother. She barely flickered her eyes in his direction. Her lips flattened into a thin line of disapproval. From the side Luke could see the emotions playing over Smits's face: first pain, then fury.

Smits had wanted his mother to hug him, too.

Luke didn't understand what he'd witnessed, or why he'd been hugged in Smits's stead. He still didn't understand why the Grants wanted him there. But he could tell that he'd just been sent to his room.

And he didn't have the slightest clue where it was.

CHAPTER *EIGHTEEN*

The chauffeur saved him. He came in just then carrying the luggage, and Luke simply followed him. Up the stairs, down a long, stately hall. Up more stairs, just a half flight, into an entirely different wing of the house. Finally, when Luke was sure he'd walked more than a mile, the chauffeur deposited Luke's luggage and Smits's luggage in adjoining rooms.

Luke hesitated in the doorway of what must have been Lee's room. He looked back at Smits and Oscar, who were still lingering in the hall.

"Just leave me alone!" Smits snarled. "I'm home now! I'm safe! Okay?"

"You think there is not danger here?" Oscar replied. "You think I believe that *you* are not dangerous here?"

Luke slipped into Lee's room, hoping the other two hadn't noticed him listening. And then, staring, he forgot everything else.

The whole rest of the house was luxurious and elegant

beyond belief. But Lee's room was the first place that looked fun. At one end of the room four couches were clustered around a large-screen TV. An entire video arcade lurked in a nearby alcove. Another alcove looked like a sporting goods store: Skis, golf clubs, hockey sticks, tennis rackets, and entire barrels of footballs, baseballs, and basketballs were arranged artfully in every corner. A third alcove held a set of drums and three guitars.

"You play?" the chauffeur asked. Luke had totally forgotten about him. But he was staring longingly at the guitars.

"Some," Luke lied, figuring that the real Lee must have. He hoped the chauffeur wouldn't ask for a demonstration.

But the chauffeur only nodded and bowed, and walked out.

Luke wandered around the room for a while, feeling lost. He looked into drawers of neatly folded clothes. He pulled out a pair of pants and held them up against his own waist. The pant legs ended about the same place as the pants he was actually wearing, but he wasn't sure what that proved. Had the real Lee been about the same height as Luke, or had the Grants secretly found out what size clothes Luke wore, and stocked the room accordingly?

Luke was really looking for something personal—some proof that a real boy had lived here. Initials carved in the bed frame, maybe, or an old drawing of an airplane that Mrs. Grant (or the nanny?) had deemed too special to be thrown out. Luke would even have settled for some signs of wear on the basketballs. But everything looked new and unused. If this had truly been the real Lee's room, he'd passed through this place without leaving behind so much as a smudge on the wall.

Or all signs of his presence had been erased.

Luke shivered at that thought. Suddenly spooked, he went next door to Smits's room, which was every bit as expansive as Lee's.

Smits was sprawled across the bed, staring up at the ceiling. Oscar was nowhere in sight.

"Smits, can you tell me . . ." Luke began.

Smits shook his head and put his finger over his lips. He pointed over to an open door, where Luke could see a figure in a black dress bent over a porcelain sink. A maid was cleaning the bathroom.

"Oh, yeah, it's great to be home," Smits said. "Home, where even the walls have ears."

"I just wondered if you wanted to go down with me and get a snack," Luke finished lamely.

The maid came out of the bathroom.

"Now, don't you boys be ruining your appetites," she scolded. "The cooks have been working all day on a fancy welcome-home dinner for you."

Nothing could have ruined Luke's appetite. Breakfast back at Hendricks School had been heartier than usual, but that had been hours ago. Still, if Smits didn't go with him, he wasn't sure he could find the kitchen. And without Smits he wouldn't have the nerve to rummage through it, looking for food.

"I'm not hungry anyway," Smits said.

Luke's stomach growled. He tried to ignore it. "Want to go outside and play, then? Shoot some hoops or something?"

"Nah," Smits said. "Outside the trees have ears."

There were gardeners, Luke guessed. He supposed that Smits was trying to warn him. He supposed that he ought to be grateful.

But what Luke really wanted to do was punch Smits right smack in the nose. It was almost as bad as if Smits really were his brother.

CHAPTER *NINETEEN*

The rest of the day felt interminable. Luke wandered aimlessly around the house and grounds for several hours. He didn't encounter either of Smits's parents again, but there seemed to be a servant around every corner. And they all seemed to know everything about him—or, at least, about the person he was supposed to be.

"Have you brought up those grades in mathematics, Master Lee?" a man Luke guessed was a butler asked him in the front hallway.

"I tuned up the engine on your motor scooter, sir," a mechanic in a grease-covered uniform told him out beside the garage, which looked large enough to hold a boat—and probably did, come to think of it.

As the grandfather clock by the front door chimed seven, a housekeeper scolded him, "There you are! Why aren't you washed up and dressed for dinner?"

"I . . . ," Luke protested. He scrambled toward what he thought was the dining room. He remembered seeing a vast wooden table in one of these rooms—now, where was it?

Mostly by luck Luke arrived in the proper room. Mr. and Mrs. Grant were seated at opposite ends of the huge table. Two chairs were arranged between them. Smits sat in one of those chairs. Luke dashed toward the other one.

"And where is your tuxedo, young man?" Mrs. Grant asked.

"Um . . . ," Luke said. He noticed that both Smits and Mr. Grant were in formal black suits, with pure white shirts underneath and black bows tied crisply around their necks.

"We didn't dress for dinner at school," Smits volunteered. "Lee probably forgot all about it."

"Indeed," Mrs. Grant sniffed. "Well, we shan't have you forgetting here. Go and change this instant."

Luke considered himself quite fortunate to be able to find his way back to his room, find a suit—a tuxedo?—in his closet, and scramble into it. He was fumbling with the tie, wondering how angry the Grants would be if he just forgot about it—versus how angry they'd be if he kept them waiting any longer—when Oscar silently stepped into the room and adeptly twisted the tie into shape. He straightened the sleeves of Luke's coat, shoved a stray lock of hair off Luke's forehead, and pushed him out the door without saying a single word.

Back in the dining room Mrs. Grant purred, "Now, that's better. That's the son I like to see." Then she, Mr.

Grant, and Smits began spooning up soup that had gone cold.

The dinner passed in a blur. Luke ate heartily of the soup, thinking it was a shame that that was all there was. So he was pleasantly surprised when a plateful of greens arrived next. But the courses that came after that were foods he had no hope of identifying. Once, he suspected he was eating white lumps of rice under some type of gravy. But Luke was pretty certain that the gravy wasn't made from pork fat, which was the only kind he'd ever eaten before.

He supposed the food was good—delicious, even—but it was hard to enjoy it sitting with a sullen Smits and Smits's icy parents. And an army of servants constantly came in and out, whisking dishes away as soon as any of them were finished. By the ninth course Luke was aware of a strange sensation in his stomach: He was too full.

"Psst, Lee," Smits finally whispered from across the table. "You don't have to eat it *all*."

Luke noticed that the others were barely touching their food, letting the servants take away plates missing only a bite or two.

"Oh," Luke said. He wondered what happened to the extra food. Did the servants eat it? Was it thrown away?

No one would be able to tell from the Grants' dining habits that there'd been famines and starvation barely fifteen years earlier, that food was still rationed across the land. Luke had a feeling that the Grants hadn't paid any attention to the famines at all.

Except for Smits's quick whisper, there was no chatter at the table, no questions from the parents, like, "How's school going?" or "When do you suppose they'll have the wiring fixed at Hendricks?" For all the notice Mr. and Mrs. Grant gave Smits and Luke, you'd almost have thought the boys were still away at school.

The Grants didn't even speak to the servants who brought and removed the food. For all the notice they gave to the servants, Luke wondered if they thought that the food appeared and disappeared by magic.

Finally, finally, the servants brought ice cream, which Luke was sure had to be the last course. In spite of his now aching stomach, he ate all of his ice cream, down to the last drop. Ice cream had been such a treat back home. He'd had it only once or twice in his life.

"Lee," Mrs. Grant hissed. "Gentlemen do not *gobble.*"

Red faced, Luke dropped his spoon. It clattered on the floor, spinning off threads of melted ice cream across the polished marble.

"May I be excused?" Smits asked in the silence that followed.

Mrs. Grant nodded.

Luke watched a servant swoop out of nowhere, grab up the spoon, and wipe away the ice cream in a flash. He gathered his nerve to speak.

"May I be excused, too?" he asked.

"I suppose," Mrs. Grant said.

Heavyhearted, Luke found his way back to Lee's room.

He threw himself across the bed, fighting waves of nausea. He'd hated Hendricks School at first, too, but the Grants' house seemed much, much worse. And yet Smits had seemed to be trying to help him. And Oscar had appeared at just the right moment to help him with that tie.

Why? Why did either of them care what happened to Luke?

CHAPTER TWENTY

Luke was sound asleep, and had been for hours, when someone began shaking his shoulder.

"Lee. Get up," a voice whispered.

Luke opened his eyes to complete darkness. It was the middle of the night, he thought. He'd fallen asleep without changing his clothes, so the knot of the bow tie dug uncomfortably into his neck. He'd been dreaming, he realized, about nooses.

"Wha—who are you?" he said, fighting a sense of total disorientation.

"Shh!" A hand clapped instantly over Luke's mouth. He'd accidentally spoken out loud. "Don't make another noise. So help me, I'll . . ." A tiny penlight switched on in the darkness. "I'm your . . . father. See?"

Mr. Grant held the tiny light below his chin, illuminating his face. But the effect was ghoulish, creating eerie shadows around his eyes. Luke felt like he was looking into a Halloween mask.

"Now, come with me," Mr. Grant whispered.

Timidly Luke slipped first one foot, then the other, out of bed. He had a flash of memory—this was like all those nights he'd been awakened by Oscar, summoned by Smits. And he'd always gone. What if he'd disobeyed? What if, just once, he'd stamped his foot and announced, "You know what? I'm not Lee, and I'm not going to pretend anymore. Leave me alone. Let me go back to sleep."

But he couldn't have done that any of the other times, and he couldn't do it now.

Silently, fighting a rising sense of dread, Luke walked alongside Mr. Grant. They went out of his room, down the hall, down the stairs. Luke might have suspected Mr. Grant of purposely leading him in circles, trying to confuse him. But the house was so much like a maze, even in bright daylight, that Luke figured Mr. Grant was truly taking the most direct route to wherever he was going.

Finally Mr. Grant stood before a closed door on the first level. Luke wasn't entirely sure, but he thought that he'd attempted to open this door earlier in the day, when he'd been exploring. The door had been locked then. But now Mr. Grant looked around cautiously, opened the door effortlessly, and motioned Luke inside. A few seconds later Mr. Grant stepped in behind him and shut the door.

"Have you activated the system?" a woman's voice asked in the darkness.

"Three, two, one . . . all set," Mr. Grant said.

Lights came on then. They were standing in an office. A massive mahogany desk stood in the center of the room, and bookshelves lined the walls. Mrs. Grant was sitting in a stiff chair in front of the desk, but she quickly stood up and walked toward Luke and Mr. Grant.

"Finally," she said.

Luke tensed, afraid that she was going to hug him again. But she only took him by the shoulders, held him at arm's length, and squinted thoughtfully at him.

"Braces, of course," she said. "And perhaps some hair dye . . ."

"Maybe contacts," Mr. Grant said.

"Do you think anyone would really notice his eyes? They're not that different," Mrs. Grant said. "Having him fitted for contacts, that'd be another person we'd have to pay off—"

"Of course. You're right," Mr. Grant said.

Luke felt like he was an object they were considering buying. Neither of them had looked him square in the eye yet or addressed him directly. Didn't they think he would have any say in the matters of braces, hair dye, or contacts?

No. Of course not.

Finally Mrs. Grant stepped back and said, "Well, *I* think

it will work. I think we ought to try it."

"Nothing to lose, eh?" Mr. Grant said.

Luke struggled to find his voice. "What do you want from me?" he demanded.

Mrs. Grant looked back at him, very solemnly, and announced, "We want you to die."

MARGARET PETERSON HADDIX

CHAPTER *TWENTY-ONE*

Luke jerked back and made a panicky grab for the door.
But the doorknob had vanished somehow.

"Oh, very nice, Sarinia," Mr. Grant said. "Now you've
terrified him. She doesn't mean for *real*," he told Luke. "We
just want to stage your death so—well, it's a long story."

"Tell me," Luke said through gritted teeth.

Mr. Grant frowned at Mrs. Grant.

"This isn't the way to get started," he said. "You'll have
to forgive us. We're still a little . . . grief stricken. It's been
very hard for us today, dealing with another boy pretending to be Lee. . . ."

Luke looked around frantically. It was the middle of the
night, and for once there were no servants in sight. Still,
his heart began pounding with fear at the thought that
someone might have heard Mr. Grant say that Luke wasn't
Lee.

"It's all right," Mr. Grant said soothingly. "This is a
soundproof, secure room. We can speak openly here."

"Have a seat," Mrs. Grant offered, turning a chair toward Luke. "We'll explain."

Luke was thinking that a soundproof, secure room would be a great place to kill someone. But what could he do? He sat down.

Mr. and Mrs. Grant sat down, too, in chairs opposite his. Mrs. Grant leaned forward.

"Our son Lee was a wonderful boy," she began in a sad voice. "Everything a parent could want. He was good at sports, musically gifted, a top student. . . ." She paused to dab at her eyes. "But he was a bit, um, idealistic."

"He was a troublemaker," Mr. Grant said harshly. "Stubborn as a rock. From the day he was born, he thought he could run the world."

Luke tried to make those two descriptions fit together. So Lee had been a perfect, gifted, stubborn troublemaker.

"Like father, like son. Right, dear?" Mrs. Grant purred.

"Aah . . ." Mr. Grant waved her question away. "When he died, he was, um, breaking the law ever so slightly," Mr. Grant continued. "He was—well, there's no need for you to know the whole story. But suffice it to say that it would have been a bit difficult for us to explain the circumstances of his death."

If Luke had only been a little braver, he might have asked, "Did the Government really kill him?" But Mrs. Grant had already taken over the conversation.

"And when he died, as you can imagine, we were distraught," Mrs. Grant added. "Simply overcome."

She sniffed daintily and let Mr. Grant continue the explanation.

"So when our friend George Talbot approached us with a possible solution, a way to make it look as though Lee *hadn't* died—and, by the way, to help you—we surely couldn't be faulted for taking advantage of that opportunity. Could we?" Mr. Grant asked.

He sounded as though he truly expected Luke to answer. Like he wanted to know what Luke thought.

"Um, no," Luke said. "And believe me, I was happy to . . ." It didn't seem right to say he was happy when they were talking about their son dying. "I mean, I'm very grateful that you made the decision you did."

"Right. And you've had, what—five, six months now of using Lee's name?" Mr. Grant asked.

"Five months, three weeks, and two days," Mrs. Grant said faintly.

Luke could only nod. Lee's mother knew exactly how long it had been since Lee died. Somehow that made Lee seem real, as much as if Luke had found pictures Lee had drawn, letters he had written, initials he had carved in his room.

Luke had liked it better before, when Lee Grant was only a name to him, a name he could hate if he wanted to.

"So here's the thing," Mr. Grant said, ignoring his wife. "We've given you these past several months of freedom. So we're just asking a small favor in return. Smits—our other son, Smits—has had quite a few problems accepting his brother's death. We asked him to keep the news secret, but—"

"Maybe it was too much to expect. Maybe it was too much to expect of anyone," Mrs. Grant said, almost to herself.

Luke could tell which one of them had decided to hide Lee's death.

"We hired a bodyguard for him," Mr. Grant continued. "We let him go meet you. We thought that might help somehow. But he's only getting worse."

Luke wondered how the Grants could know that. Had Oscar told them about Smits setting the fire? Had Smits confided in his parents?

Luke couldn't imagine Smits telling Mr. and Mrs. Grant anything personal at all.

"So we came up with an alternate plan," Mr. Grant said. "We thought we'd have some parties, show you off very publicly as Lee, and then—"

"Do I look like Lee?" Luke asked quietly.

He wanted Mr. Grant to pull a picture out of a billfold or off the top of his desk. Suddenly he desperately wanted to see what the real Lee had looked like. If only he could see the real Lee, he thought, he could decide for himself whether Lee had been a troublemaker, as his father said, or the brilliant saint Mrs. Grant had described. It mattered, suddenly.

Lee Grant, who were you?

"We think you could pass as Lee," Mrs. Grant said with

a catch in her voice. "We think. We've been debating this issue all day."

"Can I see—," Luke began, but Mr. Grant interrupted.

"Anyhow, as I was saying, we'd show you off, then stage your death. Then Smits—and Mrs. Grant and I—could grieve openly. And there'd be no danger of anyone accusing Lee of dying during any, um, illegal activities last April, because everyone would just have seen you now. In September."

Luke considered not being Lee anymore. It would actually be a relief to take on some other anonymous name—some name that didn't come with the complications of a grieving brother and powerful parents. Still, he remembered Mr. Hendricks's worries about Luke taking a name that might save some other third child in hiding, or of taking a name that carried even more danger than Lee Grant's. He wondered if he could still go back to Hendricks if he used a different name.

"Isn't there some other way to help Smits?" Luke asked. "If you kept him at home, and you talked about Lee, just the three of you—"

"What would the servants think?" Mrs. Grant asked.

"You could talk in here," Luke said hesitantly. "You could help him yourself, in private." He couldn't quite see the Grants, all cozy and grieving together. Crying together. He couldn't picture Mrs. Grant hugging Smits, or even Mrs. Grant hugging Mr. Grant. And he couldn't see this room as a place for comfort. It was too cold, too formal, too clearly a place for business deals and crafty thoughts, not raw emotions.

"No, no, you don't understand." Mr. Grant waved away Luke's suggestion. "You're just a child. You don't know what you're talking about. You'll just have to follow our plan."

"I suppose Mr. Talbot could find another fake identity for me," Luke said reluctantly.

"Oh, no," Mrs. Grant said. "You couldn't get another identity. Not after being seen as Lee. Someone might recognize you. And then where would we be?"

Luke stared at her in horror. "Then, what would happen to me? Where could I go without Lee's I.D. card?"

Mrs. Grant shrugged. "Well, wherever you were before you began passing yourself off as Lee." She made it sound like Luke had stolen Lee's identity—like he'd maybe even killed Lee himself.

"You want me to go back into hiding?" Lee asked incredulously.

And Mrs. Grant looked straight back at him and said, "Of course."

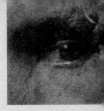

CHAPTER *TWENTY-TWO*

F or just an instant Luke let himself imagine hiding again. He could go back home with Mother and Dad, Matthew and Mark. But he'd be living in the attic, taking his meals on the stairs again, out of sight. He wouldn't be allowed to look out windows or even to walk past a window.

"I can't," Luke said weakly. "I can't go back into hiding."

"Why not?" Mr. Grant said. "You were hiding before you got Lee's name. What's the big deal about hiding now?"

"It's . . ." Luke could only shake his head. They were rich and powerful. How could they possibly understand? Having tasted freedom, having been brave, having volunteered to do something grand for the cause—he absolutely could not return now to the nothingness of life in hiding. "How would you like it if someone told you that you had to go into hiding?" he asked the Grants.

Mrs. Grant stood up with a flounce.

"Oh, this is ridiculous," she said. "I've never had to hide. I'm a legal individual. I have rights. I'm a *Baron.* It's not the same."

"Don't you think I should have rights, too?" Luke asked.

Then, looking at the two adults' stony faces, he began to lose hope. They didn't care about third children. They'd never thought about whether Luke or anyone else like him should have rights or not. He was just a pawn to them, someone they could use for their own purposes and cast aside when they didn't need him anymore.

"That's not the point," Mrs. Grant said. "The point is . . ." A sly smile crept over her face. "The point is, it doesn't matter whether you like our plan or not. If you sabotage our plan, if you don't act like Lee, you sabotage yourself. Don't think we wouldn't be happy to call the Population Police on you."

She was threatening him. Luke felt the color drain from his cheeks. He stared into Mrs. Grant's exquisitely beautiful face, still perfectly made up at three in the morning. She was even still wearing a pearl necklace. What could he possibly say in response?

"But if you want me to help in staging my death . . . ," Luke began. He was ashamed that his voice came out in a whimper.

"Oh, don't you worry about that. We've got everything

planned. We don't need your cooperation," Mrs. Grant said with a sickly sweet smile.

And then the secret meeting was over, and Mr. Grant walked Luke back to his room—to Lee's room. In a daze Luke changed out of the rumpled tuxedo and into his own pajamas. And then he lay in bed, replaying the whole conversation in his mind. The more he thought about it, the more it seemed like a nightmare.

We want you to die. . . .

You couldn't get another identity. . . .

You were hiding before. . . . What's the big deal about hiding now?

The Grants might as well kill him for real and be done with it, Luke thought. Hiding again would be practically as bad as dying.

And then a resolve began to steal over him. No matter what, he wouldn't go back into hiding. Surely he could do something, secretly, as part of the underground resistance to the Government. Mr. Talbot had hinted before at the existence of secret workers for the cause. Luke wasn't sure if any of them had legal identities or not. He remembered three kids he'd met through his friend Nina—Percy, Matthias, and Alia. They'd once been involved in making fake I.D.'s. He wasn't sure what they were doing now, but maybe he could help them.

Luke's plans were vague and shadowy at best, but they made him feel better. He wasn't a Baron like the Grants, he wasn't legal like the Grants, he wasn't even an adult. But that didn't mean he had to roll over and play dead when they said to. That didn't mean he didn't have any choices. All he had to do was get in touch with Mr. Talbot, secretly. Mr. Talbot could protect him from the Grants' schemes.

CHAPTER *TWENTY-THREE*

Comforted by his plans, Luke had fallen back to sleep when someone began shaking his shoulders once again.

"Wake up!" a gruff voice whispered.

It was Oscar this time. Luke actually had the nerve to say, "We're home now. How can Smits be homesick?"

"Shh," Oscar said. "Follow me."

Mystified, Luke obeyed. But Oscar didn't lead Luke next door to Smits's room. He guided Luke on a convoluted path through the entire house. Only when they stood before a dark door did Luke realize: Oscar had led him back to the secret office.

"Wh—," Luke began.

"Shh!" Oscar said again, urgently.

He didn't look around the way Mr. Grant had, only jammed a key in the lock. The door swung open and Oscar yanked Luke inside. Oscar seemed to be pressing buttons the same way Mr. Grant had. The lights came on once again and, Luke noticed this time, the doorknob vanished. Somehow the door seemed to have turned into a smooth wall.

"How—how did you know about this room?" Luke asked.

"Lee told me," Oscar said. "Lee gave me a key."

Lee. Luke gulped.

"I'm Lee," he said without much conviction. "I never said a word to you about, um, our house. I've never given you anything."

Oscar gave Luke a look that almost seemed compassionate.

"We're in a soundproof room," he said. "We both know the truth. There's no need for lies here."

Stunned, Luke sank into a chair, the same one he'd sat in with the Grants.

"Don't worry," Oscar said. "I'm on your side. We're fighting for the same cause."

"How do I know that?" Luke asked. "Why should I trust you?"

To his surprise, Oscar laughed. "Tough little brat, aren't you? Not like that namby-pamby rich boy I'm supposed to be guarding all the time. You're not really a Baron, are you? Let me guess." Oscar narrowed his eyes, staring directly at Luke. "You grew up poor, I bet. Really, really poor. Like me. I just don't know how *you* were picked to take over Lee Grant's identity."

Luke didn't tell him. He stared straight back at Oscar.

Defiantly. But he felt as though Oscar had seen past the fancy silk Baron pajamas, monogrammed with Lee Grant's initials. Somehow Oscar knew that Luke was nobody—and not really brave, not really confident, not really rich.

Oscar shrugged, as if he hadn't really expected Luke to tell him anything. Or as if he didn't need to know more about Luke.

"I'm going to tell you a story," Oscar said softly. "Then you'll know why you should trust me. I'm sure you'll appreciate hearing the truth."

Oscar sat down opposite Luke. Oscar was wearing sweatpants and a T-shirt that emphasized his bulging biceps, but somehow he didn't seem like a muscle-bound bodyguard anymore. He looked downright thoughtful, squinting seriously at Luke.

"The Government wants people to think that everyone's in favor of our current dictator—I mean, *president*," Oscar said sardonically. "That everyone believes that everything he does is just so wonderful and so *right*. That everyone believes the Barons deserve the privileges they get and the rest of the people deserve squat. But you and me, we know differently, don't we?" When Luke didn't answer, Oscar repeated, "Don't we, *Lee*?"

"Yes," Luke whispered. He was still stunned by Oscar's transformation. Oscar wasn't the proper, rule-obsessed servant anymore. Even his voice sounded rougher.

"When something's unfair," Oscar said, "anyone with any gumption is going to fight it. Right?"

Luke nodded. He wanted to say, "Look, I struck a blow against the Government myself. I turned in an informer for the Population Police." He wanted to impress this new Oscar, suddenly.

But he wasn't sure Oscar would be impressed by anything Luke had done.

"I was eight when I put my first pipe bomb in a Baron's mailbox," Oscar said. "By the time I was twelve, I was stealing Barons' cars. Not for my own benefit—no way! My buddies and me, we'd push those cars into the river. Can you imagine the kind of splash a limo makes? And how the police flock to the shore? We were risking our lives for the cause."

Luke swallowed hard.

"So then Barons moved farther and farther out from the big cities," Oscar said. "They all got security fences, security guards. They went crying to the Government, 'Boo-hoo-hoo. Those vandals are out of control.' And the Government listened to them. They passed new laws—did you know that it's a bigger crime to destroy a Baron's property than to kill an ordinary person? It's true." Oscar lowered his voice, as if confiding a great secret in Luke. "And meanwhile, ordinary people are starving in the streets. . . ."

"That's not fair," Luke said in a small voice.

Oscar stood up and started to pace. "That's right, it's

not fair. That's why we're doing something about it."

"We are?" Luke asked. He wondered if Oscar was going to say anything about the unfair Population Law, which forced third children into hiding. That was something else the Government had done wrong. Did Oscar know about those kids, who had even more reason than Oscar to hate the Government? Did Oscar care?

Oscar paused in his pacing and gave Luke a glance that made Luke feel about as big as an insect. And as easily squashed.

"I've been working for the underground resistance for years," Oscar said. "Our sole goal is to overthrow the Government and the Barons, and to reestablish justice. Equity for all, that's our motto." Oscar rested his hands on the back of the chair he'd been sitting in. Luke could tell that Oscar only needed to flex a muscle or two and he could have torn the chair to shreds. But Oscar wasn't moving. He was watching Luke.

"You and I both know," Oscar said, "it's treason even to say that I oppose the Government. If you reported me, I'd deny everything. And there'd be no evidence to link me to any plots."

Luke could tell Oscar was waiting for Luke now, waiting for some sort of cue to go on.

"I won't report you," Luke said. "Why would I do that?"

"Good," Oscar said. "We understand each other."

He sat down again and seemed to relax back into his story.

"I'll admit," he said. "I was nothing but a two-bit punk

in the beginning. I was poor, uneducated—how could I be anything else? But then my friends and me, we got hooked up with some other rebels. Eggheads, we called them. They thought about stuff like political philosophy. Who needs it? But they had the money to do real damage. They taught us about having more of an impact than blowing up a few mailboxes, ruining a few cars, when the Barons could always buy new. They taught us about being subtle. They even trained some of us as accountants, computer experts, electricians, all the trades. So we could create even more problems for the Government and the Barons."

"Oh," Luke said.

"You know those electrical outages they kept having on the coast? We did that," Oscar said. "Entire cities, blacked out. Because of us."

Luke had never heard of the electrical outages, but he tried to look impressed.

Oscar sprawled in his chair, as if he was totally comfortable with telling Luke this part of his story.

"Nobody was supposed to know about us, but we were famous, in our own way," Oscar said. "Who else dared to do anything? We were cool. We even started attracting a Baron kid or two, rebelling against their parents."

Luke looked up, startled.

"Lee," Luke said.

"Yep," Oscar said, nodding. "The real Lee Grant. Or

maybe I should say, the original version."

Luke leaned forward, waiting. He realized he was barely breathing.

"Lee wasn't our first Baron kid, but he had the best connections," Oscar said.

"But why would he—," Luke began.

"If your dad's the richest man in the country, and you're mad at him, what's the best way to get back at him? Mess up the Government. Such fun." Oscar shook his head. "None of us trusted him."

"Then, why did you let him join?" Luke asked.

"Don't you see?" Oscar asked. "He was Lee *Grant*. What a great weapon for our cause." He looked down. "Some in our group thought the best thing we could do was to kidnap him and ask for ransom. We could have financed our operations for years to come."

"But you didn't do that," Luke said, almost as a question.

"No," Oscar said impatiently. "We thought he'd be more useful in other ways. And he was. He . . . matured. He was turning into a fine subversive. When he was home on break from school, he relayed lots of plans he stole from his father. Plans that helped us know what the Government was up to so we could counter their activities."

"What did he do for you when he was away at school?" Luke asked. In spite of himself, he was fascinated by this new version of Lee's life. Luke felt like he was putting together a jigsaw puzzle: Here's one piece showing Lee pulling his younger brother, Smits, in a red wagon. Here's the piece from his mother: Lee as the gifted musician, the talented athlete, the brilliant student. Here's the piece from Mr. Grant—Lee as the stubborn troublemaker.

Somehow that was the only piece that seemed to jibe with Oscar's story.

"He went to one of those fancy, richy-rich prep schools. And while he was there"—Oscar chucked—"he tricked all those sons of the establishment into helping us without even knowing it. He was a piece of work, that Lee."

"But he died," Luke said. For the first time he put together what Smits and Smits's parents had said. "He was killed doing something for you. For your group." It wasn't a question. That had to be the "illegal activity" Mr. Grant had referred to. That had to be the reason a Government soldier had shot Lee. Smits hadn't been lying about that at all.

Oscar frowned.

"Unfortunately, yes. He was killed during one of our secret missions," Oscar said.

"What was it?"

Oscar narrowed his eyes, as if trying to decide how much to tell Luke. "Last spring we thought maybe we had our chance to act. There'd been an anti-Government rally in the capital. We weren't part of that—we knew it was doomed from the start. But it shook some people up. A lot of kids died, right there in public, and there were actually some officials who got upset. Public deaths are so much more offensive than private ones."

Luke wasn't sure what to make of this news. Was Oscar talking about the rally that Jen had led and died in? Had the rally had an impact after all?

"We thought we'd strike while the enemy was in disarray," Oscar said. "But we had to get weapons out to everyone in our group as quickly as possible. Some of our people were in the far north. Lee was a good cross-country skier. He volunteered to cross the mountains to deliver the munitions."

"Munitions?" Luke repeated.

"Guns," Oscar said.

Luke tried to imagine a boy his age, alone in the mountains, carrying guns. He'd never seen any mountains for real, but he pictured them as desolate places. Just snow and trees and Lee, carrying guns.

"So they caught him. The Government caught him," Luke said.

Oscar nodded. "Lee had the sense to try to escape. He knew this was life or death. If they'd captured him alive, they might have tortured him. He might have revealed our plans, betrayed our group. We might all be dead right now if Lee had talked."

If Luke had been in Lee's place, would Luke have been able to be so brave?

"But your plan," Luke said. "You didn't go through with your plan?"

"Do you see any sign that the Government's gone? That

the Barons' wealth has been given to the people?" Oscar clutched the arm of his chair—an exquisite leather chair—as if he really wanted to hand it to some poor person. "No. Without our allies in the north, with the Government suspicious after finding Lee, it wasn't worth the risk."

"Oh," Luke said.

All this had been happening while Luke was sitting at home wondering what had happened at Jen's rally. What else had been going on in the country then? How many others wanted to overthrow the Government? Maybe if they all got together—maybe that way something would happen.

"Did Mr. Talbot know about your plan?" Luke asked.

"Who?" Oscar said.

"Mr. Talbot. The man who came to school that one time. He had lunch with Mr. Hendricks and Smits and me, the day Smits ran off and said he wouldn't obey his parents. . . ."

A disgusted look was spreading over Oscar's face.

"He's a Baron. Barons can't be trusted," Oscar said.

"You trusted Lee," Luke reminded him.

"Lee was a kid," Oscar said. "He could be . . . molded. Someone like this Mr. Talbot—bah!"

Luke felt honor-bound to defend Jen's father.

"But he's helped me," Luke protested. "More than once." Did he dare tell Oscar that Mr. Talbot was a double agent, pretending to work for the Population Police while he secretly sabotaged their work?

"Are you sure?" Oscar snarled. "Are you sure he wasn't just helping himself? Will he still help you when you no longer serve his purposes?"

And Luke couldn't answer that. He trusted Mr. Talbot. Of course he trusted Mr. Talbot. But maybe it had helped Mr. Talbot to give Luke a fake I.D., to protect him at Hendricks School. Luke knew about Jen. Luke could tell the Population Police about Jen. Luke could get Mr. Talbot killed.

It had never occurred to Luke before that he had any power over Mr. Talbot.

He didn't like thinking about Mr. Talbot in that way. He forced himself to stare back steadily at Oscar, so Oscar didn't see how confused Luke was. Luke crossed his arms over his chest, trying to look certain, trying to look unfazed. Something in his pajama pocket jabbed into his arm—it was the fake I.D.'s he'd taken from Smits's room at Hendricks after the fire. Did Luke dare ask Oscar about those I.D.'s now? Was it finally time to get an explanation?

No. Luke felt like he'd already made a mistake mentioning Mr. Talbot. It was better to wait and see what Oscar would tell him on his own.

After a second Oscar sighed and said, "Never mind. This Mr. Talbot, he doesn't matter now. It helped everyone to have you become Lee Grant. It helped the Grants and it helped our cause. It protected us from the Government."

Luke could have added, "And it helped me." He could even have made it funny, like a joke. That would have defused the tension that had suddenly arisen between him and Oscar. But he couldn't bring himself to do that. He kept his lips resolutely pressed together, waiting.

"Yes, you helped us all," Oscar said. "But there have been problems. . . ."

"I know about Smits," Luke said. That seemed to be a safe subject. "I know that he told people Lee was dead—"

Oscar waved away that concern. "We can handle Smits. He's just a little boy. And he has me to watch out for him." Oscar grinned in a way that reminded Luke of a drawing of the Big Bad Wolf in the fairy tale book his mother had read to him when he was little. Hadn't there been a story in that book about how stupid it was to let a wolf guard sheep?

"Do Mr. and Mrs. Grant know that you, um, I mean . . . ," Luke began.

"That I know how Lee died? That I know Smits isn't so crazy after all—just stupid? That I work for the resistance? Do you think *I'm* crazy?" Oscar peered intently at Luke, and for a minute Luke thought he expected an answer. Then Oscar exploded, "Of course not. They don't know anything."

"Well, that's good," Luke muttered.

Oscar laughed. "Yeah, you could say that. I just 'happened' to show up here looking for work at the right time. 'Do you need a bodyguard for your sons?' I asked. 'Sons,' I said, even though I knew Lee was already dead. And it just so happened I had perfect credentials. . . ." He smirked. "Perfect *fake* credentials, of course."

"Oh," Luke said. He frowned. "Then if the Grants don't know, and you're not worried about Smits—what's the problem?"

"The Grants are being blackmailed," Oscar said.

Luke looked back blankly at Oscar. "Blackmailed? Is that where—"

Oscar didn't wait for Luke to figure out the meaning. "Someone knows what really happened to Lee. And he—or they, whoever it is—has been threatening to reveal the truth to the Government if the Grants don't pay lots of money."

Luke stared at Oscar. This wasn't just about the Grants and Lee. This was his life on the line, too.

"Are they paying it?" Luke asked.

"So far," Oscar said. "But they want to stop."

And suddenly Luke understood. Suddenly he knew why he'd been taken away from Hendricks School, why the Grants had called him into the secret room only a few hours ago, why they suddenly had a use for him after months of ignoring him.

"That's why they want me to pretend to die," Luke said. "They don't care about Smits or grieving at all. They're just trying to stop the blackmail. It's all about money." He was perfectly willing to believe the worst about the Grants. But then he remembered—should he have revealed so much to Oscar?

But Oscar was nodding grimly. He clearly knew all about the Grants' plan.

"I suspected that that was what they were telling you tonight," Oscar said. "Well, don't worry. You're not going to die. Smits is going to die in your place."

CHAPTER TWENTY-FOUR

For the longest time Luke could only stare wordlessly at Oscar. Then he managed to croak, "Just pretend, right?"

"Oh, right," Oscar said quickly. "We're going to fake Smits's death, the way the Grants were planning to fake yours. After that, the Grants wouldn't dare let anything happen to you, because it would look too suspicious to have two sons die in bizarre accidents. And as Lee Grant, you can help the cause. Think of all you can do from this base of operations. They couldn't stop you. . . ."

Luke remembered what Mr. Hendricks had said before Smits came to Luke's school: "I'd have a better chance of stopping the wind than stopping a Grant from doing what he wants." What if Luke could really act like Lee Grant, could really carry off that kind of overwhelming power? He could almost believe in Oscar's fantasy. Almost.

"But what would happen to Smits?" Luke asked.

"Oh, we'd hide him away somewhere," Oscar said. "Not

that it matters. He's such a worthless brat."

Luke tried to imagine Smits in hiding. He'd been miserable enough at Hendricks, which was a paradise of freedom compared with life in hiding. How could Luke force Smits into the same prison Luke had escaped?

"Isn't there some other choice?" Luke asked hesitantly. "Can't you just stop the Grants' plan without hurting Smits?"

Oscar laughed. "Do you really care whether Smits gets hurt or not? This is *war*. Nothing's going to be accomplished without someone getting hurt. Why shouldn't it be Smits? Is there someone else you'd prefer to see in pain?"

Luke went cold. Was Oscar threatening him? Did Oscar care who got hurt? Would he care if somebody died?

"I don't want anyone hurt," Luke said in a small voice. "Can't we do this . . . peacefully?"

This time Oscar's laughter was overwhelming. It took him a full five minutes to regain control.

"Oh, puh-lease," Oscar said, still snorting laughter. "Do you avoid stepping on ants, too? Maybe I misjudged you. I didn't take you for a sissy. I didn't take you for a Baron lover. Just another drone supporting the ruling class and the Government—"

"I don't support the Government," Luke said angrily.

"Well, sure, you can *say* that," Oscar taunted him. "But I'm giving you a chance to strike a blow for freedom, and you're scared some spoiled Baron brat might get treated a little roughly. What's Smits to you, anyway? What's he ever done for you?"

"Nothing," Luke said, but it wasn't true. Luke couldn't forget the slow unreeling of confidences Smits had told Luke all those nights back at school. Smits had shared all his memories of the real Lee. Luke had never asked for them. They didn't make Smits any less infuriating. But Luke couldn't forget them. He couldn't forget that Smits wasn't just a Baron, but a real boy, already deeply hurt, already deep in grief.

How could Luke be responsible for hurting him more?

"We don't have to decide anything tonight, do we?" Luke asked. "Mr. and Mrs. Grant said they were going to dye my hair and get me braces. Nothing's going to happen right away. We have time to think this out. Maybe—maybe if we work together we can think of a better plan. . . ."

Oscar snorted.

"I thought someone like you would jump at the chance to help the cause. I thought you were like me," he said. "I thought you had guts."

"I do!" Luke wanted to say. "I am! I would!" But the words wouldn't come. Because he wasn't sure. Of anything.

Oscar didn't give him a chance to interrupt.

"Don't you see?" Oscar said. "You don't always get time to think, time to consider carefully. We have an opportunity now that we can take or we can miss. And if we miss it, what happens then?" He stared straight at Luke. "I need your answer tonight. Are you with me or not?"

Luke gulped.

"I don't know," he said. That seemed to be the bravest answer he could give. It was, at least, honest.

But what place did honesty have around people like Oscar and the Grants?

It was too hard to sit there with Oscar staring at him, waiting for him to decide. Abruptly Luke stood up.

"What are you doing?" Oscar said.

"Um, going back to bed?" No matter how hard Luke tried to sound strong and certain—as tough as Oscar— his voice rose into a question. "I'm—I mean, a good night's sleep will help me think. Could you open the door for me, please?"

Luke was practically begging. Oscar had all the power now. If he wanted to, Oscar could keep Luke prisoner until Luke agreed to help him. What would Luke do then?

But Oscar stood up, too.

"Just one word of advice before you go," Oscar said. "Watch out for chandeliers."

CHAPTER *TWENTY-FIVE*

Luke woke to bright sunlight streaming in the windows. This, too, seemed fake somehow—like a trick. How could the sun be shining when Luke's mind was in such turmoil? He looked up at the elaborate light fixture that arced over his bed, and even that seemed dangerous this morning. "Watch out for chandeliers," Oscar had said. Did the light over his bed count as a chandelier? Was Luke in danger every time he went to sleep?

Luke shook his head back and forth on the pillow. He needed to get a grip on his fears. He remembered what Mother always said back home every time he or his brothers whined about anything: "Count your blessings. Look on the bright side." Luke's current problems were a lot worse than, say, Matthew and Mark wanting to play football while Luke wanted to play tag. But maybe he could find a few blessings even now. He began making a mental list.

1. Oscar had been kind enough to warn Luke about the chandelier.

But why? Was it a true warning or just a trick?

Luke decided to move on to the next blessing.

2. Nobody was going to blow his cover. The Grants needed him to be Lee. Oscar needed him to be Lee.

But what about Smits? Could Luke trust Smits to keep Luke's secret?

Luke frowned and abandoned his list of blessings. It was all too confusing. Every blessing hid more danger and uncertainty. It was like the reverse of that saying about clouds and silver linings: All of Luke's silver linings hid dark storm clouds.

I'll just call Mr. Talbot, Luke told himself. *He'll know what to do.*

"He's a Baron. Barons can't be trusted. . . ." Oscar's words from the night before echoed in Luke's head. Luke tried to push them away, but the doubts lingered.

Luke wished he could trust Oscar. Oscar was already right there. He didn't like the Grants any more than Luke did. It would be so easy to agree with Oscar, let Oscar do all the planning, let Oscar save Luke.

If only Oscar's plan didn't involve Smits. How could Luke, who wanted freedom so badly, help send another boy into hiding?

And was that what Oscar was really planning to do?

In that moment before Luke had asked about Oscar's plan, "Just pretend, right?" he'd seen a glimmer in Oscar's eyes.

If Luke hadn't protested, would Oscar have let him believe that Smits was going to be killed for real?

Was Oscar planning actual murder?

Were the Grants?

Luke had been wrong about a good night's sleep helping him think. His thoughts were more jumbled than ever. He was more terrified than ever.

"I *can* trust Mr. Talbot," he said aloud fiercely.

He slipped out of bed and went into the hall. He tapped on Smits's door.

"Who is it?" Smits mumbled.

"Me," Luke said. It was too hard to say Lee's name to Smits. Especially now. Without waiting for an answer, Luke pushed on in.

"Ever heard of privacy?" Smits said. "Ever heard of letting someone sleep in?"

Smits was still in bed, tangled up in his blankets and sheets as if he'd been fighting with his bedding all night long. His hair stuck up at odd angles, making him seem younger than ever. He was just a little kid. After having heard Oscar's plan, Luke found it hurt just to look at Smits.

But Luke took a deep breath and reminded himself that he was supposed to be a carefree Baron, lazing around on an unexpected day off from school. Not an illegal third child terrified of murder plots.

"It's ten o'clock already," Luke said. "How much sleep do you need?"

He was proud of the way his voice sounded so even and calm—even playful.

Smits just groaned.

"Hey," Luke said, still forcing himself to sound casual. "Don't you think we should call back to school and see how close they are to finishing the repairs? See how soon we can go—I mean, we'll have to go back?"

Luke had picked this ruse on the spur of the moment. It'd be easier to get Mr. Hendricks to seek help from Mr. Talbot, rather than trying to call Mr. Talbot directly. Nobody could deny a boy a phone if he said he just wanted to call his school. Could they?

Smits stared back at Luke as if Smits had totally forgotten about Hendricks School. Then he laughed.

"Oh, good try," he said. "But Dad'll see through it."

"What?" Luke said, suddenly scared that even Smits had figured out what Luke was planning.

"You want to make some more of those prank calls again, don't you?" Smits asked. "Remember how much trouble we got into last year at Christmas? 'Hello, is your refrigerator running? Can't you catch it?' And then Dad made it so we couldn't use any of the phones in the house at all, because they all take a special code?"

Smits was covering for Luke once again, telling him

information that Lee would have known, but Luke didn't. Why? Why did Smits want to help Luke?

It didn't matter. Either way, Luke wouldn't be able to use a phone.

"We're basically prisoners here, aren't we?" Luke asked quietly.

At that moment Oscar stepped into the room. Luke froze.

"Ah," Oscar said. "A little early-morning brotherly chitchat, I see. How pleasant." He leaned casually against the wall. Then he very deliberately pulled a headset off his ears and placed it on a chest of drawers beside him. "I won't need this now that I'm right in the room with the two of you."

Luke glanced at Smits, wondering if the younger boy got the message, too: Oscar had been listening to their entire conversation. Smits's room was bugged, and Oscar heard everything that happened there electronically.

Smits's face registered no surprise whatsoever.

"Yeah, it was pleasant until you showed up," Smits said.

Luke looked from Smits to Oscar. He felt trapped between the two of them, the muscular man and the scrawny boy. Oscar wanted Luke to betray Smits. And Smits wanted—what?

"Sometimes brothers have secrets they want to share," Oscar said. "And sometimes they have secrets they need to keep to themselves."

And Luke saw, staring at Smits's face, that Smits

thought Oscar was saying that for Smits's sake, telling Smits not to share any secrets with Luke.

What secrets did Smits know?

And what had Oscar told him?

CHAPTER *TWENTY-SIX*

Luke took a shower and got dressed. For some reason he couldn't have explained, even to himself, he transferred the fake I.D.'s for Oscar and Smits from his pajamas into the pants he'd put on. Maybe he just liked having a few secrets of his own. Or—how did he know that his room wasn't going to be searched while he was away?

Being at the Grants' house was making him totally paranoid.

Except—was it still paranoia if all his fears were justified?

On the way down to breakfast Luke passed Oscar on the stairs. Luke half expected him to stop Luke and ask quietly, "So what's your answer now?"

But Oscar only flickered his gaze briefly in Luke's direction. Otherwise, he acted as if Luke didn't exist.

He took my "I don't know" as a no, Luke thought. *And the chance to join his cause was a onetime offer.* Luke's heart sank. He wanted to grab the hulking man and beg for a second chance. But how could he? He still didn't want to hurt Smits.

"What's going to happen now?" Luke asked weakly. He meant, "Are you going to kill Smits or just hide him away somewhere? Or are the Grants going to kill me?"

Oscar didn't answer, just brushed on by.

Luke stood still, practically trembling. *Breakfast,* he told himself. *I'll feel better after breakfast.* He forced himself to continue down the stairs.

But after a huge meal that he barely tasted, he could think of nothing to do except wander aimlessly around the house. In the living room—actually, one of several rooms that Luke would have called a living room—he found an elegantly curved telephone sitting on a coffee table. Without hope, he picked up the receiver.

A maid appeared out of nowhere and scolded, "Now, Master Lee, you know your father's got those secret codes on that."

Luke got an idea.

"Tell me the code," he said. "You're the servant. I'm Master Lee. You have to tell me the code."

The maid laughed. "Sure, and you think I'd know it?" She shook a feather duster playfully at him. "Now, scoot. I've got dusting to do."

Embarrassed, Luke turned away. Master Lee. Right. And Oscar thought that if Smits was out of the way, Luke could manipulate the Grants into serving the cause?

No, Luke realized. Oscar thought he could manipulate Luke into manipulating the Grants. Luke's only choices were between being a pawn for the Grants and being a pawn for Oscar.

But Luke couldn't even choose between those two options, because he didn't know how or when the Grants or Oscar intended to carry out their plans. Why hadn't he pretended to be more cooperative during both of his sessions in the secret room? Why hadn't he just lied like everyone else?

Luke sank down onto the nearest couch. He couldn't call Mr. Talbot or Mr. Hendricks. He couldn't trust anyone at the Grants' house. He couldn't stop any of the plots boiling around him. He couldn't even tell the difference between the lies and the truths that he'd heard. For all he knew, Oscar might be working for the Government, not the resistance. Smits might always have hated his older brother, Lee. The Grants might be the poorest people in the country, instead of the richest. Or, no—Luke stared down at the finely woven carpet beneath his feet—the Grants' wealth was one fact that was indisputable.

"Lee! There you are!" Mrs. Grant suddenly swooped into the room. Lee instantly sat up straight, but she frowned anyway. "For heaven's sake, get off that couch this instant. You'll leave it rumpled, and how would that look for our party this evening?"

Luke bolted to his feet.

"P-p-party?" he asked.

"Oh, yes," Mrs. Grant said. "It'll be the social event of the season. We've been planning it for months. It's so nice that you and Smits are home from school and will be able to attend. Isn't it?"

She smiled so sweetly at him that Luke had a hard time remembering how coldly she'd regarded him the night before.

"Is it—do we . . ." Luke wanted to ask if Smits and Lee had usually attended their parents' big parties before. He wanted to ask if he'd be expected to know any of the other guests, and if so, what he was supposed to do when he met them tonight. But of course those weren't questions he could just blurt out, unless he was in the secret room. He settled for, "Do I have to wear a tux?"

Mrs. Grant laughed, making a sound that reminded Luke of breaking glass.

"Of course, you silly goose. You boys! Thinking you can get away without wearing a tux! Would you believe Smits asked me the same thing?"

And Luke looked back into Mrs. Grant's falsely sparkling eyes and thought, *No. I'm not sure I can believe you even when you tell me something as simple as that.*

"Now, come on," Mrs. Grant said. "The orthodontist and hairdresser are here. It's time for your makeover!"

CHAPTER *TWENTY-SEVEN*

By eight o'clock there were tiny lights strung in the trees along the driveway. An army of maids had made sure that every inch of the Grants' house was dust free and virtually gleaming. Dozens of cooks had prepared tray after tray of more foods than Luke had ever seen before.

And Luke had been transformed as well. Most of his teeth had been encased in silver prisons, with something that felt like barbed wire running between them. His hair had been dyed a darker brown, while Mrs. Grant had fluttered over the hairdresser, lamenting, "I can't believe you can't trust a *boy* anymore not to go bleaching his hair while he's away at school. . . ."

The braces hurt. His newly dyed—and gelled—hair felt stiff and unfamiliar. He didn't recognize himself when he walked past a mirror.

And now he and Smits were in their tuxes, standing at the top of the stairs. Waiting.

"I want both of you to make a grand entrance," Mrs.

Grant said, hovering over them, straightening Luke's tie, flattening a tiny cowlick at the back of Smits's head. "After all the guests have arrived, I'll have the butler announce you. He'll say, 'And here are the sons of the manor, Lee and Smithfield Grant.' And then you'll come down the stairs, like so."

She took small, mincing steps down the top few stairs before turning around to make sure that they had been listening. Was this part of the plot? Luke wondered. Were the Grants counting on his being so clumsy and unaccustomed to the spotlight that he'd trip and fall? Would the guests believe that he would die from such a fall?

Luke stared down the long stairway. Of course they would believe such a thing. If he tripped at the top and fell down thirty-two stairs, he might die for real.

And that would probably suit the Grants just fine.

Luke held in a shiver of fear and reminded himself: Chandeliers. Oscar had said that he needed to watch out for chandeliers. And assuming that Oscar was telling the truth about that, Luke had enough to worry about without looking for other death traps.

Far below, the front doorbell rang.

"That must be the first guests," Mrs. Grant said. "It'll be the Snodgrasses—they're always early. They have no social graces." Mrs. Grant shook her head disapprovingly and began walking down the stairs. She turned around briefly to remind both boys, "Now, remember. Be on your best behavior."

Down below, the butler was opening the door. Luke could hear his booming voice call out, "Ah, Mr. and Mrs. Snodgrass. Mr. and Mrs. Grant will be so glad to greet you. May I take your coats?"

Beside Luke, Smits slumped and sat down on the top step. Luke decided he might as well do the same. He slid down beside the younger boy. The fake I.D.'s he'd transferred into his tuxedo pocket poked his leg, as if he needed another reminder that everything around him was false.

"I can't believe they're having a party," Smits muttered. "My brother's dead, and they're having a party."

Luke glanced anxiously around. Oscar was leaning on a railing right behind them, but he seemed not to hear.

"It's been nearly six months," Luke said apologetically. "Probably that's long enough to wait before people start having parties again."

"They were having parties all along," Smits said glumly.

"They had to pretend . . . ," Luke started to say. He didn't like defending Mr. and Mrs. Grant, but he was getting panicked. Smits needed to pretend, too. What if Smits told one of the party guests that Lee was dead? What if one of the servants overheard?

"But they were enjoying themselves," Smits said fiercely. "They love their parties. They never cared about Lee."

In spite of himself Luke argued, "I thought you said they liked him better than you."

Smits fixed Luke with a dead stare. "So now you know what they think of me."

Behind them Oscar cleared his throat warningly. Luke was suddenly fed up with all the subterfuge. Without thinking, he turned around and asked Oscar, "Does Smits know who you are? Does Smits know that you knew Lee? That you can tell him everything he wants to know about how Lee died?"

Oscar's face turned a fiery red. He jerked his fists up; Luke knew that if even one of those fists hit him, he'd be knocked down the stairs for sure. But Oscar stopped just short of swinging at Luke.

Because Smits was answering.

With his eyes trained forward, Smits began reciting, "Oscar is my bodyguard. My parents hired him when I started telling lies at my old school. I'm not mentally stable. That's what my parents say. That's why I have Oscar. Oscar works for my parents."

He sounded like a schoolboy repeating facts he'd memorized but didn't understand. It was eerie.

"Good," Oscar growled. "Now we all know where we stand."

After that the three of them sat in silence at the top of the stairs until a huge light suddenly shone up at them, and the butler's booming voice called out, "And here are the sons of the mansion, Lee and Smithfield Grant."

Luke stumbled to his feet. Blindly he began descending the stairs beside Smits. The light was so intense, he couldn't see any of the guests below. But they were clapping. Luke tried to force himself to smile in the direction of the applause. The smile only pressed his lips more tightly into the braces, making his mouth ache even more.

At the bottom of the stairs Mrs. Grant wrapped first Luke, then Smits, into showy hugs. Smits wasn't slighted in the least this time.

"My sons," Mrs. Grant said, and she sounded as if she loved them both deeply.

An old, bewhiskered man behind her stepped forward to shake Luke's hand.

"My, how you've grown," the man said. "I haven't seen you since you were barely up to my knee."

"Yes, Mr. President," Mrs. Grant said, and her voice was as light and merry as a fountain. "And now Lee's going through that gawky phase, with the braces and all, so you might not even recognize him now."

Mr. President? Was this *the* president? Was Luke shaking the hand of the man who'd outlawed third children? Only disbelief kept Luke from recoiling.

"Oh, I'd recognize this boy anywhere," the man—the president?—said, chuckling. "Looks just like his lovely mother."

Luke choked back something like a giggle.

"And he'd certainly recognize *you,*" Mrs. Grant said in a voice so clogged with flattery that Luke could have gagged. "The last time we drove into the city, there were pictures of you everywhere."

"Well," the man said. "People keep insisting on pasting those pictures up. I don't even know where they get them."

"Your people love you," Mrs. Grant said soothingly.

So it was the president. In a daze, Luke shook the next hand that was thrust at him, while Smits shook the president's. Fortunately, no one seemed to expect him to say anything more than, "Hello, sir." And just as fortunately, after the first few people, somehow Smits got ahead of Luke. More than once he turned back to Luke and said something like, "Look, it's the Hadley-Perkinses!"

So Smits was helping Luke once again. Luke wasn't sure how long it would last. And no matter how hard he tried to act normal, he couldn't help glancing up every time he neared a chandelier. There was one in the entryway, one in the living room, one in the parlor—after a while Luke lost count.

And there was Oscar, constantly threading his way behind them like a dark shadow.

Was Oscar waiting for Luke to turn around and announce, "Okay, I've decided. I'll help you now"?

Or was it already too late?

Finally Smits and Luke reached the end of the row of hands they had to shake. The guests seemed to have forgotten them. They stood together off to the side. Luke finally had a chance to think. He nudged Oscar's side.

"Did you see the president?" he asked. "What if we—"

Oscar instantly clapped his hand over Luke's mouth.

"Don't even finish that sentence," he hissed warningly in Luke's ear. "There are guards everywhere."

And then Oscar released him and nodded at a man in a dark suit nearby.

"Just showing him some bodyguard moves," Oscar said calmly.

Luke wasn't even sure what he'd intended to suggest to Oscar. But how could Oscar, who wanted to overthrow the Government, stand in the same room with the president and not do *something*? How could Luke?

Then Luke looked around and noticed how many of the supposed guests had tiny wires leading into their ears, how many men kept their hands over pockets that, for all Luke knew, must have contained guns. Oscar was right—the house was crawling with guards.

Did that make the party safer or more dangerous for Luke?

"Hors d'oeuvres, sir?" a familiar voice said behind him.

A serving girl in a black dress and frilly apron held out a tray full of unidentifiable round food. Luke's face instantly lit up—not because of the food, but because of the girl. It was his friend Nina, who'd gone to the girls' school that bordered Hendricks School for Boys.

Forgetting himself, Luke blurted out, "What are you doing here?"

Nina did a better job of staying in character.

"I was just hired today, sir," she said with a small curtsy. "Mistress hired several new servants just for tonight's party. Me and Trey, and Joel and John . . . we're here to help, sir."

And Luke understood that she meant the last part completely, not just as part of her act. Luke's friends were there to help him. Not just Nina, but Trey and Joel and John. Mr. Hendricks had not sent him off to the Grants' and forgotten about him. For the first time that night Luke felt like beaming.

One of the round cheese balls or sausage balls or whatever they were rolled off Nina's tray. She bent down to pick it up, then glared up at Luke. Luke got the message. He fell to his knees as well and pretended to reach for the food. Nina leaned over and whispered in his ear, "Be careful. Most of the servants are on Oscar's side. And you better believe it's killing me to call you 'sir.'"

"That's good to know," Luke murmured solemnly.

Above him Mrs. Grant swooped in out of nowhere.

"Lee!" she hissed. "Let the servant get that! My son should not be crawling around on the floor during my party!"

"Yes, Mom," Luke said obediently, and stood up.

Mrs. Grant sniffed and steered him over to meet someone whose hand he'd somehow missed shaking.

While he was smiling and nodding and trying to act polite, he caught a glimpse of Trey opening and shutting the door to admit more guests. He saw John stacking dirty plates on a tray and whisking them away. And he saw Oscar, with narrowed eyes, talking to one of the president's guards.

The party, Luke realized, was a battlefield. The sides were being drawn in the midst of the women in their glittering dresses, the men in tuxedos holding elegant champagne glasses, the servants arranging tiny cakes in neat rows on doilies. Luke could guess at the alliances of every person in the room.

Except Smits.

The younger boy was slumped on a sofa, not even looking at the guests talking around him. Luke wondered how the younger boy felt, sitting there ignored, while Mrs. Grant crowed over Luke, "And Lee, you have to meet . . ."

Luke wished he'd been able to tell Smits, just once, how sorry he was that Smits had lost his brother.

But would Smits have believed him?

CHAPTER *TWENTY-EIGHT*

By the time the first guests started leaving, hours later, Luke felt like he'd shaken hundreds of hands, said "sir" and "ma'am" thousands of times, nodded and smiled so much that the muscles in his face ached and the inside of his lips were raw from rubbing on the braces. He'd gone glassy-eyed from forcing himself to stare directly into the faces of total strangers. And his right arm ached from the vise grip Mrs. Grant kept on it, guiding him from guest to guest.

"The president is about to leave," she hissed in his ear. "We must go outside and bid him farewell. It's protocol."

Smits came, too, this time. The three Grants and Luke walked outside and lined up as a chauffeur drove the presidential car around to the front. Mr. and Mrs. Grant stood practically shoulder to shoulder, with Smits on Mrs. Grant's right and Luke on Mr. Grant's left. A cool breeze blew through Luke's hair, and he heard a faint tinkling overhead. He looked up—right at the enormous chandelier he'd been amazed by when he'd first arrived at the Grants' house.

Luke shivered. The blazing lights seemed to blur as he fought back panic. *Watch out for chandeliers. . . .* It was all he could do not to bolt immediately. But all the guests were watching him. *The Grants won't try to fake my death if they're standing under the chandelier with me,* he thought. *And Oscar won't try to fake Smits's death if I'm here, too.* He forced himself to stand still and straight and tall, an arrogant Grant just like Smits and his parents. But out of the corner of his eye he kept track of where his friends were—Trey just behind him, off to the left, and Nina and Joel and John in a clump of servants watching through a side door as the president departed. And he noted that Oscar was just behind Smits. *Oscar's not going to endanger himself,* Luke told himself.

The president stepped out of the house. His chauffeur opened the door of his limousine and stood waiting as the president slowly moved toward the Grants. He shook each of their hands in turn and gave Mrs. Grant a kiss on each cheek.

"Marvelous party as usual, Sarinia," the president said. And then, as the chauffeur was helping the president into his car, Luke heard Nina scream behind him.

"Watch out!"

Instinctively Luke looked up. The chandelier was shaking, swaying ominously back and forth. Luke had time to move, but he couldn't suddenly—his muscles seemed frozen in fear. And then, just as the chandelier began plunging toward him, Luke felt someone knock him off his feet.

It was Trey. Trey had tackled him.

They landed safely off to the side just as the chandelier smashed down in a huge explosion of breaking glass. The blazing lights were extinguished instantly. Luke felt shards spray out against his bare hand, practically the only part of his body that wasn't sheltered by Trey. The braces bit into his lip and he tasted blood in his mouth. Somebody screamed, and then there was silence. Luke was scared to look back at the chandelier, but he glanced up at the circle of guests and servants around him, silhouetted in the dimmer lights from the windows. Everyone stood frozen in horror.

"That's what you get for teaching me how to play football," Trey said in Luke's ear.

"You saved my life," Luke muttered back. "You're the hero tonight."

"Yeah," Trey said, sounding amazed. "I guess I am."

And then he inched away gingerly, being careful not to touch any of the broken glass. His cheeks and hands were already bleeding.

Luke didn't get up yet, but he gathered the nerve to turn his head to the side, toward the fallen chandelier. Incredibly, Smits was standing out of the way, totally unscathed. But he was staring at the heap of shattered glass with an unearthly look on his face.

"Dead," he wailed. "They're all dead! My brother is dead!

My parents are dead! Oh, my . . . brother . . . is . . . dead!"

Luke scrambled to his feet so quickly that he accidentally drove more slivers of glass into his hands. He didn't bother to brush them away. He stood looking across the ruined chandelier at the younger boy.

"I'm alive, Smits," he said. "As long as I'm alive, you have a brother."

If he'd just wanted to keep up the charade of being Lee, he would have spoken differently. But he was too shocked to think about charades or pretenses or lies that had to be told. He was just trying to comfort Smits.

"I'm your brother, Smits," he said. And Smits looked past all the shattered glass and nodded.

CHAPTER *TWENTY-NINE*

The other people seemed to awaken from their trance after that. The president's chauffeur slammed the door behind the president, scurried into the front seat of the car, and zoomed away, leaving behind dozens of guards. The guards began screaming into mouthpieces, "Alert! Alert! Someone tried to assassinate the president!" They yelled at the horrified guests, "This residence is locked down immediately! Nobody shall leave until we discover who perpetrated this heinous crime!"

Luke looked around. He saw the fear in the faces of Nina and Trey, Joel and John. If they were subjected to lengthy interrogations, would they be able to tell the lies they were supposed to tell? For that matter, could he? And what would Oscar say?

Luke stepped forward. He tried to swagger every bit as much as Smits had when he'd first arrived at Hendricks. He tried to sound every bit as pompous and powerful as Mr. Grant.

"This is ridiculous," he said to the man who appeared to be the head guard. "Nobody was trying to assassinate the president. He didn't get so much as a scratch. It was my parents who died, and my brother and I who barely escaped with our lives, in this tragic accident. And it had to have been an accident. Who could have planned to have an eight-hundred-pound chandelier topple at the exact right moment? And you want to hold an investigation now, here, at the site of my parents' tragic death? When they're still, um, buried there?" He pointed toward the broken chandelier. He was trying to sound grief stricken and horrified, like a boy who had just seen his parents killed. Surprisingly, it wasn't hard. "I—my brother and I— we are the heirs to the Grant family fortune. And we say to you—you are no longer welcome on our property. Leave! Now!"

The head guard stared back at Luke. His eyes said, very clearly, *You're just a punk kid. I don't have to do a thing you say. How do I know you weren't the one who set this up just to get your parents' fortune?* But then he stepped back and seemed to be taking in the mood of the crowd. People were beginning to mutter, "He's right. How can you be so cruel to those poor orphans?" and "I'm a Baron. You're not going to interrogate *me*." And then Luke saw fear in the guard's eyes, too.

"All right," the guard said. "We'll just take everyone's names and conduct the investigation later, as we see fit."

The guests began to slip away then, the women somehow

managing to rush on their tottering high heels, the men so eager to leave that they drove off through the grass or squealed their tires on the pavement. Luke noticed that no matter how warmly the guests had talked to the Grants only moments earlier, no one bothered to stop and console Smits and Luke, no one hesitated even long enough to say, "I'm really going to miss my friends. I'm so sorry that they're dead."

Everyone was scared.

Finally all the guards and guests were gone. Luke had been standing numbly, watching the dozens of taillights depart. Reluctantly he turned around and found a hundred eyes staring straight at him. The servants were waiting for their orders. And now, improbably, he had become their boss.

Luke wanted to ask, "Who did this? And why?" But he knew he'd hear nothing but lies in response. He wanted to shout out, "Why are you looking at me? Can't someone else take care of this? Can't somebody call Mr. Talbot or Mr. Hendricks?" But there were those special codes blocking all the phones. Nobody else could take charge. Luke swallowed hard, swallowing blood, and began pointing at servants, mostly at random. "You, clean up this mess. You, take care of my parents', um, bodies. You, you, you, and you—clean up from the party."

And all the servants scrambled to do his bidding.

Luke remembered a quote from one of his history books: "The king is dead, long live the king." He'd always thought it was funny before, nonsensical even. But now it made perfect sense. The king and queen of the estate—Mr. and Mrs. Grant—were dead, and now Luke was in charge and everyone wanted to believe that he'd do a good job.

Luke turned around, and out of the blue Oscar was suddenly hugging him.

"You're a good kid, even if you aren't ready to work with me yet," he said in Luke's ear, barely loud enough for Luke to hear. "We were aiming for the president, but we held off so we didn't hit you. You owe me now."

Somehow Luke couldn't believe that. It didn't make sense. He would have been dead if Trey hadn't saved him. Oscar was just trying to manipulate Luke again, trying to turn a mistake into an obligation.

"And I owe you for sending the guards away," Oscar said. "Here's my thanks."

Luke felt something fall into his pant pocket. But it wasn't until Oscar had released him and walked away that Luke could gather his wits enough to reach in and find out what it was.

His fingers brushed smooth metal, then teeth. It was a key.

Luke knew instantly what the key unlocked.

"Smits, come with me," Luke said. "Nina, Trey—you, too. And Joel and John—you two are in charge while I'm away."

He gave them some quick instructions. Joel and John nodded numbly. This was a lot more important than leaving them in charge of the nightly games at Hendricks School, and they hadn't seemed confident enough to handle that. But it couldn't be helped.

Luke led Smits, Trey, and Nina through a maze of rooms that almost seemed familiar now. In front of the secret room he didn't even bother to look around to see who might be watching. He just thrust the key in—yes, it was the right key—and let his friends into the dark room. Luke began to fumble with the controls on the wall, but Smits took over, punching the right sequence to turn on the lights and seal the door.

"Lee and I," he said. "We used to come here sometimes, to hide. To make secret plans. Silly things like dropping water balloons on the cooks. Putting sneezing powder in our beds for the maids when they cleaned our rooms. We had so much fun before—before he died."

He looked around dazedly, as if he'd forgotten that he was speaking aloud.

"Oh, sorry, I didn't know there were servants here. You can't believe a word I say," he told Trey and Nina. "I'm crazy. Everyone thinks so."

"No, you're not," Luke said. "And it's okay to tell the truth now. Trey and Nina are my friends."

"Oh. Yes. Trey. I remember you. What are you doing here?"

"Helping out," Trey said. Smits's stunned expression didn't change.

"I think he's in shock," Nina whispered to Luke. But Smits heard her.

"No," he said. "I think I was in shock for the past six months. But now I'm—am I free now? Is Oscar gone?"

Luke remembered the way Oscar had hugged him, the way he'd slipped off into the darkness.

"I think so," Luke said.

Smits eased down into one of the chairs and stared bleakly at the wall.

"I didn't think he would kill *them*," Smits said, almost as if he was talking to himself. "He said he would destroy you." Slowly he raised his head until his empty gaze was fixed on Luke.

"M-me?" Luke stammered.

"He wanted me to help," Smits said without emotion. "Because you weren't Lee. Because you'd taken his name. Because you weren't a Baron. Oscar was a Baron, did you know that? He was just pretending to be a servant. To get revenge."

Luke's jaw dropped. "What? Oscar wasn't a Baron! He hated Barons!"

Smits didn't seem to hear Luke.

"I wouldn't help him," Smits said. "Not when it mattered. I helped you, just to make him mad. Is that . . . is that why Oscar killed them? Because I wouldn't do what he said?"

Tears began to flow down his face. He brushed them away, leaving smears of blood on his cheeks. His hands must have been bleeding, and none of them had noticed.

"Oscar was trying to kill the president," Luke said. "Not your parents. He just . . . missed."

But Luke wasn't sure that he believed that. How could he believe anything Oscar had told him?

"People try to kill my parents all the time," Smits said. "Lee and me, we weren't supposed to know, but—remember when the flaming dessert exploded? That was one time. . . . And there was a bomb once, in my dad's office. . . . But Mom and Dad, they always survived. Somehow. Maybe"—his face lit up, and he sat forward—"maybe they aren't dead now. Maybe they're just hurt really bad, and if we have the servants take them to the hospital . . ."

Luke thought about the pile of broken glass, of the way that Mr. and Mrs. Grant's bodies hadn't even been visible beneath the wreckage.

"No," he said gently. "They're dead."

Smits slumped back in his seat, back into stony silence.

"How did Oscar do it?" Nina asked. "How did he get the chandelier to fall when he was standing practically underneath it? If there'd been someone up there cutting the wires, someone Oscar was commanding, we would have seen him."

Luke hadn't even thought about that. The chandelier's falling had seemed like a tornado or an earthquake—something so sudden and cataclysmic that it didn't make sense to look for explanations.

"It was some sort of remote-control hookup," Trey said. "I bet if we looked, we'd find a release on the wires that went off when Oscar gave a signal. Or maybe he pressed the button himself. Maybe nobody except Oscar knew what was going to happen."

Luke remembered Oscar's warning: "Watch out for chandeliers." Oscar apparently hadn't given Smits the same warning. Even after Luke had refused to take sides, even after the chandelier had fallen, Oscar still seemed to have held on to some hope that Luke might join his cause. "You're a good kid, even if you aren't ready to work with me yet," Oscar had said. The "yet" kept ringing in Luke's ears.

Especially now Luke couldn't imagine ever joining forces with Oscar. Had he made a mistake, letting Oscar slip off into the darkness? Luke buried his face in his hands. His mind raced. How could he ever sort out the truth from Oscar's lies? Oscar had tried to get both Smits and Luke to help him. But it was Luke he'd given the warning to, Luke he'd hugged, Luke he'd left with the key. . . . Luke could almost feel certain: Oscar probably had been poor. He probably had blown up mailboxes. He probably did hate Barons—including the Grants.

"Smits?" Luke said gently, looking up again. "How did Oscar act around your parents?"

Smits blinked.

"Act?" he repeated, as though he'd misunderstood the question. "Yeah, it was all an act. Everything he did. He'd be all nice to them—all, 'Yes, Mrs. Grant. No, Mr. Grant.' But he was—was blackmailing them. The whole time."

"What?" Luke exploded. "It was Oscar doing that?" He'd

never suspected such a thing, but somehow it fit.

Smits didn't even seem to hear Luke. He kept talking, as if in a trance.

"They didn't know it was him," Smits said. "But I found . . . I found a check in his wallet. From them. Not his bodyguard pay. He was writing them letters, saying he knew that Lee was dead and how he had died. And he was going to tell the Government if they didn't pay up. . . ."

"Didn't you tell your parents what he was doing?" Trey asked.

"No," Smits said. His expression twisted with guilt. "I thought . . . I thought they were getting what they deserved." He was silent for a minute, then went on angrily, "They didn't even want to tell *me* that Lee was dead. 'Oh, he's too busy to answer your E-mail,' they said. 'Oh, he's just out when you call.' 'Oh, he's having too much fun to come and see his pesky little brother.'"

Luke could understand why Smits had been so upset.

"But you did find out about Lee," Nina said gently.

Smits nodded. "Lee wasn't like that. He didn't think I was pesky. He took care of me. *He* loved me. So I knew something was wrong. I started spying on Mom and Dad. And I caught Mom in here, crying. And then I made her tell me, and she made me promise to keep everything secret, but . . . I couldn't, you know? And I kept thinking, Mom was crying over Lee. And I didn't think she would cry if I died. But then tonight, when that chandelier started to fall—Mom pushed me out of the way. She saved my life. And she didn't have time to save her own. She—she must have loved me after all. And now—now I don't have any parents at all. . . ."

Smits began crying then, really hard. Awkwardly Luke patted his shoulders. Nina bent down and hugged him. Trey, who clearly wasn't any good around emotional outbursts, drifted over toward Mr. Grant's desk. He began rifling through the drawers. After a few moments Luke joined him.

"It'd be nice if we could find some papers—some proof," Trey muttered. "We can't believe what Smits tells us, can we?"

Luke glanced back at the sobbing boy.

"Yeah," he said. "He's too sad to lie."

Luke was convinced: Smits definitely believed everything he'd told them was true. He'd mostly told the truth all along—until Oscar had begun pressuring him to betray Luke, as a way to betray his parents. Smits's only lies were the ones that had come from other people.

Luke was willing to stand there and try to figure everything out, but Trey elbowed him in the ribs.

"Where'd you get the key to this room?" he asked.

"Oscar gave it to me," Luke said absentmindedly.

"How do we know he hasn't bugged the whole place?" Trey asked. "How do we know he isn't still planning to kill you and Smits?"

Luke stared at his friend. Luke's vision was starting to go fuzzy around the edges. It was so tempting to give in to that fuzziness, to slump down in a heap and let someone else figure out what to do. But he blinked hard, blinking Trey and the secret room back into focus. And Nina and Smits.

Most of all Smits.

"Think one of us can figure out how to drive?" Luke asked.

CHAPTER *THIRTY*

In the end they decided to trust the chauffeur. Joel and John sat in the front with him, ready to overpower him if he tried anything suspicious.

Trey and Luke sat in the first seat in the back, all the papers from Mr. Grant's desk spread out between them. Trey had insisted on bringing them. He was methodically reading one paper after the other with a penlight. Occasionally he'd mutter, "This is incredible!" or "Listen to this!" but Luke barely heard him. It was always something financial, something about Mr. Grant's business. Nothing Luke cared about. Luke just stared straight ahead, thinking.

Nina and Smits sat across from Luke and Trey. Or lay, in Smits's case. He'd fallen asleep leaning against Nina, but he still whimpered and thrashed about. Several times she had to grab him to keep him from falling off the seat.

Every time that happened, Luke knew he was doing the right thing.

It had been the middle of the night when they started out, so their entire trip had been in darkness. There seemed to be no light at all in the world except in their car. But by the time Trey finally gave up on the papers and turned off his penlight, the first gleam of dawn had begun creeping over the horizon. Luke stopped staring at Smits and began pressing his face against the window, trying to see something familiar outside. He couldn't get enough of staring at the landscape around him.

When the car passed a crossroads with nothing but three mailboxes in the midst of a clump of weeds, he suddenly screamed out, "Stop!"

The chauffeur hit the brakes so hard that Smits finally rolled completely off his seat.

"Sorry, sir," the chauffeur said.

"That's all right," Luke said. "You can let Smits and me out here."

"Here?" The man sounded incredulous. Luke saw him looking around at rutted fields stretching all the way to the horizon. To the chauffeur and almost anyone else who might see this scene, it would look like a vast wasteland. The middle of nowhere.

But that wasn't what Luke saw.

"You can take the others on to Mr. Talbot's house," Luke said. "Thanks."

Luke didn't wait for the chauffeur to open the door for him. He pushed his way out on his own.

"Come on, Smits," he said gently, holding the door.

Nina handed the younger boy over as if he were a mere parcel. Still, Smits stood up straight once he was out of the car. Luke saw him glance down at the dried mud streaked across the road, but he didn't say anything.

"You won't change your mind?" Trey asked. "You can still come with the rest of us."

"No," Luke said. "I've got to do it this way."

He had a feeling Mr. Talbot would disapprove. He was probably being a coward, not going to Mr. Talbot's house first. Or foolhardy for not discussing everything with Mr. Talbot before making up his mind. But Luke knew now that Mr. Talbot didn't know everything, either. Mr. Talbot was going to be stunned to learn what Oscar had done. Luke was perfectly willing to let Trey and Nina break the news.

"Okay," Trey said hesitantly.

Luke shoved the door shut and turned to Smits.

"Up ahead," Luke said. "That house. That's where we're going."

They waited until the car drove out of sight, then they began walking. Luke barely managed to keep himself from breaking into a run—he was that eager. But he had the younger boy to think about, and Smits didn't seem capable of running right now.

Finally they reached the driveway, and Luke could restrain himself no longer. He raced up to the door and pounded.

"Mother! Dad! I'm home!"

The door flew open and Mother stood there, her jaw dropped in astonishment.

"Oh, Lu—," she began, then swallowed the rest of his name and just buried him in a hug. Then she stopped and held him out from her by the shoulders, much as Mrs. Grant had held him when she was planning all the ways to change him. But Mrs. Grant had been looking for his faults, and Mother was beaming as though everything about him was wonderful.

"You've gotten taller and more muscular, and your hair's darker and—are those braces?" she asked in amazement. She didn't wait for an answer. Her face clouded suddenly, as though she'd just remembered why he'd had to leave home in the first place. "Is it safe for you to be here?" she asked.

"As safe as anywhere else," Luke replied steadily. For that, finally, was what he'd concluded. Oscar knew about Hendricks School and Mr. Talbot, the Grants' house was a Byzantine mess of mixed loyalties—if Luke was going to be in danger, he might as well get to see his family. And he wasn't going to be staying long enough to endanger them.

"Everything's different now, Mother," he said. But he couldn't say to her, "I just saw two people killed, right before my eyes. I was almost killed myself. And then the murderer hugged me. . . . How can anything stay the same after that?"

Mother gave him a searching look and opened her mouth as if she was going to ask more. But Smits reached the front door just then, a sad, slow little boy who seemed to have barely enough energy to climb the steps. Luke saw the sympathy playing over his mother's face. She didn't even know what had happened to Smits, and she already felt sorry for him.

Good.

"Mother, remember how you always wanted to have four boys?" Luke asked. "Well, I brought you another son. This is Smits. Smits Grant. He is—was—well, he's my brother now. His parents are dead."

Automatically Smits held out a hand, and for a single second Luke felt a stab of doubt. Mother and Smits looked so wrong together—like pictures cut from two different magazines and haphazardly glued together. Smits, in his fine woolen suit and leather shoes, did not belong with Mother, with her faded housedress and haggard face, her graying hair scooped back into a bun. And what had Luke been thinking, bringing Smits from his mansion to Luke's family's house, with its peeling paint and weathered wood? What must Smits think?

Mother ignored Smits's outstretched hand and drew him into a hug that was every bit as genuine as the one she'd given Luke.

"You're always welcome here," she told him.

Then Luke's dad and older brothers, Matthew and Mark, came out to see what the fuss was about. They weren't the type to give hugs, but Luke could see the joy and relief in their eyes, even as Matthew punched his arm and Mark joked, "Luke? You couldn't be Luke. I could always whomp Luke with one hand tied behind my back. And you—with you I might have to use both fists."

That was how Luke knew that Mark was happier than anyone to see him.

They all shook hands politely with Smits. Luke could tell they were shy around him.

"Have you had breakfast? We were just getting ready to sit down," Mother said.

"I could eat," Smits said in a small voice.

Matthew and Mark brought in extra chairs from the other rooms, and they all sat around the kitchen table. Such a change, Luke thought, from when he'd had to eat on the stairs while the rest of the family ate at the table. Breakfast was just oatmeal and cooked apples, but it tasted heavenly to Luke, better than the fanciest meal he'd had at the Grants'.

He wondered what Smits thought.

After breakfast everyone sat around talking, until Mother had to scurry off to work, and Matthew and Mark had to rush off to school.

"Are we going to have to put up with you when we get home, too?" Mark asked, just as the school bus pulled up.

"Probably," Luke said. "Today, at least."

"Too bad," Mark said, but Luke could tell he was secretly glad.

With the others out the door, Luke's dad asked them, "Mind if I turn on the radio? I have to check the grain report."

It was so odd that Dad would ask Luke permission for anything. Luke watched Dad twist the radio dial, and the familiar voice of the news announcer crackled out of the speaker.

"Government spokesmen report record harvests this year," the announcer said.

Luke remembered the empty fields he'd seen going from school to the Grants' house, from the Grants' house to home. He remembered all the lies he'd witnessed since leaving home in the first place. Even if the news announcer's voice was the same as ever, Luke couldn't listen unquestioningly, the way he once had. He wondered suddenly if anything the Government told the people was true.

Beside him Smits sniffled.

"They aren't . . . they aren't saying anything about Mom and Dad," he said.

"No," Luke said gently. "They wouldn't." He remembered how he'd longed to hear news on the radio about Jen, Mr. Talbot's daughter, after her rally but before he knew what had really happened. "It's better for you if they don't announce it," he told Smits.

"But I can talk about it, can't I?" Smits asked.

"Yes," Luke said. "Here you can say anything you want."

Smits fell silent then. Luke understood. But Dad glanced from Smits to Luke, his eyebrows furrowed in confusion.

"Is there something I ought to know?" Dad asked.

"Later," Luke mouthed, cutting his eyes toward Smits in

a quiet signal: *Not in front of the little boy.* Luke realized that his parents, and even Matthew and Mark, had done that around Luke all those years he'd lived at home. They'd protected him. He'd been the little boy. And now Luke was protecting Smits.

Luke half expected Dad to ask more, but he just nodded and turned back to the radio news.

"Come on," Luke said to Smits. "I'll show you around."

They stepped out the kitchen door into the backyard. Luke froze, staring out at the barn and the trees and the garden, now dried up and dying. Once, this yard had practically been Luke's whole world. Once, it had seemed huge and endless, especially when he'd been gathering the nerve to run across it to see Jen. But now—now it seemed tiny. Luke felt like he could cross the distance to the Talbots' backyard in a few quick strides.

Smits sat down on the back step.

"Your family loves you," he said. "They missed you while you were away."

"Yes," Luke said.

"I wish my parents had . . . ," Smits started, but he choked on the rest of the words and stopped. Luke patted him on the back and sat down beside him.

"My parents will take care of you now," Luke said. "Is that okay?"

After a few seconds Smits nodded. Luke slipped his hand into his pocket and pulled out the I.D. that claimed Smits was really Peter Goodard.

"Do you want this?" Luke asked. "I found it in your room at school, after the fire. I didn't know what Oscar was going to do with it, but—"

"Oscar? He didn't know anything about it," Smits said.

"What?" Just when Luke thought he had everything figured out, another surprise cropped up.

"You found it in his mattress, right?" Smits said. "I hid it there because I thought that was the one place he wouldn't look. Oscar—he searched everything I owned. Every day. He had ways of finding out everything."

He took the I.D. from Luke and clutched it in his hand.

"But that first day you came to Hendricks—you had tricked Oscar then," Luke said. "You'd locked him in the closet."

Smits flashed Luke a disgusted look. "Oscar planned all that. He set me up. He thought I'd get to Hendricks and make some big scene and betray you, and betray my—my parents. . . ."

"Why didn't you?" Luke asked.

Smits stared at the ground. "When I met you and had to call you Lee, it was like, just saying his name—I thought, what if you could be Lee? I mean, I knew you weren't really Lee, but . . . you kind of look like him. A little. And I thought maybe . . . You listened to me. Like Lee used to. But other times I would be so mad at you, and I was mean to you because . . ."

"Because I wasn't Lee," Luke finished. "Not for real."

Smits nodded.

And from that garbled explanation Luke somehow understood how it had been for Smits. He'd had no one he could trust. His brother was dead and Luke was using his name. So of course he was angry. But he'd also let himself drop into fantasy. "Can you be Lee?" Smits had asked Luke that on his very first day at Hendricks. And Luke had wondered what Smits really meant, what code Luke was supposed to understand. But Smits had meant exactly what he'd said. He'd wanted Luke to be Lee. Nothing more, nothing less.

Luke shook his head, trying to make sense of all this new information.

"But—the fire," he said. "Why did you set the fire if— and why didn't you take the I.D. when—"

"Oscar set the fire," Smits said. "Or—it was his idea. Just from what I told you that night, he figured out that I was planning to run away."

So Oscar had been listening the whole time, all those nights Smits had reminisced about Lee. And Smits might have escaped if he hadn't told Luke, "None of this is because of you. It won't be your fault. I even . . . I even kind of like you." Everything would have been different if Smits hadn't cared about Luke.

But maybe—maybe everything would have been worse instead of better. Maybe Smits would be dead now, too.

"But why did you want to run away?" Luke asked. "Where were you going to go?"

"Where I could find out more about Lee," Smits said. "I

wanted to talk to people who'd seen him right before he died. Oscar said he'd help me if I could make it look like it wasn't his fault for letting me go. Like he'd been too busy fighting the fire and saving my life to keep me from leaving. So I lit the matches, and he held his hands over the sprinklers as long as he could. . . . I thought Oscar would leave and I could grab the I.D. at the last minute. But the fire took off faster than I'd thought, and that teacher came in, Mr. Dirk. I think Oscar just wanted Mr. Hendricks to send us home, where he could make more trouble. He—he got what he wanted."

Luke was trying to sort everything out. "So you thought Oscar would help you? Why did you act like you didn't trust him?"

Smits looked weary. "Because I didn't. There were so many lies. I didn't know what to believe. Sometimes I believed him, sometimes I didn't."

Luke shivered, remembering his own confusion about Oscar. He could sympathize with Smits, trying to cope with Oscar's lies and manipulations for so long.

"I think I understand everything now," Luke said. "Except—where did you get the fake I.D. in the first place? And this other one—whose was it if it wasn't Oscar's?"

Luke drew out the pictureless I.D. for Stanley Goodard. Smits didn't look surprised to see it. He reached out and touched it gently.

"Lee's," he said. He stared out at the leafless trees at the edge of the yard.

"Lee knew there was danger," Smits said. "He said our country was going to change, and it might not be safe anymore for us. . . . So he gave me the fake I.D., just in case. He showed me that he had a fake I.D. of his own. And then he left."

"So how did you get Lee's?" Luke asked.

"I stole it from Dad's desk," Smits said, and gave Luke a defiant look, just daring him to tell Smits that stealing was wrong.

Luke didn't.

"So this was the identification Lee was carrying when he died," Luke said. That fake I.D. was what made it safe for Luke to pretend to be Lee. The Government soldiers would never have known that they'd killed the real Lee Grant.

"The resistance group must have given it to your parents," Luke said. "As proof."

Smits shrugged, as though none of those details mattered.

"But what happened to the picture?" Luke asked.

In answer Smits reached inside his shirt and peeled a small, battered piece of clear tape off his chest. He held it out to Luke.

"Mom and Dad got rid of all the pictures of Lee," Smits said. "For protection, they said. So—this is all I have."

The tape—badly bent and grubby—was stuck to a picture of a boy who looked vaguely like an older, darker-haired version of Smits. Luke gingerly took the taped picture from Smits and studied it. It was hard to tell anything from such a small picture.

"You've been carrying this around for a long time, haven't you?" Luke asked, carefully handing it back.

Smits nodded.

"I won't have to keep it with me all the time now, will I?" Smits asked.

"No," Luke said.

"But if I put it down, that won't mean I'm forgetting Lee."

"Of course not," Luke said. "You'll never forget him. And I won't, either. And someday it'll be safe to tell the whole world what really happened to Lee. How brave he was and what he believed in."

But even saying that, Luke knew that he'd never truly be sure what the real Lee had believed. Had he joined the rebels, as Oscar said, simply to get revenge on his parents? Had he been as nonchalant as Oscar about harming innocent people? Or had he been a true believer, longing to extend freedom to everyone?

Luke couldn't blame Smits for always wanting more answers about the dead. Luke would probably never know, either, if Mr. and Mrs. Grant had intended to kill him for real or if they'd just meant to send him back into hiding. If they'd wanted to kill him, how could he mourn their death?

But how could he hate them as Oscar did, when they'd given him Lee's identity?

Smits didn't seem to notice Luke's confusion. He bent the tape over the back of the picture and tucked it and the two fake I.D.'s into his pocket. Then he glanced back at Luke.

"Luke? After the chandelier—after it fell, when I yelled, 'My brother is dead,' I didn't mean to betray you. I don't think that anyone understood. But—it felt good, you know? To finally tell the truth, out loud, in front of lots of people. I feel . . . I feel better about Lee now."

"You didn't betray me," Luke said. He wondered how good it would feel for everyone to finally tell the truth. Someday he and Trey and Nina and all his other friends could stand up proud and finally tell the whole world their true names, their true stories. But somehow, even now, sometimes truth slipped out in the midst of all the lies and confusion. "And I really meant it when I said you were my brother now."

"I know," Smits said. "But you're not going to stay with me here, are you?"

It was amazing, Luke thought, that Smits had figured that out. That Smits realized that Luke, like Lee, couldn't make it his top priority to be Smits's brother.

"No," Luke said. "But you'll be safe here. You'll be ordinary old Peter Goodard, whoever that is. It's good that Mr. Hendricks is the only other person who ever saw that I.D. We can make up a story about you, about why you're here. And you don't look like the rest of the family, so no one will think that you're actually a third child with a fake I.D." He almost said, "Like they would if I stayed." But he swallowed those words and smiled at Smits. "You'll have Matthew and Mark. They're horrible brothers, but—well, they're better than nothing. And I'll stay tonight. But then tomorrow—"

"I know," Smits said.

Tomorrow Luke would march across that tiny backyard that separated his family's house from Mr. Talbot's. And then the chauffeur would take him back to the Grants' house or back to Hendricks School or maybe even someplace else. Wherever he went, there'd be danger. But there would also be a chance to work toward that day of truth he longed for.

"Hey," Luke said. "I've got an idea."

He went in the side door of the barn and emerged with a rusty old wagon.

"It's not red, and I'm not Lee, but—I made you a promise."

And Luke sat down in the little kiddie wagon. His knees were practically in his ears. Smits laughed and stood up, then grabbed the handle and pulled. Luke instantly tipped over onto the ground.

"Wow," he said. "No wonder Lee never let you pull."

They goofed off with the wagon for a long time after that, taking turns jerking on the handle and sitting in the wagon. It became a game to see who could stay in the wagon the longest, who could dump the other boy the fastest. Luke's dad came out and stood on the step and laughed at them.

"Here," he said, "I'll pull you both."

And Luke and Smits piled into the wagon, barely fitting in. Luke's dad tugged hard, and for just a minute Luke could believe again that he was just a little kid letting a grown-up determine which way he should go. But then he was on the ground again, and his dad was groaning and rubbing his arm.

"You're too heavy together," he complained jokingly. "Just the little guy this time."

And Luke stood back and watched Smits play with Luke's dad. Smits wasn't a Grant anymore, and Luke was. But now Smits would have Luke's parents, and Luke wouldn't. Luke knew he'd made a bad trade. And with all that he'd risked, he still hadn't done anything grand for the cause.

But he'd helped Smits. And for now that was enough.

turn the page to read an excerpt from the
fifth book in the Shadow Children sequence

Among
the Brave

MARGARET PETERSON HADDIX

CHAPTER ONE

Great, Trey thought. *I do one brave thing in my entire life, and now it's like, 'Got anything dangerous to do? Send Trey. He can handle it.' Doesn't anyone remember that Cowardice is my middle name?*

Actually, only two other people in the entire world had ever known Trey's real name, and one of them was dead. But Trey didn't have time to think about that. He had a crisis on his hands. He'd just seen two people killed, and others in danger. Maybe he'd been in danger too. Maybe he still was. He and his friends had left the scene of all that death and destruction and total confusion, jumped into a car with an absolute stranger, and rushed off in search of help. They'd driven all night, and now the car had stopped in front of a strange house in a strange place Trey had never been before.

And Trey's friends actually expected him to take control of the situation.

"What are you waiting for?" his friend Nina asked. "Just go knock on the door."

"Why don't you?" Trey asked, which was as good as admitting that he wasn't as brave as a girl. No courage, no pride. Translate that into Latin and it'd be a good personal motto for him. *Nulla fortitudo nulla superbia,* maybe? Trey allowed himself a moment to drift into nostalgia for the days when his biggest challenges had been figuring out how to translate Latin phrases.

"Because," Nina said. "You know. Mr. Talbot and I—well, let's just say I've got a lot of bad memories."

"Oh," Trey said. And, if he could manage to turn down his fear a notch or two, he did understand. Mr. Talbot, the man they had come to see, had once put Nina through an extreme test of her loyalties. It had been necessary, everyone agreed—even Nina said so. But it hadn't been pleasant. Mr. Talbot had kept her in prison; he'd threatened her with death.

Trey was glad he'd never been put through a test like that. He knew: He'd fail.

Trey glanced up again at the hulking monstrosity of a house where Mr. Talbot lived. He wasn't dangerous, Trey reminded himself. Mr. Talbot was going to be their salvation. Trey and Nina and a few of their other friends had come to Mr. Talbot's so they could dump all their bad news and confusion on him. So he would handle everything, and they wouldn't have to.

Trey peered toward the front of the car, where his friends Joel and John sat with the driver. Or, technically, the "chauffeur," a word derived from the French. Only the original French word—*chauffer?*—didn't mean "to drive." It meant "to warm" or "to heat" or something like that, because chauffeurs used to drive steam automobiles.

Not that it mattered. Why was he wasting time thinking about foreign verbs? Knowing French wasn't going to help Trey in the least right now. It couldn't tell him, for example, whether he could trust the driver. Everything would be so easy if he could know, just from one word, whether he could send the driver to knock on Mr. Talbot's door while Trey safely cowered in the car.

Or how about Joel or John? Granted, they were younger than Trey, and maybe even bigger cowards. They'd *never* done anything brave. Still—

"Trey?" Nina said. *"Go!"*

She reached around him and jerked open the door. Then she gave him a little shove on the back, so suddenly that he was surprised to find himself outside the car, standing on his own two feet.

Nina shut the door behind him.

Trey took a deep breath. He started to clench his fists out of habit and fear—a habit of fear, a fear-filled habit— and only stopped when pain reminded him that he was still clutching the sheaf of papers he'd taken from a dead man's desk. He glanced down and saw a thin line of fresh blood, stark and frightening on the bright white paper.

Trey's next breath was sharp and panicked. Had someone shot him? Was he in even greater danger than he'd imagined? His ears buzzed, and he thought he might pass out from terror. But nothing else happened, and after a few moments his mind cleared a little.

He looked at the blood again. It was barely more than a single drop.

Okay, Trey steadied himself. *You just had a panic attack over a paper cut. Let's not be telling anybody about that, all right?*

A paper cut indoors would have been no big deal. But outdoors—outdoors, the need to *breathe* was enough to panic him.

He forced himself to breathe anyway. And, by sheer dint of will, Trey made himself take a single step forward. And then another. And another.

Mr. Talbot had a long, long walkway between the street and his house, and the chauffeur had inconveniently parked off to the side, under a clump of trees that practically hid the car from the house. Trey considered turning around, getting back into the car, and telling the chauffeur to pull up closer—say, onto the Talbots' front porch. But that would mean retracing his steps, and Trey felt like he'd already come so far.

Maybe even all of three feet.

With part of his mind, Trey knew he was being foolish—a total baby, a chicken, a fear-addled idiot.

It's not my fault, Trey defended himself. *It's all . . . conditioning. I can't help the way I was raised.* And that was the understatement of the year. For most of his thirteen years, Trey hadn't had control over any aspect of his life. He was an illegal third child—the entire Government thought he had no right to exist. So he'd had to hide, from birth until age twelve, in a single room. And then, when he was almost thirteen, when his father died . . .

You don't have time to think about that now, Trey told himself sternly. *Walk.*

He took a few more steps forward, propelled now by a burning anger that he'd never managed to escape. His mind slipped back to a multiple-choice test question he'd been asking himself for more than a year: *Whom do you hate? A) Him; B) Her; C) Yourself?* It never worked to add extra choices: *(D) All of the above; E) A and B; F) A and C; or G) B and C?* Because then the question just became, *Whom do you hate the most?*

Stop it! Trey commanded himself. *Just pretend you're Lee.*

Trey's friend Lee had been an illegal third child like Trey, but Lee had grown up out in the country, on an isolated farm, so he'd been able to spend plenty of time outdoors. He'd almost, Trey thought, grown up normal. As much as Trey feared and hated being outdoors, Lee craved it.

"How can you stand it?" Trey had asked Lee once. "Why aren't you terrified? Don't you ever think about the danger?"

"I guess not," Lee had said, shrugging. "When I'm outdoors I look at the sky and the grass and the trees, and I guess that's all I think about."

Trey looked at the sky and the grass and the trees around him, and all he could think was, *Lee should be here, walking up to Mr. Talbot's door, instead of me.* Lee had been in the car with Trey and Nina and Joel and John until just about ten minutes earlier. But Lee had had the chauffeur drop him and another boy, Smits, off at a crossroads in the middle of nowhere because, Lee had said, "I have to get Smits to safety."

Trey suspected that Lee was taking Smits home, to Lee's parents' house, but Trey was trying very hard not to think that. It was too dangerous. Even thinking about it was dangerous.

And thinking about it made Trey jealous, because Lee still had a home he could go to, and parents who loved him, and Trey didn't.

But Lee would be dead right now if it weren't for me, Trey thought with a strange emotion he barely recognized well enough to name. Pride. He felt proud. And, cowardly Latin motto or no, he had a right to that pride.

For Trey's act of bravery—his only one ever—had been to save Lee's life the night before.

Beneath the pride was a whole jumble of emotions Trey hadn't had time to explore. He felt his leg muscles tense, as if they too remembered last night, remembered springing forward at the last minute to knock Lee to the side, only seconds before the explosion of glass in the very spot where Lee had stood. . . .

It's easier being brave when you don't have time to think about your other options, Trey thought. *Unlike now.*

He had so many choices, out here in the open. The ones that called to him most strongly were the ones that involved hiding. How fast would he be able to run back to the car, if he needed to? Would the clump of trees be a good hiding place? Would he be able to squeeze out of sight between that giant flowerpot on the porch and the wall of the Talbot house?

Trey forced himself to keep walking. It seemed a miracle when he finally reached the front porch. He cast a longing glance toward the flowerpot, but willed himself to stab a finger at the doorbell.

Dimly, he could hear a somber version of "Westminster Chimes" echoing from indoors. Nobody came. He took a second to admire the brass door knocker, elegantly engraved with the words, GEORGE A. TALBOT, ESQUIRE. Still nobody came.

Too bad, Trey thought. *Back to the car, then.* But his legs didn't obey. He couldn't face the thought of walking back through all that open space again. He pressed the doorbell again.

This time the door opened.

Trey was torn between relief and panic. Relief won when he saw Mr. Talbot's familiar face on the other side of the door. *See, this wasn't so bad,* Trey told himself. *I walked all the way up here without my legs even trembling. Take that, Nina! I am braver than you!*

Trey started thinking about what he was supposed to say to Mr. Talbot. He hadn't worried about that before. Words were so much easier than action.

"I'm so glad you're home, Mr. Talbot," Trey began. "You won't believe what happened. We just—"

But Mr. Talbot cut him off.

"No, no, I do not want to buy anything to support your school's lacrosse team," he said. "And please do *not* come back. Tell the rest of your team that this is a no-soliciting house. Can't you see I'm a busy man?"

Mr. Talbot's eyebrows beetled together, like forbidding punctuation.

"But, Mr. Talbot—I'm not—I'm—"

Too late. The door slammed in his face.

"—Trey," Trey finished in a whisper, talking now to the door.

He doesn't remember me, Trey thought. It wasn't that surprising. Every time Mr. Talbot had visited Hendricks School, where Trey and Lee were students, Trey had been in the background, no more noticeable than the wallpaper.

Lee, on the other hand, had been front and center, talking to Mr. Talbot, joking with him, going off for special meals with him.

Mr. Talbot wouldn't have slammed the door in Lee's face, Trey thought. Was Trey jealous of that, too? *No. I just wish Lee were here to talk with Mr. Talbot now.*

Trey sighed, and began gathering the nerve to ring the doorbell again.

But then two things happened, one after the other.

First, a car shot out from under the house—from a hidden garage, Trey guessed. It was black and long and official-looking. Its tires screeched, winding around the curves of the driveway. Trey caught a glimpse of two men in uniforms in the front seat, and Mr. Talbot in the back. Mr. Talbot held up his hands toward the window, toward Trey, and Trey saw a glint of something metal around his wrists.

Handcuffs?

The black car bounced over the curb and then sped off down the street.

Trey was still standing there, his mouth agape, his mind struggling to make sense of what he'd seen, when the car he'd ridden in—the car that Nina, Joel, and John were still hiding in—began to inch forward, under the cover of the trees. Trey felt a second of hope: *They're coming to rescue me!*

But the car was going in the wrong direction.

Trey stared as the car slid away, just a shadow in the trees, then a black streak on the open road.

Then it was gone.

They left me! Trey's mind screamed. *They left me!*

He was all alone on an uncaring man's porch—an arrested man's porch?—out in the great wide open where anyone in the world might see him.

Without thinking, Trey dived behind the huge flower-pot, to hide.

magine a world where families are allowed only two children.

llegal third children—shadow children—must live in hiding,

for if they are discovered, there is only one punishment:

Death.

Read the Shadow Children series by

MARGARET PETERSON HADDIX

Simon & Schuster • www.SimonSaysKids.com

— THE MISSING —

"Fans of Haddix's Shadow Children books will want to jump on this time travel adventure. . . . An exciting trip through history." —*Kirkus Review*

MARGARET PETERSON
HADDIX

FOUND	SENT
978-1-4169-5421-7	978-1-4169-5422-4
Available now	Coming August 2009

FROM SIMON & SCHUSTER
BOOKS FOR YOUNG READERS

PENDRAGON

Bobby Pendragon is a seemingly normal fourteen-year-old boy. He has a family, a home, and a possible new girlfriend. But something happens to Bobby that changes his life forever.

HE IS CHOSEN TO DETERMINE
THE COURSE OF HUMAN EXISTENCE.

Pulled away from the comfort of his family and suburban home, Bobby is launched into the middle of an immense, interdimensional conflict. It's a journey of danger and discovery for Bobby, and his success or failure will do nothing less than determine the fate of the world. . . .

Coming Soon: Book Ten

From Aladdin Paperbacks • Published by Simon & Schuster

ENTER THE WORLD OF

EREC REX

Books 1 and 2 in stores now

THE DRAGON'S EYE   THE MONSTERS OF OTHERNESS

And Book 3 coming in June 2009

THE SEARCH FOR TRUTH

Travel into magical new worlds with

The Chronicles of the Imaginarium Geographica!

**HERE, THERE
BE DRAGONS**

**THE SEARCH FOR
THE RED DRAGON**

THE INDIGO KING

**THE SHADOW
DRAGONS**